HOLLICOTT CROSSING

James Richard Langston

authorHOUSE®

AuthorHouse™
1663 Liberty Drive
Bloomington, IN 47403
www.authorhouse.com
Phone: 1-800-839-8640

First published by AuthorHouse   11/23/2011

ISBN: 978-1-4670-4181-2 (sc)
ISBN: 978-1-4670-4180-5 (hc)
ISBN: 978-1-4670-4179-9 (e)

Library of Congress Control Number: 2011917443

Printed in the United States of America

Art work by: Carrie Simpson Petty [www.csimpsonmurals.com]
Dan Libisch [www.cactus3d.com/Home.htm]

To the precious memory of Launa Gay

CHAPTER 1

JB hated buzzards. To him, they were nothing but filthy scavengers that flew around the countryside and ate maggot infested, putrid flesh. He couldn't think of much that was more disgusting, except maybe a snaggled tooth, overweight woman, spitting a rope of slimy tobacco juice through the snaggle. He and his outfit was still an hour away from water. The large winged birds were floating on the upper currents of hot air above the dry semi-desert landscape; a landscape that had claimed untold numbers of men and beasts, keeping the damn buzzards fed. *'They're just waiting for one of my cows to die, the bastards,'* he thought. The heat of the day was bearing down on man and beast, alike. It was hot enough to blister a lizard's belly, if he turned loose and laid down on a flat rock. The air was close and humid along the river, bottom land. Off in the distance, there was a black formation of ominous looking storm clouds hanging over the western horizon, shooting out threats of bony skeleton fingers of lightning. The storm was background against a late afternoon sky and was creeping toward them. JB rode the point position to pick the best route for his herd of white-face cattle as they trudged on to water. A layer of dry, thick dust floated along with the herd as if it was riding on the cattle's backs.

He had sweated at least a gallon in the last two hours and was looking forward to dipping his body in the river when they got there and bedded the cattle down. His shirt stuck to his back like a layer of painted on cotton, covering an unseen river of sweat that flowed down his spine like an underground river, spotting the top of his jeans. The sweat that trickled down was, really, helping to keep him cool. He was carrying a layer of Texas dust on the exposed parts of his body that made his skin look like he had been rolling on the ground for a week. He reined his horse to a halt atop a small ridge overlooking the river basin. Removing his Stetson, he took a bandana from his back pocket, wiped the sweat band and his forehead and then returned the hat to his shaggy head. It was an old but good hat and it kept the sun off his face and neck and out of his eyes. The river basin was covered with rich, lush grass that grew tall, drinking the rain that seemed to fall mostly in river basins and it was a deep green as opposed to the sun baked brown grass of the open plains.

He squinted at the buzzards once more, clucked his horse forward and rode to catch up with the cattle before they reached the river. He wanted them to stay in a close group and not spread out too much up or down stream. The sun was still hot but there was a cool breeze blowing, ahead of the storm, that fluttered the ends of the bandana that he wore, tied around his neck. Evaporation of the sweat that collected there helped to keep his neck skin cool as did the river of sweat running down his back. He yelled at the other riders that they needed to flank the cattle and hold them in close. They would have to quicken the pace if they were to reach the river by nightfall and get bedded down and settled before the storm that threatened, got there. The sun had already been blacked out by the clouds and the gloom of stormy weather blanketed the countryside.

The seven riders other than himself were Buck Parker, Dusty Walden, Chuck Jackson, Abe Rivers, Joe Vaughn, Tom Cranston and Jocke Atchley. They pushed the herd to move it a little faster with yelps and the slapping of cow butts with their coiled ropes. Each pop of a coiled rope brought a puff of trail dust from the hide of the cow popped. A lizard scurried from the dangerous onslaught of the cattle's hooves and sought refuge under a piece of flat slag. A little earlier on, the sun had fallen from noon high to late afternoon as if gravity had a hold on it with an iron grip and was pulling it down against its will. The cattle were easily moved, now that they had caught the scent of water and just naturally headed toward the river. Although they were tired, their pace was quickened by their need for a long drink.

The whole herd kicked and stamped their way to the river's edge and some of them plunged into the water and waded out to belly deep. The herd of five hundred and ninety four cows and six bulls spread out slightly when they hit the sandy bottom of the river bed, others started to mill about the water's edge, wetting their dry throats. Some of those in the water were relieving themselves into the water while they drank. The men eased their mounts to the water's edge to let them drink. The men would drink their own fill as everything gradually settled down.

A tall, full bodied cowboy in his early thirties, JB had gotten out of the way of the charging, thirsty cows and trotted his cayuse in behind the last of the herd as his seven riders flanked the cows, keeping them from spreading too far.

****

JB Johnson was six feet, even, bare footed. He had a set of shoulders that were as wide as a door and with some doors; he had to turn slightly sideways to get through. His body was thick with muscle. His chest tapered down to the small waist of a rider. He had narrow hips and walked with a slight bow in his legs. He was handsome in a rugged sort of way from a woman's point of view, though he never considered himself to be much of a lady's man. He had dark, sun baked skin, from endless days in the saddle. His eyes were milky green, the green of a turquoise stone, with a sparkle, so deep set that it was, sometimes, hard to see unless you looked real close. On a clear day his eyes had a penetrating glow. He had sandy colored hair that was bleached by the sun for he loved to ride with the wind through it from time to time, hat hanging down his back. He was hell on earth with a handgun.

A neatly trimmed mustache offered a contrast to the hard lines of his face. Lines that made him seem much older than he was. He sat a fine looking Appaloosa stallion. The horse was a mouse color, light from the head, deepening in color as you looked to the hind quarters. His back end was as spotted as a freckled faced kid. He had an off blond tail and matching mane and three white stocking feet. He was a beautiful animal to see and he and JB seemed to mesh with each other as though they were one. This was JB's first herd and though small, he was as proud of it as a child would be of a new, store-bought toy on Christmas morning. He just hoped Pepper Cladderbuck, his partner, would do as well with the longhorns down in the south of Texas. The white faces were shipped from Kentucky and offloaded from flat bottomed, river barges on the Red River, north of Dallas.

****

He hired Buck Parker, Dusty Walden and Jocke Atchley at the stock yards in Fort Worth and picked up the others in Dallas, through the Cattlemen's Association, to ride for him and help with the herd until he could get it settled on the grass of his homestead in the Texas panhandle. Clancy Jones, his home cook was tending chuck for the drive. Before now, Clancy and JB were the only two on the ranch, but until now, he had no cattle to take care of. He had gotten acquainted with Buck Parker, Jocke Atchley and Dusty Walden on the trail between Fort Worth and Dallas and found out a few things about each man.

Buck was of medium build and carried his weight like one who knew how to handle himself. He was an inch or two shorter than JB and was straight of back with the small hips of a cowboy who had spent his share of hours in the saddle. He wore a holstered .44 Navy Colt, tied down and was extra good with an eight foot long, bull whip. The holster he wore was worn slick and shiny from much practice and some use. The .44 was held in place by a rawhide thong, looped over the hammer. Buck was good with cows as well as horses. He was a serious minded individual that hated to see a horse, woman or child mistreated. He had a streak of mischief, but a good sense of humor could be found just under the surface and he was deadly with the .44 Navy.

Jocke Atchley on the other hand had very little sense of humor and wasn't given to pranks. He had been raised in a large family and had been overshadowed by an older brother after their Pa was tortured, scalped and finally killed by Comanches. The older brother had taken over the running of the family at the death of their Pa and Jocke decided to leave and be on his own so he pulled up stakes and lit a shuck. He never looked back. After what happened to his Pa, he harbored a strong distrust of Indians, bordering on hate and was glad that most of them now lived on reservations. It made no difference to him what kind they were. To Jocke Atchley, an Indian was an Indian.

Jocke was an inch or two taller than Buck, right at the same height of JB but appeared shorter because he walked loosely on legs, bowed much more than J.B.'s. He also carried a tied down pistol, though the holster did not show near as much use as Buck's did. A large, tobacco stained, brush mustache tickled his grub, bite at a time. It was yellowed from many years of tobacco smoke and somewhat bleached by the sun to boot. He'd been smoking quirlys since he was eight years old.

Dusty Walden…well…Dusty was a trip. He was quiet, acted like he didn't understand most anything that came up but actually was a very deep thinker. He was slow to get involved in other folks' differences but if need be, would put a .44 slug in a person as quick as a wink, there again, if need be. He, too, was very good with cattle and he had a tremendous like and respect for horses and women. He loved dogs but hated cats. JB had not had the time to get closely acquainted with the rest of his outfit, beyond knowing them by name and sight. He knew that time would fill in the gaps.

****

JB filed on a section in the northwest corner of Texas the year before and was in the process of proving it up. His section was situated almost in New Mexico Territory. It was a good watered piece of land and a fine place to raise any kind of livestock, especially cattle and horses. When he found the land, filed on it and started to make his improvements, he had written his old school friend, Pepper Cladderbuck, in St. Louis, explained what he had in mind and offered to go partners with Pepper in the cattle business. He remembered that Pepper owned a piece of land further west, around Santa Rosa, New Mexico

If interested, Pepper was to swing down to San Antonio, buy and bring fifteen hundred head of prime longhorn breeding stock to include a couple of bulls to the ranch, with Pepper's land in New Mexico, they could have two bases of operation, multiplying their chances for success. He had not heard from Pepper for a long time but finally his answer came. Cladderbuck was on his way, by way of San Antonio. He was going to get the longhorns and bring them on to the ranch, so JB left the ranch, went to Fort Worth and found three men and then on to Dallas where he hired Chuck Jackson, Abe Rivers, Joe Vaughn and Tom Cranston to help him and continued on up to the Red River and picked up his whiteface breeding stock. Abe Rivers was a Negro and had at one time been a slave on a plantation back in Virginia, but he fit right in with the rest of the crew.

The land on which JB had filed was really a whole lot more than a section when you considered all the open range that surrounded his section, on which they, he and Cladderbuck, would be able to graze their cattle. The ranch, proper, would be six hundred and forty acres but; they would have access to thousands of acres, stretching over into New Mexico Territory. There was plenty of grass and water. The water, used by the ranch headquarters came from a year around spring that flowed from the base of a hill as an artesian well and was added to by the runoff of many canyons and arroyos that fingered out of the surrounding hills and crisscrossed the countryside like giant snake trails. The hill with the spring was covered with cedar and pine. The waterways that JB enjoyed were lined with many kinds of growth but mostly gum, pecan, oak and cottonwood, but all of these were outnumbered by many different kinds of willow trees.

The water that came from the spring was cold enough that a pool of it, shaded all day from the sun, above the ranch house, was used to keep foods cooled in the summertime. JB had placed large rocks in the pool, created by a small dam, so that the surface of the water came up to the tops of them. Clancy kept things like butter and eggs in covered dishes, sitting on the rocks. The overflow from the pool ran down to and over a ledge into a watering trough for the livestock with a 'y' off to feed the house needs.

****

JB sat his horse and looked to the southwest at the circle of buzzards that floated on the currents of the damp wind, blowing ahead of the storm, a few hundred feet above an out-cropping of rocks, maybe a quarter mile from the river and looked to be maybe a mile upstream. Atchley eased his horse up close to JB's side. They both looked at the buzzards for a moment.

"What do you make of it, Boss?" Jocke asked. "It looks like them Buzzes are zeroed in on something to eat."

"No telling what it is, probably a coyote or the remains of a cougar kill, Jocke," said JB, "As soon as we get these critters bedded down, we'll check it out. There ought to be enough light left by then for a look-see."

They rode off the bank, together and hazed the cattle on across the river. The water level was down from a shortage of summer rain. The crew circled and stopped the herd on good grass, a stand of young, tender blades that grew well along the river basin with ample water to keep it thick. Some of the cows remained in the river, water up to their bellies, to cool their blood.

While Buck gathered dry wood along the river bank for the camp fire, JB and Jocke Atchley rode to the outcropping of rocks to see what was so attractive to a flock of buzzards. Dusty was putting a camp together including spreading a tarp between three trees with the forth corner tied to a bow of the chuck wagon, for cover from the impending storm. He also tied a picket rope between two other trees to tie the horses to and have them close to their camp. Abe Rivers had found a tall pole which he used to prop the center of the tarp up so the rain would drain off. The rest of the outfit was settling the cattle down.

JB and Jocke rode through the rocks to a lonely, dead tree where a man hung from one of the high up branches. He evidently had been hanged some time before because the buzzards had torn away most of the clothing and was well on their way to devouring the carcass. JB dismounted and picked up a battered old wallet lying on the ground next to the tree trunk. There was no sign of a horse, dead or alive. Jocke rode over close to the tree where the other end of the rope was tied and cut it, dropping the man to the ground. The buzzards squawked and flapped around with their huge, back heavy wings, irritated that their meal had been disturbed. There was no money in the wallet but it did contain a bill of sale for twenty head of cattle from a man in Albuquerque. JB and Jocke saw no cattle anywhere around, other than their own and no sign anywhere close to the rock formation.

"What are we to do with this mess?" Jocke ventured.

JB thought for a minute. "Nothing," he said.

"Nothing? You mean we're just gonna leave him here on the ground like this?"

"There's nothing we can do for him, now, might as well let the buzzards and coyotes finish their job. By the time the coyotes get through, there won't even be a bone left. This poor devil will be recycled into coyote and buzzard crap and left in splatters and piles, full of tumblebugs, all over this countryside."

"Any mention of who he was in that wallet?" asked Jocke.

"No, there's nothing in here to tell who he was and no money in it either, only the bill of sale and a tin type picture of a rather attractive woman. The 'to line' on this bill of sale is blank. The man that signed it has an address in Albuquerque, I get a chance, I'll write him and see if I can find out who bought these cows mentioned in this bill. I don't know what good it'll do, though, we don't have the cows to pass on to anyone. Whoever hung him, probably took his cows, horse and anything else he owned in addition to his life. The only thing we can do, maybe, is let his next of kin know what happened to him."

"Them damn birds are still looking for something further on over in them rocks, yonder," said Atchley. He thumbed in the direction he meant.

"Let's take a look," said JB. They rode over to the spot of interest to the buzzards.

There was no sign of an entrance into the rocks that would accommodate a horse on the side they approached so they dismounted, ground hitched their cayuses and climbed into the rocks. Squeezing between two large boulders, JB spotted the body of an Indian stretched out on the ground in a little clearing almost completely enclosed by stone. He was lying face down in a pool of black, dried blood and was not moving. His first thought was that the Indian was one of a party that had attacked and hung the man they had found, but on second thought, he realized that Indians didn't hang a person, that wasn't their way. Jocke came squeezing, sideways into the pocket.

Upon closer examination, they found that he had been shot through the left side and had evidently lost a lot of blood. There was no sign of a horse. The Indian was dressed in buckskin. A knife was lying to one side. Jocke took the knife and pushed it between his chaps and his gunbelt. The Indian was still alive but JB found his pulse to be very weak and his breathing was shallow.

"Get my canteen," he said to Atchley, who immediately squeezed back through the crack and returned to the horses outside the rock outcropping. Soon, he was back with the canteen and handed it to JB.

They turned the Indian over, raised his head and JB offered him water. In a state of half-consciousness, he almost strangled on the first sip.

"Take it easy," said JB. "Take it easy."

The Indian blinked and squinted through pain stricken eyes to see who was befriending him. He slowly looked from one to the other and jerked with recognition of white men only to grimace with pain from his wound. Sensing that he was not in danger, he motioned for another taste of water.

"That's it," said JB, "take it slow. You've had a hunk of hot lead rip through your side."

Helping him to his feet, they were able to negotiate the rocks and make it to the horses. Once in the saddle, the Indian slumped over the neck of JB's big Appaloosa. JB walked and led the horse back to camp. Dusty was helping Clancy get supper ready. He stopped and spread a blanket close to the fire. JB and Atchley eased the Indian off the horse and stretched him out on the blanket. Clancy heated some water in a pan the men usually used to take a bird bath and bathed the Indians wound. The Indian lapsed back into unconsciousness but he moaned when JB poured whiskey on the wound, in an effort to stop or head off any infection,

"He's showing signs of fever and might pass a critical point sometime tonight," said JB. "When he reaches that point, he will either come out of it or we could wind up having to put him in the ground. It might help if we can get some whiskey down him in the meantime."

They held his head up and poured a little of the whiskey down his throat. The first sip went down wrong and the Indian coughed himself awake spitting the whiskey back up. Then he accepted a few swallows and seemed to relax. He went off again and JB covered him with a couple of blankets in hopes that they would help to sweat the fever out of him.

"What do you suppose he was doing out here by himself without a horse and who do you think put that hunk of lead through his side?" asked Buck.

"Your guess is as good as mine," said JB. "I'm still trying to figure out what happened to that poor fellow we found hanging from that tree and what he did that put him on the wrong end of a rope. Whoever shot this Indian could have taken his horse as well as that of the man in that tree, and his cattle. I'd say they took any money the fellow had and left his wallet laying on the ground."

"Well, I for one don't cotton too much to no damn Injuns," said Atchley. "They give me the willies, besides, you can't trust'em and there ain't nothing they won't steal, they catch your back turned. You won't ever catch me turning my back on one."

"Well, it's for sure this Indian won't be giving anybody any trouble, stealing anything or taking any scalps for a few days," said JB, "that is, if he makes it at all."

The outfit all stood around the fire and drank coffee as the sky of purple gradually turned to black velvet and the stars started to wink on. The bank of storm clouds kept, slowly hiding the stars in the western sky. Buck spiked his coffee with a touch of whiskey. The wind picked up and fluttered the brim of his hat. He squinted in the direction of the storm clouds and then turned and sat down on a deadfall close by and thought on it all. He was scheduled to take the second watch. As the storm got closer, the wind picked up and whipped the flames of the fire. The water trapped in the wood, crackled and popped, kicking sparks into the air. Out in the darkness, lightning bugs could be seen, darting to and fro, trying to attract a mate with the light of their tails.

Atchley meanwhile sat close to the fire on a blanket and took his Navy Colt .44 apart, cleaned, and oiled and then reassembled it. He loaded it, spun the cylinder on the sleeve of his shirt and put it back in its resting place. He poured himself a cup of coffee and headed for the herd to stand his watch. He led his horse, saddled, and carried his Winchester in the crook of his arm, being careful to not spill the rich black brew in his tin cup. His chaps made a swishing sound as they swept back and forth through the tall river bottom grass, his spurs softly jingled, musically, as he walked into the edge of nightfall.

The call of a whippoorwill sounded in the night and all up and down the river bank, he heard, what sounded like thousands of frogs and untold numbers of crickets and other insects, blending in a symphony of night sounds. Off in the distance, a coyote yelped and another answered him in kind and the night settled in with the whole pack on the chase. The night sounds were a good indication of what was going on in the wild. It was amazing how the presence of imminent danger would shut the sounds off. The storm to the west hung over the horizon a while and then broke up and faded away as if it went to sleep with the coming of nightfall. The whole crew was glad to see it dissipate.

JB felt the need to clean his gun, also, but decided to wait until another time. A good thing, too, for not half an hour later, they had company.

From the darkness a voice rang out. "Hell...ooou the camp, mind if we come in?"

"Come closer," JB said, aloud, "slowly."

Two men on horseback slowly materialized out of the darkness. When they were well inside the light circle of the campfire, JB could see that they were both hard cases.

"We're lookin fer our Injun," said one of the men, with a curl of smoke from his cigarette drifting into his eyes, making him squint. He leaned forward and rested his forearm on the horn of his saddle. He was sitting a Texas rig with a rope coiled and tied with a rawhide thong on the right side of the horn and a saddle gun wrapped in a fringed scabbard under his leg on the right, stock forward. He took the cigarette from his mouth and grinned through greenish, yellow stained teeth. "I see you caught him for us," he said.

"Are you the ones who shot him?" asked JB.

"Sure as hell are," said the other rider, "we put lead in'im first, so that makes him ours! Ain't that right, Goesto?"

"Yep, that's about the size of it, Lucas," said Goesto.

"Wait just a minute," said JB. "Let me get this straight."

"Wait fer what?" asked Goesto? "We got a long ways to go to collect and we ain't wasting all night jawin with a bunch of simple minded cowpokes."

"What do you mean, collect?" asked JB.

"The bounty," exclaimed Lucas, the second hard case! "Tell him about the bounty, Goesto."

"Shut up Lucas," said Goesto, "you want the whole country to know about it?"

"Tell me about this bounty," JB spoke with a cool tone, keeping his eyes fixed on Goesto. Jocke strolled back to the fire from his watch about then, stopping to the side, just inside the circle of campfire light. Dusty was just finishing his grub. He laid his plate aside, stood up and hooked his right thumb over the top edge of his gun belt. Goesto was talking.

"Well, there's a rancher west of here, about a hundred mile or so, pays fifty dollars a head fer Injuns, dead, Lucas gets his half, twenty dollars and I get the other half."

"Thet's right," said Lucas, "I git half." JB turned his head a sixteenth of an inch left and then back right in total disbelief at the stupidity of Lucas.

"Thet rancher don't want no live ones. All he wants is the head, so's he'll know we got one. You can do whatever you want with the rest of him. Taking the whole carcass back would be a stinkin job, which I don't intend doin, course, if'n you want, we'll haul him out a ways a'fore we cut the head loose."

JB fought back the sick feeling he had and tried without much success to hold back the anger that began to rage within him; it overflowed. He spoke with a cold, dangerously angry tone to his voice.

"You boys missed this one," he said.

Lucas dropped his hand to the butt of his gun and had it clear of leather before JB moved. In less than a quarter of a heartbeat, JB's .44 Navy Colt was spewing fire and burning hot lead. The upper arm of Lucas jerked from the impact of the heavy metal, traveling at about eighteen hundred feet per second. The force turned him in the saddle and rendered him unable; not only to lift the weapon, but even to hold it and it fell from his relaxed grip and hit the ground. Jocke Atchley's .44 was pointed at Lucas also, but his trigger finger was resting on the trigger, without tension. When Goesto turned to find Buck, he discovered Buck's Winchester .44-.40 was pointed at his belt buckle. The noise of the pistol blast frightened a screech owl that took wing and left its perch to seek a quieter place to sleep. Dusty was just standing there with his arms crossed, watching the whole show. Goesto's hand was on the butt of his gun but he opened his hand widely and slowly raised it slightly up in the air in a show of surrender. The round was lost to him so why get killed over it? He backed his horse as Lucas did his and once outside the light of the camp fire, they wheeled their mounts and rode out without looking back.

****

"I told you we should'a brought the rest of the boys," Lucas spat past his pain with gritted teeth, when they were out of earshot of JB"s camp.

"Ah, shut up," said Goesto with a sneer. "How'd I know we'd run into a camp of salty drovers, and them with that stinking redskin sprawled out by their fire. We'll get the boys and come back fer that Injun; lay us away some cowboys at the same time, too."

****

Back in camp, Buck picked up the gun Lucas had dropped, blew the dust from it, checked the action and load then stuck it behind his belt buckle.

"Do you think we've seen the last of them two?" he asked.

"I doubt it," said JB, "we'd better take our watches just a hair more seriously. Expect anything. I hope I'm wrong but I expect them to come back to get the Indian and they might have friends they can bring along, they won't come back to talk, either. We'll lay bedrolls around the fire, fill'em with cedar boughs and then pull back into the brush to bed down. Leave the bedrolls stuffed with those cedar boughs to look like a person sleeping and do one for the Indian. Buck, give me a hand, let's move the Indian back into the brush, with us."

They lifted the Indian and carried him back into the brush. Dusty snatched up the blanket, ran ahead and spread it for them to lay him down on. Then they all returned to the fire, stuffed their bedrolls, drained the coffee pot and set it aside. They then took their cups of coffee and some beef jerky back into the brush and stretched out. Jocke returned to post on watch and stayed close to the cattle. He tied his horse, saddled, to a low branch of a tree and sat down against the tree. Every now and then, he got up and casually walked around and among the cattle to keep them calm. There wasn't much danger of a stampede but it was possible for something to spook them, so Jocke kept a sharp eye out. He whispered, hummed and even sang to them, very softly, which seemed to always sooth the critters, even though his singing left a whole lot to be desired, according to Buck and Dusty. JB stayed out of it. He had learned early in life not to get between two men at odds with each other. He had known a man named Elrod that was trying to break up a fight between two of his friends and one of them bit his nose off, spit it out and a dog snatched it up and swallowed it whole. He recalled how old man Elrod looked like a turtle the rest of his life.

Soon the first watch was through and the second almost over and nothing had happened to that point. Then, somewhere between one and two in the morning, all of a sudden, there was a blaze of rifle fire from the line of trees that ran along the river bank. The bedrolls in camp were being cut to pieces with flying chunks of hot lead, fire from the barrels of rifles, flashing like orange lightning across the area, the thunder of exploding gunpowder, rolled up the river bed. A cloud of heavy, acrid smoke filled the air and was swirled and whipped around by the soft early morning breeze. The screech owl was off somewhere else, sound asleep.

Jocke was caught off guard by the sudden blasts of rifle fire. He was on the opposite side of the cattle from his horse. The cows were restless and expressed their confusion with loud bawling and the walling back of their eyes in a sign of fright. He talked his way through the herd, trying to keep his own excitement concealed and reached his horse just about the time of the second round of gun fire. The second round was answered by what he figured was return fire from his own outfit. The karumbaboom of sound reverberated through the branches of the trees of the basin, helping the breeze in its tireless effort to move the leaves.

Buck, Dusty and JB waited for the second round of fire so they would have the flashes from the muzzles of their would-be assassins to aim at. They leveled chunks of .44 lead at as many flashes as they could with their hand guns. It was surely close enough for pistol work and from the yelps and later, breeze brushing silence, it was pretty sure they had scored some deadly hits. In only a minute or two, Buck hallooed the camp and came in, waving his hat to clear the smoke from the air. It was about then, that they heard the rattle of the hooves of at least two horses, urged into a fast gallop, going away.

"Light that lantern and let's see what we have here," said JB.

Dusty put a Lucifer to the wick of the coal oil lantern and everyone walked out into the darkness, Dusty holding the light high. There, in the tall grass, close to the tree line, they found one horse, saddled, standing, nervously, to one side with an empty rifle boot. They also noted the tracks of four horses leaving the area. Two of the would-be bushwhackers lay sprawled on the ground, one looking wide-eyed at the stars but seeing nothing, a bullet hole half an inch above his right eye. The other was face down in the wet sand with his fingers clinging to a hand full of it, a large exit hole in the center of his back, torn by a splattered out fragmented hunk of hot lead.

"Neither one of these is either Lucas or Goesto," said JB. "If it was them, they're the ones we heard leaving. They may be back but I doubt it. Put that hoss in with ours and gather up their weapons and ammunition. Take their gun belts and check their pockets and the saddlebags on that hoss. There's no sense in leaving anything we can use," he said. "Come first light, find a place along the bank of that dry wash to put their carcasses and stamp the bank down over them. We ain't got time to dig them a hole and besides, the varmints deserve a treat every now and then, so let them have what's left to pick over.

One of the men had eleven double eagles in his pocket and the other had five. JB split the money between the seven men. He kept the guns and ammunition for future use along with a bottle of Tennessee whiskey, found in the saddlebags that were on the horse. Not having any room in the chuck wagon to carry extra freight, he decided to keep the saddle and let the extra horse carry it each day. He figured they could build a travois to haul the Indian and tie it to the tail end of the chuck wagon, until the Indian was well enough to ride. When the Indian was well enough, he might just give him the extra horse and let him be on his way, but first things first. The bushwhackers had to be dealt with.

"We can go on as we are and wait and watch for those hombres to return, which they may never do, or we can go after the bastards and put a stop to it once and for all," said JB, "what do you'al say?"

"Well, I for one would like to put it to rest, once and for all," said Buck.

"Me too," Atchley chimed in.

There were unanimous nods from the whole crew.

"Then that's settled," said JB, "Buck, you go and pick up their trail. The rest of you see to the cows and horses and we'll keep the camp and hold where we are until Buck gets back."

Buck was stepping into the leather when JB turned and said, "Don't try anything with them unless you are a hundred percent sure you can handle it. If you're not sure, come and get us."

"Okay, boss," said Buck, over his shoulder as he rode out. He was casting back and forth in the general direction the horses sounded as they rode out and soon he was on the track and off in search of the bushwhackers. It was just getting light but the trail was clear. The hard cases hadn't had the time to cover their trail and a blind man, with one eye closed, could have followed it in the dark. It wouldn't have mattered too much for Buck was a skilled tracker. Some folks said he could track a snowflake over the mountains in the middle of a winter blizzard and catch it before the spring thaw. Buck was indeed a western man in the know. He grew up on rattlesnake meat and mare milk. He was shooting a pistol by the time he was old enough to hold it up and point. He had tight, browned skin and went clean shaven. Short rawhide chaps covered the front of his faded jeans and a deer-skin vest wrapped his long sleeved wool shirt to hold the body heat in. A Stetson that showed quite a bit of wear capped his head. Thus he sat his Texas rig on his favorite horse, a bay gilding that had an abundance of cow sense.

After a couple of hours, he was getting a little weary of the trail for there was a sense of ambush that he felt very strongly. He cut from the trail and rode a mile or so to the right of it. He then turned in the direction the trail was taking and proceeded parallel to it. He continued for a couple of hours in the same direction and then cut back to where he figured the trail would be. When he had gone a mile or so, he cast around in circles, looking for sign. Finding none he rode back toward his own camp searching for where the outlaws had either stopped or turned off.

He had only gone a short distance before smelling the faint odor of wood smoke. He knew then the outlaws had stopped for some reason and had built a fire. Catching sight of the smoke, he rode a wide circle until he was downwind from them. He stopped in a thicket of mesquite, tied his horse and continued on foot after changing from his boots to moccasins that he always carried in his saddlebags, for comfort as well as quiet movement when the occasion called for it.

There was no reason to alert their horses that he was anywhere around. Holding to the heaviest growth, he made his way to within ear-shot of the camp of the owlhoots. He circled the camp looking for a lookout but found none. '*What a fool thing to do*,' he thought. '*Pulling a stunt like they did and not putting out a guard. They must not have been expecting anyone to follow them.*'

He heard one of the bushwhackers talking.

"Them damn cowboys have cut our number in half. I figured we had them dead to rights," said Lucas, "what happened?" He asked. He skewed his face from the pain in his arm.

"I don't know," said Goesto. "They got one of our horses, too." He was furious. "I tell you what we're gonna do. We're gonna find us some more men and go after them lowdown cowpokes and burn us some hide, make'em wish they had never, ever, heard of Goesto Church."

"Not me," said Lucas. "I still have a few hours of daylight and I'm making tracks for parts unknown. I've had all I want of them Texas cowboys."

"Why you yellow skunk," said Goesto. "I guess you aim to take part of the grub with you and half of them damn cows we took off that pilgrim we hung?"

"You can keep my half of the bounty on that Injun, if you can get him away from them cowboys."

Buck had eased to within twenty yards of the camp, keeping concealed in the brush. He stepped out into the clearing and spoke.

"You Gents have been busy, lately," he said.

The outlaws turned as one to face Buck with startled looks on their faces. There was what seemed like, a ten minute silence when nobody moved. Buck had his .44 out and the owlhoots were looking down the dark hole in the end of the barrel. He directed his speech to the second outlaw.

"You say you want to ride, Lucas?" he asked?

"Yes…yes Sir, I do."

"Well, you climb into that saddle and get out of the country. I ride for JB Johnson and I'm not so sure he would be as generous as I am in letting you go. Now get!" He twitched the barrel of his gun, slightly, to encourage Lucas to move.

"I'm going Mister. Just let me get my saddle on a fresh hoss and I'm gone," he said as he proceeded to remove his saddle to put it on one of the horses that had belonged to one of the downed riders.

Buck thought about making him walk but that would have been cruel. A man in that country without a horse was as good as dead. As soon as the owlhoot unsaddled the mount he'd been riding and saddled one they were leading, he stepped into the leather. Buck spoke.

"Let me see you in this country again and you can keep your appointment with the Devil," He then turned his full attention to Goesto, whom he had been watching from the corner of his eye.

Lucas reined his cayuse around and pointed him south and laid spurs to his sides.

"Now, Goesto, what's all this talk of more men and all your lip about getting you some cowboy hide?"

"You talk big with a .44 in your hand," Goesto whined.

Buck eased his weapon into the holster and pushed the brim of his Stetson back a notch, using his gun hand purposefully. He stood there with his feet spread; shoulder width apart, a grim look in his eyes and a soft smile of confidence eased across his lips. A scared look came into the eyes of Goesto. He was staring death in the face but he was committed. His hand went down to the butt of his gun and he was fast. He swung the pistol up and fired. He felt two kinds of bucking. One was the pistol in his hand. The other was a hunk of lead tagging his left shirt pocket. Then memory of the Buck was gone.

19

CHAPTER 2

Pepper Cladderbuck still wore the Smith & Wesson .44 that he had the night his father was killed and when the hired gun, he now faced, reached for his weapon, Cladderbuck's hand swung forward past his holster, his trigger finger slipped into the trigger housing, pulling his gun up and forward at the same time his thumb cocked the hammer. So fast that it was almost impossible for the human eye to see and was impossible if that eye blinked. Those present, only thought, they saw it. One minute, Cladderbuck was standing there, empty handed and in less than an excited heartbeat, he was standing there with a smoking .44 in his grip. One quick twirl put the weapon back in its resting place. It had swung, barrel up, in a line straight to the chest of the gunman, hammer back with Pepper's trigger finger pressing half a hair on a hair trigger. Then the blast of gunpowder that over-lapped the movement seemed to have all happened in one lightning fast movement. The gunman stood on his tiptoes, his pistol hanging on his right index finger, hammer eared back but he seemed to lack the energy it took to lift the gun, much less to pull the trigger, a neat round hole appeared in the center of his chest, as if by magic and his life's blood pumped out in spurts.

Cladderbuck walked over, knocked the pistol from his hand with the barrel of his own pistol and the hammer of the gunman's weapon fell on the round in the chamber, exploded a chunk of hot lead through the man's groin, down and through the lower side of his left boot and lodged in his heel. He sank to his knees. Pepper stood looking down at the man. The gunman looked up with the glaze of death, slowly capturing his eyes. He blinked away the sweat that ran down into them. He said in a blood foaming gurgle, "I should have taken you, Cladderbuck."

Pepper looked him in the eye and whispered so that only he could hear, "You judged the wrong name."

"What… do you mean…wrong name."

"I'm not only Pepper Cladderbuck," said Pepper, "but someone else, also."

"Who else?" the gunman asked in a, half breath, whisper.

"I'm the Saw Tooth Kid," Pepper said.

The gunman knew the legend. Now he knew the Kid.

"You...Saw...Tooth...Kid..?" He gurgled the question, as a crimson trickle oozed from the corner of his mouth.

"Yep." said Pepper.

The gunman gasped, expelled his final breath and fell forward with an expression of fear on his face as if he had been scared to death.

The witnesses present, all told the same story to the deputy sheriff who had been called to the scene. 'Cladderbuck had fired in self defense.'

"Put him in the ground and send me the bill," Cladderbuck told the deputy that investigated the incident, who was going through the man's pockets.

"There won't be any expenses," he said, "this hombre's got ten Doubles here. That'll be more'n enough to put him in a pine box on boot hill, with a bunch left over. What should I do with it?"

"What do you suggest?" asked Pepper.

"Well, why don't I give it to the church for the orphan's fund? I growed up an orphan," he said. "I know firsthand just how badly they need it."

"That sounds like a real good place for it," Pepper said.

****

The attempt on his life tied the sack as far as he was concerned. He had to get away from everything for a while, if not for good and pull things back together. As luck would have it, he received the letter from his, only, friend from school, JB Johnson, that same day. After sending an answer, he took the train the next day and like a magnet, the urge to return to the west, was pulling him and all he could think of was the valley where he and his father had spent many long hours together; growing up hours for him. Now he had the deed to that valley, obtained many years earlier. It was time for him to do something with the valley and JB's offer sounded just like the ticket to that end.

The train car in which he rode was one of typical design for the period. It had iron framed seats with wood slats. The wood had a thin pad of cotton, covered with a, paisley design, heavy cloth. The arm rests were exposed metal and left a lot to be desired in comfort. Feather stuffed pillows could be rented from the conductor, for a penny, that could be used as a pillow for sleeping, padding for the arm rests or extra padding for the seats. There were kerosene lanterns that hung from the side walls between every-other window. The alternate side panels were, each, covered with a long strip of mirror, about six inches wide. The floor was constructed of hardwood, penetrated with cotton seed oil and usually strewn with cigarette butts and pieces of discarded trash. The windows were two-paneled solid glass.

Pepper had been staring out the window, with his deep brown eyes, most of the day. It was as though he could see his past in the reflective glass and in his mind's eye, he could, hardly seeing the countryside as it flew by. He was at the same time, looking at the reflections of the others who shared the railroad car with him. There was the drummer with the coat that was or seemed to be two sizes too small for him. Pepper thought that he looked like so many other drummers with his round derby hat, bow tie and slicked down hair. Always with a small satchel that contained samples or pictures of his goods, ready to show to anyone in whom he might create an interest. Then there were the three cowboys that were probably on their way back to their home range after delivering cattle to the stock yards in St. Louis. The older lady and surely her husband, sitting close to her, headed for who knows where, probably to see grandkids, or returning from such a visit.

His muscles tightened ever so slightly but tightened none the less, when he glanced at the man in the last seat, near the rear door. He knew that this was the one who needed watching. The man was the only one, other than himself, maybe, who seemed separate and apart from the rest of the passengers. Then there was the young woman with the initials, GP. She was dressed in a leather riding skirt and a matching waistcoat that complimented her trim, designed, hand tooled boots. She was evidently a western woman who would have looked, totally, out of place in an eastern city dress. She wore a round brimmed, flat crowned hat that matched the color of her outfit. Her red hair was bunched into a ball and laid on the back of her neck. Cladderbuck's eyes lingered on her reflection for some time and there was a stirring in his loins.

He didn't need to see the countryside for he knew it. He had spent many long hours in the pursuit of jackrabbits, deer and antelope all through country just like this. The buttes, arroyos, cliffs and ledges and forests in the foothills of the great mountain range that continued into the Rockies to the northwest and the beautiful mountain streams, fed by springs and high-up snow melt, all of these things were part of the enormous playground he enjoyed as a child, and closing his eyes, he could feel, see and smell the memories of those years of the past.

Summers in the west could be and usually were very hot but it was a dry heat. They were not like the humid summer days back east. A hundred degrees back east felt like a hundred and ten, but in the southwest, a hundred degrees felt more like ninety. The difference was in the humidity. Johnson had said that his ranch was in the northwest part of the panhandle of Texas. It was a little short of New Mexico, where Pepper had grown up, but still it was the west, one hell of a lot further west than St. Louis.

The sulfur odor of burning coal filled the air with pungent fumes that caused his eyes to water just a little. His thoughts moved to the scene just a few days earlier, when he'd had that close brush with death, and he couldn't help thinking about it. When a man comes to the realization that death is as strong a possibility as living, he reflects on a very many things. He comes up with a lot of questions for which answers are sometimes hard to find.

Question number one, why had he decided to return to the west to sort out his life? Maybe it was Johnson's invitation or maybe something deeper. He really didn't know. He wasn't afraid of Metcalf but in St. Louis, he was on Metcalf's turf. Out west, he would be on his own ground, giving him the advantage. He knew, finally, that you just didn't turn your back to enemies like Craig Metcalf who would stab you in the back and you never turn your back on friends like JB Johnson, who would toe the line for you, when they need and ask for your help. He had no proof but he was almost completely sure that Metcalf was behind the hired gun he had faced the day before he took the train.

On the surface, Pepper had tried to convince himself that he was not too fond of the west, that St. Louis was the place he belonged. He thought he had succeeded in convincing himself, but now, some strange force was drawing him back to the rooting place of his life, a feeling of excitement inside him gave him realization that he had been fooling himself all along. He had begun in the west; maybe he would find himself there. Sure, he had built a fortune and a whole different life style back in St. Louis; yet, here he was, on his way to a section of the country that was just barely beyond the savage stage. But first, he had to pick up those cattle in south Texas and get them to the other side of the state. He felt elated about the mission and couldn't wait to get on with it. Time passed and the day faded softly into night and after sandwiches and coffee, provided by the railroad, time poured black ink on the countryside and trying to look out the window only produced reflections of the inside of the car and stars above the blackness of the land.

He gazed at the window of the railroad car as if watching the countryside fly by, but it was like the coal they were feeding the engine and the only thing he could see were the reflections of the five men and two women who shared the car with him. *'I wonder what that good looking heifer is doing out here in this hard country?'* He thought to himself about GP, whatever those initials stood for. The wick lamps provided very little light but he could see the passengers slumped in their seats in restless half sleep as the train cut through the murky darkness of the early morning hours. The night was clear and there was a chill on the wind that wrapped the train like a frosty blanket.

The women in the car had gotten on at St. Louis, as well as the three drovers. GP was a good looker and appeared to be a couple of years younger than Cladderbuck, but he realized that it was hard, sometimes, to tell just how old a person was, since you couldn't look in their mouths like you could a horse's. She had a beautiful mouth. He had noticed also that she was traveling alone and he had heard her tell the conductor that she was headed for Albuquerque which would require a change of trains in Dallas. Cladderbuck's close observation of people was, for the main part, to single out those he felt he needed to keep an eye on. He saw only one on the car, the tall, lean man with the look of an animal that killed only to eat and he looked like he was getting hungry. How much, he thought, like himself, except Pepper Cladderbuck, only killed to protect Pepper, or those who could not protect themselves, like most women, children and animals, other than that, he pretty much let everyone tend to their own snake stamping.

The train rocked on through the night, into early light and made its way into a valley that spread a few miles to a small mountain range that reminded him of the San Jacinto Mountains, out in New Mexico Territory. The coiled trail of black smoke, from the engine, blended with the dark of night and cast, goblin like, shapes against the background of cloudless, pale blue skies that stretched from horizon to horizon.

About that time, the door at the forward end of the car opened and the conductor came in, letting a blast of cold air in at the same time. The frigid air wove its way around and under the seats. He had a pot of hot coffee in his fist and a bunch of tin cups with a string through the handles, hanging on his arm. He looked from each passenger to the next as he walked, with a sway caused by the motion of the train, down the aisle until he came to the center of the car. He placed the coffee pot on top of the potbelly heater, took the poker, swung open the door and poked a couple of chunks of coal in.

Hanging the cups on a nail next to the heater, he turned and said, "Coffee's here if you want it." Then he turned and went back out the door, letting in another blast of cold air that challenged the little bit of warmth in the car.

Cladderbuck read the woman as one with the courage to look a man in the eye with the conviction of truth without being forward in any way. Her eyes revealed that she knew what men were all about and that she liked them. She was medium height, not too tall but slender, with an air of self sufficiency. To put it another way, she was very much the lady but one who could take care of herself in a pinch. He had noticed her initials embroidered on her luggage earlier before the conductor had taken them to the baggage car. Glancing at her, on his way to pour a cup of coffee, he wondered what the initials stood for. Picking up the pot, he turned to her. "Coffee?" he asked.

"Why, yes, thank you," she replied, watching as he stood before the heater and wondered, '*what of this man.*'

He poured a cup and handed it to her and then after pouring one for himself, he put the coffee pot back on the heater top and returned to his seat. She felt a slight letdown that he had not asked if he could sit with her. The heat increased and laid a barrier against the frigid weather outside. The heat, washing the inside of the cold windows, caused them to fog up a bit and Pepper wiped the window with his sleeve. The wiping action left a band of streaks that beaded up with moisture. The droplets of water streamed down the glass, leaving more streaks that crossed those, streaked across the window. '*Damn, I got my sleeve all wet,*' he thought and almost voiced. He glanced at the woman to see if she had seen his dumb mistake. If she had, she didn't show it. He wondered to himself why it made any difference whether she did or not.

His thoughts turned to when he had walked into the trading post that night with his father, and was hardly noticed by anyone. It was a night that was burned into his memory and would be with him the rest of his life; a dark, wet, stormy night. He had sat down in the corner behind the heater to keep warm while his father, George Cladderbuck, traded the pelts they had brought, for food and ammunition. The large one room trading post, the Saw Tooth Trading Post, had that wonderful blend of smells that a person could only get in a store like Sal's, the smells of new leather, coffee, new clothes and the faint odor of coal-oil burning in the lamps. He thought of how he had settled in the corner behind the heater and smelled all the smells. He had hardly been noticed by anyone.

He was noticed by everyone though after the roar of his repeater left four men stretched out dead on the floor and a fifth one half down, hanging onto the counter, dying. The drovers who shot George Cladderbuck did not even know Pepper was on the place until they heard the click of the hammer on his .44 being cocked. Within seconds, the sawdust on the floor was soaking up their blood. Silence settled in as the echo of the gunfire fled the building and bounced off the walls of the town's buildings, and fell across the room as Pepper bent down, picked up the bleeding body of his father and carried him, through the swirling remains of gun smoke, into the night. What had happened that night became a legend as the story was told over and over again. Cladderbuck became known as 'The Kid at the Saw Tooth Trading Post', and later, as the story was told over and over, he became known only as the 'Saw Tooth Kid'. Nobody knew the man or the boy, who carried him out. The two of them faded into the black of night without a trace; a violent storm washed away any sign and nobody was able to even tell which direction they had gone.

The story told was that the man had come into the trading post with a bundle of pelts he wanted to trade. One or two of the people in the trading post had noticed the boy going to the corner but that was all. The man was at the counter talking with Sal, the owner, when the drovers walked up behind him. One of them tripped over the bundle of pelts on the floor and got mad about it.

"Why don't you keep them stinking animal skins out of folk's way?" The drover said.

"You might watch where you put those big feet," Cladderbuck said.

One thing led to another, and two of them grabbed George's arms and the one that had stumbled said, "Nobody talks to me like that and gets away with it." He then shot Cladderbuck, twice, at point blank range. The other two, turned him loose and let him drop to the floor and the one that did the shooting, spit a thick, amber stream of tobacco juice, hitting the dying man's head.

Then there was a long moment of silence, with the acrid odor of gun smoke permeating the room. The deafening sound of silence was broken by the click of metal on metal of a gun being cocked. The drovers all turned to look into the black muzzle of a .44.

Without a word Pepper stood with his feet apart as the fire of exploding gunpowder spewed from the barrel of his gun. Two of the four, killed in the first round of fire, were shot between the eyes, two others in the throat and the fifth man, hit in the chest, whispered two words "help me" to the owner of the trading post just before he lost his grip and slid off the counter to the floor and died. The thoughts of the fight kept coming back to Pepper's mind from time to time.

****

The lonely sound of the train whistle, trailing off into the emptiness of the plains, pulled Cladderbuck back to the present. He sat a few moments and listened to the clickity-clack of the train wheels on the steel rails where the sections of track were joined together, clickity when they left one section and clack when they hit the next. The train was slowing on a grade. After the climb to the top there was a half mile run to a place the conductor called Lizard Springs. He put a cigar in his teeth, stuck a long splinter of wood from kindling in a box, next to the heater, through a small air hole in the heater door, brought the flame up to his face and lit the smoke.

He took a deep draw and taking the cigar from his lips, blew a ring of smoke that drifted through the still air to encircle one of the coal oil lamps that hung from the section of wall between two of the windows. The lines on his face showed a quick glimpse of a lot of years of fighting for the right to live his own life. He blew out the fire and threw the splinter into the ash pail. For a moment though, while he lit his cigar, the woman with GP on her luggage caught the hardness in his eyes, hardness but with a spark of kindness that was so deep, she had to look a second time, after blinking, just to see it.

He kept his saddlebags and his Winchester .44-.40 at his side. His bed roll and saddle were in the stock car, where his horse was stalled. The cold air might arouse the other passengers when he opened the door to leave but he needed some fresh air. He walked slowly toward the door at the end of the car. On his way down the aisle, he glanced at himself in one of the strips of mirror that filled the panels between the windows. His face was lean and tight and was flanked by black sideburns that cut in line with the lower part of his ears. His dark eyes gave the impression that he was the kind of man that asked no quarter and gave none. The only part of his face that gave expression was his eyes. His hardness had been acquired over the ten years since that night at the Saw Tooth Trading Post.

His father, George Cladderbuck, was carrying a pouch with close to five thousand dollars worth of pure gold nuggets when he died that cold wet night, not more than five miles from the trading post. Pepper buried him between two giant oak trees on the upper bank of a fresh water stream. With that kind of money, it was easy for Cladderbuck to settle and start a business in a town like St. Louis.

The whistle of the train sounded. He turned to see if the sound had disturbed the other passengers. The only one that seemed to be awake was the woman GP. "Are you restless, too," she asked. A polite smile was written on her lips. He smiled back with one corner of his mouth. "If a man wasn't restless every now and then, he would never get anything done," he said. "That is, anything worth doing."

"True," she said, "very true."

She turned away to continue her fruitless effort to sleep. Then she turned once more to glance at the man. He looked tight and strangely savage in a gentle way. Grace Pritchet was confused. She watched as the man went to the door, rubbed the fog from the glass and peered out into the darkness. Then he returned to his seat for a spell. All of a sudden, he was thinking about the woman more than he was thinking about fresh air. His thoughts were jumping around, all over the place.

Ten years was more than enough time for him to build his business into one of the largest in St. Louis. He had made an untold amount of money. Friends were easier to count than enemies. The count was friends, one or two and enemies, many. One of the two most dangerous of his known enemies were Craig Metcalf, who, in one of Pepper's unguarded moments, had tried to have him killed. The other was Metcalf's silent partner, Howard Stewart, who just happened to be the town Marshall. One of the most dangerous combinations there could be, to have the town marshal, who was a known gun hand, hooked up with the likes of Metcalf, a class 'A' crook. They remained free as birds because nobody had ever been able to prove anything against either of them. The train sliced its way through the night.

Cladderbuck was glad to be shaking the dust of St. Louis from his boots, but he was surely going to miss the challenge of business pursuits. The one thing he could not have foreseen was the fact that Metcalf had instructed Stewart to following him. He didn't realize either that he and Metcalf were on separate courses that would bring them face to face, one last time, down the trail. Fate has a strange way of correcting itself, sometimes.

Twenty nine years had passed since he received his first slap on the butt, the first time in his life that he cried. The second and last time he cried was the night he buried his father. He never knew his mother who died in childbirth. His first cry had to have been for her. He got once more to his feet and walked to the door. He took one quick glance at the other passengers. All were still. He stepped out the door and closed it behind him. A cold breeze curled around his boots and its brother whispered past his ear. The night was crisp and clear with at least a million stars winking at him. He judged that it was close to two in the morning from the position of the stars.

He watched the smoke from the engine trail off into the night like a misty cloud between him and the stellar display. His eyes traveled over the mail car, just ahead, then the stock car, and then the tender, which was the tail end of the engine. The tender was half filled with coal. It had only been a short few years since the trains had been converted from burning wood to burning coal. Just ahead of the tender, the engine was smoothed out, beyond struggling, not having to contend with any grade, to speak of. The window in the door of the stock car had an orange glow with the light from a coal oil lamp. Cladderbuck thought of his horse which had, on many occasions, been his only companion. There was an attendant in the stock car to take care of the animals. He was responsible for on and off loading any animals as well as luggage, which was stowed in the mail car.

Shortly, the train slowed to a stop under the spout at Lizard Springs. A night owl, disturbed by the train, left its perch on the tank, popped its large, soft feathered wings, against the early morning air and flew off, into the darkness. The engineer climbed to the platform on the water tank and guided the spout to the water intake on the engine. It took only a short time to fill the tank on the train and they were ready to go. Dallas was the next stop and Cladderbuck would change to a train going south to San Antonio. Pepper stood on the platform of the passenger car as the giant wheels of the engine slowly turned over and strained against the weight of the train. Then after slipping and spinning a couple of times, they caught and hugged the steel of the tracks. For a moment, he stood watching the stars. The owl returned to its perch where it resumed its patient wait for a rabbit or field mouse to come to the tank for a drink of the sweet, water overflow that trickled to the ground beside the tracks.

He heard the sound of the next whistle blow from the train and then nothing but the clickity-clack of the wheels on the rails. A feeling of longing swept over him. He wanted, very much, to see the place where he had grown up, a place he had come to think of as Sparkling Water Valley.

Pepper Cladderbuck was returning to the land of his birth, in a round-about way. He stood now alone as he had stood ever since the night of the trading post shootout. The longing in him steered his thoughts to the beautiful woman inside the car. He had a momentary stirring in his loins, again. What was it with this woman?

He was getting sleepy and tiredness was beginning to catch up to him. There was something about traveling that relaxed him and it wouldn't be long now before he would be able to drop off into a sound sleep, just as soon as he got settled on the train south, out of Dallas. He thought of the cattle he had to buy and the drive west. Howard Stewart peeked through the glass in the back door of the car, at Pepper, to make sure that he was there and settling down, then he returned to his seat in the next car. He would not venture another look unless the train stopped for any reason.

****

Grace Pritchet sat quietly as her train rocked a little back and forth. She had not been able to get back to sleep since switching trains in Dallas and the tall man had stayed on the train, going south. For some reason, she was unable to get him out of her mind. As far as she could tell, none of the others had even realized that he was no longer with them. The three cowboys were on the train, west, as was the rough looking man, who again, was seated at the back end of the new car. The older couple had left the southbound train in Dallas and must have stayed in Dallas or took another train to some other place. Grace got up and made her way to the heater, poured herself a cup of coffee and continued on to the front door. She stood by the door and peered out into the darkness, sipped her hot coffee and wondered who the mysterious man was, where he was at that moment and where he was headed. She stood there until the first light of dawn began to glow in the eastern sky, chasing the train from behind. She took another sip of her Arbuckle. In a few hours, the train would make it to Amarillo and then on to Albuquerque.

CHAPTER 3

It was just dusk and the edge of the western horizon had become a golden stripe from the northern most peaks to the southern rim when Buck rode in with two horses, one on a lead rope and the other, bridled and saddled with gear tied on including saddlebags. Jocke and JB stood with cups in their hands and had just filled them with fresh coffee. Dusty and Chuck Jackson were keeping an eye on the cattle while the rest of the crew was knocking around camp. There was a curl of dust behind Bucks horses that filtered the scant light from the late afternoon sky creating a light tan vale backdrop for Buck's shadowy figure. He pulled rein and stepped down from the saddle. Jocke and JB watched as Buck led the horses to the picket line, stripped off the saddles and let them roll. He then tied them to the rope and went to the fire. Taking his hat off, he stuck a finger through a bullet hole in it. With a big grin, he pointed the finger at his amigos.

"How'd you get that hole in your hat?" asked Atchley.

"Goesto put it there about half an eyewink after I slipped a pill into his left shirt pocket, for safe keeping."

"How many were there?"

"Just two," said Buck as he strolled up to the fire, picked up a tin cup and reached for the coffee pot. He, slowly, poured the tin full of the rich, hot, black brew.

"What happened to the other one?" asked JB?

Buck took a long sip of his hot coffee and winced at the hot. Then in a matter of fact tone he spoke.

"They didn't know I was on the place and I heard Lucas tell Goesto that he wanted no part of us, so I let him leave the country. I don't think he'll be back, Goesto was a different story."

"I'm glad you brought those hosses back with you," said JB, "we can use them." He strolled over to take a closer look at them, his tin cup in hand.

"All in a day's work, Boss," Buck said, "where's Dusty, with the herd?"

"Yah, he and Chuck are nurse-maidin'em right now," JB said.

"We've built a travois to haul the Injun on," said Jocke.

"How's he coming along?" Buck asked curiously.

"Well, he's still out of it with fever but it seems to be not as high as it was, said Jocke. "JB thinks he's coming out of the woods, I guess he is, at that."

JB came back to the fire about that time and said, "Jocke, you and Buck take the next watch, let Dusty and Chuck come in and eat. Tom and Joe can relieve you two in four hours. Abe and I'll relieve Tom and Joe about two in the morning." The night passed without incident and everyone was refreshed and ready to go at first light.

"Buck, tie the travois to the back of the chuck wagon.," said JB. " Clancy, take it easy and try to avoid any deep holes or large rocks and don't drag our Indian friend through any water. Jocke, Dusty and the rest of the crew will be taking care of the cattle and horses. You go ahead and get out in front of the herd. We don't want these cows stomping on the tail end of that travois."

They lifted the Indian onto the travois and tied him in place with rawhide strips. Then JB and Buck moved to their positions. Dusty fell in at drag, his favorite job. They slapped a few hides with coiled lariats, adding shouts and whistles and started the cattle on their way. Buck took outrider and JB moved out to point. One good thing, bunch quitters were not that many. The absence of summer rains not only left the river low but seemed to double the amount of dust that covered the planes country, but high winds kept it swept along. There were still some old buffalo wallows around though most of the buffs had been killed off. The wallows sometimes had water standing in them but not this year. At least, not since early summer. Water wouldn't be a problem for them for there were a number of streams and rivers between where they were and the homestead. The Sweetwater, Palo Duro, Wolf and Canadian all had water in them.

Their days were filled with, not only dust but, the never ending effort to keep the pressure necessary on the herd to move on. The country around was fairly flat but looks were deceiving, for there were swells, arroyos and dry creek beds that couldn't be seen until almost upon them. There had to be a constant watch for ambush. Some of the arroyos could hold an army of savage Indians that could overrun them in minutes. JB left his point position about the middle of the afternoon and rode around the herd to see how everybody was holding up.

"Man, it's as dry as the heart of the bad lands in August," said Atchley.

"You've got that right, Jocke," said JB. "I don't think I've ever seen it this dry before. We could sure use some rain."

As if saying it, willed it, for before nightfall, a thin layer of clouds appeared on the western rim and by dark, lightning flashes could be seen reaching their ghostly fingers to the ground as if in search of something, lost. The roll of distant thunder could be heard from time to time, sounding like muffled Indian drums being beat in a cave somewhere, far off. He and Atchley were sitting their horses, looking in the direction of the flashes.

"We'll have rain before morning," said JB, "if it don't give up, lay down and die like the last one."

"Well, me for one will welcome each and every drop," said Jocke.

"Maybe we can find some shelter before it gets dark. Somebody up there must be listening." He pointed skyward with his thumb.

The only shelter they could find before dark was a gnarled up old cedar that was full enough to block most of the wind and blowing rain. They spread the canvas tarp that Clancy always carried, folded up and stowed in the chuck wagon. It was about eight feet square and when used to block the rain from their camp fire, it served them very well. The fire was small but large enough to broil bacon and boil a large pot of coffee. They all gathered under the tarp, ate their supper, drank their coffee and listened to the roar of the rain on the tarp and surrounding layer of ground-top dust.

The Indian had come around by then. The whiskey they had been able to get down him had evidently done the trick. His fever was gone. He stood close to the fire and drank hot, black coffee with the rest of them. He was quiet but it was noticeable that he was becoming more trusting of everyone. Jocke was in turn, beginning to put some trust in the Indian as well. By the time they pushed the herd into the basin where JB's homestead was located; Vicious Dog was riding well and seemed to enjoy chasing the bunch quitters, though it mattered not after they were in the valley.

Topping a knoll that overlooked his spread, JB reined up and sat his horse, looking the countryside over. Buck and Dusty rode up and stopped beside him. The rest of the outfit was hazing the herd on down onto J-C Connected range. The J for Johnson and the C for Cladderbuck, the name JB had decided on when Pepper agreed to partner up with him.

"That's it," said JB, "we're home."

There was a pause while Buck and Dusty took it all in. The place was a good one. Jocke came trotting up and stopped to take it all in. Vicious Dog stayed back behind the herd and bounced the cattle back and forth trying to keep them bunched, having more fun than a kid with a new toy at Christmas time. There were clumps of trees here and there and grass that was belly deep to a sixteen hands horse. On the west side of the basin, they could see the cabin JB had built at the base of a rolling hillside. The hill was covered with cedar and pine.

"See that hill behind the cabin?" he asked. "There's a spring that comes out of that hill that is cold enough to freeze your tongue, and sweet? You have never tasted water as sweet as that water, almost as if it flows out of a sugar coated cave."

Buck just smiled and kicked his mount into motion. Dusty and Jocke rounded the herd and broke up their little milling session and helped push them on down the slope toward the ranch house.

"We might as well get these critters on down there," Dusty said over his shoulder as he moved away. JB followed Buck and went off the rise at a trot.

They had questioned the Indian after he had come out of his feverish state many days before and found out his name, translated, was "Vicious Dog", named so because he was born in the middle of a vicious dog fight, going on, just outside the teepee, when he was delivered. They also found out that he had been shot while trying to help a stranger who was being robbed and hanged. He saw them hang the man, thinking that he, Vicious Dog, was shot dead. He had crawled into the rocks and later heard them curse and yell something about losing two hundred dollars. In hindsight, it might have been wiser to have given the whole affair a wide birth. To him, as an Indian brave, stealing a horse was an honorable thing to do, a test of manhood, but stealing cattle was something al-together different. He knew quite a bit of English and what he didn't know, he made do by filling in with signs. He was fully aware that he was welcome to stay and work the range for JB. He felt obligated to help those who had helped him, so he stayed.

Buck, Dusty and Jocke were not too happy with what came next. Like most cowboys, anything that couldn't be done from horseback was foreign to them, and they were not able to cut and stack hay and fire wood from horseback. There were fences and corrals to be built, and a bunkhouse for them all to sleep in. The cabin was just not big enough for the ten of them. Clancy returned to the cabin to get supper started. After cooking in the open from the back of a wagon, having a kitchen that didn't move or go no place was a quieting feeling for him.

****

All of that had taken place two months before and the boys had found out that JB was not fooling about Clancy's cooking. He turned out some pretty danged good grub once he got settled in a real kitchen, of course, they all thought he had done a pretty dog gone good job on the trail. He was turning out tubs of bear sign that would melt in a cowboy's mouth. In fact, it was the best bear sign Buck, Dusty and Jocke had ever tasted. Vicious Dog said nothing about the grub. The rest of the crew was all in agreement with Buck, Dusty and Jocke.

"That danged Injun is going to eat us out of house and home," Clancy fussed. "I ain't been able to fill him up. He must have two hollow legs he takes turns filling up or a dependent tapeworm."

JB just laughed and everybody else joined in. Vicious Dog stopped eating long enough to look at everyone but not knowing what they laughed about, shrugged and returned to his challenge to eat everything in sight.

The days and weeks went by and the weather began to change. The evenings became cooler and the shadows of autumn stretched across the homestead which by then included a larger cabin, a barn and a bunkhouse. Vicious Dog was becoming a regular cowboy. He could already throw a steer or ride a bronc as well as most everyone and still could put down more grub than anyone. By the time the first snowflakes fell, there was plenty of hay cut and stacked in the fields and the hay loft well filled. Water holes were cleaned out and a dam had been reinforced in expectation of spring thaw. There usually wasn't that much snow in the Pan Handle country but the wind in winter could play havoc with nature's creation as well as man's construction. JB and his outfit would settle in for a cold winter and it wasn't that far off.

"Buck, why don't you and Vicious Dog see if you can track down a couple of deer? We can hang them in the back end of the hay loft to age and by the time they do that, it will be cold enough to keep the meat until we can get it cooked and eaten."

"Sure thing boss," said Buck. "Come on Vicious Dog. Let's go get us some deer meat."

He and the Indian left the breakfast table, put on their sheepskin coats and gloves and turned to leave. The wind whipped through the open door as they left the kitchen. It swirled through the cabin in search of a warm corner. The flames in the big open fireplace whipped and sputtered as the frigid fingers of winter's chill reached and tried to strangle them. Then the door was closed behind the departing men and the cabin returned to normal. JB cut a small grin as he sipped the hot coffee. He was pleased at how the crew was coming together.

Buck and Vicious Dog crossed the yard to the barn and entered. The horses that were stalled there all turned their heads and a couple of them walled their eyes to see who had entered. Upon recognition of the two punchers, they returned to their soft munching of hay. Buck liked the smell of the hay and fresh horse manure intermingled. It somehow triggered a sense of being home.

"Vicious Dog, which way do you think we ought to go this morning?"

The Indian was still a little slow in picking up just what was being said by all of his fellow punchers at the ranch but he was getting more and more familiar with the lingo as time passed.

"We go to shining ridge, we find deer there," said Vicious Dog.

"You may be right," said Buck, as he flung his saddle over the back of his cayuse. They finished tightening and looping the latigo straps and Buck went for a little pinto mare in the last stall in the back of the barn and put a pack saddle on her. They led the horses out of the barn. Mounting, they rode off; leading the pinto, toward a place called Shining Ridge because the water that trickled down the face of the cliffs, which dropped from the ridge, sparkled when the morning sun topped the horizon and reflected off it. The water pooled at the base of the cliffs, where game came to water and then formed a stream that ran off toward the main ranch headquarters. It joined with other small creeks that formed the main source of water for the cattle to drink.

The two men came in behind the ridge and picketed their horses. They slipped their Winchesters from their saddle boots and climbed the ridge without making too much noise. Once at the crest, they settled down to wait for their quarry to appear at the watering hole most used by the deer. It wasn't too long before a couple of doe and three bucks appeared in the clearing by the water. It took only two shots. Two of the bucks were down. Buck and Vicious Dog mounted and rode down the arroyo to where the ridge petered out and rounding the end of it, they rode back up the draw to where the deer lay. They gutted the deer after cutting the musk pouches off the hind legs and then tied the carcasses on the pack horse. They were about ready to mount when they both heard the faint knicker of a horse. They instantly grabbed the muzzles of their horses to keep them from answering the call.

The sound had come from the mouth of the canyon and before long; they saw the source of the knicker. A herd of wild mustangs was picking its way up the canyon floor with a big black stallion pushing them on, cutting them off from straying and nipping at them to keep the mares in pretty much a straight line to the water hole. Some of the mares still had half grown colts tagging along behind, still wanting to suck teat.

Buck and Vicious Dog had dragged the guts of the deer to a tree, back a ways from the water but there was still enough of the blood odor to alert the stallion. He circled the mares and started them milling while he checked out the area. He was bothered, there was something not right. He just had not figured it out, yet.

"He's a smart one," said Buck in a whisper. "Just look at him. Now, there's a fine looking hoss."

"He smells blood," said Vicious Dog. "He not bring other horses to water with odor in air."

"No, I guess not, but just look at how beautiful he is."

Buck had no more than said that when the wind shifted and all of a sudden, the stallion was down wind of them and evidently caught a full nose load of man, horse, deer and blood. His head went up, ears pricked, nostrils flared and he let out with a scream that could be heard a mile away. The entire herd wheeled toward the mouth of the canyon and the stallion was right on their tail.

"I'm going to see if I can get me that hoss later," said Buck.

CHAPTER 4

Cladderbuck stopped the conductor and asked what time they were scheduled to arrive in San Antonio.

"We should be in there around ten o'clock," the conductor said after pulling his pocket watch out and checking it. He wound it a few turns and returned it to his watch pocket. He continued on up the aisle, collecting unused pillows so that he could rent them to someone else. The pillow rental concession belonged to the individual conductors, a way for them to make a little money on the side. Pepper got up and poured himself a cup of coffee and returned to his seat. He sat down and sipped the rich, black brew, looked out the window and thought about the woman GP, still wondering what the heck those initials stood for. '*What a waste of time,*' he thought, '*I, probably, will never see her again.*'

He wanted to ride around some of the country and look at some of the local cattle after he got settled in San Antonio. Later on, he would have to round up some men to help him move the critters. The train slowly chugged into the San Antonio station, bell clanging a rich tone and came to a labored stop, spewing out steam on both sides from the relief valves like smoke from the nostrils of a fire eating dragon. It was a necessary action to relieve the pressure on the pistons. While Pepper gathered his trappings, his horse was led from the stock car, tied to a hitch ring on a corner post of the station platform; his saddle blanket and saddle were put down on the platform, next to the post. After leaving the train, Cladderbuck stood on the platform and watched the passengers coming and going for just a minute. He picked up his saddle and blanket and carried them down the steps to the hitch post. He had not seen Stewart, leave the train on the opposite side and make his way around the engine and behind the station building. He saddled his horse, stepped into leather and rode in search of a hotel, where he could spend the rest of the night.

San Antonio was a thriving town. It boasted two hotels with three floors and an even dozen saloons. There were two livery stables, a theater and seven eateries. He found a hotel by the name of 'The Oakland' and checked in. While signing the register, he asked, off handedly, where he might find a scout for a trail drive. The desk clerk directed him to the local law enforcement office.

"I'm sure the sheriff can give you that information a whole lot better than I can. I just don't travel in those circles," the hotel clerk said as he handed the room key to Pepper.

At the sheriff's office, he was told that there was an Indian that had worked for the Texas Rangers as a scout from time to time in the past, but the rangers no longer used him because they were becoming so spread out thet there were units, practically all over the state.

"They just don't seem to need scouts much, anymore," the deputy said.

"Where might I find this Indian?" Pepper asked.

"He hangs around the livestock pens a lot, down at the railroad tracks," the deputy answered.

"Do you happen to know his name, by any chance?"

"I believe it's Tawkawa…yah, that's it, Tawkawa.

"Thanks," said Pepper, "is there any place to get a bite of supper, this time of night?

"No place except the saloon. They have a free lunch at the saloon, the other side of the livery barn, three doors going right out the front door. Sometimes, they have leftovers to all times of the night, don't cost nothing to ask."

Pepper left the jail and stood on the boardwalk for a minute, took a cheroot from his inside vest pocket, struck a Lucifer on the heel of his boot and lit his smoke with hands cupped around the flame, blew out the match and thumped it into the street. He took in the street of half light and deep shadows. The livery was across the street and down a couple of buildings. There was a coal oil lantern hanging next to a sign painted in uneven letters of black on white, grayed with age and weather, that read: 'FIND YOUR OWN STALL– 4 BITS A DAY – GRAIN EXTRY'

He led his cayuse across the street to the door of the livery and glanced at the sign again as he pulled the door open. There were a couple of lanterns hanging in the hallway. The doors of individual stalls that were vacant, were hanging open. Horses in the closed stalls hung their heads out, looking to see who was coming down the hall. Their eyes rolled back, reflecting the orange light from the lanterns, ears pricked for any unwanted sound. It only took a second for them to realize that they were not on call and most of them returned to their hay munching routine. Pepper put his horse in one of the empty stalls and scooped him a couple scoops of grain. The manger was full of fresh hay, already and the water trough was about half full. He placed his saddle on the wooden horse in front of the stall and hung the bridle on a wooden peg on the stall door post. He left to the grain munching sound generated by his pony and went next door to the saloon and was able to get a couple of sandwiches and some cold beer. *'Just what the doctor ordered,'* he thought as he chewed on the sandwiches. He then returned to the hotel and sacked out.

Morning came with a fresh feeling of empty, having processed the sandwiches from the night before. Pepper walked from the hotel to a café, named; The Western Steak House, went in, found an empty table and sat down, his back to a wall from habit. A middle aged woman with a strand of dark hair hanging down across her forehead and a pot of hot coffee in her fist, walked up to the table almost as soon as he got settled.

"Coffee?" she asked.

"Yes, thank you," said pepper, looking into her smiling eyes.

"New in town?" she asked in general conversation as she poured the hot, rich, black, steaming brew.

"Yep," he said, "just blew in last night."

"Well, welcome to San Antonio, what can I get you?"

"I think I'm gonna eat light this morning," Pepper said, "I think I'll have a half dozen eggs with a full slab of country ham, grits, gravy and biscuits with a smathering of churned butter and wild honey, if you have it."

"We got hive honey and wild honey. We also have plenty of gooseberry jam, if your taste runs in that direction."

"No, I think I'll stick with the wild honey."

"Coming right up," she said, turning for the kitchen. "If that's eatin light, I'd love to see what you eat on a heavy day," she said over her shoulder and chuckled to herself.

Pepper couldn't help but notice the full body movement of a mature nature. She had a nice shape and he enjoyed it all the way to the kitchen door. *'Like two young cougars tied up in a feed sack,' he thought.* His mind was snapped back to even as the thought of the woman GP flashed in his head and she walked through his mind. After breakfast, he walked down to the railroad station, looking for Tawkawa. He approached a man with a tally sheet in his hand, a pencil behind one ear and cow manure encrusted boots on his feet, pant legs stuffed inside, no spurs.

"I'm looking for an Indian by the name of Tawkawa," he said.

"What you want with him?"

"Fellow down at the jail said I might be able to hire him to scout my trail drive." Cladderbuck said.

"That's him over by the loading ramp, wearing the leather hat with a turkey feather stuck in the hatband, says it's eagle bur anybody with any savvy a'tall, knows it's a damn old turkey feather, home grown at that, not even a wild one." He went back to counting cows as Pepper walked to the loading ramp.

"Howdy," he said as he approached the man.

"Howdy," the Indian replied.

"Are you Tawkawa?"

"That's me," Tawkawa slitted his eyes at Pepper who was back grounded against the early morning sun. "What can I do for you?"

"I'm putting a cattle drive together and I'm in need of a good man to scout the trail and keep an eye out for trouble and help find water for the cattle. You interested?"

"I'm your man, Captain," Tawkawa said, enthusiastically. "I've been hangin around this town way too long, where we bound for?"

"I'm headed for west Texas, just about as far as you can go and stay out of New Mexico Territory. In fact, I'll be using some of the open range over in New Mexico Territory."

"That sounds good to me," Tawkawa said. "How many head you movin?"

"I'm planning on about fifteen hundred," Pepper said.

"Huh, good sized herd, how many pokes you have?"

"Don't have any, yet," said Pepper.

"It's off season," said Tawkawa, "you not have much trouble finding good men. I'll help you look for them."

"I plan to take care of that, later, for now, I'm going for a ride around the countryside and see what I'm looking at. I want to see what kind of livestock is available. Would you care to ride with me? You probably know the country better than most. What I want are longhorns"

"I will go with you," said the Indian. He went to his horse and led it back to where Pepper stood. They went to the livery and Pepper saddled his cayuse and the two of them rode out of town and spent the day looking at cattle from one outfit to another. They returned to town in the late afternoon.

The Western Steak House was where the two of them stopped to get a meal after washing up from the trail. Tops on the menu were beef, beans and potatoes. Seating themselves in a back corner, they were approached by an attractive strawberry blond who looked to be in her early thirties. She placed a pot of hot coffee on the table and waited for the men to order.

After they were finished with their meal, they went across the dusty street to the Bird's Nest saloon. Pushing their way through the batwing doors, Pepper noted that there was somewhere in the neighborhood of twenty men in the saloon. Approaching the bar, he ordered a beer and turned to Tawkawa, who nodded his head.

"Make that two beers," Cladderbuck said.

As the bartender placed the mugs of beer on the bar, a big, haggled looking man stood up at the table where he had been playing poker and said, "We don't allow Injuns in here when we are."

No sooner said and Cladderbuck's toe caught the back of the man's heel and with a quick jerk, the big man tumbled back over the table from which he had arisen. It collapsed under his weight and he sprawled in the floor. He came to his feet with amazing speed for such a big man. His hand fell to the butt of his gun only to be looking into the mouth of Cladderbuck's .44. Large beads of sweat broke out on his upper lip and forehead. His face and neck turning flame red with anger. He stood there for a long moment and then decided to wait for a better chance. His hand moved ever so slowly away from his holster, for he knew he was staring death squarely in the face.

"We're not looking for trouble," said Pepper, "but we can handle any that might come our way. Since you don't allow Indians in here when you're here, I suggest that you find yourself another place."

When the big man and a couple of his buddies had left the saloon, Cladderbuck dropped his weapon into its resting place, turned to the bartender and spoke.

"I'm here to buy cattle and find drovers to help me drive them to west Texas, any suggestions?"

"What kind of cattle are you looking for?" The bartender asked.

"Two year old longhorns," said Pepper.

"If you want good stock, your best bet is the Lindsey ranch. It's located about twenty miles southeast of here, just beyond Crater Lake. Going that way, you can't miss it; road goes right by the place. As for drovers, there's a few around, left over from the war. More drifters than anything but they're Texans, all."

"Could you pass the word for me? I'll be staying at the Oakland hotel. My name's Cladderbuck, Pepper Cladderbuck."

"Sure thing Mr. Cladderbuck," the bartender said as he picked up a container of pickled eggs and wiped the bar underneath.

Pepper and Tawkawa left for the hotel. Upon arriving and asking for a room, the desk clerk gave Tawkawa a funny look but before he could say anything, Cladderbuck placed his stone hard eyes on him and said, "We're not going to have any trouble with my friend, being an Indian are we?"

The clerk swallowed hard and broke out in little beads of cold sweat.

"No sir," he said as he turned the register to look at the name written there. "No sir, Mr. Cladderbuck. No sir-ree."

In the room, Tawkawa was having no part of the bed. He spread his blankets on the floor and soon was asleep. Cladderbuck removed his boots, hat and gun belt, stretching out on the bed, and was soon asleep himself.

The next morning they went to the café for breakfast. Then they went to the mercantile, where Pepper bought a six-gun and holster along with a Winchester for Tawkawa. He also purchased enough ammunition to add to what he already had to last them the trip to the panhandle. While in the store, a couple of men came in and approached Pepper.

"We understand you are looking for drovers to take some beeves to the pan handle." The one doing the talking was a wiry, square jawed man that stood about five feet eight inches, tall.

"Where'd you hear it?"

"I got it from Gus, over to the saloon. My name is Shotgun Boyd and this is my twin brother, Noble."

"I can see the resemblance, but there are some differences."

"Yeah, we're twins but not identical twins. We both know cows and horses bout the same."

"I'm offering forty and found which includes all the ammunition you might need. We'll be going through country with outlaws and Indians and it, more than likely, won't be a picnic."

"If we were looking for a picnic, we'd stay here and go to Sunday school."

"Do you boys have guns?" asked Pepper.

"We both have .44s and .44-.40 Winchesters."

"That ought to do it then," said Cladderbuck. "By the way, this here is Tawkawa. He'll be riding with us."

The Indian nodded.

Noble turned to Cladderbuck, "We have some friends of ours that I'm sure would like to come along. I'm sure I can get Rob Taylor and if you're looking for a cook, there's Curly Miller down the other end of town. He slings grub in the Greasy Plate café. Used to be a drover himself before he got all stove up from being throwed once to many times."

"Can he cook?"

"Can he cook? He's probably the best danged cook this side of the Great Divide. Makes bear sign like you've never tasted in your life," said Noble.

"If he can make bear sign that good then I hope he'll come along," said Pepper.

The next day Cladderbuck and Tawkawa went southeast out of San Antonio in search of the Lindsey ranch. By high noon, they were sitting their horses on a small butte, above the wagon road that trailed down in front of the gate. They rode on down and into the ranch yard. The house set back from the road, four or five hundred feet and Pepper noticed a group of good-looking horses grazing in the pasture by which they rode. It was a fairly well kept place; no rawhide outfit for sure.

"Light and set," said the man on the porch. He was dressed like a rancher and had the manner of a gentleman. "We are just now taking a nooning."

"The name's Cladderbuck, Pepper Cladderbuck. This is Tawkawa, he works for me."

"Yes, I know Tawkawa. I've seen him around town," Lindsey said.

"I'm Damon Lindsey. Won't you join us for a bite to eat? Have your man check in at the cook shack, there ought to be plenty to go around."

Tawkawa knew where he stood and he turned his horse, took Pepper's reins and headed for the cook shack where the ranch hands were lined up.

The ranch house was a sprawling Spanish style house with a large veranda to one side. They seated themselves at a table on the veranda and two Mexican women appeared to serve them.

"What can I do for you?" asked Lindsey.

"I'm in the market for fifteen-hundred head of two year old stock, longhorns. I'm going to start raising beef on a place in Oldham county, out in the pan handle," said Pepper as he picked up his cup of coffee and took a large swallow. "I'll need five good bulls and the rest cows, if you have them."

"I have almost that many. I tallied fourteen hundred and forty three two year olds just the other day. I could fill in the rest with three year olds."

"That's fine," said Cladderbuck, "providing the price is right."

"I can let you have them for fourteen dollars a head."

"Ten dollars is closer to my pocketbook," said Cladderbuck.

"Make it twelve and you've got yourself a deal."

"Deal," said Cladderbuck. They shook hands on it and returned to their meal.

"One thing," said Pepper. "I'll need to leave them here until I get my outfit together. It shouldn't take more than a week."

"That's fine," said Lindsey, "they'll be right here whenever you're ready."

Returning to San Antonio, Cladderbuck learned that Shotgun had another five drovers lined up for him. He introduced them around. "This here's Bill Terry and his older brother John. And over here is the youngest of the group, Hal Jeffreys.

"I may be the youngest," said Hal, "but I can out work these over the hill boys any day of the week and twice on Sunday."

Everyone guffawed and Hal's face turned a bright shade of red.

"These last two are from up in the panhandle, they pretty much know that country. Meet Jim Heart and his son, Jay."

"Howdy," said Jim Heart. Jay only nodded his head, but with a big sheepish grin.

"What kind of fire power do you boys have?"

He made a mental list of what the men all had and figured what he needed to buy to fill in what they would need.

CHAPTER 5

Five years in the gold fields of Colorado had fattened JB's poke and after fixing the homestead up, he still had enough money left to increase his herd and maintain the ranch for a long time. He had decided to cross breed his white face stock with the range hardy shorthorn cattle from the Kansas and Missouri country in addition to the longhorn cattle from south Texas. With that in mind they were getting ready to leave for Kansas. He was counting on Vicious Dog to go along and be his wrangler, seeing to the horses, because the Indian was a wonder with the animals and they would need a forty five or fifty head remuda on the return trip. JB planned to put Vicious Dog in charge of the remuda, coming back. He still was not sure when Pepper Cladderbuck would arrive with the Longhorns.

Meanwhile, as they were preparing to leave, a scene was taking place in a saloon in Amarillo. Lucas, who once rode with Goesto Church and was given a chance to leave the country by Buck, had not taken it and was leaning on the bar, sipping a whiskey and talking loose-mouthed to the tender. He was telling all about his run-in with the JB Johnson outfit, slanted in his favor of course, when Bert Rawlings just happen to overhear him mention the name of Johnson.

"Pardon me, friend," Rawlings said, "could I buy you another drink?"

Lucas turned and stared through blurry eyes, for he had already had more than his share of Redeye that night. Squinting through thin slits, he spoke.

"Don't mind if I do," he said, knocking back his last bit of whiskey to make room for the forthcoming shot. "Who are you friend?" he asked.

"Name's Rawlings, Bert Rawlings. Who is this fellow you mentioned, Johnson, was it?"

"Yah, that's what I said, Johnson. Do you know him?"

I don't know, might though. I was just curious. Did this Johnson have a front handle," asked Rawlings?

"Don't know for sure, seems like he had just initials or something."

"Could it have been JB?"

"Yah, that's right. JB Johnson was what his hand called him," Lucas said as he held his glass steady with both hands, for the bartender to pour his drink.

"And you say this cowhand of Johnson's walked into your camp and drew down on you for no reason at all?"

"That's right," said Lucas. "He acted like he knew Goesto. He told me to saddle my cayuse and ride." He took a sip of his drink, coughed slightly and cleared his throat. "I don't mind telling you, when you're looking down the business end of a .44, well, I was glad to have the chance to move on."

"What happened to, this, Goesto fellow?" asked Rawlings.

"Don't know," said Lucas, "and don't care. I saddled my cayuse and rode hell bent for leather until I was out of sight of that camp. I heard a couple of shots about the time I got out of sight. Really, it sounded almost like one shot, they were so close together. I didn't go back to see. I just kept right on moving."

"Sounds as if this Johnson is taking a pretty high hand up in that part of the country," said Rawlings. "Think I'll mosey up that way and see for myself."

"Yah, you do that," Lucas said, as he pushed his glass toward the bartender for a refill.

"I might," said Rawlings. "Say he's up northwest of here?"

"Yah," said Lucas, "I think his spread is up around Hollicott Crossing, some place. If you see him, you tell him ole Lucas is next to gone from this country. In fact, I'll be out of this country by the time you can get it all said. I'm pulling out right now. I just stopped in, long enough to have one for the road." He finished his drink and headed for the door.

"On second thought," he said over his shoulder, "don't say anything a'tall about me. Just pretend that you never saw me." He hiccupped as he pushed the batwing doors open and was gone.

Rawlings had long been at odds with JB Johnson. His lack of age and experience, he told himself, had caused him to take water from JB Johnson a few years back and it had been eating at him ever since. Maybe he could ease up-country and check ole JB out. Find out what the story was and maybe get his pound of flesh. Early the next morning, he went to the livery after breakfast and saddled his horse. He packed his saddle bags with enough provisions to last him a week and a half. He then stepped into leather and left town at a trot and headed out of town, going south.

When he had gone about three miles or so, he circled around the town to a west, northwesterly direction. Three days later he broke camp and ventured to within sight of the ranch house of the "J-C Connected Cattle Company". He noted the sign that displayed the name over the gate that marked the entrance to the ranch. There was no fence leading up to or away from the gate. It stood alone across the wagon tracks going through it.

"Did you see the stranger beyond the meadow?" asked Buck.

"I caught the glint of sunlight off his metal or telescope," said Clancy as he stepped into the back yard of the ranch house and threw his dishwater across the ground. He turned and squinted in the direction he had seen the glint. A small flock of chickens and a couple of Ginny hens covered the area where the dish water splashed and were picking around for any tidbit of food, washed from the dishes.

"Yah," said Buck. "He's staying back in the trees." He paused a moment and then said, "Well, whoever he is, he's keeping his distance."

"Maybe he's just bashful," said Clancy

"Anyhow, tell the boss about him when you go back inside."

"Sure thing," said Clancy as he headed for the back door. He paused at the step and half turned to Buck and said, "I'm whipping up a batch of bear sign for supper. Tell the boys."

"What boys?" said Buck, with a chuckle? "I'm pretending that I'm the only one. I hate sharing your bear sign with a bunch of unworthy cow nurses, you old broken down puncher."

Clancy just grinned to himself at the cowboy humor as the screen door hit him on the butt. He set the dish pan on the table and went to find JB.

"Boss, there's a stranger hanging back in the trees on the back side of the meadow. All we can see of him is a glint from either glass or metal. He may have one of them telescopes."

"Well, if he hangs around too long, tell Buck or Jocke to circle around and get a backside view of him. See what he's up to."

"Okay, boss," said Clancy. "By the way, I'm making bear sign for supper, I was afraid Buck might not tell you. He said he might want to hog them all himself." They both chuckled.

By dusk though, the watchful eyes of Bert Rawlings fell not on the ranch house of the J-C Connected ranch but on the one street that ran through Vega. With only a few log building and some tents, Vega could hardly be called a town. One of the log buildings was a trading post run by a Sweed and his Indian squaw. It was no surprise to Rawlings that the owner was called Sweed, being one. Rawlings, upon entry into the building, spoke to the owner.

"My name's Rawlings, Berton Rawlings. I was wondering if there's a place in town where a Gent could lay his head."

"Sur, der iss, Mister Rawlings" said the Sweed. "Der thurd tent ohn der left, goin dat-a-vay." He pointed up the street with a big fat finger as he spoke.

Rawlings bought a small coffee pot, a tin cup, a pound of coffee and half a pound of sugar in addition to the other supplies he had picked out. Leaving the trading post, he added the item to his saddle bags except the cup and coffee pot. He placed the cup, wrapped in a bandana, inside the coffee pot and tied the handle of the pot to his bedroll with a rawhide thong. He then took the reins of his horse and walked down the street to the sleeping tent. There was a sign above the door that read "Sleep $1". He went inside and found it to be one large room, filled with beds made of rough, small trees that had been put together with nails and laced crisscross with rawhide strips about two inches wide with a feather mattress, some two inches thick rolled at the end of each unoccupied bed.

There was a man sitting by a potbelly heater to one side of the door, the only door as a matter of fact. He spoke to the man.

"I'd like to reserve a bed for tonight."

"Sorry, no reserved beds. It's first come, first served," said the man. "You get here after eight o'clock and most likely you'll be sleeping on the floor. Floor is only two bits."

Rawlings turned and walked back to where his horse was tied; unwrapped the reins from the hitch rail and went to the saloon he had spotted earlier. He found a table in the back corner, ordered whiskey and sat, sipping and thinking of what he would do about JB Johnson.

****

With the hay cut and stacked, JB, unaware that Rawlings was plotting against him, decided to go ahead with his plans to buy more cattle to put his cross breeding idea into action. He figured that the sturdy short-horns would cross well with the heavier white-face. He called his small crew together to announce that they would be going to Kansas City and be bringing back a sizeable herd of short-horns.

"Men, we're leaving in a couple of days for Kansas City to buy some more cattle," he said. "We'll all be going and I'm concerned about leaving the ranch with nobody to look after it. Any suggestions as to what I can do about it?"

"Why don't you get old Jeb Andrews to hang around until we get back?" asked Clancy.

"Good idea," said JB. "You know him best, Clancy. Why don't you ride into town and ask him? Tell him we should be back before winter sets in."

"Sure thing boss," said Clancy. "I'll go in first thing tomorrow."

"Wait a dog gone minute," said Jocke. "You do mean after breakfast, don't you?"

"Yah, Clancy, let's do breakfast first," said Buck.

"Well, dang it all," stormed Clancy. "Of course I meant after breakfast. For two reasons; one is, none of you yah-hoos can cook worth a dang and second, I don't want anybody messing around in my kitchen, besides, I ain't trapsing off to town on an empty stomach."

The next morning, after breakfast, Clancy left for Vega. JB and Buck saddled their horses as Jocke hitched a team to a wagon. They piled the tools that they would need for the day's work into it and headed for a pond that needed some cleaning. JB was never one to give orders and set back and do nothing. He pitched in on whatever job needed doing. He, like Buck and Jocke, was in excellent shape, physically and he more than carried his weight in the day to day work that had to be done, but he put his foot down on milking the cows. If he grabbed hold of a teat, it wasn't going to be on a cow.

Clancy slapped the rear end of the horses lightly as they passed the coral at the end of Main Street at a slow trot. He continued on passed the livery that stood with both its front doors wide open. Clancy noticed an old yellow dog stretched out on his side against the south side of the barn, soaking up the sun. The dog raised his shaggy head, just long enough to see who was passing, opened his mouth in a wide yawn, licked his tongue out and down and then curled it up, over and back into his mouth, popping his teeth softly together as he closed his jaws, blinked his eyes and laid his head back in his depression in the dust. Nothing short of a nice meaty bone was going to move him from his chosen spot.

Vega was a busy town and Clancy had to work his way through all the traffic of the street. He stopped at the mercantile located just passed the Last Well, one of the town's saloons. He had to find Jeb Andrews, but that could wait. First, he had a few supplies to pick up and by his figuring, a man who worked as hard as he did, needed a cool drink once in a while. Therefore, after rounding up his supplies, he would be heading for the Last Well.

He stamped up onto the boardwalk, slapped his legs with his hat to dislodge some of the dust that had settled there. He ran his fingers through his bushy hair, wiped the sweat band of his hat with a bandana, placed his hat back on his head and entered the store.

"Well, help my time, if it ain't Clancy Jones.

Clancy squinted through weather leathered eye lids to see who had spoken his name. Coming in from the bright light of day, it was a moment before recognition lit his face with a wide grin.

"Do my old eyes deceive me or is it Joe Collins?"

"Clancy, you old broken down excuse for a cowboy. What have you been doing with yourself?"

"I give up nursing cows," said Clancy. "I took up cooking and I'm cooking for, you'll never guess who." He paused just a moment with a secretive grin on his face. "JB Johnson... I'm cook on the J-C Connected ranch, just a day's ride from here. He's took on a partner, Pepper Cladderbuck."

"JB... Why that son-of-a-gun. Got himself a place of his own," Collins said with a grin. He then turned to his side and called to a young woman who had been looking at bolts of cloth.

"Hope, come over here a minute."

She walked to where the two men stood.

"Hope, honey, I'd like you to meet an old friend. This here is Clancy Jones. Clancy, meet my daughter, Hope."

"Proud to make your acquaintance, Ma'am," Clancy said with a smile.

"I'm pleased to meet you, Mr. Jones," said Hope.

"Please, just call me Clancy. Mr. Jones was my Dad. How'd you turn out so pretty with an ugly old cuss like him for a Papa?" Clancy asked, nodding at Joe Collins, with a wink of his eye?

"She takes after her mother, God rest her soul," said Collins. "Now tell me about JB. What kind of an outfit does he have?"

"There's just ten of us, counting JB. He and eight new men including one Injun, one Negro and me, of course, came in a while back with his first cows. Six hundred head of the prettiest white faces you ever saw. I'm in town to get a man to watch after things while we all go to Kansas for more stock."

"What kind of stock will he be looking for in Kansas?" asked Collins.

"Short horns," said Clancy. "He wants to cross them with the white faces and some longhorns his new partner, Cladderbuck, is bringing up from south Texas." Clancy paused a moment. "By the way, are you still with the Texas Rangers?"

"No, I retired last month," said Collins. "I decided to settle here in Vega. Being the county seat, I know a lot of people from when I was with the rangers. I always liked this area. Hope is a seamstress and she plans to open a shop here. Me? I'm just going to take it easy and let the Texas Ranger organization run itself."

Clancy lifted the corners of his mouth in an all-knowing grin and said, "If I know you, you won't be able to just sit still."

"No, he won't," said Hope Collins. "Put him in a rocking chair and he'd be out of his mind within a week's time."

The three of them laughed heartily. Clancy laughed the loudest and felt a little foolish when he stopped to realize it.

"Say, why don't you and Miss Hope come out to the ranch with me and see JB?" Clancy asked. "We'll be leaving in a couple days, but you could visit for a day or two with JB while the rest of us get things ready to go."

"I'd like that," said Collins. "I'd like that very much." Then turning to Hope he said, "Would you like to go along or stay here and get things organized?"

"There isn't anyone or anything that could keep me from going with you," she said. "It'll give us a break from the routine of setting up a sewing shop. I hadn't realized how much work there is in such a, seemingly easy, business just to make a few garments. Besides, I want to meet this JB Johnson. Dad has said so much about him that I have him pictured as nine feet tall, at least."

"He's not nine feet tall, more than likely six feet and two inches. But I reckon it's six feet, two inches of man which makes up for the extra two feet and ten inches," said Clancy, chuckling a little.

Joseph Collins and Hope both joined Clancy in a little laughter. Then Clancy nodded at the interior of the store and said, "Well, I guess I'd better get my supplies together. How's about meeting me at the café in the morning and we can head out, right after breakfast. Say six o'clock?"

"Sure thing," said Collins, "are you sure it will be okay with JB?"

"It'll be okay," said Clancy, "JB would skin me alive if'n I said it wouldn't be."

"Do you think you'll be ready by then, Hope?" Joe asked.

"I'll be ready," Hope said with a little flare to her words, as if to reflect the notion back to her father. "Question is, will you be ready?" She knew full well that Joe Collins beat the rooster up every morning.

"I think so," said Joe. "I have been getting a little lazy since I left the rangers."

Joe Collins and his daughter left the mercantile and Clancy busily gathered the things he needed but thinking all the while about that cool drink that awaited him in the Last Well saloon.

CHAPTER 6

The next morning Pepper went to the mercantile and bought enough ammunition for their drive. He also paid for two kegs of black powder, five Winchesters and four new handguns and holsters. Now he had enough guns for his outfit to have a Winchester and at least one handgun. With a couple of Winchesters extra, he had already asked Miller to be his cook and he, at the same time, made arrangements, with the store owner, for Miller to stock a chuck wagon for the trail.

From there he went to the café where Curly was working. As he seated himself, Curly came out of the kitchen and sat at Pepper's table.

"Curly, do you have any idea where we can come up with a chuck wagon in four days?"

"I think so," said Curly. "George, down to the freight company, has an extra freight wagon I think I can get. Course, it'll need some reworking but I think I can handle it with a little lumber, hammer, saw and a few nails. I'll need a canvas to build a top for it."

"Okay, check it out. I've already told them at the Mercantile that you'd be stocking up. I'll leave it up to you as to what you get but get enough for the whole outfit plus one, just to be sure."

"Today's my last day here at the café," said Curly. "I'll see to it first thing in the morning. I'm plum tickled at the prospect of getting back on the trail. Living in town may be for some folks but I don't much cotton to it."

"That's fine about the wagon," said Pepper. "Just so it's ready for the trail in four days. We'll be heading out at first light Thursday. You'll get your chance to kick the dust of this town off your boots. I'll have to admit, I'm a little excited about the trip, myself."

On Tuesday, Pepper sent Bill Terry out to the Lindsey ranch to see where they stood on putting his herd together. On Monday, Curly had started on the chuck wagon and by midday Tuesday, he had it ready for loading. He drove it down to the Mercantile, climbed down, with a broad grin on his satisfied face and went in to shop. He got coffee, beans, bacon, sugar, flour, salt and a stand of rendered lard. He also stocked a barrel of dried apples and an ample supply of tobacco.

"Never seen a puncher what didn't like fried pies," he said, to nobody in particular, as he loaded the apples onto the wagon. Curly also added all the plates, cups and utensils that they would need, a Dutch oven, three large coffee pots and an assortment of pots and pans to do the job of feeding a bunch of hard working, hungry cowhands. Curly was ready to go.

On Wednesday, Pepper took his drovers to the Lindsey ranch to pick up his cattle. He paid for them in gold, got a bill of sale and fell in with his men as they headed for the holding point he had selected just west of San Antonio. When they arrived at the holding point, Curly was waiting with coffee on. That night, Pepper left three men with the herd and took the rest of the outfit to town for one last café meal before they took the trail. After eating, they returned to camp and let the others go in. Upon the return of the whole outfit, he set up night watches in three shifts of three men on each shift.

"We'll keep up the four hour watches with two men on the cattle and one man to be with the horses. We'll rotate every week, each crew moving forward to the next shift. As the first nighthawks left camp after supper, the rest of the men hit their bedrolls for they knew the work they had ahead of them would require as much sleep and rest as they could squeeze in. Cladderbuck had his bill of sale for the herd and they seemed to be in pretty good shape, not knowing that Jake Moran and his henchmen had already left San Antonio and were planning to meet up with ten more owlhoots that were coming from across the border. Moran had his eye on those cattle and figured he'd get twenty dollars a head in Kansas City or Dodge. It seemed like a small job for men like the members of his gang.

The dawn of gray sky paled against the expanse of the wide-open country, into which, Cladderbuck and his outfit were to drive his cattle.

"Head'em up, move'em out," he cried as the sun first peeked over the horizon. With shouts and whoops, drovers laid doubled lariats on the dusty hides of the cattle. The herd began to move and Pepper took the point. Curly was to stay out in front of the cattle and Tawkawa was even further in front of Curly with the horses.

Pepper swung back and fell in beside Jim Heart who was riding the right flank.

"Jim, I'm riding on ahead and scout for water. Pass the word on back."

With that, Cladderbuck swung by the chuck wagon and told Curly the same thing. Then he was off past the remuda and before long was out of sight of the herd. He rode at a careful pace, keeping to low land and watching for any sign of Indians or outlaws. He knew the risk they were taking and he was counting on his outfit not coming on more than small parties of Indians. The Indians, he knew, mostly traveled in small groups. That way they could live on what food and water they could find and did not have to carry a large amount of either with them.

After riding for, what he judged to be, ten miles, Cladderbuck crossed the trail of at least a dozen shod horses. Was it a Calvary patrol or outlaws? He figured no group of men, if they were not military, would be riding in that part of the country unless they were up to no good. He decided to back track them to see where they might have come from. A few miles to the south, the back trail split into two trails that had come together. There were three horses that had come from the east and had joined ten others that had come up from the south. The ten riders from the south almost had to have come from Mexico. He high-tailed it back to where he had first picked up the trail, and continued on in search of water. He had only gone three miles further on when he came to a stream that gurgled over rocks, pebbles and sand and came from a source back up in the hills, somewhere high up, probably a spring. There was a natural reservoir that would provide plenty of water for the cattle and everyone else. Curly could fill the two large barrels that he had mounted with bracing to the sides of the chuck wagon. They would be able to leave the waterway with full barrels, canteens and bellies, water wise.

He rode back to the herd and passed the word. He sent Curly and Tawkawa on ahead to water the horses and get them on a graze beyond the stream before the herd arrived and Curly was to set up camp and get supper ready.

When the herd arrived at the stream, supper was just about ready. The drovers had just enough time to water and bed down the herd by dark. Tawkawa was helping Curly out by carrying water to fill the barrels while Curly cooked.

"Come and get it," yelled Curly, "or I'll throw it out to the coyotes." He chuckled to himself. He loved ribbing the punchers about their grub and he used the same threat three times a day. In actuality, he had never thrown out the first morsel to the dogs of the night.

After supper, the nighthawks on the first watch went to the herd and everybody else settled down for some well deserved rest. Curly let the cook fire die down to a bed of red-orange coals on which a large pot of coffee sat. That would be enough for the nighthawks. The first night on the trail went without incident and Curly had breakfast ready an hour before sunup. By sunup, everyone was in the saddle and the cattle were moving out slowly. A big brindle steer, with one broken horn, had seemed to take over as the leader and was setting a good pace that kept pressure on Curly's chuck wagon.

As before, Pepper rode out looking for their next camp sight. The thought that kept plaguing him was that out there ahead of them somewhere, there was a band of twelve or thirteen men who by all indications were outlaws and he had to assume that they had an eye on his cattle. In light of that assumption and the fact that there were bands of Indians that they might encounter, kept his caution honed to a keen edge with every move he made. Pepper Cladderbuck was an Indian in his mind; dating back to the years he had spent moving through the New Mexico territory with Screaming Eagle, an Indian brave with whom he was friends, during the early years of his life. He thought like an Indian. He moved like an Indian and when the occasion required, he fought like an Indian, with one goal in mind, that being, to win.

When he had gone, what he judged to have been between ten and twelve miles, by the gate of the black horse he rode, he came upon a small canyon that opened up into a meadow some four or five hundred yards long. There was a stream that ran through it, sufficiently filled with fresh, crystal clear water to furnish the camp and water the stock. It ran down across the meadow into an arroyo where it disappeared into the ground but above the point where it ran into the arroyo there was a small pond which was almost in the center of the meadow, created by an abandoned beaver dam. There were a lot of Aspens and around the edge of the meadow on the north side, a stand of Lodge Pole pines covered the side of the hill that bordered the meadow. There was plenty of graze for the herd as well as water.

Returning to the herd, Pepper caught sight of a group of riders approaching from the southwest. They rode in slowly, eyes on the riders with glances at the cattle. Pepper drew up at the point position where he was joined by the point man, Jim Heart and his son, Jay who came forward from left flank. Jay had all the indications of being a salty young man but not quite as salty as his Pa. The three of them spread out with about ten to fifteen feet between each.

"Howdy," said the leader of the band of men as he and his group reined their horses to a stop, kicking up a small cloud of dust that swirled around their horses and settled on the flat.

"Howdy," said Cladderbuck. He waited for the man, he recognized as the one he had forced to take water in the saloon, back in San Antonio, to speak.

Jake Moran crossed one leg around the pommel of his saddle and pulled a sack of tobacco from his shirt pocket and started to roll a quirly.

"I hope you Gents realize you're crossing our range, and your cows are eaten our grass as they go." He paused to lick the paper on his cigarette. He put it in his mouth, struck a match on the pommel and lit his smoke. Shaking the match to extinguish the flame, he squinted one eye from the smoke, tossed the spent match to the ground and said, with traces of smoke coming from his mouth, "I spect we'll have to cut your herd to pay for the grass they done et, unless'n you have the dinero to pay the grazing fee."

"Which is," said Pepper.

"I spect we can let you off with, say, two bits a head."

Cladderbuck sat his horse with his right hand resting on his thigh only inches from the butt of his gun. Jim Heart had his Winchester laying across his saddle bow with the hammer back and the barrel pointed at the stomach of the man to Moran's right. Jay had his thumb hooked behind his belt, just right of the buckle.

Cladderbuck spoke with a deadly tone in his voice, like the rhythmic rattle of a sidewinder that has just been stepped on.

"I don't think so," he said.

Without a first thought, much less a second one, Moran dropped his hand to his gun, almost a fatal mistake. The men, aligned with him, were not expecting him to move so soon and all of them were caught flat butted in their saddles. Moran's gun was out and rising when Cladderbuck's .44 spewed flame. His shot impacted the top of Moran's shooter, busted the cylinder, ricocheted off to the right and creased Moran's left shoulder. His horse jumped sideways and crashed into the two men just to his left and the men behind him had trouble controlling their mounts. Jim Heart lifted his .44 and Jay pulled both of his. Between the two of them, Moran's men were covered. The horses settled down and they all sat still for a long, angry moment. The threat of death, hung heavy on the air. Just one wrong move would open the ball and everybody was ready to dance.

"You boys can all just drop your gun belts and shuck those rifles, easy," said Cladderbuck. "Then you can ride, or we'll leave your carcasses right here for the buzzards and coyotes, your choice."

The anger on Moran's face was ugly but the thoughts behind that face were even uglier. He knew they had these three outnumbered but he also realized that he more-than-likely would not survive if his men tried to reopen the ball in such close quarters. Every man in the group dropped his gunbelt Moran swore softly, jerked his mount around and as one, the group rode away.

"We ain't heard the last of them boys," said Jim Heart.

"No, you're right. We haven't," said Cladderbuck. "Pick up all those guns and gun belts. We can use them."

Jim and Jay gathered the guns, took them to the chuck wagon and returned to their positions with the herd.

Pepper rode on back to fill the rest of the outfit in on what he had learned about their camp site for that night and to let them know what the shooting was all about. Fortunately, the shot had been far enough away from the cattle that they hardly even jumped from the sound of the report. If they had been much closer, the shot could have started a stampede.

After supper, Pepper called everyone together before the first watch left camp and they talked about the events of the day and considered ways they might avoid trouble with the outlaws further on down the trail. He was almost sure they would be there, just waiting for the herd to arrive at their selected, rustling spot.

"Hellfire and damnation," said Noble Boyd, "is what those owlhoots deserve."

"Yeah, and that's just what they'll be getting once they each get plugged full of holes," said Bill Terry.

"I say we don't wait for them to come after us," said Noble. "I say we cut'em down afore they find some guns and come back when we least expect it. They could pick us off, one at a time, while we're spread out on the trail and we'd wind up going to the dance with them pickin the music."

"Maybe your right Noble," said Pepper.

"You danged right I'm right," said Noble.

After a long moment's thought, Pepper said, "I tell you what we're going to do, men. I'm sending Tawkawa to scout their camp. If they have more guns and pose a threat to the cattle or us then we'll move against them. If we do move against them, it'll be just before first light and we'll all move as one and it'll be for keeps, but first, we'll wait for Tawkawa's report.

Tawkawa left camp while the moon was still up. He had gone about seven miles when he smelled wood smoke and in no time spotted the outlaw's camp. Getting within half a mile of the camp, he dismounted and tied his horse to a small tree in a thicket to keep him from being seen. Tawkawa was well aware of the threat of other Indians coming upon his horse which they would not hesitate to take. Satisfied that his horse was concealed well enough, he set out on foot, right after moonset, for a closer look at the outlaw camp. From a vantage point in an outcropping of large boulders, he was able to determine that none of the men seemed to have a gun. He slowly scanned the desert in all directions and then eased to the ground on his stomach and crawled to within a few yards of the circle of light from their fire. From there, he could hear everything they were saying.

"There's no way we can go agin that bunch without guns." A big heavy set hombre was saying. "I'm not so sure we ought to mess with them even with guns."

"What's the matter with you, Hagen, you scared or something?" asked one of the others.

"I ain't a'feared of nobody," said Hagen, anger flushing to his face.

"You two, shut up," said Moran. "Hagen's half right. Them boys are salty and we have to be real careful about how we approach them from now on. We can't do anything without our guns. First thing we got to do is get some guns and then we got to figger out a way to get them cows. I ain't letting them just slip through my fingers. Them cows would bring twenty dollars a head in Kansas City or Dodge."

"What are we going to do?" asked another of the gang.

"I don't know just yet," said Moran. "But we'll figger it out. Just you wait and see, soon's we get ourselves some guns."

Tawkawa had heard all he needed to know. He eased back to the boulders and then made his way back to where he had left his horse tied. By the time he reported what he had heard to Pepper, it was about three hours till first light. Cladderbuck felt he should have gone after the outlaws but gunning down a bunch of men, who were unarmed, rankled. He decided not to attack the outlaws and everyone turned in to get a little rest before daylight. By sunup they were all in the saddle as soon as the last shift of nighthawks finished their breakfast.

"Head'em up, move'em out," Pepper cried and with the usual whoops and lariat tossing, the old brindle steer led out, set the pace and the rest of the herd followed suit.

CHAPTER 7

The range grass spread across the Texas Panhandle like a diamond studded carpet with many hues of brown, tan and light green, the droplets of early morning dew giving it sparkle. The day dawned with a clear blue white sky. There were birds singing everywhere, in every key, as the trio of riders left town passed the livery and corral where Clancy noticed the big yellow dog had already taken his post next to the south wall. This time though, he didn't even raise his head from the dust. Clancy had divided his few supplies into two gunny sacks that he laid across the horse, in back of his saddle and secured them with a rawhide thong.

Joe and his daughter, Hope joined Clancy and the three rode out of town at a brisk trot. They kicked their mounts to a mile eating gait that the animals could hold all day with a few periods of rest along the way. Before night fall, they were at the ranch. They reined up in the ranch yard and stepped from their saddles, with a couple of tail wagging dogs barking, not at them but sending a signal to the house. Buck had stepped out the back door with a toothpick in one corner of his mouth, walked out and reached over to take the reins of the horses.

"I'll see to the hosses," he said, eyeing Hope Collins all the while. Clancy grinned and hoped Joe and Hope hadn't noticed Buck's attention to her.

"Boss inside?" asked Clancy.

"Yah," said Buck. "He's just finishing up supper. Are you folks hungry?"

"We could use a bite," remarked Clancy, looking around at Collins and his daughter. "This here helpful fellow is Buck Parker, folks." Looking back to Buck, he said, "Buck, meet Captain Joe Collins, fresh out of the Texas Rangers and his daughter, Hope."

"Howdy," said Buck as he took the outstretched hand of Joe Collins and then tipping his hat to Hope, he said, "Ma-am." He then turned with the reins of the horses in hand and headed for the barn, trying to sneak a peek at Hope, without her noticing and almost stumbled over one of the ranch dogs. In the barn, he unsaddled them and let them roll. He took each animal in turn and rubbed them down with a, burlap, feed sack and putting them in individual stalls, gave each a portion of grain. He then forked down hay, from the loft, to each. He was working as fast as he could, for he wanted to get to the house and find out more about the very attractive woman that graced their ranch with her presence, but, no rancher, owner or cowboy neglected their horses.

In the meantime, Clancy had shown Joe Collins and his daughter into the dining area, separated from the kitchen by an invisible line that Clancy had established with the toe of his boot.

Under normal circumstances, nobody was to cross that line and enter his kitchen even though it was all in one big room. Upon recognition, JB burst out with a, big as all outdoors, grin, the corners of which seemed to touch his ears on each side of his face. He was up from the table and across the room with one bound. Taking Collins' outstretched hand and shaking it vigorously, he extended a welcome to his old friend.

"Joe, you ole hoss thief," he said. "Where in the world did you shake from? Man, it's good to see you." Pausing and looking at Hope, he continued, "and who is this lovely lady?"

"JB, I'd like you to meet my daughter, Hope."

It was as if the world tumbled down around JB's ears. He looked into the eyes of Hope Collins and all of a sudden, his entire being was lost to whatever else was going on around him. After a moment, he realized that he was staring and his face reddened a shade darker, leaching out through the summer tan that he had.

"Miss Collins, I'm so glad to make your acquaintance. May I say that I've never met any lovelier than you?" JB surprised himself with his own words. Turning to Joe Collins, he said, "It's just great to see you, Joe. How long are you going to be in this territory? Are you here on Ranger business?"

"I'm not in the Rangers since a month ago. I resigned and moved to Vega. Hope is going to open a millinery shop there."

"Hey, Joe, that's great," said JB. "Maybe we will get to see each other more often than before. I knew you were married but I never dreamed that you had such an attractive daughter."

Hope returned the blush which was more pink than red.

"Yes, my thoughts, exactly," said Joe, about seeing more of each other. "We can get in a little hunting maybe."

"I do a lot of my business in Amarillo. The nearest little town, Vega is so small that there's not a lot of choice of goods to buy," JB said, "in fact, it can hardly be called a town."

"Funny you would say that," said Joe. "I just mentioned to Hope that we might be better off if we resettled in Amarillo. It may be a much better place for her business."

"That might be best," said JB. "You being in Amarillo will still give us a chance to get together from time to time when I get into town. Talk about hunting, don't leave out fishing."

"The Sheriff in Amarillo has already asked if I'd be interested in filling in for him when he has to be gone for any reason," said Joe. "I told him I might, as long as it's not a full time thing."

Feeling like Hope was being left out of the conversation; JB directed his next question to her. "What do you think of our Pan Handle country, Hope?"

"I don't think I've been anywhere that could compare to the beautiful landscape that I've seen here in the Pan Handle. There doesn't seem to be as much dust as where we came from, and it's not nearly as hot."

"Hope's been getting spoiled since we got here. Austin seems so far away with all its saloons and people. Austin has a lot of dust and noise. It's gotten almost unbearable and nigh impossible to nail anything down," said Collins.

They talked into the middle of the night and finally closed their conversation with 'good nights' all around and turned in after a nightcap with Joe offering up a toast to the success and safety of JB's upcoming trip.

****

JB was snaked out of bed by the smell of rich, strong coffee about first light and when he went into the dining area, he found Joe Collins had already beat him to a cup of Clancy's strong, black brew. Early morning talk picked up pretty much where it had left off the night before.

"When are you and your crew lighting a shuck for Kansas City?" asked Collins. "Clancy mentioned that you'al were headed that way."

"We were planning to leave at first light tomorrow morning. It'll probably take us five days to get there. I've got Jeb Andrews coming out later today so we can fill him in on what he needs to do while we're gone."

"I haven't met this Jeb Andrews. Is he a good man for the job," asked Joe?

"Yah, I guess so," said JB. "He's a little gimpy from being thrown too many times, but he seems to get around pretty well."

"How long you figure on being gone?"

"Well, let's see," said JB, rubbing his chin in thought. "Say five days going and you can figure five days returning for every one day going so that would put us about twenty five days returning. All in all, I'd say we should be back in six weeks to two months, on the outside."

The whole crew trouped in for breakfast and Jocke spoke.

"Are we still leaving at first light tomorrow," he asked?

"Sure thing," said JB. "Do you'al have everything ready?"

"Everything is all set and ready," said Buck. He looked around the room and finally asked, "Where's Miss Hope?"

"She's sleeping late. She was so tired when we finally went to bed, I didn't have the heart to wake her," said Joe. "I'm sure she'll be along soon." He had no more than said it when Hope Collins walked into the room. All eyes turned in her direction for she was a beautiful woman. She blushed at the full attention she was receiving.

"Good morning everyone," she said. "I can't remember when I had a better night's sleep. There's a lot to be said for this frontier living and I have to give a lot of credit to that feather bed, that thing just swallows you whole."

JB smiled as he arose from his seat and meeting Hope, he took her hand and offered her the seat he had just vacated. "Sit here," he said.

The day went fast and before anyone realized it, supper was being put on the table. Buck had spent the most of the afternoon showing Jeb what all had to be done around the place while they would be gone.

"I'm glad you decided to stay over another night," JB said to Collins. "We can ride part of the way with you and Hope before we turn east. There's an old cattle trail that stretches from south Texas all the way to Kansas City. We have to ride a few miles south, then east to pick it up."

"That's fine JB," said Joe. "Hope and I are much obliged for you showing us such great hospitality."

"Think nothing of it," said JB. "The pleasure was all mine and you're welcome at the J-C Connected, anytime."

They all said their good-nights and retired. The next morning, at first light, everyone was in the saddle and headed south. Five or six miles down the trail, JB and his crew said their good-byes to Joe and Hope Collins and cut east to pick up the cattle trail while Joe Collins and his daughter turned in more a southeast direction and headed for Amarillo to look around before making their final decision on whether to move there or not..

The cattle trail that JB and his boys would be taking north was still in use from time to time and it was possible that they might come across herds going north. The sun was closing fast on the noon position when they came to the trail. They decided to take a nooning in an out-cropping of rocks alongside the trail.

"I've been watching those gray clouds banking up in the western sky," said Buck. "We'll most likely have rain by morning."

"Yes, I noticed them myself and you're probably right," said Abe Rivers, who was riding close by. "We might be able to out run the rain if that storm is moving to the southeast. If it does, it may go south of us, all together. If it goes northeast instead, we probably will get our butts wet."

Before too long, it became evident that the storm was moving in a northeast direction and by morning, the whole countryside was soaked like a sponge left in the watering trough over night after using it to wash a dozen horses. They made it to a water source before dark and well before any rain reached them. While JB and Clancy tied a tarp between trees, Jocke and Dusty snaked in a couple of deadfalls and pulled one of them under the tarp to keep it dry and provide a place to sit and eat their evening meal.

They made a ring of stones and soon had a good cook fire going, warm and comforting from the storm. A pot of coffee was soon on the fire. Everyone gathered under the tarp and had their supper. Somewhere outside the camp, a hoot-owl made its presence known by its usual question, 'Who? Who?' The light from the cloud-hidden sun had faded into a soft gray milky hue that melted into an ink-black blanket that spread out and settled upon the land like a home sewn quilt of velvet patchwork. The stars were blistering white against a depth of a sea of black. A pack of coyotes yelped through a dry creek bed in search of a late night snack. Soon, the soft night sounds of millions of insects, all participating in their own nighttime symphony and before long, the show was called off because of rain. It stormed for an hour or so and soon moved on to wet the countryside to the east, northeast..

Morning light shook everyone awake and as soon as everybody was dried out, they lines up for breakfast.

When they were finished eating and the camp shelter removed and the fire put out, they mounted their wet saddles and moved out in a hanging fog. Clancy moved back under the canvas top of the chuck wagon and sat on a box to drive the mules. He was high and dry, under the cover. There had been no lightening and very little wind from the storm; just rain.

"If we stay on the move, we'll be in Kansas City by the end of the week," said JB.

"Yah," said Buck. "I'm going to see if I can't find me a bath, a steak and then a woman."

Everyone chuckled. Buck was always talking about the women but all knew he was shy around them and usually went from the bath and steak to a saloon, a bottle and a poker table. Vicious Dog was so quiet that everyone hardly realized he was with them. They didn't see much of him. He was, most all the time, scouting ahead for any sign of trouble and seemed to be, forever bringing game to the cook fire.

Five days and four nights from the time they left the home ranch, they arrived in Kansas City. They stopped at a livery and left their horses, paying for grain and a rubdown for each. They took their Winchesters, bedrolls and saddlebags and headed for a hotel just down the street. Noticing a café across the street from the hotel, JB suggested that after checking in, they go there to eat. Vicious Dog and Abe stayed at the livery, wanting no part of white man's town or hotel, knowing that they wouldn't be welcome. JB made arrangement for them to sleep in the hay loft. Most of the hotels did not allow Negros, pets or Indians. A practice JB wished would one day be changed, but he wasn't in the mood to start a movement to accomplish a goal of that nature. His objective, at the moment, was to secure the cattle necessary to implement his plans and get them back to the ranch.

"Get everything put away in your room and we'll all go eat," said JB.

They took four rooms on the second floor at the front of the hotel and two of the rooms had windows that looked out over the street. After a few minutes, they had stowed their gear and all met in the lobby. Crossing to the café, Buck noted the sign on the front door that read '**No Negros, Indians, Pets or Ponies Allowed**'. They found a table in a corner that would accommodate the eight of them, JB, Buck, Dusty, Jocke, Chuck, Joe, Tom and Clancy.

A stocky man approached their table. He had a cloth tied around his middle with a smudge of, what looked like, gravy on one edge of it. Other than that, he appeared fairly neat.

"What'll you Gents have?" he asked, with a lilt of English accent tripping his words.

"What you got?" Clancy asked, ever the gourmet critic.

"We 'got' the same thing we had yesterday," said the waiter, with just a twinge of sarcasm, "steak, potatoes, cornbread and coffee. Then for desert we have deep-dish apple pie, penny a slice."

"Sounds good to me," said Buck.

"Yah, bring us eight rounds of what you have," said JB. "After eatin old Clancy's grub day in and day out, anything, other, has to taste good." He chuckled at Clancy's expense, as did everybody else.

"That's easy for you to say, seein as how you have this chance to eat town cookin and all, but you just wait till we get back to the home ranch and we'll see who can cook an' who can't. You can't always tell, my gal-dang cookin might get worse," he sputtered and spit out his words as though he was mad as the dickens. But inside, he was chuckling to himself. He had been at this game a long time. He called it "rag the cook", and really, at heart, didn't take any of it as a serious offense, truth be known, he worried about his recipe if he didn't get ragged.

They all sat in friendly conversation while they put their supper away. Settling back after eating, Buck rolled a smoke and passed the makings over to Clancy, who immediately rolled his own and passed the makings back to Buck. JB and Jocke were both pipe men except on occasion, JB would smoke a cheroot, and kept a package of them in his vest pocket but he preferred a pipe after supper and even at times, rolled his own quirlys. They were on their last cup of coffee when JB spoke.

"I'm going down to the stockyards first thing after breakfast in the morning."

"Do you want any of us to go with you?" asked Buck.

"No, I'm just going to see about the availability of the short-horns we want. I'm sure the yard super can steer me right. You stay around the main part of town. Let's all meet back here for our nooning. It was getting late and they were all tired so they went back to the hotel and hit the hay. Buck forgot all about the women and stayed to get plates of grub for Vicious Dog and Abe.

The next morning, they were off on their individual quest after meeting for breakfast. Buck and Dusty walked down to the livery with grub for Vicious Dog and Abe. The rest of the outfit was lounging around the hotel and later some strolled down to the stock yards to look at the livestock. JB headed for the stockyard in search of information about the purchase of cattle to his liking, he instructed Buck to try and round up some more men for the drive. At the yards, he found the man in charge, leaning on the top rail of a holding pen. JB walked up to the fence and spoke.

"Could you tell me where I might find the person in charge of the yard?"

"That'd be me son," the older man said. My name's Frank Carpenter. What can I do for you?"

"My name is Johnson, JB Johnson and I'm looking to buy a few head of shorthorns. I thought maybe you could put me on the trail of someone selling."

"Sure I can, Mister Johnson," said Carpenter.

"JB," said JB. "Just call me JB."

"Well, JB, you've come to the right man. Just how many do you want?"

JB rubbed the stubble on his chin and said with a serious tone to his voice, "Now that all depends on the price. I want to buy all I can with what money I have allocated to the purpose."

Carpenter looked JB straight in the eye and said, "There's a glut in the cattle market right now and I've got holding pens full of shorthorns. I'd say I have close to four thousand of them on hand right now. I can let you have them for," he paused in thought, "say...ten dollars a head... feeding them is killing me."

JB did the arithmetic quickly in his head. Of the fifty two thousand he had left of his gold field money, the purchase of the cattle would take forty thousand, leaving him twelve thousand for start-up money plus what Pepper would inject into the partnership. He rubbed his chin a moment and then spoke.

"Let's have a look at those cows," he said.

"This way," said Carpenter. He stepped away from the fence and started walking. JB fell in step and they headed for the pens where the cattle were being held.

"This is just a part of them. The rest are in a number of holding pens. As you can see, this pen will only hold a certain number of head." Carpenter was saying as they approached the first pen.

JB took a good look at the cattle, paused for just a moment and said, "If they're all like these, it's a deal, Mister Carpenter."

"They all came in the same herd," said Carpenter, pleased with JB's acceptance of the transaction, proposed by him.

They went back to the office where Carpenter drew up the necessary paper work and they headed for the bank. As they were leaving, Buck showed up with three men. JB told them to wait for his return. At the bank, the papers were witnessed and JB gave Carpenter a draft on the bank in Amarillo for forty thousand dollars.

"Give me a day or two to get the rest of my outfit together and we'll be taking those cows off your hands," said JB.

"That's fine," said Carpenter, "whenever you're ready. Keep in mind though that I'll have to charge for all feed from now on since they are your cows now. I'd not do it but for the owners of the yard. They are real sticklers for keeping everything, strictly business. No charge for the use of the pens though."

"Thanks Frank," JB said in a business tone. "It won't be more than a couple of days."

They walked back to the stockyard office where they found Buck and the three men he had brought plus four more ride-bys that knew the first three and decided to join the group with Buck's invitation after he had talked to them all. The cowboys Buck had chosen thus far were all from the same cattle drive that had come in from Texas just a couple of days before. Texans all and trail wise. JB thought Buck had done a good job getting those kinds of men and decided to make him Segundo of the J-C Connected. Dusty was satisfied just being a drover and none of the rest of the men showed any interest in giving orders. Buck introduced the one who seemed to be the spokesman for all seven of them.

"Boss, this here is Charlie Estell. I'm gonna let him introduce the rest of these Gents. Men, meet JB Johnson."

JB removed his glove and took Estell's outstretched hand and shook it. He said, "Pleased to meet you Charlie."

"Likewise," said Estell. "These Gents are Ben Campbell, Waco, Winston Yates, his baby brother, Billy Yates." Billy's ears turned red and he had a sheepish grin on his face. Turning to the next man, Estell continued, "This Gent is Bret Mosby and last here is Wilford Teague."

"Glad to meet you Gents," said JB. "I guess Buck has filled you in on what's to be done and what I'm paying."

They all nodded their response. He continued, "Do any of you know of anyone else who might want to sign on?"

Billy Yates raised his hand and said, "They's four others what rode in with us. They might be interested. You want me to round'em up?"

"Four more is about what I had in mind," said JB. Why don't you go and see if you can find them."

Billy was off in the direction of the saloon section of town. In less than half hour, he was back with the four other men. He spoke. "Mister Johnson, these men are." He pointed to each as he named them; "Bert Young, Pablo Vega, Thad Brooks and John Hanks. Men, this here is JB Johnson."

They each touched their hat brims in turn and waited for JB to lay out the deal.

"Men, I'm taking a herd of shorthorns to a spread west of Amarillo, just a few miles from the New Mexico Territory. I'm paying forty and found plus ammunition. Are all of you armed with pistols and rifles?" They all nodded and he continued. "Good. If Clancy, our cook, can get the chuck ready by then, we'll take to the trail at first light the day after tomorrow. Get your loose ends tied up, any man not ready, then, will have to look for another job. Is that clear?"

They all shouted their understanding.

"Good. Let's all meet in the café, yonder and have supper at six o'clock. I'll round my other men up by then."

That night at supper, JB asked Clancy about the chuck wagon.

"How you coming on that wagon, Clancy?"

83

"I've just about got everything ready," he answered. "I just need to pick a few bags of grain to feed them long eared mules along the way. I'll be ready on time."

"Good man. You'll do just fine cause I think you're just as stubborn as those mules," said JB. "You've done chuck before and knowing you, if those mules give you any trouble, we might wind up having strange meat for supper," He guffawed at Clancy's expense and after a sputter or two, Clancy joined in the laughter.

"Yah to your comment, I have done chuck a lot of times but it's been a while," said Clancy, "I mean for a crew this big."

"You can handle it," said JB. "Remember I have to move the cattle by day after tomorrow. I gave Carpenter my word they'd be gone in two days."

"That won't be a problem," said Clancy. "I have the wagon ready and stocked with supplies."

"That's fine," said JB. "Now let's finish supper and get some shuteye."

CHAPTER 8

Berton Rawlings and his right hand gun, Jack Potts, sat in the Branch Water saloon in Amarillo, sharing a bottle of Tennessee whiskey. Potts was dealing hands of five card stud to himself and three imaginary players as Rawlings looked on. Potts spoke.

"What's with you and this Johnson Gent?" he asked Rawlings. "You sure have a red ass about something. He must have messed over you real bad at one time or the other."

"Never you mind why, Jack." Rawlings sneered at Potts. "All you need to know is, I want his stinkin hide nailed to the barn door. I've got my reasons. You'd be better off mindin your own business."

"What are you plannin on doin?" Potts asked, tossing out another round of cards. He lifted the corner of his own card.

"I haven't figured out exactly how, yet, but when I'm through with Mister JB Johnson, he'll wish he never even thought about poppin out of his mamma," Rawlings spit out the words as if they were burning the inside of his mouth like a spoon full of chili peppers. He knocked back another glass of the Tennessee whiskey and hissed through his teeth as it went down, and then poured another.

"Word has it Johnson is gone to Kansas to buy cattle," he said as he picked up his glass and held it half way to his mouth while in thought.

"That's it," he hissed. "Soon's he crosses out of Indian Territory, into Texas, we're gonna take possession of those cattle, pay Johnson in full with hot lead and take them through New Mexico territory and sell them across the Mexico border. If we pay nothing for them cows and sell them for ten dollars a head, depending on how many we have to sell, we could both be rich beyond our wildest dreams. All we got to do is get a few boys together, to help handle the herd till we can sell them."

"What about having to pay them boys?" asked Potts?

"We just tell them they'll be paid when the cows are sold. Then, when we get the money, we'll get the outfit drunk and when everybody's drunk out of their minds, you and I will just disappear, money and all. By the time they all sleep it off, we'll be long gone."

"Yah," said Potts with a renewed enthusiasm for the deal. "Won't nobody know the difference until it's too late. I really cotton to that idea. You know, you're a mean son of a bitch, Rawlings."

Rawlings didn't mind being called that name for it was a badge of honor, coming the way it did. He had a smug expression on his sinister face.

"But, first things first," said Rawlings with a satisfied grin at the offhanded compliment paid him by Potts, "we have to do good ole Johnson in and if he gets killed in the process, well, that's all the better." He laughed deep in his chest, a crazy laugh and turned up his glass. Potts turned his glass up likewise, sat it hard on the table and cracked a grin in the corner of his mouth, then wiped it away on the sleeve of his shirt, smile gone; he started to deal another hand of cards.

"Did you see that new chunk of woman flesh that blew into town?" he drawled. "She and her old man have rooms down at Murphy's boarding house."

"I sure did," said Rawlings. "I been meaning to drop in on the little lady and get better acquainted, so to speak. As a matter of fact, I think I'll do just that right now." He winked at Potts and got up from the table.

He slipped his hat on, turned and knocked back one last drink, then headed for the door, Potts on his heels, both of them weaving from too much whiskey.

Hope Collins was standing on a chair, putting stock on a shelf when she heard the bell, attached to the wall above the door, ring. She was just stretching to place a box on the shelf and she turned her head and tried to look over her shoulder to see who had come in. She could see the two men but because of the angle of vision, she couldn't tell much about them. She spoke.

"I'll be right with you," she said. "I just need to place this box."

She froze at the response she got from the floor behind her.

"That's all right. The view from here is just fine," said Rawlings with a thick tongue. "Just you don't fall off that chair. I wouldn't want you gettin hurt before we become better acquainted." There was a tone of self confidence and boastfulness in his voice as if it would be all her pleasure just to meet such a fine specimen of a man.

Hope stepped from the chair and turned to see Rawlings and Potts both staring at her figure and not looking her in the eye. She had a mixed feeling of anger and embarrassment and she knew her face had reddened.

"What can I do for you," she asked?

"Not a question of what you can do for me," said Rawlings, "more what I can do for you."

"I'm sorry, but I don't understand."

"Oh. You will," said Rawlings as he reached and took her arm, gripping it tightly. She was standing behind a counter and her other hand had slipped under it. Before Rawlings knew what was going on, she pulled a hand iron, made of cast iron, from under the counter and smashed him across the arm with a driving blow. His face drew up in an agonizing scowl and he let out with a scream that could be heard a block away. He let go of her arm and she quickly headed for the front door.

Potts had moved to block her exit from the store and she backed into a corner, looking for anything she might use as a weapon to defend herself. Rawlings meanwhile had gradually overcome his pain and walked slowly toward Hope.

"Nobody, not even a woman does something like that to Berton Rawlings and gets away with it," he said as he sliced her with his eyes.

The opening of the door was a sudden shock to all concerned. Two women walked right on into the shop as Rawlings and Potts withdrew to leave. "We'll discuss it later, ma-am," Rawlings said as he pulled the door to.

Hope was almost in a state of shock.

"Is there anything wrong?" one of the ladies asked.

"Ah...no, no," Hope said as she regained her composure, "what may I do for you ladies?"

When she had finished waiting on the two women, Hope locked the door after them and went to the back of the shop for her hat. Returning to the front door she unlocked it, went out, turned and locked the door, left the shop and went straight to the boarding house where she and her father were staying. Finding him gone, she sat in her room with the door locked and cried while she waited for his return. When he returned and heard her story, he was furious at the liberties the man had taken with his daughter. In the west, no man molested a woman...no man, and lived to brag about it. He, with her description of the two men, left to try to find them.

While he searched through the towns saloons, looking for the two, Rawlings sat in his room with cold compresses on his arm. He swore one oath after the other.

"I'll get even with that bitch if it's the last thing I do," he said. "Nobody, I mean nobody, does something like this to Berton Rawlings and gets away with it." His arm had turned color to red, purple and yellow, bordering on green. "Damn that woman, it's a wonder she didn't break the damn bone."

Potts just leaned against the wall watching and listening with a half smile on his lips, though inside, he was laughing out loud, but he would never let Rawlings know he thought it was funny at the risk of being shot on the spot. Meanwhile, Joe Collins had given up his search and returned to the boarding house. He spoke to Hope.

"I think I'll hire someone to work in the shop with you," he said.

"That won't be necessary," she said. "I don't think I'll have any more trouble."

"Never-the-less, I insist on someone being with you during shop hours. I mean it, Hope, I don't want you there, alone."

From then on, there was another woman, hired by her father, in the shop with Hope all the time the shop was open.

Joe Collins couldn't get the incident out of his mind. Time went on and the description of the two men that had bothered his daughter grew dimmer. He was sure he would have to have definite proof before accusing anyone so he, finally, put it on a back shelf of his mind. But, he resolved to keep a closer eye on things from then on.

Rawlings's arm was getting better, but still pained him quite a bit. He sent Potts, with enough provisions to last a couple of weeks, up the trail to locate Johnson's outfit. He wanted more than anything to destroy Johnson. He had already gotten a commitment for the purchase of the cattle through a local Mexican. He would be driving them through New Mexico territory into the southeastern corner of Arizona, through the San Pedro valley, directly between Tombstone and Bisbee. He was to meet his buyer, a representative of the Mexican government, in Nacho, Mexico. What a sweet setup for himself, he thought. He was already entertaining the idea of double crossing Potts.

Potts was having his troubles with the mule he had rented to carry his pack.

"Come on you dumb headed son of a stall sick mare. We got to get gone up the trail. I ain't got time to pamper you all the way, either." He pulled and forced the mule forward with outstretched neck.

Camping by night and traveling all day, in a little over a week, he still was two days out of Kansas City and had seen no sign of the Johnson herd. He made camp that night by a small stream. Sitting by his fire, sipping on a cup of black coffee, he thought about the money he and Rawlings would have and all the things he was going to do with it. The darkness was filled with lightning bugs and off in the distance, a coyote howled a lonesome sound. Potts shivered at the thought of being so alone and determined to buy himself a fine woman to spend his time with; soon as he got his money. Finally he finished his coffee, threw the butt of his quirley into the fire and rolled into his blankets as late night darkness closed in.

That night, JB and his riders were spending their last night in Kansas City. The chuck wagon was stocked and ready. JB had hired enough new riders, along with Clancy, Jocke, Vicious Dog, Dusty and Buck, to push the cattle; he had bought, to the home range.

On the morning of departure, JB and his outfit all piled into the café as the first pale gray of dawn crept over the horizon, like a sick incandescent wooly worm. They were soon surrounding large platters of fried eggs, country ham, bacon, sausage, grits, gravy and biscuits with a smathering of churned butter, wild honey and homemade gooseberry jam. All being washed down with what seemed like gallons of scalding hot coffee. When they were fully fed, JB stood to give them a last minute set of rules that would be obeyed by one and all while on this cattle drive. There were only two hard clad rules. One was to do your job. The other was no whiskey except what Clancy kept for fever and snakebite but he could overlook a snifter in their coffee every now and then. JB was lucky, he thought, to have grabbed a Texas trail outfit that was right at home with a herd and the Texans were lucky to have come across someone who would pay them during their trek back toward their home range.

They all left the café and headed to where their horses were and saddled up for the start of their day. The cattle were being held in a row of pens down one side of the stock yards. The men rode down the sides of the pens and one by one, the gates to the individual pens were opened and the riders entered the pens, eased around the cattle and hazed them out, mixing into one large herd. When all the cattle had been merged into one group, the drovers started them in a column, about thirty abreast, toward Texas. JB was out front on point, Buck and Atchley were out riders and the new riders flanked left and right and filled in at drag. Dusty rode drag by choice, mainly because, for some odd reason, he liked the smell of dust and cow manure blended together, he had no earthly reason why. Clancy had the chuck wagon behind the drag riders and was eating a mountain of dust. His mouth even tasted gritty.

Vicious Dog had been sent ahead with the horse herd. JB had assigned a man to help with the horses so Vicious Dog could scout for water and possible trouble from time to time and return to help with the horses. They didn't expect an awful lot of trouble until they got close to Indian Territory. Never-the-less Vicious Dog kept his eyes peeled because, in that time and place, you just never knew what was just around the next bend in the trail.

So the J-C Connected Cattle Company was on the move, kicking up a cloud of dust into the early morning skies of Missouri, headed south, southwest toward Indian Territory.

Early in the afternoon of the first day on the trail, Vicious Dog rode back to the point position to report to JB.

"There is water for cattle six or seven miles," said Vicious Dog. "I saw tracks of unshod horses along water's edge. The tracks are a day and a half, maybe two days old. No fresh sign along creek bank, either side. Tracks I find go to the setting sun."

"Good," said JB. "Go back to the horses and get them to the water and put them on any good grass you can find close. We'll be slow getting grub ready tonight but I'm making a change in the line-up starting tomorrow. We're moving the chuck wagon to the front of the herd, between the herd and the horse remuda. That way, Clancy can get the wagon in place and have the coffee and grub ready for the outfit a lot earlier, we won't be trying to find our mouths in the dark."

Vicious Dog grunted his understanding and wheeled his horse and headed back to the horse herd. JB rode to the right flank and informed the man riding there that they were about six or so miles from water and camp. "Pass the word," he said. Then he rode to the rear of the herd, told the drag riders and went on to the chuck wagon, further back.

"Hey! You ole lazy wagon rider," he called out to Clancy, putting a big wide grin on his face.

"Who are you calling lazy. You ought to have to ride on this hard flat seat all day. It gets to where you can't even feel your butt, it gets so numb, once it gets passed the sore as a risen stage. What's up, Boss?"

"We're about six miles from water where we'll make camp. Get the grub ready as soon as you can. I'll be talking to you about a change I've got in mind at supper."

"I'll get'em all fed just as soon as I can," said Clancy.

By the time the riders had gotten the herd watered and milling on the grass that grew along the banks of the stream, Clancy had two big pots of coffee boiled and pulled back from the fire to let the grounds settle. The men all gathered around the camp fire as the horse herd mingled with the cattle, cropping at the grass. There were three men assigned to stay with the herd while the rest of the outfit had their supper. Then they were relieved to come in for their grub. Supper was ready a little before sundown and the men held their plates while Clancy filled them. The last couple of hours before night time purged the sky of all light, the men sat around the camp fire and told tall tales of their exploits, mostly of the women they had known and all who listened, knew that the tales were stretched almost to the breaking point, but that was the fun in it all.

"What ever happened to that little redhead you knew down in Dallas, Ben?" Thad Brooks asked with a little chuckle to his voice.

"Ah, hush up about that," said Ben Campbell.

"Shoot, it ain't nothing to be ashamed of, Ben." Thad went on, "You boys ain't never heard the story about ole Ben, here and the redhead from Dallas, have you?"

"Now hush up about it," said Ben. "You know dang good and well if I'd a- knowed she was married, I'd of never said boo to her and just because her husband was six and a half feet tall and weighed at least two hundred and sixty pounds don't mean I was scared of him, neither."

"I didn't say you were," said Thad. "I'll have to admit, a man would have to be a fool to tackle a man that size, with just his hands."

Everyone laughed at the expense of Ben, but Ben laughed also and the camp fire humor continued.

JB walked over to the chuck wagon where Clancy was washing the plates and utensils, listening to the men rib each other. He had a cup of coffee in his hand and he took a sip as he stopped by the tailgate of the wagon. Putting his coffee cup on the tailgate, he took out the makings and started to roll a quirley. He spoke.

"We'll be changing the line-up starting tomorrow. I want you to move the chuck wagon up ahead of the herd. We'll give you a good head start before we poke the cows. Stay well ahead and when you reach our next camp site, I want you to set up and have the grub ready when the men get the cattle settled down for the night. That way, there won't be all that pressure at the last minute. How does that sound?"

"I was wondering when you was going to get me out of that dust cloud behind that bunch of smelly cows," said Clancy. "It sounds just fine to me. I'll have time to whip up a batch of bear sign every now and then."

"If I'd known that, I'd of done it from the start," JB said with a chuckle.

JB walked back to the fire. He spoke to the men. "Listen up," he said. "I've made a list of who will be on which watch. We'll have four shifts. Vicious Dog will be sleeping with the horses and the rest of you will keep an eye out for trouble and try to keep the cattle quiet. I want Charlie Estell, Ben Campbell and Waco on first watch from nightfall to nine o'clock, Winston and Billy Yates and Buck Parker will be on from nine to one, Bert Mosby, Wilford Teague and Bert Young take it from one to four and then Jocke Atchley, Pablo Vega, Thad Brooks and John Hanks will take it to first light. We'll have breakfast as soon after first light as possible then I plan to have the herd up and moving by an hour after first light, but make sure Clancy has the chuck wagon well ahead before we start the herd, any questions?"

Nobody voiced a question so it was left at that. The men on the first watch left for their duty and the rest of the men began to roll in their blankets for the night. A couple of the last watch men stayed up and talked over coffee and smokes. Finally, they, too, slipped between their blankets.

The next morning JB arose while the first thin line of light crept slowly over the far eastern horizon. There was a cool feeling to the early morning, and JB breathed in the fresh cool air like taking a drink of pure mountain spring water. Early morning made him feel good, all over. The daytime birds were coming awake and flitting from bush to bush, singing as they went. A slight mist lay close like an, almost transparent, blanket across the ground and mingled with the wispy smoke from the camp fire. He stood for a minute as Clancy arose and started to build the fire up for breakfast.

"Mornin, JB," he said.

"Mornin to you Clancy," JB responded. "Is that coffee hot?"

"It's still pretty warm, want I should heat it up, only take a minute?"

"Yeah, it's probably as strong as a muscle toned mule but I like it that way."

Clancy pushed the pot close to the fire and proceeded to get breakfast ready. He filled the other large coffee pot with water from one of the kegs that he had fitted to the sides of the chuck wagon. He intended to refill both of the kegs before leaving the stream by which they had camped.

JB could see above the ground fog that Vicious Dog was up and seeing to the horses. As the rest of the outfit eased out of their blankets, JB strolled down to the creek to freshen up a bit. The water was clear and cold and it took only a splash or two in the face to chase away all feelings of sleepiness. A mourning dove cooed to its absent mate and received no answer. As he turned to walk away from the water's edge, Vicious Dog was coming down to the creek with the horses all grouped around him like a bunch of loving pets, each seeking his attention. He was talking in low tones, soothing Indian yammering that the horses seem to understand. They all came easily down to the water and drank. JB wondered at the ability of Vicious Dog to communicate with them. He thought there was no better way to tame horses than to have a person who understood them and who they, in turn, understood, to gentle them without taking away their spirit.

Soon, after each man had cut out his mount for the day, Vicious Dog and his helper were off to the south with the horses and on short order, the day broke with a flood of light from the rising sun when the shout came, "Head'em up, move'em out!" With whoops and shouts and ropes popping bovine hides, the clear air above the ground fog began to fill with dust kicked up as the herd slowly arose and started their daily trek southward. The chuck wagon was already out ahead of the cattle, following the horses. JB was at point.

As soon as the J-C Connected cattle drive was underway, Vicious Dog ranged ahead to scout for any sign of trouble and to look for a likely place to camp for the coming night. The drag riders had all covered their noses and mouths with their bandanas to cope with the dust. There were quite a number of bunch quitters, causing the flank riders and drag boys to work harder to keep them all moving in the right direction. It was just a given for the herd to take a few days to become trail wise, and things would settle down as time went on and the work of chasing quitters would slack off, or at least everybody hoped so.

Vicious Dog had gone what he judged to be about fifteen miles before he came on the tracks of two shod horses. The tracks were headed west toward the foothills of a low mountain range on the horizon. He could not tell if it was one or two riders. Could be one rider leading a pack animal. Not much farther on, he came onto a naturally formed tank, shaped like a huge gourd dipper with a stream leading off from one side like a curved handle. The tank was fed by a spring on the up side.

The reservoir had a considerable amount of water collected in the basin of solid rock, more than enough to water the cattle and horse herds. It would be easy to collect enough clean water from the spring at the point where the fresh water entered the tank to fill the kegs on the chuck wagon and for the men to all fill their canteens. He thought again of the tracks of the two horses then he wheeled his horse, after he and his mount had drank their fill and he had filled his own canteen, and headed back to the herd.

Potts had spotted Vicious Dog's approach and had changed his direction and headed west. He rode in that direction for a few miles and then turned north. It wasn't long before he came in sight of the dust from the herd. He waited in an outcropping of large boulders and rode out as the herd approached and rode at a slow trot to the chuck wagon.

"Howdy," he said as he pulled rein by the wagon.

Clancy pulled the team to a stop and pushed the break with his foot.

"Howdy, where you headed?" said Clancy.

"On my way to Kansas City," said Potts. "Any sign of trouble back that way?"

"We didn't run into any trouble," said Clancy.

"My name's Potts, Jack Potts. What outfit is this?"

"The owner of these cows is JB Johnson, out of Oldham County, Texas."

"Never been there," said Potts. "Well you take care. I best be getting on up the trail, so-long."

Clancy touched the brim of his hat in response and sat a moment watching Jack Potts ride off to the north. He popped the reins on the backs of his team and was off toward the horses.

Potts was pleased with himself. He had done what he had been ordered to do. He had located the Johnson outfit and now he had to circle wide of the herd and return to Amarillo to report his findings to Rawlings.

Vicious Dog reported to JB that he had found water enough for the herd and fresh spring water for the chuck and men.

"I see tracks of two horses between here and there that go west," he said.

"Were they shod or unshod?" asked JB.

They were tracks of shod horses," said Vicious Dog. "I not find sign of them at tank. They not find water."

"Go ahead and take the horse herd to the water and get them on grass, if you can find any. It's getting a little scarce on this cattle drive trail. Clancy will be right behind you and we'll try to pick up the pace to get there before dark."

With that, JB pulled his mount around to pass the word to step up the pace. It would be up to the drag riders to push the tail end of the herd so the rest of them would have to move faster just to keep the horns of the others behind from sticking them in the butt. The cattle arrived at the tank just after the sun dropped behind the silvered horizon. They crowded around the water's edge to wet their dry throats. By the time they had watered and been circled for bedding, supper was ready and the smell of bear sign floated on the early evening breeze that caressed the countryside. It intermingled with the aroma of fresh coffee. A night owl hooted twice, far enough away for the sound to be just barely heard from camp. While the men ate, a whippoorwill whistled softly into the fast approaching darkness.

Beyond the tank runoff, the land stretched out and looked flat to the eye for it was hard to determine where the low places were. They were there and sometimes caused problems when it came to running cattle across them. Some had steep banks and a cow could break a leg going off them. But that was tomorrow. The now of tonight faced the outfit and everyone was aware of it. Tired from a hard day, most of the men ate their supper topped off with a handful of Clancy's bear sign and a cup of fresh, hot, black coffee, they rolled into their blankets and soon the camp site was quiet except for an occasional snore. Clancy was still up finishing the dishes and JB sat alone by the fire with his cup in his hand, sipping black coffee and thinking of the days to come. He finally stood and slinging the dregs from his cup into the fire, turned to his bedroll.

"Good night Clancy," he said. "See you in the morning."

"Good night Boss," Clancy said over his shoulder as he continued to clean up, it would be only a few minutes before he, too, would be in his blankets. Clancy slept under his chuck wagon for two reasons, it was the driest place, usually and cowboys were bad about pilfering food at night. They were the eat'inest congregation of people ever assembled in one place and that place at the moment was a cow camp.

The night shifts came and went and the night passed without incident. At first light, everyone was saddled and ready to ride right after a breakfast of bacon, flapjacks with syrup and plenty of strong black coffee.

"A breakfast like that sure sets good on the ole stomach," said Ben Campbell.

"Yah," echoed Bret Mosby. "You keep feeding like this and you might not be able to get rid of us Texans when this drive is over," he directed his comment to JB

"Well," said JB, "it's for sure, with these cattle added to what I already have plus what Cladderbuck is bringing and us runnin a two base operation, We're going to need a few good men to help with the ranching. When we get all these cattle on the home range, there's a lot of work to be done to insure the success of the J-C Connected.

"They's some of us got family back in Texas but some are foot loose and fancy free. May be that some of us will stay on with you," said Bert Young.

"Well, let's count it when we get there, I think Clancy is far enough out for us to get started," said JB. He turned from his conversation and let out with a yell, "Head'em up, move'em out!" The day's drive was under way as the golden light from the sun pushed the misty grays and purples from the recessed areas of the foothills in the distance. The cattle moved at a slow pace to begin with, stretching the night's kinks out of sleeping muscles. The first indications were that it was going to be a beautiful day. As the day wore on, that seemed to be a false prediction. For in the western sky, a bank of dark clouds rolled up over the horizon, pulling its self along with long jagged fingers of blue, white lightning that threw muffled explosions of angry thunder across the wide open plains like the rumbling of a game of tenpins being played by a bunch of short-legged leprcons.

"Going to have rain by nightfall," said Buck as JB rode up beside him. The bunch quitters were almost none and the flank and drag riders struggling, to keep from going to sleep in the saddle.

"Yah," said JB. "I can smell it. I'm going to range out a little and see if I can meet up with Vicious Dog and find a place where we can have a little shelter from the worst of it." With that, he spurred his horse and galloped off toward the south. He passed the chuck wagon and the horse herd and on about five miles before he spotted Vicious Dog, sitting his horse atop a butte. He rode up to the Indian and nodded a greeting.

"How's it look ahead?" he asked.

"I find water two miles from here but cattle reach it by middle of afternoon. That will not give us long day. We could go more miles before dark," said Vicious Dog. "I find more water ten miles. We cannot get there before dark comes. We would be better off with a short day than dry camp." Vicious Dog sat his horse and waited for JB's decision.

"I guess you've noticed the dark clouds in the west," said JB. "What do you think?"

"I think we get wet by time dark gets here," said Vicious Dog, "if we don't find shelter."

"Is there any kind of shelter at the close water?"

"Yes, a little," said Vicious Dog. "Not enough for cattle, but camp site could get under cottonwoods that line water's edge. Stream flowing from sunset to sunrise and there is much used buffalo crossing."

"Good," said JB. "Let's stop at the first water and set up camp under the trees. You go ahead and water the horses and get them on grass. I'll tell Clancy before I go back to point." With that, JB wheeled his Appaloosa and rode back to the chuck wagon. Clancy saw him coming and pulled back on the reins and stopped the mules that pulled the big wagon, as JB eased his horse to a stop.

"Clancy, there's a storm coming," he said, "I guess you've noticed it.

"Yah, I saw the clouds forming. Looks bad," said Clancy.

"We're going to make camp about seven miles from here. You go on and set up. Take that large canvas and spread it between the trees as best as you can and be sure to stay to the west of the place where the horses water. Get Vicious Dog to give you a hand setting up. The stream is flowing toward the east and it'll be clear to the west. I'm sure the eastern flow will be full of horse apples by the time you get there." He spurred his Appaloosa into an easy trot and headed back to the herd. Upon arriving at the herd, he circled around and notified everybody of their plans and eased back to his point position at a trot.

The storm moved closer, threatening to overtake them before they could get the cattle to the camp site. As the sky darkened and the wind increased ahead of the storm, the sun was dimmed and the late afternoon got much cooler. JB loved the fresh feel of wind just ahead of a rain storm. It smelled so sweet and clean. It also, coming from the west, blew the dust eastward and gave some relief to the drag riders, much to the dislike of the left flankers.

CHAPTER 9

Potts rode into Amarillo at a slow trot. He almost rode his horse over a dog that was sleeping in the late afternoon sun. The weather was getting a little cooler and the warm sun probably felt good to the hound. He jumped up just in time to get out of the way of Potts' mount. He stood off a few feet and growled a low throaty growl. The dust from the horse's hooves puffed into his face and he sniffed and sneezed and turned to walk away. Potts went to the livery and left his horse to be cared for and, finally, got rid of the stubborn mule, he'd fought for days.

"Sorry bastard, it'll be a cold day in hell when I rent you for a pack mule," he said as the attendant led the mule away. Taking his saddlebags and rifle with him, he made his way to the saloon where he had a room, upstairs over the bar; up where all the ladies-of-the-night plied their trade. Getting his key from the barkeep, he proceeded up the stairs, entered his room and putting his gear down, he stretched out on the bed. He decided to rest a while before going to find Rawlings. He figured

Rawlings would be in the saloon later that evening, and figured that he had plenty of time.

Unknown to Potts, Rawlings had been out to spy on the ranch house of the Johnson spread that day and when he returned, he headed straight for the saloon just as Potts had thought. He had no more than seated himself at a back table alone and started to shuffle a deck of cards, when Potts descended the stairs. Seeing Potts, Rawlings motioned for him to come to the table.

Potts walked to the table about the same time the barkeep walked up.

"What'll you boys have?" the barkeep asked.

"Bring us a bottle of that good Tennessee whiskey and two glasses," said Rawlings, then turning to Potts he said, "Well what's the story?"

Potts leaned over the table and started to say something when the barkeep walked up with their bottle and two glasses. Potts leaned back, reached and took up his glass and held it for Rawlings to fill, which he did. The barkeep walked away with the shiny coin Rawlings had flipped to him. The bartender put a tooth mark in the coin from force of habit to make sure it was really gold.

"Well?" Rawlings spit between clinched yellow stained teeth.

"He's got a pretty good sized herd of shorthorns. I'd say maybe three...four thousand head."

"How far out are they?"

"I'd say maybe five weeks. They can't make more'n twelve to fourteen miles a day, at the most, with that many cows. He's got fourteen riders besides himself and the cook," Potts said. He turned up his glass and knocked back the smooth Tennessee whiskey, spun his finger around the inside of the glass and then licked the whiskey off of it. Puckering up a bit, he then let out a half hiss and half sigh through his teeth and grinned wide. "Man, that's good whiskey, smooth as silk." He paused a second, looking at the glass. "I could tell that some of them cows are springin, hell, he's gonna have some calves on the way here, from the looks of it."

Rawlings reached over and poured Potts' glass full again, but this time Potts just sipped at the glass's contents. They sat, sipped and talked in low tones.

****

JB intended to throw in the shorthorn cows and cross them all down the way, with his white faces and the longhorns, Cladderbuck was bringing up from the south. What he hoped to get for his effort was a strain of cattle that could survive the harsh conditions of the pan handle plains and yet produce a bigger, meatier steer for market. Some thought he was dreaming in his hat. They thought that his schemes would never work. Some even told him so. Yet, he was determined to try and by doing so, prove that it could be done, he just wasn't quite sure of the results. That was yet to be seen.

Clancy rolled the chuck wagon in under the cottonwoods that lined the banks of the stream. It flowed west to east and he positioned the wagon a good distance from a buffalo crossing. He, first thing right off, filled the kegs on the chuck wagon with fresh water from the stream, using a bucket made of oak with a rope handle. Then he stretched the large canvas tarp between three trees and tied the fourth corner of it to the wagon bed after spreading it over one of the hoops that held the wagon top in place at the rear of the wagon. He not only sheltered the camp fire area but also the tail gate of the wagon so that his fixing place would stay dry, any good cook hated to have it rain on his fixing place, at least to Clancy's way of thinking.

By the time he had a fire started and supper under way, the rain set in. First a few large drops, each containing at least two tablespoonfuls of clear, sweet water, beat rhythmically on the canvas wagon top and the spent leaves, on the ground. The sound on the wagon top and canvas was like a smathering of Indian drums in a sacred ceremony, echoing from, and far back up in the foothills. At the height of the ceremony, as if it were a rain dance, a steady downpour set in. The sound of it made the campfire seem all that much warmer, cozier and secure.

There wasn't much wind and the rain seemed to be coming straight down. The lightning subsided as if someone in the heavens had awakened a God-awful snoring giant. The herd was brought up to water and then pushed on across the stream because, sometimes, a lot of rain upstream would overflow the banks of such waterways and JB didn't want the cattle to go back the way they had come from in case of a stampede, besides, pushing them across deeper, fast rushing water after a storm, could pose a host of problems, the worst of which could be the loss of life of both men and cattle..

The cattle were restless because of the storm but not so to the point of breaking into a stampede. The men were all soaked to the skin and the dry spot under the tarp was very much welcome. They all crowded under it with a lot of room to spare. Winston Yates, Pablo Vega, John Hanks and Buck Parker were left to see to the cattle while the rest of the outfit ate their supper. JB stood just under the edge of the cover with a steaming cup of black coffee in his hand. He was apprehensive for some reason. Maybe it was due to the fact that they would be going into Indian Territory in a day or two. He knew the possibility of either Indian attack or rustlers, either way, there was danger for his men, and the immediate threat of the storm didn't help any.

"I'm glad we pushed the cattle and hosses on across this stream. If this keeps up, we may have more water than we need come morning. It's a good thing you decided to pitch camp over here also, Clancy. Getting the chuck wagon across was smart. If the water rises, it could have been a mess trying to cross. We're high enough here to avoid a flash flood, don't you think?"

"We'll be alright here unless Noah is building another ark. I figured it was best to cross and get out of the way before the cattle got here," said Clancy. "All you fellows gather around. I've got fresh bear sign to go with your coffee."

The men all gathered to the tail end of the chuck wagon and each got a handful of Clancy's famous donuts. They mingled around under the tarp and ate the donuts and sipped their hot black coffee. The rain had drowned the usual night sounds and all that could be heard was the soft padded sound of the rain.

"You'al that are not on watch first thing had better get some shuteye. It'll be morning before you know it and we'll be moving out by sunup," said JB, "rain or shine." Turning to Clancy, he said, "Do you still have plenty for the other four to eat?"

"Sure do," Clancy said.

Not long after that, Buck and the others poked into camp, soaking wet and they all stripped off, dried off, laid their wet clothes over the deadfall, next to the fire, to dry, redressed in long-johns and sat down on their blankets and ate. After their supper, a couple of the men rolled in their blankets and was off to sleep. Buck and John Hanks sat up a while, eating bear sign and drinking coffee. After a while, John rolled in his blanket and Buck rolled a quirley and leaned back, watching the rain run off the edge of the tarp and smoked. Finally, he too rolled in.

The rain kept up its pouring as each man spread his ground sheet and rolled out his bed roll. There was just enough room for everybody to lay in under the tarp and stay pretty much out of the rain. Almost everyone used his saddle for a pillow and most had their hand gun lying next to his head. Some of the riders stripped to their long johns but most only removed their boots. It wasn't long until snores were heard and they were intermingled with the soft sounds of night rain. An occasional fart broke loose; a testimony to Clancy's good cooking. It was a close fit but everyone was able to fit in under the tarp well enough to stay dry, for the most part. The camp fire died down. There was still coffee in the pot that sat in the edge of the fire for the night riders as they went to relieve the others. Everyone who came in camp wanted a sip or two of the hot black brew before they turned in. It was amazing to Clancy how many cowboys took a tin of coffee to bed with them.

Dawn broke with a faint pale gray line across the horizon. The early morning was cold enough to have a light dusting of frost on the exposed countryside. The riders rolled out of their blankets with shivering and shaking. Clancy was starting to build up the fire, stirring the coals, creating puffs of red sparks that lifted into the air. The men got dressed, shook out their boots, in case a critter had taken up residency during the night, and pulled and stamped them on. Soon the campfire was roaring enough to put out the heat necessary to warm the men's hands and backsides as they stood and turned their butts to the flames. Breakfast would be ready soon. Clancy had to work between the men as they warmed themselves. They drifted to take care of their horses, get them saddled and then pack up their bedrolls and tie them on behind their saddles. Sometime in the early morning hours, the rain tapered off and finally stopped and the sky began to clear.

"You know," said Buck to nobody in particular, "It's amazing how many farts a body can hear in a cow camp during the night."

"You know there is a moral to that," said Bret Mosby. "My Pa used to say, 'A mule that farts will never tire and a man that farts is a man to hire.'"

"Shit, Bret, what in the world does that have to do with a cow camp and a bunch of farting cowpunchers?"

"I don't know," said Bret, "but that's what he used to say."

"What he probably meant," said Clancy, "was that a man that farts can put out a lot of hard work like a mule. Come and get it."

The men then all gathered around the chuck wagon tailgate and Clancy filled their plates with fried bacon, sourdough biscuits, grits and gravy. In their cups, he poured black scalding coffee. They all milled around or sat on the ground, where the tarp had been and ate their breakfasts.

"I could eat at least a dozen eggs if we had them," said Dusty.

"Trouble is," said Abe Rivers, "We ain't got none."

"I want every man to wear his side arm from now on. There is too much danger of being attacked; the closer to Indian Territory we get," JB said as he finished off his own breakfast. "I want all you drag riders to switch places with the outriders and the flankers. We'll hold that way a couple of days and then switch back. That'll give everyone a break from the same old job. You men on the horse remuda stay where you are and I'll be on point. Keep a sharp eye. Any rider you see, let it be known, shout it out to the other men. From here on in, we don't trust anybody. I don't care if he comes in dressed like a preacher, challenge him."

After Vicious Dog got the horse remuda started well, he ranged on out to look for water, leaving his helper to see to the horses. Clancy fell in behind the horses and when he had a far enough start, the herd was started.

"Head'em up, move'em out," shouted JB.

There were yelps and whistling and slapping of ropes on cow hides and the cattle moved out slowly at first and then began to kick up clods of mud. The drag riders all had their neckerchiefs pulled up over their noses, more to block the odor of fresh cow manure. They all rode straight in the saddle like most all western men did but they all had their necks pulled down in their wool lined coats that came down almost to their knees. The weather was turning colder after the rain went through. There were very few bunch quitters by that time and the jobs of drag and flanker were getting a little tiresome just from sitting in the saddle all day. The men almost wished more of the cattle would break and run. It would give them something more to do and help in their struggle to stay awake.

The trail south was easily found by the point rider for it had been trampled by so many herds moving north from Texas. They picked up a stray steer every now and then that had been lost from one of those northbound herds. JB was sure he would leave some of his cattle that strayed from the herd, cattle to be picked up by other herds or found by settlers or Indians. On balance, he expected to arrive home with pretty close to what he started with in KC.

"Round'em up, bed'em down," was the cry, and the men echoed that cry across the small valley in which the herd had been driven for the night. Everyone was dog tired from a long day in the saddle and was glad for the respite.

Clancy was busy over his pots and pans. He had two hanging from triangles of iron that allowed him to place the pots directly over the fire. He had built two cook fires and on two sides of one he had a couple of Dutch ovens and on two sides of the other, he had placed two large pots of coffee. Squeezed in between the coffee pots, he had a large four inch deep pan with two inches of fat simmering. One of the pots contained beans and the other had a mixture of dried vegetables and wild onions that he had found along the way, boiling in salted water. He started to lay tenderloin steaks that he had rolled in flour, into the deep fat. The scent of the food cooking was enough to drive the men wild.

"Dang, Clancy, that chow smells almost good enough to eat," wisecracked Charlie Estell.

"You bet your bottom dollar it's good," whipped Clancy, trying to sound irritated. He always swelled inside a little when anyone bragged on his cooking, for he knew Charlie was only using a little cowboy humor. "If you broken down old cowpokes'll be nice about it, I'll mix up a batch of bear sign and pop them into this here fat when I'm through with the steaks and as a special treat, I'll roll them in sugar, to boot."

The men lined around the fire and poured themselves scalding, black Arbuckle coffee. Taking their tin plates, they filed by the pan and Clancy dished up the steaks. He let them spoon out their own vegetables and beans. Charlie Estell sat down on the stump of a dead fall and was joined by Billy and Winston Yates. Billy, the youngest of the threesome, spoke in a low tone.

"Don't rile Clancy too much, Charlie or he might not make them bear sign."

"Ah, don't worry none about that, Billy. Ole Clancy knows I was just spoofing."

"Still just the same, I'd sure hate to miss them bear sign tonight," said Billy.

Charlie just laughed and dug into his plate of grub.

There was no moon that night and it was so dark you could hardly see your hand before your face. The cattle were restless and there were a lot of nervous bawls and grunts from them. The camp was quiet and the fire had died down to just embers that glowed orange red in the dark. The smoke from the fire rose and seemed to hit a point where it lifted no more but drifted to form a layer six or seven feet from the ground. A lone wolf howled in the distance and seemed to moan when his howl was not answered. The night air was filled with the sounds made by the critters of the dark. Crickets chirruped, frogs croaked and an untold number of other insects made their own individual sounds to harmonize into the sounds that were natural to the night.

When this night sound was interrupted, Vicious Dog was awake instantly listening to the silence. To him, it meant that someone or something was about that shouldn't be. He arose to investigate but as soon as he was on his feet, all hell broke loose. The first thing that happened was the thundering sound of hooves moving through the edge of the cattle herd. The cattle, already nervous, were on their feet and moving before any of the nighthawks knew what was happening.

"Stampede!" Vicious Dog cried.

The men were scrambling for their clothing and boots. The cattle were headed for the horse remuda and would take the horses with them if they couldn't be turned. The nighthawks were racing to do just that but it appeared they were a little too late. There was no way they could get ahead of the mass of beef that plunged eastward.

JB quickly saddled one of the horses that were hobbled near the camp and stepped into leather before everyone in camp except his Segundo. When he rode up to Buck, he shouted to make himself heard above the noise of the thundering cattle, the leading edge now a thousand yards away from where they started.

"What in hell happened?"

"I just found this," Buck said. He held up what was left of the carcass of a coyote. It hung on a rawhide strip by which it had been dragged through the edge of the herd. "This scared yesterdays grass out of them cows," he said.

"Well, there's not much we can do about it tonight," said JB. "Round up all the riders and let's get some rest. We'll head out at first light on however many horses we can find and start rounding those boneheaded critters up."

"Whoever pulled this stunt, took the horses with them and all we have are the ones the night hawks have and two others that were hobbled," said Buck.

"Well, we'll just have to do the best we can, with what we have," said JB. "We need to be away from camp by the time it gets light enough to move. Take the five mounts we have and start rounding up what cattle you can find and bring in any horses so the others can start looking, also."

Buck headed out to round up the riders as JB wheeled his horse to return to camp. He still had the coyote carcass Buck had given him when he arrived in camp. Handing it to Waco, he said, "Here Waco, take this and find a place for it where it won't scare any more stock."

Waco took the carcass and walked off into the night with it.

"Who do you think ran those cattle off," asked Thad Brooks. He more or less addressed his remark to Pablo Vega who was standing nearby.

"I think it was a band of Indians, myself."

"Indians?" questioned Thad.

"Yah, Indians," said Pablo. "They don't care much for beef but they'll eat it, comes to that. My guess is they were after the horses and Clancy's mules. They'll eat the mules, if they can catch them. I guess about the best meat in the world to some Indians is mule."

JB was listening to the talk while he thought on it. He spoke.

"I think Pablo is right. Dragging a coyote carcass to scare the cattle is something I've heard of them doing. Everybody get some shuteye, if you can. Whoever can find a horse in the morning will be heading out to round up the herd. Everybody riding keep an eye out for horses and bring back any you find so the rest of us can ride. If Indians did pull this off, they will be trying to round the horses up pronto. We'll have to be quick at it if we're to get them back. Now everyone turn in, Clancy, how about you keep some coffee on for anyone who can't sleep."

Not many were able to step passed the excitement, to catch the Sand Man.

CHAPTER 10

Pepper realized that they were way passed the heat of the summer and the water supply was getting scarcer as the days went by. Central and west Texas pretty much dried up in the summer months but fall and winter rains would usually remedy that. It wouldn't be long though before they reached the Nueces River. Once they crossed it the water would be spaced pretty well apart to allow them plenty for every camp, provided nothing went wrong. They were half way through their second week on the trail and Pepper had figured, at best, on making the trip in ten to twelve weeks, since they had to push the herd a total of some seven hundred and fifty miles from start to finish. He felt even a stronger need to scout ahead, not for water as much as for any sign of possible trouble from Indians or outlaws.

On their eleventh day, Cladderbuck was out some twelve to fourteen miles ahead of the herd. It was about ten o'clock in the morning when he rounded a butte protruding from the side of a mesa that stood naked in the middle of wide open country. The walls of the mesa were about seventy-five to one hundred feet above the arroyo in which he was riding. His first sight on the other side of the butte was a flock of buzzards that had landed and were closing in on the figure of a man stretched out on the floor of the arroyo. There was no sign of a horse or anyone else. Upon closer examination, he could see that the man had been mutilated and he was sure that it had been done by Indians. Casting around, he found the prints of three shod horses and the tracks of another seven that were unshod.

From the tracks of the shod horses, he was able to determine that two were ridden by very light people or one or both were pack animals. The tracks of the other shod horse, being without a rider, indicated that he was the one that had brought the dead man into the arroyo but had been led away with the other two without a rider. He dragged the body to the edge of the arroyo and pushed it back up under the overhang of grassy dirt. He climbed up on top and kicked at the edge, caving in the dirt, sufficiently to cover the body and prevent the buzzards from recycling the man into buzzard crap and spreading his remains all over the plains. His last kick proved to be a mistake. He was leaning in the wrong direction and he tumbled off the bank and rolled to the bottom of the arroyo. With no apparent serious injury, he mounted his horse, took off his hat and ran his fingers through his hair, returned the hat and picked up the reins.

Pepper decided to follow for a while and see just what the story was. If the Indians had pack horses then he was willing to let well enough alone but if they had a hostage, that would be a different story all together. From the freshness of the tracks, he figured that the Indians had left the arroyo within the hour, which meant they would have probably a four or five mile lead on him. He put his big black into a perky trot. He approached every rise or ridge with caution and stopped just short of seeing over where he would take off his hat and get just enough of his head over to see before he topped the rise and proceeded, only after knowing that the way was clear.

It was over one of these rises that, when he looked, he saw a faint wisp of dust settle over the next rise. He topped over and down to low ground and turned sharp left going parallel to the next rise. He rounded a curve and was confronted by a cluster of large boulders that had tumbled from the walls of the butte on his right. He figured the Indians had to be on the other side of the butte. He dismounted; ground hitched his horse, took his Winchester and climbed the rocky face of the butte. At near the top he could see through a thin crack that the Indians had dismounted in a, boxed in, space between the butte, and the rise over which they had crossed just minutes before. They were circling the small figure of a woman who looked to be in her early twenties. Her hands were tied with rawhide and her face was twisted with stark fear.

Cladderbuck mentally counted his shots. He had fourteen rounds in his Winchester and six more in his .44. His cover was excellent and he had the element of surprise on his side. He made a quick decision that he had thought he would never make and that was to attack as many as seven Comanche warriors single handed.

"Oh… shit," he whispered softly to himself.

He had spent many hours as a youth growing up when he had shot fast and accurate enough to knock down four quail out of a flushed covey before they could get out of range, with a handgun and that skill came to the forefront unconsciously as he opened fire on the seven warriors. He shot as fast as he could lever in the shells and the noise of the rifle shots boomerang off the surrounding rocks was like the noise of a Gatling gun shot from inside a cave. He had not even thought of the danger a stray or ricochet might be to the girl.

In just a matter of seconds it was all over with five Indians dead and one wounded. The seventh had gotten away on one of the saddled horses as the unshod horses broke and they and the pack horse scattered in all directions. The other shod horse with a saddle was ground-hitched and only sidestepped about ten yards away before stopping. The girl was cowering against a boulder with her hands, still tied together, on top of her head and tears of fright streaming down and streaking her dust-covered cheeks.

The wounded Indian was trying to recover his footing when Pepper reached the box. Throwing a quick foot to the legs of the Indian, Cladderbuck put him flat on his back where he stayed, realizing the position he was in.

Pepper went to the girl and placed a hand on her shoulder. She was shaking badly, like the last of the clinging leaves on an almost bare aspen in an early winter storm, as she looked into his dark eyes. Realization of what had happened brought her to her feet with her arms over Pepper's head as she sobbed into his chest. The Indian only laid still and stared at Pepper. Cladderbuck's .44 was pointed to a spot, dead center the Indian's forehead, just above eye level.

After reassuring the girl as he untied her hands, he retrieved her horse and when mounted, the two of them rode off in the direction which would take them back to the herd. Pepper figured the Indian that got away would soon return with others and they could take care of their wounded and dead. He just didn't want to be around when they got there. Water for the cow camp that night had not been found, which meant a dry camp.

When the herd had been bedded down for the night, supper finished, and the first nighthawks out, Pepper sat on the tongue of the chuck wagon, which was laid out pointing toward the North Star, making it easier to keep their right direction, come daylight and talked to Shirley Covington. Miss Covington had gone to live with her aunt and uncle when her father had passed away and her uncle was taking her to live with her brother, she hadn't seen in ten years. Her brother lived in El Paso and they were on their way there from Dallas when they were attacked by the band of Comanches.

Shirley Covington only recently became of age. She was a very attractive young woman and that fact was noted by everyone in camp. All of the young bucks felt a stirring in their loins just thinking about her, let alone looking at her. Pepper noticed that Jack Archer seemed to have a bit more interest than anyone else. Lightening Jack, as they called him, was a young, rugged but handsome man who was, at twenty-two, already a top cowhand. He had learned early how to use a gun, but not only how but when to use it and most important of all, when not to use it which made him, not only a top cowhand but a top gunman also.

The, dry camp, night passed without incident but with a lot of bawling from the cattle to show their irritation at not having a drink before bedtime. By sunup the herd was moving, with the big brindle steer out front. They had water the next night and the next day they brought the herd to the banks of the Nueces River. There, on the west bank, they bedded the cattle down after watering them. The sun was about half covered by the western horizon and the men gathered around camp, waiting for Curly to finish getting the grub ready.

"There's a small settlement by name of Rock Springs about ten miles northwest of here," said Pepper. "Jim, after supper, you and Jay ride in with me. I'd like to get the latest on Indian movements in these parts and we could use some more supplies I'm sure. Curly, make me out a list of what you need and throw a pack saddle on one of the horses."

"Pepper, you know much about the water between here and where we're going?" asked John Terry.

"Well," said Cladderbuck. "We should be able to avoid any more dry camps from here on. Going on what I remember about the last surveyor's map I saw, there's about a day's drive between each source of water till we hit the Red. We've got the Guadalupe, the Llano, Colorado, Concho, Wichita and then the Red. Once we hit the Red, we'll go west of Palo Duro Canyon and work our way up to the Canadian. That'll put us just a few miles from the ranch. That's where we'll be running our brand to start with."

Later that night, Pepper, Jim Heart and his son Jay rode into Rock Springs.

Rock Springs was just the beginning of a town. Most of the structures were log and adobe. There were a few dugouts, a few small tents and one large tent stretched atop seven foot log walls and divided into two sections. A regular door went into the general store side and a batwing door that went into the saloon and eating establishment side. Cladderbuck and the Hearts stopped in front of the large tent. They tied their horses to the hitch rail and when Pepper tied his horse with a slip knot in case of the necessity of a fast exit, the Hearts did likewise. Stepping upon the boardwalk, they hitched their gun belts to a more comfortable position on their hips. An old blue tick hound stood from sleep as the men crossed the porch and padded softly away.

Intending to get a meal before going into the store for supplies, they went through the batwing doors into the saloon and eating section of the tent. Pepper wanted to ask about the movements of Indians of late, also. They were eyed by everyone in the place as they went to one of the three long tables that filled the most part of the long narrow room. Seated on a bench made of a split log and fitted with legs, they each ordered their food after the bartender came over and told them what was on the menu.

"All we have is beef, beans, potatoes and sourdough bread," he said.

"Then that's what I'll have," they all said as one.

"And bring us a round of beer to wash it down with," said Jim Heart.

The saloon had an old tin panny sounding piano that sat in one corner and a couple of smaller tables for poker or whatever. There was a big buffalo head mounted on the wall above the center of the bar, which was three wide planks laid across the tops of three whiskey barrels sitting in a row. The floor was dirt with a layer of saw dust covering it. In the front corner opposite the bar was a potbelly stove that would put out the heat they would need in the winter months. One step up, went to a rough plank floor that covered the store side of the structure. On both sides of the step was a railing that separated the store from the saloon. The buffalo head had a woman's garter hanging on one of its horns.

After finishing their meal, Pepper and the Hearts went into the store and were in the middle of selecting what they needed when a fancy dressed young man with two tied down, pearl handle, guns left the saloon and in walking past Jay Heart, bumped into him and sent him sprawling across a stack of ax handles, creating a loud racket, clattering across the floor.

"Why don't you watch where you're going," the young gun said. "You walked right into me."

Jay picked himself up from the floor and with a cool soft voice he said, "You were the one walking."

"Are you calling me a liar?" the young gun slick asked with a tight half grin on his face.

It was evident that the youngster was looking for enough trouble to build his reputation. He was just plain itching to kill someone and he had picked Jay as his target.

"I got no quarrel with you mister," said Jay, which only made the slick more confident in his quest for a fight. To him, Jay's remark was a sign of weakness and he pushed even harder.

"I say you're a rotten, yellow bellied, coward," he said. With that he dropped his hand to the butt of his gun and there was no question, he was fast. In fact, he was a little too fast. He fired well ahead of Jay but his aim was hurried and his bullet went through the upper left shoulder of Jay and the latter, being a little slower was much more accurate with the placement of his .44 slug. It pushed the young gun's shirt button, which was located an inch above his belt buckle, into his guts. The slick stood on his tiptoes for a moment, his gun dangling loosely on his finger, looking at Jay with a knowing expression on his face that he was a dead man as his life's blood ran down his legs into his boots. He took one half step forward and the blood in his boot made a squishing sound. He then dropped to his knees and slowly fell forward on his face, crushing his nose. Almost immediately, his bowls moved and a puddle of blood and urine spread out from under him.

"Someone get the sheriff," said Cladderbuck.

"We ain't got no sheriff," said the storekeeper. "The sheriff was shot and killed just a week ago."

"Well then, who is this young fool, coming in here looking for trouble?" asked Cladderbuck?

"That there's the one what shot the sheriff. Don't know who he is. He just rode in here a week ago and right off picked a fight and when the sheriff stepped in-between to break it up, that kid pulled iron and shot him. Nobody in town was brave enough to call him when they had seen how fast he was."

"Well, he's had his last stomachache," said Pepper.

The smell rose from the body and intermingled with the acrid odor of gun smoke.

There were two other men in the store who had witnessed the whole thing, standing by the counter with their hands cupped over their mouths and noses. Cladderbuck turned to them and said, "Do you Gents agree that it was self defense?"

"Yes sir," said one, as the other nodded. "That kid on the floor got, just what he deserved, after killin our lawman the way he did."

"Then you Gents write down what happened and sign it as your statement, just in case there's ever a question comes up about it later," said Pepper.

One man went to the counter for pencil and paper and started to write out his statement. The other one turned to Cladderbuck and said, "I can't write or sign my name neither."

"Can you make your mark?"

"Yes sir, I can," he answered.

"Then you put this Gent's name on there with yours," he said to the other man. "When you finish and sign it, write this man's name on there and let him make his mark by his name."

Finished, the man handed the piece of paper to Cladderbuck, who turned and stuffed it in Jay's right shirt pocket.

"Hang onto this," he said. "Now we'd better get a Sawbones to look at that shoulder."

"We ain't got no sawbones, neither," said the storekeeper.

Cladderbuck helped Jay off with his shirt and took a look at the wound.

"The bullet went all the way through and it looks like the bleeding has stopped on the front where it went in. You still have some bleeding on the back. It left a handsome hole just outside your shoulder blade."

Taking a long piece of muslin cloth, from the store counter, Pepper folded it into two square pads. He soaked them with whiskey and tied them into place with more muslin. Each pad had been smeared with sulfur salve and Pepper got Jay a new shirt from the store stock and helped him put it on.

"If you can ride, Jay, we'll get on back to the herd. We can see to that wound just as well there as we can here. I don't think the bullet broke any bones and it was too high up to have hit any vitals."

With his arm in a sling, Jay joined his Pa and Pepper after they had loaded their supplies on the pack horse, and headed out of town.

It turned out to be a long ride for Jay. By the time they arrived, he was weak from loss of blood for his wound had broke open and was bleeding again. Resting in the floor of the chuck wagon, just behind the seat, Jay only winced and gritted his teeth when his Pa cauterized the wound on his back. There was no bleeding from the hole in the front and Jim didn't think it needed attention.

Shirley was quick to pitch in and help with the care of Jay and he seemed to be resting a little easier as the night drew on, but by morning, he was out of his head with fever.

"Get as much of this whiskey down him as you can," Cladderbuck said to Shirley. "We're going to stay here today and see if we can break his fever. We'll see how it goes after that."

The next morning broke with a beautiful clear sky. Jay was still out of his head and the fever had not broken. The day dragged on. The outfit milled around except those on watch with the cattle and horses. About the time they were all about halfway through supper, Jays' fever broke, his pores opened up and the sweat flooded out. He felt cooler to the touch. Before too long he was asking for water and something to eat, a wonderful sign to Shirley.

"I never was shot before," he said. "I didn't know it would give you such a gosh-awful headache."

"Weren't the shot that give you that headache," said Rob Taylor with a grin on his face. "You got the headache from the half bottle of whiskey Shirley poured down your gullet to chase the fever away."

"I don't know which would be worse," said Jay, "being dead from the headache or the gun shot."

Everybody laughed at the attempt of Jay at being funny.

"Being dead from the bullet would be worse," said Curly. "You can get over a hangover but just try shucking that coffin after you've been fitted for it."

"If you feel like riding in the wagon a ways, we'll get this outfit on the trail at first light in the morning," said Pepper.

"I think I can make it okay," said Jay. And dressed with fresh bandages after breakfast, he lay in the chuck wagon with Shirley to see after him as they took the trail.

CHAPTER 11

The dawn broke with rain clouds banked across the western sky. The threat of rain made things look a lot worse than the night before. Tracks would be washed out and make it a lot more trouble to round up all the cattle.

"We had better get as many as we can before that storm gets here. It will hit us before dark from the looks of it," said JB. "Everybody grab a bunch of that jerky. We may be in the saddle for a long time before it's over."

Clancy had a container of jerky on the tailgate of the chuck wagon and the men filed by and stuffed their saddlebags. Clancy spoke to all.

"I'll keep the coffee on and anyone who is around, I'll feed."

There were a total of nine horses so six of the riders had to stay in camp and wait for one of the other riders to bring them horses, when and if they caught any. The chances of them finding any of the horses were just as good as the Indians finding them. Every man was told to shoot any Indians on sight if they were after the horses, and every man had his sidearm as well as his Winchester.

Just before they all rode out, Vicious Dog came riding in at a full gallop. He pulled rein and threw his legs to one side and hit the ground, out of breath. He spoke.

"I see prints of sixteen unshod horses. They are behind herd."

JB spoke from the back of his horse.

"Men, let's not waste anymore time. Move out."

They all thundered in the direction of the long gone herd. There was heavy dew on the grass of the plains and their horses were wet to the belly. The tracks of the herd were easy to follow but the storm on the western horizon was definitely moving their way. Once it hit, the cattle and horses would be harder to find. The men had only ridden four or five miles when they started to see cows browsing. They were spread out and soon John Hanks came riding toward JB, with JB's Appaloosa in tow. JB swung out of the saddle and started to unsaddle the horse he was on. As soon as he had saddled the Appaloosa, he was on his way again after telling Hanks to take the other horse back to camp and get another rider mounted for the roundup.

By the time the storm hit, they had rounded up most of the horses and two of the riders had taken shots at some Indians. A head count showed that out of the forty six horses and four mules, they had recovered all but one mule and six horses. A count was taken on the herd just before the rain set in and they were still missing about seven hundred and fifty. It's lucky for them that there was no lightening or thunder in the storm, just rain, rain and more rain. Clancy had spread the tarp once more and at least they had a dry place to eat and sleep. The cattle were satisfied to mill and eat. The sky grew darker and it soon became pitch black. There was no opening in the cloud cover to let in any starlight or moonlight. The nighthawks were draped in their slickers and rode around the herd, water dripping from the wide brims of their Stetsons.

The rest of the outfit milled around under the tarp with tins of hot, black coffee and talked of the coming day. They still had a lot of cattle to find. JB knew it would take some time to accomplish that task but he couldn't take a loss that big, so he and his men would just have to search until the missing cattle were found. No matter how long it took; he guessed a week or more. But as luck would have it, by the end of the third day, a head count showed only one horse and twenty or so cattle still missing. JB decided to call a halt to the search and head, what cattle he had, home.

By dawn on the fourth day after the stampede, the cry was heard, "Head'em up, move'em out!" And the J-C Connected trail drive was underway once more.

JB rode ahead to talk to Vicious Dog before he moved out to look for water or trouble ahead. He spoke.

"Vicious Dog, the water is not as important as sign of any trouble ahead. If you spot sign of possible trouble, forget the water and head back here on the double...pronto. Savvy?"

"I see trouble, I ride back like wind," said Vicious Dog. He wheeled his horse and was off at a trot. JB sat for just a moment and watched him go. Then he heeled the Appaloosa and returned to his point position. '*Good man*,' he thought.

The next week or so was as routine as it gets on a cattle drive, and by the end of the week, they were well into Indian Territory. JB topped a rise and saw a group of riders coming his way. He estimated eight or ten in all. He pulled rein and waited for them. They rode up at a slow trot and pulled rein about ten feet away.

"What outfit is this?" the apparent leader asked.

"Who wants to know?" asked JB

"Don't get smart mouthed with me, puncher. I'll ask you just once more, what's the name of this outfit?"

JB saw no profit in making the situation worse so he, being outnumbered, answered. "This herd belongs to the J-C Connected Cattle Company. We're moving them to the ranch a little west of Amarillo."

The leader leaned on the horn of his saddle and grinned through tobacco stained teeth. He turned his head to one side and spat a stream of tobacco juice to the ground, keeping his eyes on JB. Turning back to face JB, he said, "Well, you ain't moving them cows passed here until we cut out our share."

"Your share?" questioned JB.

"Yah, we get our share, for you crossing our land and them cows eating our grass. I figure we take about five hundred head ought to square it."

JB knew better than to argue with them at that time so he said, "I'll have to go back and talk to the boss. He's a reasonable man."

"You do that, cowboy."

JB wheeled his Appaloosa around and rode back toward the herd. He had no intention of paying these outlaws. Approaching the herd, he waved his hat to signal the men to circle the herd. The outriders and flankers started to do just that. JB rode in hard, pulled rein as the men from the drag position came forward to meet him and the rest of the crew. As they pulled in tight and circled him to see what was up, he spoke.

"There's a group of outlaws wanting to cut five hundred head of my cows for the privilege of crossing what they claim is their land."

"What are we going to do, Boss?" asked Winston Yates. "Are we gonna let them have five hundred head?"

"Hell no, not on your life, we ain't going to pay one cow let alone five hundred. Every man leaves the cattle to mill and we all ride to give them our answer," said JB.

When confronted by the entire outfit, the hard cases were not quite as sure of their position. The leader asked, "What say you?"

"The boss says he ain't paying for crossing government land."

"Under the circumstances, we're pulling back but you ain't heard the last of it," said the leader of the outlaws. They all, as one, wheeled their horses and retreated.

As they rode away, Buck spoke.

"He said it. We haven't seen the last of those bastards."

About then, Vicious Dog came riding up. He spoke. "I find water one hour from here and more seven hours, at the speed the cattle are moving."

JB sat his horse and rubbed the stubble on his chin in thought. He needed a shave and so did a lot of the other cowboys.

"We'll be stopping at the first water. I know we still have a few hours till dark but stopping at the first water, it will give us all a chance to shave if you like and to do a little cleaning up. I know all of you have at least as much dust as I have tucked away in the creases of your hide and elsewhere, not to mention the stink. We want to look pretty for them outlaws, if and when they come calling, sound good to you'al?"

The men all agreed vocally as they wheeled their mounts and headed back to the herd. On the way back to the herd, JB stopped and informed Clancy of their plans and Clancy clucked the mules and headed on to set up camp. Vicious Dog went on forward to drive the horse remuda. By the time all was settled, they still had more than three hours before dark. The men took advantage of the respite and got their clothing washed and themselves bathed and shaved. There was banter among them as they went about their personal chores.

"Billy, what are you going to do with that razor?" asked Bert Mosby. "Surely you ain't gonna scrape it across your face."

"Ah, Bert, leave him alone. You know there ain't no cats around to lick that peach fuzz off," said Charlie Estell.

"Why don't you old broken down cowpunchers mind your own business," Billy snapped.

"Ah, don't pay'em no never-mind Billy," said Waco. "It ain't been no time since they had to call up the cat."

There was laughter all around and even Billy joined in.

JB left four riders to watch the cattle and two to keep an eye on the horses while everyone else settled down to the evening meal. While they all ate, JB took his Segundo aside for a talk.

"What do you think about our friends out there wanting five hundred head of my cattle?" he asked.

"Well, Boss, I think about the same thing as you, probably. We can't let that bunch get away with it. They have no right to take part of this herd. If we go to giving a few hundred head to every group of trash that comes by, we'll arrive at the ranch, cows in the hole."

"That's my thinking for sure," said JB.

"Then what are we going to do about them?" asked Buck.

"You're Segundo. What would you suggest?"

"I say go after them before they come after us," said Buck.

"I think you're right, Buck. When it gets dark, I want you to leave five men to watch the herd and horses. Then we'll take the rest of them and go hunt those owlhoots down and put a stop to their thievery. Go ahead and get you something to eat."

After supper, Buck rose and spoke to the men. "Winston, Charlie, Ben, Waco and Billy, you five stay with the herd and horses. The rest of you, wear your sidearms and carry your Winchesters. We're going after those outlaws and wipe them out before they come back and catch us off guard. Vicious Dog will be scouting ahead so we don't ride right upon their camp by accident. Vicious Dog, you go ahead and move out. As soon as you locate their camp, hightail it back and we'll all go in together." He took his hat off and lightly brushed it against his chaps. "Everyone, leave anything that jingles or makes a sound, here in camp, including your spurs."

As Vicious Dog disappeared into the darkness of the night, the rest of the men, except those staying in camp, removed their spurs, stepped into leather and rode off in the same direction, JB in the lead. Moon-rise was only an hour away and by the time the man in the moon looked upon the land, the J-C Connected outfit had traveled six or seven miles from camp. They kept to a slow pace, waiting for word from Vicious Dog. A couple of miles farther on, JB still in the lead, they heard the soft sound of hooves coming back from the way they were headed at a slow, careful pace. JB pulled rein and the rest of the men did likewise. They all sat their saddles, silhouetted against a moon lighted sky and waited for the rider to reach them.

Vicious Dog rode up at a slow trot. Pulling rein, his horse dropped his rear end slightly as he came to the sudden stop kicking up a small puff of dust that shown white in the moonlight.

"Did you find them," asked JB before Vicious Dog had a chance to say anything?

"I find camp," said Vicious Dog. "They are in shack at head of canyon, three, maybe four miles. They have put fence across head of canyon and have many cattle inside. There is small coral next to cabin with horses. I count sixteen horses."

"A damn nest of sidewinders," JB exclaimed.

JB motioned the men forward and they all rode to within a half mile of the cabin and there dismounted and proceeded on foot. Every man was carrying his Winchester. They were close to moon-set when they eased up and surrounded the cabin. There was a curl of white smoke, like a ghost from the past, shining silvery in the bright moonlight, rising from the chimney which was at the back of the cabin where it backed up against the side of a slope. JB studied the situation for a moment then motioned for Vicious Dog. Vicious Dog eased over beside him and JB whispered to him.

"See if you can get up the bank behind the cabin and onto the roof." He quickly removed his shirt and handed it to Vicious Dog. "Take this shirt and stuff it into the top of the chimney."

Vicious Dog studied what JB had said for just a moment and then he nodded acknowledgment, took the shirt and stole into the dark shadows toward the bank, staying out of the direct moonlight. A coyote yelped in the distance but the insects in the immediate area hushed with the movement of men but voiced their presence, again as men moved off or got still. Before long, Vicious Dog was in position and he reached over, one foot on the bank, the other on the edge of the roof, and stuffed the shirt into the chimney. It only took a few minutes and all hell broke loose. The door of the cabin burst open and the outlaws fought over each other to gain access to the fresh air of the out-of-doors, dragging their drawers.

All of them were bending over or hanging onto each other while they coughed in an effort to expel the smoke from their lungs. They had no more than congregated in front of the cabin than JB spoke to them in a stern tone.

"Ease those irons out and drop them to the ground."

His words echoed loudly in the stillness of the night, boxed in the small canyon. Before thinking about it, some of the owlhoots swung toward the sound of JB's voice pulling their weapons as they turned, those who had them. The thunder of gunpowder exploded and the flashes of fire from the barrels of many weapons lit the faces of desperate men, the walls of the canyon and the smoke-filled cabin. The cattle in behind the fenced in area were up and moving around, restlessly. There was a splattering of blood as the JB Johnson outfit returned their fire.

The sound of men groaning and the yelps of men surprised by the pain of hot lead ripping through their bodies could be heard as the echoes of the gunfire bounced off the canyon walls. The shots of the outlaws were high, whining off into the night for all of JB's men had positioned themselves prone on the ground.

When the smoke cleared after the sudden end of gunfire, there were only two of the outlaws left alive and they were limping up the road to Boot Hill. JB directed his question to his men.

"Is anyone hit; sing out if you're okay."

Everyone responded with a negative answer to his question and remarkably, nobody in his outfit was hit. When the last of the outlaws put his foot to the bucket, JB spoke.

"Drag them all back into the cabin and set fire to it. We don't have time to dig holes for this scum. The coyotes can have their next meal, Bar-B-Q'd. Gather up all their weapons, ammunition and anything else we can use before you torch it. There's no use in letting anything go to waste or letting it fall into the hands of other outlaws or Indians. Look through their pockets."

A search of their pockets and saddlebags turned up seven hundred and twenty dollars in gold coin.

"Probably money they stole from others or received from the sale of cattle they had cut from herds previously," said JB. Later he would split the money between the men of the outfit. The guns and ammunition were placed in the chuck wagon upon returning to camp. The outlaws' horses were herded back with their saddles placed on their backs, no sense in letting good tack go to waste and besides, without a rider, the horses could carry the tack without strain. The cattle were unfenced and driven back to camp and put in with the herd.

In camp, "What happened?" questioned Billy in his youthful excitement.

"It was like this Billy. We walked right up to those owlhoots and when we spoke to them, well, they just up and died of fright," said Thad Brooks. "Ain't that right, John?"

"That's right," said John Hanks. "Just up and killed over right in front of us, dropped their guns, pissed their pants and dropped dead."

"Aah. Come on you two. Didn't no such thing happen," said Billy. "Come on now, what really happened?"

The men were all gathered around the camp fire that night and the story of their encounter with the outlaws was related, finally, to Billy's satisfaction except that he was a little hot under the collar because he wasn't with them.

"You guys have all the fun," he remarked. "While I had to stay here and play nursemaid to them blamed cows."

"Now, Billy, you know that's what you was hired for," said Wilford Teague with a friendly sounding chuckle. He grinned when he said it and Billy about half grinned and said, "Aah, shucks."

CHAPTER 12

Fairly well assured of having water for all of their future camps, Pepper still rode ahead to scout for other kinds of trouble. Tawkawa's report of the outlaws going after more guns posed a threat of future encounters with them as well as the threat of meeting up with bands of hostile Indians. Cladderbuck loved the western part of the country. One day, not too far in the future, he knew that law and order would prevail in that land and the day of the gun would pass and the gunfighter would become extinct. He, himself, would be out dated, that is, if he lived long enough to see that time arrive. He was every bit a gunfighter except that he did not live by the gun. His reputation lay with the fact that he was the Saw Tooth Kid but nobody knew him to be so the reputation lived on its own.

Jay's shoulder had healed enough that he was back in the saddle. Shirley Covington had blended in with the group and Curly had taken it upon himself to be her protector from all comers and that included one Jack Archer who tried at every turn to spend time with her.

Another week passed without too much of anything out of the way when all hell broke loose. In the early morning hours, the camp was awakened by the thunder of hoof beats racing back down the trail they had just come over the day before.

When everybody gathered after the herd had disappeared into the black of night, it was evident what had happened. The carcass of a steer lay where the edge of the herd had been and the smell of fresh blood had put the cattle into a full-fledged stampede. There were hoof prints of Indian ponies close to the steer and a lance had been left sticking in its side.

"Not much we can do till daylight," said Cladderbuck. "We'll go after the cows at sunup. Everyone get as much sleep as you can by then. We'll need it before we get those critters rounded up."

The next morning everyone except Curly and Shirley were out looking for the herd and by mid morning, they had rounded up about half of the cattle. By sundown they had all but about a hundred head back and Pepper called off the hunt until the next day. After supper Pepper decided to check out the creek bank before it got too dark. Riding downstream, he was shocked by his luck. On the opposite side of the creek was a lone cow but the tracks showed a large group had crossed at that point. As he crossed the water, the cow turned into a thicket of brush and following, Pepper broke out into a clearing in the middle of the thicket where he found eight cows grazing on the long grass there.

Crossing the clearing, he began to haze the cattle back toward the herd when he spotted the tracks of a number of unshod horses following a large number of cattle that had gone out the other side of the thicket. He knew that the Indians who had stampeded the herd had cut out the remaining steers he was still missing. He returned to camp with the few head he had and called a meeting of the outfit.

"I saw where the rest of our herd went," he said. "The Indians have headed north with them. They crossed the creek a ways south of here, went a short distance and then turned back north. I can't afford to lose that many head so we're going after them."

"When do we get started?" asked John Terry.

"We can get started right now," said Pepper. "I want Curly and

Shirley to keep the camp and Shotgun, Noble and Jack to stay with them and keep an eye on the herd. Keep the horses bunched close to the herd and Curly; you keep plenty of coffee on. When we teach those redskins a lesson, we'll be back. Okay, mount up," he shouted. And they rode out at a gallop. Pepper motioned for Tawkawa to ride ahead and scout. He wanted to try to take the Indians by surprise but he wanted it to be a surprise to the Indians and not to him.

After they left camp, Jack went to the fire for a cup of coffee before he headed for the herd. Shirley filled a tin and handed it to him. The coffee was strong and black and Jack sipped it slowly wanting to linger close to Shirley as long as he could get away with it.

"How can Tawkawa, being an Indian, ride in pursuit of other Indians with white men," asked Shirley? "It seems like he would feel guilty in doing so."

Oh, that's easy," said Jack. "You see, Tawkawa is an Apache and those skins that they're chasin are Comanches. Now...the Apaches hate the Comanches about as much as the people of Ireland hate the English. Don't ask me why, they just do."

He finished his coffee and handed the tin to her.

"Well, Miss Shirley, I guess I'd better be getting on out to them cows," he said with a stiff voice like he was in charge of the world, to impress the woman and turning to go, he tripped over the tongue of the chuck wagon and landed face down in the dust. Shirley and Curly, both, broke out in almost uncontrollable laughter. Jack's ears turning red and he puffed up like a bullfrog, full of gas from a bate of campfire beans. He stamped to his horse and climbed into the leather and was gone, Curly's and Shirley's laughter ringing in his ears, especially, Shirley's.

****

Pepper and the rest of the outfit came to a halt when Tawkawa came out of a stand of trees close to the creek bank. They had been following the trail of the cattle which had gone parallel to the creek for some six or seven miles.

"The cattle are just over on the other side of that mesa in a coral of brambles. The Indians number fourteen and they have set up camp just on the outside of the entrance to the coral. There is one guard on top of the mesa. I will take care of the guard. Then we can get very close before the rest of them know what is happening."

Tawkawa fell silent and turned and looked in the direction of the mesa, then said, "I go now to send the guard to visit his ancestors."

"As soon as the guard is out of the way," Pepper said, "we will stampede the cattle from the back side of the brambles. Let's remove just enough tangles to get one horse through at a time. When we're all through and in position, we'll pop a few .44 pills into the air and send those critters through the entrance on a rush, right over their camp. I'm sure the Indians' horses will fall right in with the cattle and should put those redskins afoot. I've never seen a damn Indian yet, to put hobbles on his damn horse."

When Tawkawa had eliminated the guard, he gave a double whippoorwill call. Pepper and the outfit eased in behind the bramble barricade and removed just enough sticks and boughs to make room for them to enter with their horses, one at a time until all were inside. With the cattle being used to the drovers, by sight and smell, they showed little concern at them being there and when they were all in position, they, as one, climbed into the leather and with a whoop, they fired their .44s and the cattle bolted for the entrance and the Indian camp.

Smashing through the camp with churning hooves, the cattle raced on as what was left of the Indians scrambled for cover. Most of the thirteen in the camp were caught under the deadly hooves but two or three escaped with their lives. The horses had, as Pepper had predicted, fell in with the cattle and not only had they recovered the last of the missing cattle but had come off with fourteen fine Indian mounts to boot and Pepper knew Tawkawa would have no trouble getting them broke to the saddle and ready for use by the outfit.

Everyone was in high spirits the next morning when they hit the trail. A quick head count put the number of cattle at thirty six hundred and ninety seven. They had gained a hundred and ninety seven head in almost seven weeks on the trail, including what they had come away from the outlaw camp with. The next day they would reach the Pecos

River. Little did any of them know that Jake Moran and his band of outlaws were already at the Pecos, waiting for them.

****

The day they reached the Pecos river, it was misty. The morning had dawned with a brilliant red sky and Pepper thought of that old sailor's rhyme, 'Red sky at night, sailor's delight; Red sky in the morning, sailor take warning.' He had seen the build-up of dark clouds in the western sky and the day gradually turned gray and dismal.

"We'll be soaked to the bone by this time tomorrow if we don't find shelter by then." He said. "We had better start looking for a place to get out of the storm. We need a halfway decent shelter for the cattle, also. There'll be less chance of lightning and thunder sending them to hell and gone again if we can bunch them with a little bit of cover."

Cladderbuck rode on ahead to the banks of the river and turned northwest along its course. Within five miles he came on the tracks where a group of shod horses had crossed.

Looking the area over, he spotted a piece of cloth hanging on the end of a broken limb on a bush at the edge of the water. He eased his horse down to retrieve the cloth and leaned out of the saddle to get it when he heard the whine of a bullet cut through the air where his head had just been. Leaning over to get the piece of cloth is all that saved his bacon. He heard the bark of the rifle, just a fraction of a second later. Being in a leaning position at the time gave him a head start in his effort to get off his horse and roll into the brush. His black trotted off a few yards and stopped. His Winchester was in the saddle boot and out of reach. From the time between the bullet and the sound of the rifle, he was able to determine that the shooter was well out of range of his .44 hand gun.

The outfit had bunched the cattle and spread the tarp and set up a camp. Curly was just getting the fire started under the trees along the river bank when they all heard the shot. Bill Terry and Jim Heart were first to ride in that direction to see what had happened. When they appeared, Pepper waved a hand for them to lay low and come in carefully, which they did. Both had their Winchesters and they popped

135

a couple of shots in the direction Pepper had indicated in hopes of getting return fire so they could pinpoint the location of the ambusher. All was quiet. No more shots came so they all backed away from the brush along the river bank. It was almost dark, so they mounted and rode back to camp.

****

"You fool," growled Jake Moran. "Now we've lost the element of surprise by you taking a shot at Cladderbuck. What in the world were you thinking of? No, don't answer that. That's just it. You weren't thinking. In fact, I don't believe you have anything to think with." His anger was evident and it was directed at the hard case that had taken it upon himself to fire the shot.

****

Cladderbuck sat sulking to himself with a cup of hot, black coffee. He seemed to be in deep thought. He was getting tired of having to be on the lookout for Indians and outlaws and trying to find water all at the same time. He should have finished Moran and his bunch when he had the chance. He was almost sure that was who he was confronted with now. He was brooding also, because he didn't like being used for target practice.

He motioned for Tawkawa to join him. They stood on the edge of the fire circle of light and talked for a few minutes. Then Tawkawa left camp and faded into the night.

Pepper went to the fire, refilled his cup with coffee and called for everyone to gather around him. When they were all in close enough to hear he began. "I've sent Tawkawa to scout the camp of whomever it was that took a shot at me today. That is if he has a camp and Tawkawa can find it."

"What're you planning to do?" asked Jim Heart.

"I think it's high time we rid ourselves of the threat of whoever it is. I think it's Moran and his gang. We've given them their last chance to leave us alone. I was a little slow before, going against unarmed men, maybe a little too slow. So, what we're going to do is wipe'em out, once and for all."

"Hey, that's the way to talk," said Jack Archer. "I always said; do them afore they can do you, I think that's in the bible somewhere."

"That's not quite what the Good Book says," said Shotgun. "It says 'Do unto others as you would have them do unto you."

"Well, it all means the same," Jack said in defense of his statement.

Shotgun just closed his eyes and shook his head.

"Well, ain't it?" asked Jack.

About two hours after moonset, Tawkawa returned with the news that it was indeed Jake Moran and his gang. That settled it.

"We're going after them tonight and I want to hit them about sunup." Pepper said with the sound of determination in his voice. A night owl hooted and then hooted again as the camp went silent.

About four o'clock in the morning they were ready to go. "Noble, you, Shotgun and Bill stay here and keep the herd as tight and as quiet as possible and keep the horses in close. We'll be back just as soon as we get this job finished."

"Aah, foot-fire," said Bill. "I'm gonna miss all the fun again."

Everyone else rode out of camp following Tawkawa. Pepper had an outfit of serious fighting men. They cut up a lot and had their share of fun but they were men who rode for the brand, Texans all. They each knew that this could be their night to die, but they had a job to do and they would do whatever needed to be done. The sounds of the night, the insects and the wind were interrupted by the sounds made by the riders; the creak of saddle leather and, from time to time, an occasional click of an iron horse shoe on a stone. The man sounds were sandwiched in with the night sounds; a slight contrast.

When they were about half a mile from the outlaw camp, they dismounted and taking their Winchesters, proceeded on foot. Even though they were downwind of the outlaw camp, Pepper wanted to take no chances on being heard or smelled by the outlaw's horses. They, themselves, could smell a faint odor of wood smoke. Pepper decided to leave Jay Heart to watch the horses. There was too much danger of losing them if they were spotted by Indians and there was, also, the ever present danger from wolves or cougars.

There was just a faint hint of light in the eastern sky when they reached the camp and circled it. The only guard was leaning against a tree close to where the horses were picketed. His cigarette was lighting up and dying back, like a lightning bug, trying to attract a mate, on a warm summer night. With his last puff on the cigarette, he tossed it to the ground and rubbed it out with the toe of his boot. That was the last thing he ever did. Tawkawa put his knife to the guard's throat and left him to drown in his own blood.

Just about the time a couple of the outlaws began to move around, one sitting on a log, watching the other stoke the fire and put coffee into the boiling water, Pepper and his outfit cut loose with their Winchesters. Some of the outlaws started returning fire. They were firing at the muzzle flashes of their attackers. The firing lasted for only a couple of minutes and then all was quiet. The air hung heavy with the acrid smell of gun smoke, strong enough to make the eyes of the men burn and a low hanging misty fog, intermingled with the smoke, added to the cold eerie look of the camp site. There was not one of the outlaws left alive.

"Anybody hit?" Pepper questioned.

"Yeah," was the return. "John took one through the stomach. He's hit pretty hard."

"Rob is hit in the shoulder but it's not too bad," said Jim Heart.

They all gathered around the camp fire and John Terry was brought to the fire and put on one of the outlaw's empty blankets. He had a half smile on his lips. Pepper offered him a cup of coffee from the pot the outlaw had just fixed a few minutes before.

"Boss, I tried not to let the outfit down," said John.

"Hey, Old Son," said Cladderbuck. "You're one to ride the river with. We'll get you back to camp and fix you up. Shoot. You'll be back in the saddle in a few days. We'll lay you in the chuck wagon and Shirley can look after you and there won't be no holding you back."

Pepper knew what he was saying was not true except the part about John being one to ride the river with but by the time he was finished saying it, John Terry was gone. They returned to camp bedraggled and tired. After Shirley patched up Rob Taylor's shoulder, they all lingered over breakfast with a heavy feeling of loss hanging over the camp. John was liked by everyone and he would be missed.

After a while, Pepper got to his feet and said, "We'll go ahead and bury John under that big sycamore yonder and then we need to get those cows on the trail."

They laid John to rest and Curly read from an old bible that he had just about worn out. The sun was shooting bolts of golden light through the sycamore when Curly turned the chuck wagon up the trail and the old brindle steer led out. The herd was getting trail wise and fell right into their daily march without much pushing. Jim Heart took the point and Tawkawa was out in front of the chuck wagon with the horses. Cladderbuck rode on ahead to scout the trail. The sun was well on its way to high noon before Pepper reached the next likely camp site where they would spend the night. He rode along the near bank of the Pecos on the way upstream a ways, crossed the river and rode back downstream, looking for any sign, whether it be trouble or not. There was no sign of anybody being in the area, at least not since the last rain. The river was about two feet deep in the middle where he crossed to check the bank on the other side. On his way back across, he stopped once more to let his horse drink and then headed back to the herd.

CHAPTER 13

As Clancy stirred around the cook fire with his preparations for breakfast, the morning came with a glorious golden orange in the eastern sky. The cowboys were all at their duties. He had sliced a large quantity of bacon into a large frying pan and had two Dutch ovens in the fire with sourdough biscuits almost ready to come out. There were the usual large pots of coffee hanging over the fire boiling. He soon removed the coffee from the fire and set them in the edge of the coals to let the grounds settle a might before filling everyone's tin cup.

When breakfast was over, the camp was deserted before long except for Clancy who was putting the final utensils away for the journey to the next camp site. The cattle were on the move and there was a cloud of dust for Clancy to drive through in order to go ahead of the herd. The horses were way out in front of the cattle and Clancy, as usual, was to fall in-between the two herds. '*Sometimes, I feel sorry for those drag riders,*' he mused to himself. '*But on the other hand, I've et my share of trail dust over the years, so why should I want to deprive them of theirs?*'

Vicious Dog had gone on ahead as usual, looking for water and any sign of trouble. JB was at point; Buck and Jocke were the outriders. The morning drug on and about eleven o'clock, Buck came trotting across the path of the herd, headed for JB's point position. He slowed his mount to a walk and fell in beside JB. He spoke.

"I just now came up with a trail of fresh sign headed in the same direction we're going. Looks like a pretty good size band of Indians, unshod horses."

"How long?" asked JB.

"Two, maybe three hours," said Buck.

About then, Jocke came trotting from their left. He pulled rein and fell in with the other two riders and looking out between the ears of his horse he said in a casual tone, "We got us a flanker out beyond were we can see from here. Whoever it is, he's riding alone, seems he is sometimes ahead of us and then he drops behind for a while. He's riding a shod horse that throws his left front hoof out about an inch or so."

"Have you seen him at all?"

"Nah, I came on his tracks a couple of hours back. I waited to make sure before I came over to let you know."

JB thought for a moment. Then he said, "Swing back out and pick up his sign. It's sure worth checking him out. He could be scouting the herd for a larger gang of rustlers. Buck has picked up Indian sign on our right flank. Let's look alive on this. Buck, you ease back and keep an eye pealed for that bunch of redskins, but don't take any chances. I'll ease back and let everyone know what's happening."

As Buck and Jocke each headed for their outrider positions, JB swung his Appaloosa around and headed back to alert the outfit to the possible dangers.

"We may run into Indian trouble ahead," He shouted to each rider as he made his way back along the east side of the herd. Cutting across behind the cattle, he filled the drag riders in. Then back up the west side of the herd and across the path of the cattle, up to the chuck wagon.

Clancy pulled rein on his team of mules. He set the brake and looked JB in the eyes. He spoke.

"What's up Boss?"

"Clancy, there could be some trouble ahead. Buck has spotted Indian sign on our right flank. Keep a sharp eye out."

"Don't you worry about me, I've got ole Betsy right here between my legs, and she's loaded for bear," roared Clancy.

JB heeled his horse on forward to let the horse wranglers know what was in the air. While he was talking to Waco, Vicious Dog came in at a trot. It was about noon.

"I find water but it's too far to reach today. We have dry camp tonight," said Vicious Dog.

"Did you see any sign of trouble?" JB asked.

"I saw no sign of trouble."

JB sat his horse in silence for just a moment. He rubbed his whiskered chin. Then he spoke.

"Buck came across sign of an Indian band on our right flank. Good size band, according to Buck, ranging out two or three hours ahead of the herd."

"What do you reckon they're up to?" asked Waco.

"Can't tell," said JB. "Whatever it is, I want every man ready. I've already alerted everybody else."

He wheeled his horse and rode back to the drag position, thinking that if they were attacked, it would be from behind. They pushed the cattle on for another four hours or so with no sign of attack. No one even saw an Indian. They had no idea what the lone rider off to their left, earlier, was doing.

"Round'em up, bed'em down." was the cry. There was only two hours or so until nightfall and since they would be in a dry camp, JB wanted to make sure all precautions were taken in case a nighttime attack came. Until that time, he had given all of his thoughts to the Indians. He had all but forgotten about the lone rider Atchley had found sign of. In camp, he stated that he still hadn't caught sight of the rider.

The drovers had rounded the cattle into a milling position and they began to bawl their disapproval of their treatment. They wanted water but there was none to be had. So, with much noise and stamping around, they finally settled down and began to quietly graze on the bunch grass that had become plentiful as they neared the Texas border.

The men all gathered around the camp fire to hear what JB had to say. Clancy was almost ready with supper and four of the men had been left with the horses and cattle. JB spoke.

"Men, as I told you, we have a good size Indian band dogging the herd. It's important that we sleep with one eye open, as it were, until they make their move. Every man sleep with your boots on tonight, leave your horse saddled and tied close to your bedroll. There will be only two watches tonight. I want the unsaddled horses brought in close to the camp fire and seven men on watch at a time. The first watch will take it to midnight and the second take it from midnight to first light. If we have no trouble by then, we'll have a short breakfast, and then we move out."

"Come and get it," said Clancy. "Or I'll throw it out to the coyotes." It tickled him to see the men so hungry. They all lined up and filed by to get their plates filled. Clancy had made cornbread and had a pot of beans. He had seasoned the beans with bacon drippings and wild onions he pulled along the way that day. He also fried up a batch of Antelope steaks. The cowboys were all hungry after their day's work and they dug in like a bunch of half starved lobos. Clancy just chuckled.

"Don't get too full on them beans," said Clancy. "Save some room for bear sign."

Everyone had a tin cup of scalding black coffee to wash it all down with, and there were more than a few grins at the mention of bear sign.

"We should be crossing into Texas by late tomorrow," Said JB to Buck as they leaned against the chuck wagon after supper. JB filled his pipe, tamped it down and struck a match on the iron rim of a wagon wheel and held it to the bowl of his pipe. He drew on it, removed it from his mouth then blew smoke out through his nose.

"Then maybe we can relax our watch a little tomorrow night," said Buck, "seein as how we will be out of Indian Territory."

"Maybe," said JB, "we'll see. We still don't know what those Indians, that have been dogging us, have in mind."

"Well, it's for sure they won't be following us too far into Texas," said Buck. "They're smarter than that."

"I hope you're right, Buck."

The crew was on edge while going about their duties throughout the next day and on up into the dusk that settled on them with a beautiful Texas sunset. There was a distinct sign of relaxation on the part of everyone when they began kicking up Texas dust. JB changed the watch from seven man watches to three men, with three time periods, dusk to ten, ten to two and two to dawn.

It was about mid-way through the two to dawn watch that Bert Rawlings and his men attacked the camp. Jack Potts had lined up a bunch of ner-do-wells; a crew of dangerous men. He had six men to take care of the nighthawks while he and the rest saw to the camp site. It was a disaster for the JB Johnson outfit. While the men slept, chunks of hot lead tore into the bedrolls. Two of the nighthawks, Charlie Estell and Ben Campbell were both knocked from their saddles while the third nighthawk, Pablo Vega, was shot through the right thigh. He was lucky for the bullet went clear through without hitting a bone. It angled up under Pablo and lodged in the leather of his saddle. Charlie and Ben fell in the path of the stampeding cattle and there wasn't enough left of them to bury.

Winston Yates, Bret Mosby and Thad Brooks were killed in the hail of rifle fire that riddled the camp site. They were all three shot to doll rags. John Hanks was shot in the right shoulder and it looked like maybe his collar bone had been cracked or broken. Waco had a crease along his left rib cage but not deep. The rest of the outfit seemed to be in good shape. JB quickly made the rounds of the camp, checking on everyone. Buck was with him.

"Clancy," shouted JB.

"Yah Boss," came the answer.

"You okay?"

"Yah, Boss," said Clancy. "I didn't get a scratch. I was under the wagon.

"Good, get some water on to boil and pull out a batch of that white muslin we brought. We have a bunch of wounds that need tending."

As soon as it was light enough to see well, the total effects of the night raid on the camp became a belated nightmare for the survivors. Five of the outfit were dead. Two more had serious wounds and a third with a slight crease on his side. The herd was gone and JB seemed to be at a loss as to what to do right then, but, he was actually in deep thought as to what he was going to do. He felt an anger rising from deep down that he hadn't felt in a very long time, an anger that rose to possess him. He had fought at times before to control it and for the most part, he had been able to. Now that dark anger threatened to consume him completely. Those were his men that had been killed without forethought on the part of the raiders. They must be made to pay for their actions.

"Buck, call all the men in. Have them gather around the fire. I have something I want to say."

Buck called the men together. They came to the fire, some half dressed, some with a tin cup full of coffee, and some leading their horses. They all milled around JB.

"Men, I don't have to tell you what's happened here. You were all in the middle of it. You know as well as I that a blood thirsty bunch of bastards have rustled my cattle and left five of our number dead and three others wounded." He got quiet and still for a long moment. Then he slowly gazed into the eyes of the outfit, one man at a time and tightened his lips against his teeth. He swore bitterly.

"We're going after those sons-of-unwed-mothers and make them pay a steep price for what they've done. Are you with me?" He bit off his words as if they had a bitter taste.

"We're with you," said Buck. There was a round of agreement voiced by the entire outfit.

"Okay, then," said JB, "as soon as we get our men buried, everybody get your horse and each man take an extra horse on a lead rope. We'll have a chance to rest the horses as we go without too long of a stop each time we transfer the saddles. Clancy, you stay with the chuck wagon and see to all our gear. But first, fix each man a pair of saddlebags of jerky and hardtack. Cram them full and fill a couple of extras with coffee and sugar. I'll tie a coffee pot on the back of my saddle with my bedroll. The rest of you men all get your bedrolls tucked and get ready to move out. They already have a head start on us. Everyone stick as much ammunition as you can in your pockets and saddlebags. Push the jerky aside."

****

A few miles southwest of the Johnson camp, the rustlers had the cattle on a hard run and they continued to push them even harder. They intended to put as many miles as they could between themselves and any pursuit. Rawlings was leading them and he had decided to drive the cattle right through the J-C Connected ranch and pick up what cattle Johnson had on the place, including the White Face stock JB had intended to cross with the shorthorns. To that end, Rawlings had left two of his men at Hollicott Crossing to round up all the stock on the J-C Connected ranch and have them ready when he came through with the rest of the herd. He had already planned his route across the panhandle of Texas, through New Mexico Territory, across the southeastern corner of Arizona into Mexico. He figured he and his men could handle any pursuit because he figured they had killed most of Johnson's outfit.

****

"Boss, we are not that good on ammunition," said Buck. "We're going to be out-gunned and out-manned if we don't find some help along the way."

"I know, Buck," said JB. "We'll just have to play the cards as we're dealt them. Are the men ready?"

"Yes, they are."

"Then let's move out."

Clancy stood by the chuck wagon and watched them all ride out of camp, wondering if he would ever see them all again. He had his job and that was to get the chuck wagon back to the home ranch with the remaining, wounded crew and gear. JB set a mile eating pace that the horses could handle and they kicked up a cloud of dust that could be seen for miles. The blood veins stood out on the faces of the men revealing their determination as they rode into the wind. The sun beamed down on the countryside, lending a brassy look to the scene. A jackrabbit scurried away, creating his own dust cloud, as the horses raced by. Here and there, the small animals of the plains were removing themselves from the path of these hell bent for justice men.

Onward they rode, following the path left by over sixteen thousand hooves. At the close of the day, with no moon to guide them, JB called a halt to their pursuit until first light the next day. They gathered twigs and dried flower stalks of Yucca plants and dried cow chips to build a fire to warm them from the chill of the night and to make coffee. With nothing else to do they sat around the camp fire, most within their own thoughts, some talking in low tones and sipping their scalding coffee. They chewed on jerky and hardtack as they sipped their Arbuckle. The mood among the entire outfit was the same. They were bent on finding and punishing those responsible for the death of their fellow ranch hands.

"Everyone try to get as much rest as you can tonight. We'll have a long day tomorrow. I plan on leaving at first light."

****

While the Johnson outfit rested, Rawlings was awake in the saddle. He and his men kept pushing the tired and restive cattle on through the night. He was taking his direction from the stars and not being able to see the bunch quitters, he was sure that some of the cattle would be lost and he was willing to take the chance that a rider's horse might step in a prairie dog hole, break a leg and possibly throw and kill the rider. Since the cattle hadn't cost him anything, he wasn't worried about losing a few head and since he planned to double cross the men in the end, he really didn't give a damn if any of them did break his neck. He and his men could rest when they had crossed the Mexican border.

Finally, after two days and two nights of driving, Rawlings' crew of hard cases reached the J-C Connected ranch. The cattle that were on the ranch were rounded up and ready to mix with the shorthorns for their drive on to Mexico.

CHAPTER 14

As JB and his men continued their pursuit, it became more and more apparent that the trail was leading them directly to their home ranch.

"What do you make of it," JB?" asked Buck.

"It looks to me like they are headed straight to the ranch," said JB.

"I'd say you're right, Boss," said Buck. "But I sure can't make any sense out of it."

"Well, let's keep on their tail. We're bound to catch up to them soon. They can't move that many cattle that quickly and keep it up forever."

When they arrived at the ranch, the cattle were long gone. Rawlings was moving them as fast as he could. He wasn't worried about the weight the cattle were losing or how many were falling by the wayside. He was concerned, only, with getting away with the cattle and more importantly, his hide.

JB rode up to the ranch house and dismounted in the front yard. He called to Jeb Andrews who was left to watch the ranch until their return.

Not getting an answer, JB went on into the ranch house. There he found Jeb, shot to doll rags under the front window seal, where he had tried to hold off Rawlings' two gunmen.

JB went back into the yard and spoke.

"Jeb is dead. They shot him to pieces. We'll rest here long enough to bury him."

"Boss, it looks like they took what cattle you had here on the ranch also, I believe they got all of the whitefaces."

"Damn," said JB. "There seems to be no end to what they will do. I'm thinking that it was someone from around here who has it in for me. Otherwise, why would they come to the ranch and get the rest of my cattle?"

"The trail is headed toward Amarillo," said Atchley.

"Surely they wouldn't try to sell cattle wearing the J-C Connected brand in Amarillo," said Buck.

"I don't think so," said JB. "They must be headed to some point beyond Amarillo. They're probably making for New Mexico territory, or even beyond."

"It has to be New Mexico territory," said Buck. "There's no market beyond there until you get to the west coast. Surely they're not trying to take them cows to California."

"You forget about Mexico," said Atchley. "If they're headed for Mexico, and they make it across the border, we may never see them cattle again."

"We're going to stop in Amarillo and stock up on food and ammunition. That is probably what the rustlers have in mind. Then we're going after those bastards and we're going to catch them even if we have to follow them all the way to South America." JB spat his words through clinched teeth.

Arriving in Amarillo, JB told his men to hit the mercantile store and load up on jerked beef, hardtack and ammunition.

"Tell them that I said to put it on my account," he said. Then he went looking for Joseph Collins. He stopped by the boarding house and was told that Collins was in his room. He went to the head of the stairs where he was told Collins' room was and knocked on the door. It was answered by Collins who had a moment of surprise on his face.

"JB," he exclaimed. "Come in."

JB entered the room and Collins closed the door behind him. JB spoke.

"Joe, I just got into town a few minutes ago. I'm after a bunch of rustlers."

And then he told Collins the whole story in a short time and then he asked about Hope.

"Hope's doing fine," said Collins. "Now, what are you planning to do about the rustlers?"

"My men are at the Mercantile right now stocking up on ammunition and food. We're heading out right away. I came by to ask you a favor."

"I'll do whatever I can," said Collins. "What's the favor?"

"I'm short of men," said JB. "Do you know a few good men that might be willing to ride with me? I'm paying fighting wages plus a bonus when my cattle are recovered."

"I think I can round up maybe ten men in, say, an hour's time. That's nine plus me," said Collins.

"I can't ask you to go along," said JB.

"I'm not waiting for an invite. I'm counting myself in," said Collins.

"Okay, get those men, Joe. I'm going down to the Mercantile. Bring them down there and I'll make sure they're outfitted properly."

Within forty five minutes, Joe Collins was at the Mercantile with the nine men he had promised. JB spoke to them.

"Men, I guess Joe told you I'm paying fighting wages. I want every man to have at least one hand iron and a rifle. If you don't, get them here along with a couple hundred rounds of ammunition, each. It'd be best if you have weapons that take the same ammunition. Stay with the caliber I've selected."

Turning to Joe, he said, "You ready to go?"

"I just have to go by and tell Hope where I'm going. Come along and say you're howdy." He turned and left the Mercantile, JB on his heels.

The sun beat down on the town but the weather was cool for it was well passed the fall of the year. The odor of dried, powdered horse manure mixed with Texas dust was noticeable in the air. The two of them walked side by side down the boardwalk toward the little shop that Hope ran. An old blue tick hound, lying on the edge of the boardwalk, turned his head and watched the men as they passed. He popped his big, long tail once on the foot-worn planks of the walk and then laid his nose back down between his two front paws and returned his attention to the street. The two men walked on to the door of the millinery shop, opened the door and went in.

Hope Collins was busy with a customer but she looked up and smiled an acknowledgment to her father and JB. Soon, she was finished with her customer and she walked from behind the counter to greet the two.

"Hello Dad," she said, "and a good day to you Mr. Johnson."

"Please, just call me JB."

"And to what do I owe for this nice visit?" she asked, pleasantly.

"JB has had his cattle stolen and Jeb Andrews plus five of JB's drovers have all been killed."

"Oh, no," she gasped. "When did it happen?"

"Three days ago," said JB. "At least that's when they jumped our camp, killed five of my men and ran off with the herd. They drove the cattle to the ranch and took the rest of my stock and killed Jeb in the process. They came close to here, probably for supplies, and then headed southwest."

"I'm going with them to track the rustlers and murderers down," said Collins.

"No," exclaimed Hope. "This is not your fight, Dad." She then turned to JB and with a spark of anger in her eyes; she said in a cool voice, "This is not his fight."

"Now, listen honey," said Collins, "the country they're headed for was out of my jurisdiction but I had many occasions to go into that country and I know it pretty well. I can be a help to JB and his men."

Hope was puffed up and she looked again at JB. "You have no right to let my father ride into danger on a chase that is none of his business."

"That's enough Hope," Collins said in a scolding voice. "Upholding the law is everybody's business. Where would we be if nobody sought justice where there was injustice?"

She stood there for just a moment more. Then tears welled up in her eyes and she turned and ran into the back room and closed the door. Collins and JB just looked at each other.

"Women," Collins said in frustration. "Come on JB, we're losing time. She'll be okay as soon as she gives it a little thought. She's a reasonable person and she will realize that I'm right."

The two of them left the store and headed to the livery for Collins to get his horse.

"Get a second horse, Joe. We're all taking an extra horse for change up."

Joe stopped at the office of the livery and told the hostler that he would need an extra mount. He then went to the stall where his horse was and led him out into the runway. He saddled him and mounting, he went to the front door where the hostler had his extra horse on a lead rope. While he was doing this, JB had walked back to the Mercantile to replenish his own ammunition and food. Soon, Collins appeared and did the same. He had a repeating rifle and a .44 that took the same size ammunition as the rifle. The rifle was in the saddle boot and he had the .44 resting on his thigh, tied down.

The rest of JB's men gathered around and JB gave the order to move out. They rode up the street, passed the saloon and the millinery shop. Hope was standing in the doorway with a handkerchief to her eye. She blinked back the tears and stood watching them disappear in a cloud of dust to the southwest of town. The old blue tick hound got up from the boardwalk, stretched, licked his tongue out and down in a wide yawn, scratched himself and walked across the street. The wind whipped around the corner of the building and into the street, kicking up a small dust devil. Hope stood staring into the distance as the dust devil danced down the street and the gust of wind that held it, turned loose. The swirl of dust lifted slightly as if taking one last shallow breath and then dropped to the ground in a soft, flat puff.

The men rode out across the plains, seventeen strong, Texans all, headed on the trail of the stolen herd, west by southwest, toward the New Mexico Territory.

"There won't be a moon tonight," yelled Buck to JB as they rode in a fast trot.

"Yah, I know," said JB. "We will have to slow our pace after dark. There's too much danger in riding off into an arroyo that could kill a man, his horse or both."

"Why don't we call a halt after dark and all get some rest," said Collins. "Then get an early start in the morning. It's going to be too dark to follow their trail and we don't need to go off in the wrong direction."

"You're right, Joe," said JB. "We'll make camp just at dark and be in the saddle as soon as it's light enough to see sign. Buck, pass the word. We'll make camp at dark. Be sure everyone knows to be in the saddle at first light."

"Consider it done," said Buck.

They rode on for a couple more hours into the purple of dusk. There was a bank of dark clouds on the western horizon as they pulled down for the night. Some of the men gathered what wood and dried cow chips they could and built a fire. Soon, there was hot coffee and the men settled down for the night. They sat around the fire and drank their scalding coffee and ate jerked beef and hardtack. The night was cool and each man was glad he had blankets. JB lay awake, long into the night, looking into the heavens at the stars there. Joe Collins lay close by, he too, looking at the stars.

"You know, JB, I read in the Bible one time that God, not only made all the stars, but He has them all named and can call them by their names," said Joe.

"Aah, go on now, Joe, there ain't that many names in the world.

"You're right, JB, there ain't, but there are that many and more in the heavens."

"Hummph," JB grunted. His thoughts turned to the cattle and catching and punishing the rustlers. Along about midnight, his thoughts shifted to Hope Collins, as he drowsed off to sleep. He, in his mind, could see her standing in the doorway of her shop, as she was when they rode out of town. He thought to himself how beautiful she was, and his thoughts gradually transcended into dreams and he slept.

Day began with a thin sliver of light filtered through the mist of early morning. The clouds in the western sky had dissipated into a vapor appearance, without substance or threat. Everyone arose, dressed and was ready to move out. They had gotten up earlier and had their hot coffee with a breakfast of jerky and hardtack and they all realized that what they had to look forward to until this job was done would be more of the same.

"Move out," JB shouted. "Vicious Dog, range on ahead and find the direction the trail is taking."

With a commitment of purpose, the outfit moved out to pick up their pursuit.

****

Meanwhile, Rawlings and his gang had the cattle on the move and were pushing them as hard as they could. He had no way of knowing but he was ahead of JB's men by two full days. The cattle were bawling their complaints at being treated like they were. No rest, no water, and very little graze.

"We're going to have to find water soon or we're going to start losing a bunch of cows." Potts shouted to Rawlings. "They need a drink, now."

"I know," said Rawlings. "We'll be on water in another hour. Don't you think I checked out the route ahead of time?"

"That's good," said Potts. He swung out to head off a bunch quitter, cutting him off and hazed him back into the herd. As Rawlings had promised, they were watering the herd an hour or so later. Watered, the herd settled down some and they were driven another two hours after dark before Rawlings called a halt to the drive for the rest of the night. The next night, there was a new moon. Just a sliver of silver in the star filled sky. A lone wolf voiced his acknowledgement of the sliver and off across the expanse of time, his call was answered.

****

The day after that, JB and his men started seeing dead cows along the trail. The fact that they had come to water wasn't enough. The cattle needed graze and they were being moved so fast that they had little time to even nibble at the grass, what little there was, along the trail. Some of them were starving to death. By the time JB's outfit came on some of them they were already starting to swell putrid.

"Whoever is leading that bunch of owlhoots must be crazy. He'll have them push those cattle till he kills them all," said Buck. He leaned against a large rock and rolled himself a quirly. They were taking a short rest at noon. JB just nodded, a shoot of bunchgrass hanging in the corner of his mouth. It had gotten so bad that they could almost follow the trail by the buzzards in the sky.

"Mount up, men," said JB.

They rode out three abreast. JB was in the lead with Buck Parker on his right and Joe Collins on his left. By the middle of the morning the next day, they could see the dust that was being kicked up by the herd. Vicious Dog was ranging out ahead of the rest and shortly after JB and his men had stopped to make camp for the night, he came in to report.

"The herd is bedded down three hours ride from here," he said.

"Did you get a chance to find out how many men are with the herd?" asked Jocke.

"I counted thirteen," said Vicious Dog. "There could be more. I not think they know we follow."

"That's good. We may be able to surprise them and that would be to our advantage," said JB. "We will have a half moon tonight and moonset will be around three in the morning. We'll strike right after moonset. Vicious Dog, you will lead us to within half a mile of their camp. We'll go in from there on foot. We need to be on the downwind side of their camp. I don't want their horses picking up on us before we're ready to strike. All you men relax a while. We'll be moving out a little while before moonset."

All of the men milled around the camp fire. It had been located in the bottom of an arroyo to prevent the rustlers from seeing light from their fire. There was hot coffee and JB allowed a little whiskey to be mixed with it to knock the edge off the cold night air that negotiated their coat collars and whispered passed their ears. There would be no sleeping to speak of because the men were all keyed up for the fight before them. JB and Joe Collins sat with their backs against the bank of the arroyo chewing on jerky and sipping black coffee. JB spoke.

"I was just wondering if Hope is mad at me for letting you come along on this chase."

"She may be a little upset with you but she'll take it all out on me. She thinks, just because I've retired from the Rangers, that I can't take care of myself anymore."

"I'll tell you, Joe," said JB. "I'm more than just a little taken with that daughter of yours. I'd like to come calling on her after this mess is all over. That is, if it's okay with you."

"JB, there's nobody in the world I'd like better for a son-in-law. You know you're more than welcome."

They got quiet for a while and sat and drank their coffee. There were the yelps of a coyote pack off in the distance. The late purple of dusk gradually faded into the darkness of night and everyone was on edge in anticipation of the early morning attack. The sky was soon filled with stars and around nine o'clock, the moon was directly overhead. It cast enough light that every object on the plains threw its shadow against the sandy soil. The ground, with its alkali content, looked almost white in the moonlight. The hours drug on and before long it was time to mount up and ride. Someone kicked sand on the fire and with their gear all tied behind their saddles, they moved out, Vicious Dog in the lead.

CHAPTER 15

The longhorns were a sturdy breed of cow and Pepper's outfit kept them prodding on as the sun elevated the temperature to a comfortable level on the plains. The drag riders had eaten and breathed, what they felt was, at least a ton of dust, each. There were very few bunch quitters at this stage of the drive and the drovers' hardest job was to stay awake in the saddle. It seemed as though the farther they went, the more time dragged and the longer the days became.

They were a day from crossing from Texas into New Mexico Territory, where they would travel north, along a small river that ran out of northwest Texas. Up that river is where the J-C Connected ranch lay, just a few miles inside the state of Texas. The thunderstorm of all thunderstorms came rolling out of the western sky.

"Boy howdy, they're really catching it over yonder, west of here." Hal Jeffreys spoke up after supper was all but over. "Reckon we'll get any of it here?"

"Can't ever tell," said Curly. "Sometimes them clouds will build up like that, stay put, and rain on the same spot for days. Then again, they'll sweep across the countryside so fast that it'll no more than start to rain when it quits. It'd be my guess that we're in for a lot of lightning, thunder and strong winds, might even get a little hail out of that one. I just hope we don't get no twisters."

Hal had ridden over close to the chuck wagon to see if Curly might have an ole loose biscuit or donut lying around. Curly accused Hal of having a straight gut. He just couldn't seem to fill Hal up. All he had on hand was a little bit of hardtack that he handed to Hal, along with one long strip of jerky.

"Thanks a lot, old timer," said Hal, with a mouth full.

"I swear, that kid must have one hollow leg that hangs down in the Jake," Curly mumbled to himself. Shirley just chuckled, softly, to herself.

As the day drew on, the sky kept getting worse and worse. By the time they made camp, it was almost as dark as night but time wise; they still had an hour before sundown. Cladderbuck decided not to continue but instead, take the time to secure against the storm. He also noticed the cattle were already getting nervous.

They pulled the chuck wagon alongside two large sycamores and stretched a canvas tarp between the wagon and the trees, this would give them a place out of the rain to cook and eat. If there was anything a puncher hated, it was to have his grub floating in water. Curly was sure, if the wind didn't get too strong, they would be able to maintain a fire throughout the night.

"Some of you snake in some fire wood," said Curly. "That is if you want supper tonight and breakfast in the morning."

He had no more than said it and Bill, Rob and Jay were mounted and riding out in search of wood, shaking out loops with their lassos. By the time the storm broke and sent sheets of rain sweeping the countryside, supper was ready and everyone had a dry spot to eat, under the tarp. Pepper had put his saddle on the ground, under the edge of the chuck wagon and he sat next to it and leaned on it while he had coffee after supper. The rain continued most of the night but they were lucky that the threat of lightning and thunder did not materialize. It started to taper off about the middle of the early morning hours. The sky began to clear and a few stars peeked past the clouds like a bashful child and were joined by more and more of their friends. From the stars, Pepper was finally able to determine that it was about three in the morning. It wasn't long after that when the Indians launched their attack.

The attack began and ended with an arrow in the chest of Shotgun who was night hawking with the horses. Before anyone knew Shotgun was in trouble, the horses had all been driven away and the only ones left with horses were the other nighthawks who were working the cattle. The whole outfit was alerted when they heard the pounding of hooves as the horses thundered out across the desert floor with the band of Indians driving them on.

After calling the nighthawks in, Pepper spoke to the group. "They were not concerned with the cattle like we were. If we'd had three men on the horses and one on the cattle, we would have been better off. By the way, who was watching the horses?"

"Shotgun was with them," said Jim Heart. "He relieved me at midnight."

"Where is he?" asked Pepper. "Has anybody seen him?"

Nobody had, so a couple of the men went to see about him and finding him down with an arrow in his chest, they gave a shout which prompted the outfit to run to the shout. Curly and Shirley waited at the camp fire until the men returned, carrying Shotgun. They placed him on a blanket next to the fire where it was dry. There was no sign of froth on his lips and that was a good indication that the arrow had not hit a lung. Turning him sideways, Curly noticed a small knot on Shotgun's back. He felt of it.

"That arrow head is pushing the skin out here on his back. It's well clear of his spine. I think we can push it on through without too much trouble."

"I know you're not a drinking man, Shotgun, but this whiskey is all we have for pain," Pepper said as he lifted Shotgun up so he could drink.

"That's okay," said Shotgun. "I'd as soon have the pain in my chest as in my head from a hangover. Save the whiskey for some other purpose.

Just go ahead with it. It can't hurt any worse coming out than it did going in."

He eased over on his side more and Pepper broke the shaft from the arrow and taking his .44, he emptied the cylinder. He held the barrel and using the butt like a hammer, he drove the arrow on through with three licks. Shotgun groaned with each blow of the gun butt and sighed with relief at the knowledge that the arrow was finally removed.

Shirley took over to clean and dress the wound and Pepper went to the front of the chuck wagon and sat down on the tongue. He had no more than sat down when Curly handed him a tin cup of scalding black coffee. It tasted good.

By that afternoon, Shotgun was feeling better and it looked as if he was going to skip right passed having a fever. In the meantime, Pepper, Tawkawa and Hal had taken the three remaining horses at daybreak and started tracking the Indians. It was not hard to follow the trail of so many horses. The Indians had made off with twenty-seven of their animals and there were the tracks of ten or more Indian ponies as well.

It was evident that the Indians had only been interested in the horses. They had not wanted scalps or cattle, just horses. Pepper realized that without those horses, the drive would end there until the animals could be replaced. They had to have horses to continue. The day drew to a close with Pepper, Tawkawa and Hal still well behind the Indians, but closing the gap.

They were passing through some of the most beautiful country Pepper and the others had ever seen. There were buttes standing tall against a bright blue sky, like gothic cathedrals of old, with cacti, scattered as far as the eye could see, with their prickly arms reaching toward the heavens. Cliff walls of multicolored sandstone jutted up out of the desert floor to form jagged edged ridges. Arroyos cut through the desert like the tracks of giant snakes. Still they followed the horses until it was too dark to see the trail. They made camp after finding a deep arroyo where they could build a small fire that couldn't be seen from far off. They prepared and ate their supper and had a pot of coffee to share.

They lay awake until late, talking in low tones because sound carries so far in the desert at night and they didn't want to be heard by their quarry. Most battles were won by the side that surprises the other and they didn't want to lose the element of surprise. Finally, they all turned into their blankets and slept.

It was still pitch black when Pepper was awakened by a hand on his shoulder. He did not move as he cracked the lids of his eyes to a very thin slit to see who had touched him. His hand was on the .44 under his blanket. Through the slits in his eyes, he saw Tawkawa leaning close with his finger across his lips to indicate that they should be quiet.

"They come." He whispered so that only Pepper could hear.

Pepper eased out of his blankets, .44 in hand. He touched Hal who followed suit. Tawkawa pointed to Hal and then to his left. Then he pointed to himself and then to the right. Then he pointed to Pepper and then in a third direction. They went into the darkness. Each moved like a ghost. Once in the black of night, they positioned themselves so they could see the camp area. They waited.

The first Indian into the circle of light received Tawkawa's knife, hilt deep, in the middle of his chest. The other three that had come for the scalps of Pepper, Tawkawa and Hal, were caught cold in a cross fire. One got off an arrow that went wild. Then he was standing on his tiptoes, having been straightened up by a slug from Hal's Winchester. He lingered for half a heartbeat and then fell like a giant oak tree, to his face. Pepper and Tawkawa accounted for the other two.

Following the back trail of the Indians, at daybreak, led them to four Indian ponies which after shod, would make good mounts for the outfit. At least they'd have seven men on horseback. But Pepper did not intend to let anybody be without a mount and to work a herd the size he had, they needed all the horses they could find, at least two per man and better still, three. So, continuing, he, Tawkawa and Hal went after the rest of their horses once the four they had were picketed on a patch of grass in a small flat that shot off the arroyo in which they had found them.

They rode with great care not to skyline themselves. On the air of the next morning, they smelled wood smoke. Only a faint wisp of it but it was there none the less. They stepped down from leather in a small arroyo and proceeded on foot, leading their cayuses. Pepper and Hal removed their spurs and proceeded forward as quietly as possible.

The air was cool and crisp in the predawn light. There was a layer of smoke mixed with fog that blanketed the Indian camp. The smell of roasted meat permeated the surrounding area. There were eight tepees, three community fires that had died down to smoldering ash with orange, red coals peeking through smoke cracks and a few pole stands for stretching hides and drying meat. It was good that they were downwind of the camp for there were three or four dogs, that they could see, wandering around camp. There was a coral of poles and brush on the far side of the camp from where Pepper and the others crouched. It contained not only their missing horses, but what looked like forty or fifty others.

"There couldn't be that many braves in that camp. They've been busy stealing horses from Lord knows who," said Pepper in a whisper. "There's no telling how long it took them to accumulate that many."

"What're we gonna do?" asked Hal

"We're going to take every horse they have," said Cladderbuck.

"How are we gonna do that?"

"We're going to get around behind those horses, slip the gate poles out of the way and stampede them right through their damn camp before they all get out of bed. We're gonna throw a handful of justice into their dreams."

The sun was not quite up though it had been light for some time when they went for their horses. They circled around on foot, leading their mounts to keep a low profile until within forty or fifty yards of the back of the corral. While Pepper and Hal stayed with the horses, Tawkawa worked his way around the corral and slid the gate poles back. He made no effort to excite the animals in the corral. He eased back to his horse and as they all three stepped into the leather and eased around the corral. Tawkawa entered the corral and made his way to the rear where he pulled his .44 and fired.

As the horses left the corral gate, Pepper and Hal fell in behind them and all three rode hell bent for leather behind the herd of horses right smack dab across the Indian camp. The charging animals caught the camp still half asleep and tore it from one end to the other. Indians screamed and scattered in every direction. By the time they recovered enough to fire at Cladderbuck, Tawkawa and Hal, the three of them were out of range. The Indian braves were left afoot and Cladderbuck meant to see to it that they stayed that way.

Pepper and Hal flanked the horse herd while Tawkawa rode drag and they headed for the camp of the night before, picked up the four Indian ponies and pushed the whole bunch back to the herd. When they rode into camp, everyone raised their hats and shouted a good ole Texas congratulation welcome. Shotgun was up and around as if he had never been hit. The whole outfit had really come together during the past few weeks on the trail.

"We're going to double up on the night watches," said Cladderbuck. "Shotgun, Noble, Jim, Jay and Bill take the first watch. We'll relieve you at midnight. Hal, you, Jack, Rob and Tawkawa will join me on the midnight to dawn watch. We all need to keep in mind that the tighter we keep them bunched, the better off we'll be."

The next week went by without any trouble beyond a few bunch quitters that tried to travel down the back trail. When cows get thirsty, they have a natural instinct to return to the last water they had. The weather held and they pushed the herd into the valley and closed in on the ranch.

"Take them on past the Canadian and hold up on the graze on the other side. Move them on out about five or so miles," Pepper said to Jim Heart who was at point.

Heart just nodded and touched his finger to the brim of his Stetson. Pepper rode on to inform Curly and Tawkawa so they could settle the horses on graze and get the camp set up. Shirley rode the wagon with Curly and he was as proud as punch to have an attractive woman by his side, even though he felt more like a father than anything else. He was determined that Lightening Jack Archer was going to treat her with respect, which Jack intended to do all along.

After the cattle had been watered in the Canadian and driven to graze about five miles beyond, Pepper split the outfit, half to stay with the herd so the others could go into town for some owl hooting and just blowing off steam. He figured it would take about an hour for them to get the trail dust off. Most of the outfit was really fond of cutting up and having fun. They split and went in every way to Sunday when they hit town. Amarillo was too far away so they had to settle for a turn in Vega, a small weather-beaten town. There was only one saloon and eatery.

Pepper headed for the barber shop for a shave and a bath. He had saved a change of clothes that he had stashed in the chuck wagon. It was good to get cleaned up and some fresh cloths on. The way it turned out, he had to shave himself while sitting in a large wooden tub in the back yard of the barber shop.

Eight days later, Pepper and his drovers pushed the cattle onto J-C Connected range.

CHAPTER 16

They were on the downwind side of the camp and even at a distance of half a mile, they could smell wood smoke. The fragrance of coffee drifted across the night and teased the noses of the men. JB and the whole outfit fell in behind Vicious Dog, on foot, to approach the camp, hopefully without notice. A night owl made his presence known with a soft hoot and then the popping of its giant wings as they beat against the cool night air. All around them were the songs of the night creatures, the profusion of insect sounds, joining with the fiddling of crickets and chirruping of many different kinds of frogs. A whippoorwill offered up a solo to complete nature's performance. The darkness was filled with those usual noises and every man in the outfit was aware of them, seeming to be louder than normal because of the tension in the air.

They heard the swoosh sound of the night owl in his decent on a small creature of the plains. Then the squeal of that creature as the owl's talons closed around it. Off to their right, at some distance, was the cry of a wolf, calling to another of his kind. And a moment later, the answer. The men crept through the growth of the plains slowly so as not to break even one twig. They knew that sound carried loud and long distances at night on the plains. At the slow pace they were taking, it took them about half an hour to make the half mile. When they were within a couple hundred yards of the camp, JB touched the arm of Vicious Dog and whispered to him.

"Vicious Dog, you and Buck take two others and circle around the camp to where the horses are. Ease in among the horses and make sure they are not hobbled or tied. When they are ready to run, start them in a stampede toward the camp. You should be able to get the cattle going in the same direction at the same time. We'll wait until they have destroyed the camp before we close in."

Vicious Dog and Buck selected Bert Young and one of the new men Joe Collins had rounded up. They eased off into the dark of night to circle the camp. There was only one nighthawk on the horses. Vicious Dog held up his hand and putting one hand to his lips to signal for silence, he used the other hand to motion the other three to lay low. He then took his knife and placing it between his teeth, crawled off into the dark. In a few minutes, he returned. He whispered to the others.

"The nighthawk with the horses is no more."

The four of them then formed a semicircle behind the horses and when all were in place, they pulled their .44 pistols and started firing into the air. The horses bolted in stark fear toward the camp and in doing so, they charged into the herd of cattle. The cattle had already started in the same direction and they and the horses formed a sea of animal flesh moving in one gigantic wave over the camp site. There was the bawling of cattle and the screams of horses and men as total destruction ripped through the Rawlings camp.

Rawlings, remembering how he and his men had devastated the Johnson camp, had laid his blankets out from the main camp along with Potts. They each had his horse hobbled close to him and when the stampede started, the two of them, realizing what was going on, saddled their horses and climbing aboard, rode for their lives.

"What about the cattle?" yelled Potts?

"To hell with the cattle," Rawlings spat out through clinched teeth.

They rode into the dark of the early morning, headed toward Amarillo. As they rode away, JB and a couple of his outfit walked their horses into the camp area behind the thundering herd of cattle and horses. The camp had been flattened and there wasn't a man left alive that was asleep in the camp area. Of the four nighthawks on the cattle, two were shot and killed and the other two rode for their lives. Not a single one of the Johnson outfit got a scratch.

"Men, let's get back to our horses. As soon as it's light enough, we're going after those cows. The way they've been pushed, I don't think they will run too far," said JB. "I just wish we had found out which one of these bastards was behind this whole thing."

It wouldn't be long before daylight, and being all keyed up, the men knew it was no use to try to get any sleep so they built a fire where the owlhoots coals were still smoldering. Then they made and had coffee to pass the time until dawn. As soon as it was light enough, they were all in the saddle and riding out to round up the herd. JB's prediction had come true. The cattle had not gone too far before they started to mill and graze and from the looks of it, they had not spread too awfully much. Even so, it took them all day and still they did not have them all.

"Maybe the ones missing will drift back to that last watering place," said Atchley, a few minutes after he had ridden in from the round-up. "A cow may be the dumbest creature on this earth but they do remember where they last fed and drank."

"You could be right," said Buck. "We'll find out soon. If they are going to do that, they will do it when it gets close to dusk. Let's push what cows we have back to that stream where they must have watered last."

JB was on his horse, following the herd when Vicious Dog rode up.

"I fond horse tracks of two riders leaving the area of the outlaw camp. They were on top of the tracks of the herd when it came to this spot. The tracks were going back toward Amarillo."

Sure enough, when the riders approached the stream with the rest of the herd, they began to see cows. By the time darkness set in, it was too late to take a head count so the cowboys circled the entire herd and bedded them down for the night. At dawn, everyone was up and around, chewing on jerky and drinking hot, black coffee. Soon, they were assigned the task of counting the cattle. Three men took individual counts and they averaged the three and it came within one hundred and ten of what there should have been.

"Men, I guess it was to be expected. Such a loss can be accounted for owing to the fact that we saw a lot of cows dead along the trail. It's almost impossible to find those that are still alive in this country since there are so many arroyos where they can hide. We'll call an end to the search. Let's head these cows home, slowly. I want them to put on as much weight as they can between here and there." They had about a hundred and fifty miles to go to get home. JB figured the cattle would put on a lot of weight if he didn't push them more than ten miles a day so they headed northeast through the New Mexico Territory.

"What's the closest town from here where we can get supplies," JB?" asked Joe Collins.

"The closest I know of is Santa Rosa. It's just a few miles northeast of here."

"Would you mind taking a couple of the extra horses and see if you can find a couple of pack saddles in Santa Rosa and load them down with supplies to get us home?" asked JB.

"No, I don't mind in the least," said Joe.

"Take Bert Young with you. The two of you can handle it okay." JB turned and called Bert Young over to them. "Bert, I want you to go with Joe here. You two are going into Santa Rosa for supplies. And don't get drunk and wind up in a fight or in jail."

"Now, Boss, you know me. I don't even like the stuff," said Bert.

"I know," JB said with a chuckle. "That's why I picked you to go with Joe."

They had only gone about five miles since first light and it was almost noon when Joe Collins and Bert Young rode out for Santa Rosa. Before they left, JB had made sure they knew where the herd would be by sundown. For when they returned it would be after dark. The rest of the crew was too busy popping bovine hides with coiled ropes to notice the two ride off.

The cattle were taking their time browsing as they went and the cowboys were not having to work near as hard as on a normal cattle drive. There wasn't a problem with bunch quitters. JB had taken the point and since there was no chuck wagon to worry about, or horses in any great number, Vicious Dog was scouting ahead for water. He was, out of habit, looking for any sign of trouble. They were a little too far west for Cheyenne Indian trouble, there was always, this far west, the possibility of Apache hunting or even war parties. It seemed that the Apaches were at war with someone over one thing or the other, year around.

It was an hour or so after dark when Joe Collins and Bert Young rode back into camp. They had the two pack horses on lead ropes and handing the ropes to two of the other men; they dismounted and walked to the fire to warm themselves.

"You have any trouble?" asked JB, as they walked up.

"Not a bit," said Collins. We saw the sheriff and told him about the trouble we had been having with the rustlers."

"What did he say?"

"Said we did the right thing and as far as he was concerned, the matter was shut and closed," said Bert. "He said that the coyotes and buzzards would save us all a lot of trouble."

"That's good," said JB. "Now all we have to do is get these cattle home."

The men all sat around the fire, except the nighthawks, and laughed and talked and sipped hot, black, Arbuckle coffee and chewed on beef jerky. Soon the day's work took its toll and the men rolled in their blankets to get some well deserved rest. Off in the distance the sound of a whippoorwill could be heard and the men were sung to sleep by the chirruping of the night insects and the soft murmur of the wind. A pot of coffee was kept on the fire for the men coming off and going on nighthawk duty.

With morning, came the smell of bacon frying for Collins and Bert had brought a large skillet with the supplies from Santa Rosa and Jocke Atchley was making good use of it. After some six skillets full of bacon had been consumed, the supplies were all packed on the pack horses and the fire put out. Everyone was rested and ready to take the trail. JB issued the order in a loud voice.

"Head'em up, move'em out! Let's take'em home."

The noises of over four thousand head of cattle, on the move, filled the air. Dust swirled from the thousands of hooves kicking the New Mexico Territory soil. Vicious Dog had gone forward in his usual search of water and trouble and JB, on his big Appaloosa was at point. All seemed to be back to normal and would have been if it hadn't been for Bert Rawlings and Potts on their way to Amarillo. They were yet to be a problem to Johnson. JB wasn't aware that his old rival, Rawlings, had been behind the rustling of his cattle.

The weather was turning colder and JB was worried that they might have an early snow before he could get the cattle back to the ranch beforehand. Two days out of Amarillo, a bank of dark, mean looking clouds formed in the northwest sky and there was a cold wind blowing ahead of them.

Vicious Dog rode up to JB and said, "We have snow before nightfall. I can smell it."

"I was afraid of that," said JB. "Pass the word down the right side of the herd. I'll take the left." They met at the drag position behind the herd.

Buck had traded off with Wilford Teague at drag. JB swung his horse in beside him.

"Buck, looks like we're going to get a little advance winter weather. Vicious Dog seems to think that the clouds on the horizon represent snow."

"I wouldn't doubt it at all," said Buck. "How soon do you think we'll be hit with whatever it is?"

"Vicious Dog says by nightfall. His nose is predicting snow."

"If that's the case, there's not much we can do about it. I just wish we'd come a little better prepared."

"You and me both," said JB. "It looks like we'll all have to make do with slickers. But I do wish I had my sheepskin coat."

Two days later, JB called a halt to the drive on the outskirts of

Amarillo. He told Buck to have the men push the cattle on out to the ranch while he and Joe Collins went into town.

"I won't be long," he said. "Just time enough to square myself with Hope."

Buck and the outfit turned the herd toward the ranch and pushed them on.

JB and Joe Collins both unsaddled their horses while Vicious Dog roped two fresh ones for them. After saddling the fresh mounts, the two men mounted and headed for Amarillo. It was only five or so miles to town and they arrived well ahead of the storm that was brewing. They went directly to Hope's shop. Upon entering, they saw Hope in the back with a couple of women. One of the women was being fitted with a new hat and they all three turned to see who had come in. Hope excused herself and came to the front of the shop with a big smile on her face. She did not have the same look about her that she had displayed toward JB when he and Joe left on the chase. Evidently, she had come to grips with the fact that she wasn't going to be able to run her father's life to suit her and neither could she run JB's life. She loved her father very much and really all she wanted was to make sure that he was safe. He was all she had. Little did she know that JB was thinking of becoming part of the family. She didn't know that Joe had said that it was okay with him if JB wanted to come courting Hope.

"I've been worried out of my mind ever since you left," she said to Joe. "Did you'al catch up to the rustlers?"

"Yes, we did," said Joe, "not only that but we got the cattle back and not a man in JB's outfit was scratched."

"I'm so glad," she said. "What are you going to do now Mr. Johnson?"

"Well, I guess take the cattle back to the ranch. We have so much work to do and so little time in which to do it from the looks of the weather. We'll be into winter before you know it. I just wanted to make sure you were okay and ask if I might come calling sometime."

"If you like," she said.

With that, JB said his goodbyes and headed for the door. He went out on the boardwalk and looked up and down the street. The mercantile store was just across the street and he went across over and into it. There he bought a coat for each of his men who all were about the same size. Medium size would fit each except two who were taller than the average and for these two, he bought a size larger. He went to the livery and bought a horse and pack saddle. He would have to haul the coats on the pack horse. Loaded, he walked his horses to the hitch rail in front of the saloon. He knew that saloons were the news rooms of the west and he needed some information on the yahoos who had rustled his herd if there was any floating around.

Easing through the bat-wings, he stepped to one side to let his eyes adjust to the dim interior. A minute or so passed and his eyes were adjusted enough to see the people inside, well. He walked to the end of the bar closest to the front door. Leaning on the bar with his forearms, he looked the bartender in the eye as the latter questioned him about the preference of drink.

"What'll you have friend?"

"I'll have some good Tennessee whiskey," said JB.

The bartender reached under the counter and came out with a bottle. He slid a glass over in front of JB and proceeded to pour it about a fourth full. JB picked up his glass with his left hand, leaving his gun hand free and knocked back the drink. He set his glass down and when the bartender started to pour again, JB covered the top of the glass with his spread out hand. He spoke.

"No thanks, one is enough, just enough to get the dust out of my throat. Have you heard anything around about the Johnson outfit?"

"Come to think of it, I have," said the bartender.

"Oh?" questioned JB, "anything of interest?"

"Well, seems there was a gang of men rounded up to ride herd on that outfit. Recruited right here in Amarillo a few weeks back."

"Do you have any idea who was doing the hiring?"

"If I remember correctly, it was a man named Potts. Don't know if he was asking for himself or for someone else," said the bartender.

"Any idea where I might find this Potts fellow?" asked JB.

"Nope," said the bartender. "He used to stay upstairs here but I haven't seen him in quite a while. Don't even know if he's still in town."

JB left the saloon and mounting his horse, took the lead rope and rewrapped it around the saddle horn and rode out. At least he had a name to go on. He continued on to the ranch headquarters where he spotted Pepper standing on the porch of the ranch house when he rode into the ranch yard.

"Pepper, man, it's good to see you," said JB as he stepped from the saddle and extended his hand. "I saw some of those longhorns out in the grass when I rode onto the place."

"JB, it's good to see you, said Pepper. "I was getting a little apprehensive, not finding any cattle here when I got here, but then your men came in with all those whitefaces and shorthorns, I felt a little better about everything. Your men filled me in on what happened. They said that your guide found tracks where a couple of the rustlers got away."

"I reckon so," said JB.

A few days passed and the men spent the time necessary to divide the cattle putting two herds together with half the longhorns, half the whitefaces and half the shorthorns in one here and the other halves in the second herd. While this was being done and all the brands changed, Pepper saddled up and with a pack horse, headed to the land he owned in New Mexico. One of the herds was to be driven to that location after all the preliminary work was done, by the men Pepper had hired in the south of Texas. Pepper was going on ahead, alone.

It was early morning, the day he headed out for New Mexico Territory and in short order; he was getting into country familiar to him. Soon, the day was well spent and he was looking for a place to lay his head. He found a concave place in the side of a ridge, fifty or so feet above the tree line. It was a perfect site for a camp.

He built a small fire and carried cedar boughs up to make his bed. Thoughts of his soft warm bed he had left in St. Louis, many months before, crossed his mind as he spread his bed roll on the boughs, but only for a moment. He removed his gun belt, wrapped it around the holster, and tucked it under the edge of his saddle. He sat close to the fire and warmed his hands while he chewed on a piece of tough jerky. All his money was of no use to him now. There were no stores, no restaurants and no bath parlors, just beef jerky, hardtack and coffee.

For the most part, the brush and rocks blocked the cold wind from his camp but his boots were the only thing he was going to sleep without. He crawled between the covers, sheepskin coat and all, laid his head on his saddle, pulled his Stetson down over his eyes, felt the pistol butt with one hand and drifted off to sleep.

A sound wrestled him from the grasp of the Sandman. He listened quietly, unmoving. There, he heard a second yell, this time with his conscious mind. Then two gunshots in rapid succession, echoed in the distance and another yell, then silence. He somewhat dismissed it because it was off some distance and didn't concern him anyway.

Daybreak came and Cladderbuck was mounted and ready to ride at sunup. He wondered what the commotion he heard during the early morning hours was all about. He had heard some far off yelling and gunshots. Leaving the rocks of camp, he swung around the point and took a trail made by the animals of the area that kept well below the top of the ridge. There was no reason for him to be easily spotted and even less reason to be an easy target in the event of trouble. The day turned out to be warmer and dry. It felt good where the sun struck on the downwind side of his face.

He stopped from time to time to check his back trail. He saw nothing but the usual birds and small animal life that were also enjoying the warm sunlight. By early afternoon, he had covered about ten miles as the trail winds. He had just crossed from the side of one ridge, down through a shallow draw and up the side of a hill, covered with small scrubby trees when he rode smack dab into the middle of a necktie party. Five men, three on horseback, and two on the ground; one with a noose around his neck and the rope thrown over a limb of an old dead tree. The other one was kicking trappings around as if looking for something.

Cladderbuck stopped his horse. Sat still and looked at the situation for a moment before he was noticed by the men. Everything was dead still, quiet, as they all stared at each other, then.

"What's going on here?" asked Cladderbuck.

"What does it look like?" asked one of the men.

One of the men on the ground raised his hand to the one that had spoken as if to shut him up. He then looked at Cladderbuck, his head cocked a little sideways with curiosity; his eyes squinted from the sunlight.

"Who are you?" He asked, turning his head just slightly to spit tobacco on the blade of a cactus close by.

"I asked you first," Cladderbuck spoke with no lightness in his voice.

"What has this man done?" He asked.

"I usually ask the questions around here," said the man, "You had best mind your own business, stranger."

Cladderbuck paused for just a moment, and then said, "The killing of a human being is everyone's business. Are you the law?"

"No, we're not the law, I'm John Watson, and I own this land and these are my drovers. They have a right to be here, I have a right to be here but this stinking cattle thief and you, stranger, have no right at all to be on my land."

"What makes you think this is your land? Do you have a deed to it?" asked Cladderbuck. "I was under the impression that this is government land."

John Watson was a pompous little man, with a long black handlebar mustache that stuck out like the horns of the cattle Pepper had brought up from south Texas. His skin was rugged and browned by many long hours of exposure to the elements. He wore a pistol, but carried it a little too high to be very fast with it. He ran a spread that backed up to the nearby mountains and he claimed to own all the land you could see east of the crest, which included land on both sides of the railroad.

"I don't need a deed," snapped Watson.

"You do if you plan to run me off this land," said Cladderbuck.

One of the riders turned his mount as if to get in a better position to draw his piece.

"I wouldn't try it if I were you," said Cladderbuck. Then, looking at Watson, he said, "You're just like a lot of other little men who think that just because you have a little money, that everyone dances to your tune."

Watson's blood was just about to boil by then.

Cladderbuck continued, "Since you are not the law and you don't have a deed to this land and I don't remember ever seeing a hanging law that says just anybody can carry out justice without a courtroom trial. I suggest that you turn this man over to the law or turn him loose and get your arrogant butt out of my sight."

"You must be stupid, there's four of us," Watson said with his lips creased tight over gritted, tobacco stained teeth, a half grin on his face.

"True," said Cladderbuck. "I may not be able to get all four of you or even three but it's for dead sure I can get one. I'll let you figure out which one that will be, but don't take too long to think about it."

Watson glared at him for a long breathless moment, then turned to the man with the rope wrapped around his saddle horn and said, "Let him go."

After his hands were untied, the man wasted no time in taking the rope off his neck and leaving with his horse kicking up a cloud of dust, passed Pepper and down his back trail. Watson mounted, wheeled his horse around and looked at Cladderbuck. "You haven't heard the last of this, stranger," he said. With that, all four left at a gallop.

Cladderbuck wasted no time in getting off the ridge in the opposite direction. He wasn't afraid of John Watson and his men, but there was no sense in waiting for him to return with more men and he was mad enough to do just that. Cladderbuck eased his way down the slope to a stream that flowed passed the bottom. He took to the water for a while so as not to leave a trail if he could help it. He rode downstream to keep from sending debris down to be seen. He was good at tracking and just as good at not leaving a trail for someone else to track. By nightfall, he had put another five or six miles between him and the place Watson had lost his trail by the stream. He left the water on a slab of rock that got him well clear of the bank before making any prints that could be followed. He decided to sleep without a fire that night.

CHAPTER 17

Bert Rawlings had found a cabin that was deserted back in the far reaches of nowhere. It had most likely been used for a line cabin at one time but it had been a long time since. He and Potts had moved in and were thankful for a place out of the weather. Winter was closing in and it was getting as cold as a well diggers butt in Utah. Their supplies were running low though and it wouldn't be long before one of them would have to pack some in. They drew straws to see which one would go to Amarillo for supplies. Rawlings held the straws and he held two short ones to insure that Potts would have to go. Potts hadn't the sense to know the difference, besides, he trusted Rawlings, which was a failing on his part.

"Listen now," Rawlings said. "You go straight to the mercantile, get the things we need to make the winter. Then go to the saloon and get us a dozen bottles of that good Tennessee whiskey. I don't intend to spend the winter without something to warm my innards. And stay away from them women. You know how you are when it comes to women; you ain't got a lick of sense. And keep your mouth shut. Don't talk to nobody you don't have to. And don't say where we're hold up to anybody, hell; don't even talk to yourself about it."

"You don't have to worry about me."

"But I do," said Rawlings. "You couldn't keep your mouth shut if it was laced together with rawhide."

"Honest," said Potts. "I won't tell anybody."

They had gotten their first snowfall and there was about a foot on the ground when Potts saddled up, mounted and rode off. Two days later, he rode into the town of Amarillo. He did just as Rawlings had said. He went straight to the mercantile and placed his order with Seth Williams, the owner. Seth and his wife, Martha busied themselves with the order and Potts left, while they got it together, and went to the saloon. There, he bought the whiskey Rawlings wanted and the bartender put the whiskey bottles in a burlap bag. Taking the bag, Potts left the saloon, hung the bag over his shoulder and went to the livery where he rented a wagon and team of mules. He tied his horse to the tailgate of the wagon and climbed to the driver's seat. He drove to the mercantile and picked up his supplies. After loading them in the wagon, he spread a tarp over them, climbed to the seat and headed out of town. He had probably a three day trip back to the cabin for the wagon would be slower than horseback. He kept one of the bottles of whiskey out to keep him company on the way.

When he arrived back at the cabin, Rawlings was pacing the dirt floor. Potts drove the wagon up to the front door, got down and started to unload the supplies.

"It's about time," Rawlings shouted from the door.

"I made it as fast as I could," said Potts.

"Did you bring that whiskey?"

"Yah," Potts said as he picked up the burlap bag and handed it to Rawlings. "I got twelve bottles just like you said."

"Did you see anything or hear anything about Johnson's cattle being rustled?"

"I talked to the bartender and the mercantile store owner and neither of them said a word about Johnson, but the man at the livery said he was in there asking about me. He knew my name and everything."

"Did he mention anything about me?" asked Rawlings.

"Didn't say so," said Potts. "Give me a hand with this stuff."

The two men unloaded the wagon and hauled the supplies into the cabin and stacked them against the wall, next to the open fireplace. The sky had been clear the past few days but there was still snow on the ground though some of it had melted off. Rawlings had a good fire going in the fireplace. The cabin became warmer as the heat from the fire started swallowing up the cold let in when the men brought the supplies in. After a while the two of them settled down to two handed poker, while outside the wind howled as it rearranged what snow was left. Far off in the night, a coyote barked and the tall cactus plants cast long shadows across the snow covered plains. The moon was almost as bright as day. Winter had arrived.

****

JB and his men had settled in for the winter. There would be a lot that had to be done because of the cold weather. The watering holes had to be kept clear of ice around the edges so that the cattle could drink. Hay had to be thrown from the storage places to keep them fed. Saddles, bridles and other equipment had to be mended and one chore nobody liked, firewood had to be chopped and stacked close to the house and bunkhouse to supply the necessary heat through the winter.

JB brooded a lot during the cold days over who had rustled his cattle and killed five of his men. He couldn't get it out of his mind. Buck had noticed his moodiness but said nothing. Then on the first day that the weather let up, JB rode into Amarillo. He wanted to see Hope Collins. He also wanted to mill around town, in the saloons and cafes to listen for any kind of clue to who might have been responsible for the death of his men. In all likelihood, whoever was behind the raid had been wiped out in his retaliation when he and his men had recovered the herd. In the back of his mind, though, was the remark Vicious Dog had made about two riders that might have gotten away. He rode his big Appaloosa into the edge of town and swung into the livery. The hostler came up through the runway of the barn to take charge of his horse. "Howdy," he said.

"Howdy, Pard," said JB. "Rub him down good then give him a helping of oats and one of corn."

The hostler took the reins and led the Appaloosa through the runway to an individual stall. He removed the saddle and bridle and put a halter on him, rubbed him down and then led him into the stall and gave him the oats and corn requested by his owner. While he was doing this, JB made his way to the quarters of Joe Collins. He passed a number of saloons on his way, stopped at the house, stepped to the door and knocked.

There was noise of movement within the room then the door swung open. Joe Collins stood in the doorway. The warmth of the room rushed out in the face of JB and felt good against the cold in which he had been riding.

"JB," said Collins. "Come in man. It's too cold out there for men, maybe small, furry nocturnal animals, but not men. It's good to see you."

JB wiped his feet as best as he could and entered the room. Inside, he looked around. He was in a sitting room with a dining area to one side and a kitchen beyond. Two other walls, each, hosted a door. JB guessed that those doors lead to the sleeping quarters. He took a couple of steps into the room and turned as Joe closed the door. Joe spoke.

"How have you been, JB?" he asked?

"Things couldn't be better."

"What brings you to town in this miserable weather," asked Collins?

"Two things," JB said with a thin smile. The main reason was to see you and Hope. Mainly Hope."

"Ah ha," said Joe. "What is the other reason?"

"To see if I can get a handle on the bunch that rustled my cattle and killed five of my men. As you know, Vicious Dog found the tracks of two of them that could have gotten away, the tracks he found indicated that there were riders aboard."

"Any idea who the two might be," asked Collins.

"The bartender gave me a name. A fellow named Potts. I checked with the hostler at the livery and he put a first name to him. His name is Jack Potts. I plan on milling around town, ask a few questions and find out if Potts had a sidekick. I thought maybe Hope, you and I could have supper together and afterwards, you and I might make the rounds in the saloons with our ears open and ask a few questions. What do you say?"

Collins rubbed his chin for a moment, in thought. Then he spoke.

"You know, it just might work. It won't hurt to ask around. Of course Hope and I will be more than glad to have supper with you."

"I have some errands to run this afternoon. I have to see the banker on a matter and see to ordering a few supplies we're running short of and make arrangement for a room."

"The El Dorado Hotel has some nice rooms and they're clean," said Joe.

"Thanks, Joe. I think I'll get that room first and then take care of the rest. What time should I meet you at the café?"

"The best place in town to eat is Ma Pratt's place," said Joe. "How about we meet you there at, say, six o'clock."

JB placed his Stetson on his head as he said, "That's fine." He turned to the door and opening it and strode out into the arms of the cold wind. He had not removed his sheepskin coat while inside and the warmth of it felt good. He walked down the boardwalk to the hotel, entered and walked to the counter. The clerk looked up from a copy of the Dallas Sentinel and spoke.

"Good afternoon, sir. May I help you?"

"Yes," said JB. "I need a room."

The clerk turned the registration booklet around to him and cracked a thin smile.

JB took the pen offered and signed the book. "

"I would like a hot bath, also."

"Yes sir. I'll have the man prepare your bath whenever you want."

"I'll be back by four o'clock. I'll be ready for the bath by four fifteen," said JB.

"It'll be ready, sir. Your room is on the second floor. Go to the top of the stairs, back down the hall to the front of the building, it'll be the last door on your left. It has a door that opens onto the balcony that looks down on the front street."

JB took the key and went to his room. He entered the room and placed his Winchester on the bed and taking his saddlebags; he stepped out in the hall, locked the door and went out of the hotel. His first stop was the bank. He entered the bank and walked to the railing which fences off the manager's desk area from the lobby. He spoke to the manager, a Mr. Burgett.

"Good afternoon Mr. Burgett."

Burgett looked up to see JB and smiled his usually warm smile he had for all the bank's customers.

"Good afternoon Mr. Johnson. It's good to see you. What can I do for you today?"

"I need two thousand dollars in double eagles," said JB.

"Yes sir, I'll just be a minute," said Burgett. He left his desk and went to the rear of the bank. He returned in just a moment, with a cloth bag, which he set on the desk. He reached in and counted out a hundred double eagles to JB.

JB picked them up and put them in his saddlebag, fifty in each for balance. He thanked the banker, as he signed for the money and left. He made his way to the mercantile store and there settled up with Seth Williams and gave him a list of what he would need before he left town.

"When will you be leaving?" asked Williams.

"I'll let you know," said JB, "probably in a couple or three days. In the meantime, I'll need a pair of Levies, a shirt, one pair of socks and some long johns."

"Just let me know and I'll have the rest of your supplies ready," said Williams.

JB waited for his new duds, and then touching his finger to the brim of his hat, he turned and left. He returned to the hotel where he put his saddlebags in the hotel safe. It was right at four o'clock and he reminded the clerk that he would want his bath within fifteen minutes. He headed for the stairs as the clerk called for his helper to start preparing the bath water. The clerk called after JB.

"Mr. Johnson, the bath room is at the far end of the hall next to the back stairs, on the right."

JB never looked back. He just raised his hand in acknowledgment and proceeded up the stairs. Reaching his room, he laid out his new duds and taking his razor, he went down the hall to the bath room.

At five minutes before six, he walked into Ma Pratt's café. Joe Collins and Hope had not arrived so he went to a table in the far corner where he would be able to see the front door. He sat down and was approached by a sweet little old lady he guessed was in her sixties.

"What'll you have cowboy?" she asked. She was used to calling everybody without a necktie, cowboy.

"You must be Ma Pratt," said JB with a wide smile.

"That's me. What'll you have?"

"I'm expecting Joe and Hope Collins to join me for supper," said JB. "Why don't I just have some coffee while I wait?"

"I can take care of that," Ma said, and left. She had no more than disappeared into the kitchen when Joe and Hope walked in the front door at six o'clock on the button. Spying JB at the table in the corner, Joe took Hope by the arm and guided her to it.

"Good evening," said JB as he rose from his seat in greeting and respect for Hope. "I was just fixing to have some coffee."

Hope sat in the chair that JB pulled out for her and held. Joe sat across the table from her and she had her back to the door. JB had just sat down when Ma Pratt returned with his coffee. She spoke.

"What can I get for you two lovely people? Would you like something to drink?"

"What all do you have?" asked Hope.

"Well, we have coffee of course and water but the best thing to my mind is fresh tea I made this afternoon and it's been setting out in the snow for about an hour now. Ought to be cold enough to make your teeth hurt."

"That sounds good, I'll have some," said Hope.

"Me too," Joe chimed in.

Ma Pratt turned and was gone before you could say Jack rabbit. In a moment, she was back with two large glasses full of bright amber tea. She spoke.

"Have you thought about what you folks want to eat, yet? Before you make up your mind, Will Miller and his sons killed hogs not long ago and he sold me some of the best pork chops you ever tasted. I can serve them up with mashed potatoes, gravy, beans and beets out of the root cellar, stewed in butter with hot biscuits or corn pone."

They all three looked at each other and nodded.

"Looks like we all want just what you named," said JB.

Before long, the food came and they were all engaged in their meal. So much so that nobody noticed Jack Potts when he entered and sat at a table next to the door. He looked into a mirror on the wall at the same instant that Hope looked and her instinctive reaction caused him to ease up and out the door. Her reaction was noticed by Joe and he said, "What's wrong, Honey?"

"That man that just sat down by the door, he's one of the two that came in the shop that time." She just barely got it out.

Joe turned and looked, seeing nobody there. He spoke.

"There's nobody there."

"But there was a minute ago." She said with a nervous tone to her voice.

Joe and JB both got to their feet and dashed out the door. The evening being young, there were a lot of people in the street and along the boardwalks and it would have been impossible for Joe to pick out anyone. He had all but forgotten the description Hope had given him so many weeks before. They returned to the table and resumed their meal but none of the three were all that hungry after that.

Jack Potts was running scared. Rawlings had sent him to town to buy more whiskey and Potts had decided to have a good meal while he was in town but now he wasn't thinking about food. He slammed into the saloon, out of breath. The bartender grinned at him when he approached the bar. He spoke.

"You look like the devil himself was after you. What's up?"

Potts was sweating even though it was cold outside. He fidgeted for a moment then blurted out, "Whiskey!" Then settling down a little, he said in a more controlled voice, "Give me a dozen bottles of that good Tennessee whiskey." He looked all around, especially at the door. "Put them in a burlap bag."

The bartender went to the back room for he didn't have that many bottles up front. In a few minutes he returned with the burlap bag and set it on the bar.

"That'll be twenty four dollars," he said.

Potts paid him and grabbed the bag, turned to the door and left in a huff. He went to his horse, tied the burlap bag to the saddle horn, mounted and left town in the opposite direction than the hideout. South out of town, he came to a stream. He rode his horse into the middle of the stream and turned up stream, a while later, he left it. He circled wide and went around the town, to gain his true trail, in case somebody watched him leave. He put about five miles behind him before he stopped for the night. He had planned to get him a room and a woman for the night but he was too scared to try that. He wound up sleeping on the ground next to a camp fire. The night air was so cold; he had trouble keeping warm enough to sleep except in short spurts between putting more wood on the fire.

After supper and a smoke with after meal coffee, JB and Joe Collins walked Hope to the boarding house. They then proceeded to the closest saloon. Entering, they walked to the front end of the bar which ran almost the length of one wall. It was made of dark mahogany with a brass foot rest, eight inches or so off the floor, stretching the entire length of the bar. Behind the bar was shelving filled with bottles of all sorts. The shelving was separated, in the middle, by a large rectangular mirror and above the mirror was the picture of a mustang horse, racing across a mesa. It was easy to figure out the name of the saloon. Mustang Saloon was scrolled across the top of the painting for those who could read.

"What'll you Gents have?" asked the barkeep.

"Do you carry that good Tennessee whiskey?" asked JB. "Jack Daniels by name."

"Sure do," said the keep.

"Joe?" asked JB. Joe nodded his head. JB continued.

"Give us two of that Tennessee whiskey."

"Coming right up," the barkeep reached under the bar and came out with a bottle. He slid two glasses to them and proceeded to pour each a drink. Finished doing so, he sat the bottle down between them, picked up the coin JB had laid on the bar and turning, he walked away to tend to other customers.

An old Indian staggered through the batwing doors and demanded, "Whiskey!"

The bartender came around the end of the bar, took him by the nap of the neck and the seat of his pants and thrust him out the door, to the boardwalk. The Indian got up on weak legs, staggered out into the street and disappeared into the night.

"He comes in here almost every night," said the barkeep. "He never gets a drink in here. I have no idea where he gets it but he is always drunk." He picked up a glass and started to wipe it with a cloth he had laid across his shoulder. Looking at Joe he spoke.

"How do you like retirement, Mr. Collins?"

"Now, I've told you to call me Joe," said Collins. "I don't think you know my friend here, Hank, meet JB Johnson. He has a ranch out northwest of here, over close to Hollicott Crossing. JB, meet Hank, ah, ah. Dang it Hank, I don't think I've ever heard what your last name is."

"Steelman, Hank Steelman," said the barkeep. I'm one of the Steelmans that came out here from Kentucky. I have a brother who settled on land about a hundred miles southeast of here and a cousin over to Santa Rosa in New Mexico Territory."

"It's good to know you Hank Steelman," said JB. "You serve a mighty fine Tennessee whiskey here."

"I also have some of the best, smoothest Kentucky bourbon you'll ever find."

"Do you sell a lot of this Tennessee whiskey?" asked JB. He was just being curious.

"Yah, I sure do," said the barkeep. "Why just tonight I sold ole Jack Potts twelve bottles of the same brand."

JB's ears perked up. He glanced at Collins, then at Hank Steelman. He spoke in a low, level voice.

"Did you say Jack Potts?"

"Yah, Jack Potts, he came in here not more'n a hour ago and bought twelve bottles and had me put them in a burlap bag. He said something about keeping the cold off or something like that, and then he left. Strange thing too, he left here, earlier after having a drink or two, said he was going over to Ma Pratt's and have a good meal but he was back in five minutes, out of breath, buying the whiskey. I kind of wondered about that so I walked over to the door and watched him mount up and ride out of town."

"Which way did he go?" asked JB.

"He rode out of town, headed south. All he had with him, that I could see, was his bedroll and that sack of whiskey. I just hope he don't freeze to death. It's mighty cold out there on the flat."

"Did Potts ever have a partner, someone he hung around with a lot?" JB asked.

"Yah, as a matter of fact, he did," said the bartender, "a fellow by the name of Rawlings. I heard his first name a time or two but I just can't quite get it."

"Could it have been Berton or Bert?" asked JB.

"Yah, that was it, Bert."

JB's face lost a little of its color for an instant. Then, it turned a shade redder than normal. He was silent for a long moment.

"Do you know this Bert Rawlings?" asked Joe Collins.

"I should say so," said JB. "We had a run-in way back. He was whipping a horse for no good reason and I put a stop to it. We faced each other and he finally took water. I wouldn't be a bit surprised if he's not in back of the rustling of my cattle. It's just like something he would do to get back at me and at the same time, line his pockets. He and Potts could very well be the two who molested Hope in the shop, also."

"What are you going to do?" asked Joe. "Whatever it is, I want to be in on it. I've got as much score to settle with them as you do."

"The first thing I'm going to do is get a good night's sleep. I can't follow his trail tonight but I hope to pick it up at first light. If you're going with me, be ready to go at first light. Meet me at Ma Pratt's café for breakfast at five. First light will be around six."

"I'll be ready," said Joe.

JB then went to the hotel. He was dead tired and as soon as his head hit the pillow, he was asleep.

CHAPTER 18

The sun was about an hour from setting when the buckboard Hank had picked Grace Pritchet up in came out of the canyon, turned the road at Snake curve and descended to the valley floor. The entrance to the valley was at the head of a deep canyon that snaked from the other side of the mountain. The canyon wound its way through the mountain with barely enough room for a buckboard and team at some points. It climbing as it went, and came out at a point which overlooked the stream that cut through a gorge to form the deep canyon. Inside of the canyon was moist and damp with moisture that rose from the stream below as vapor. The passage wound through the mountain, back and forth. It was dimly lighted from the diffused light that came in from above.

She had seen the ranch house from the point but now all she could see was cottonwoods, scrub timber and bushes which surrounded the huge valley of grass that came up to a horses' bellies. The valley was at least five miles wide and went on for some forty odd miles before it tapered down to a narrowing canyon that went out to the edge of the desert.

The countryside was beautiful and seemed to wrap itself around her like a protective blanket. She felt the warmth and security of the valley. It had been her home since her father had first found the valley by accident and moved his whole operation, cattle and all to it. They had never actually measured the valley but had estimated the distances and it was completely enclosed by cliffs and mountains. The only way in or out that they had found was the passage through the deep canyon at one end and the smaller canyon to the desert. They stopped in the stream, pausing long enough to let the horses drink, and then continued on.

Off to the left of the road was a narrow field rolling over into a draw that had a creek which flowed down to the stream they had just crossed. On the opposite side of the creek, the land sloped up to the foot of a twenty-five or a thirty-foot rock ledge. Grazing in the field was a small group of cattle, being hazed by one of the ranch hands. Grace threw up her hand and her gesture was returned by the waving of a Stetson in the air. A little puff of dust flew from the wheels as they went on.

There was a golden, purple hue to the countryside as the sun disappeared behind the hills. Then the black blanket of night settled on the land with only the orange glow of kerosene lamps breaking through the darkness. Grace had been told that her father was checking on the line camps but she couldn't help but be concerned any time he was gone for long without a word.

It was during supper when they heard the cry, "Rider coming in."

Everyone turned to see who, as the rider dismounted and came toward the house. It was Pete Pritchet. Grace stood to face her father when he entered the room. "What is wrong, Daddy?" Her question prompted by the expression of fear mixed with anger that distorted his usually smiling face. He stood for a moment in the silence of the room and then threw his hat to the floor and stomped into the next room, slamming the door behind him.

"What's eaten him?" Hank asked. He sat with his fork dangling loosely in his fingers.

"I have no idea,' said Grace. "I've never seen him like this."

They all knew not to bother Pete under normal circumstances, when he wanted to be left alone and they surely were not going to butt in when he was that upset.

In a short while, Pete Pritchet came out of his room. This time he entered the room normally. With a slight smile on his face, he looked at Grace. "I'm sorry daughter, I..."

"Oh, Daddy,' she said. She rushed over, threw her arms around his neck and kissed him on the forehead. "That's okay, but what's bothering you?" she asked.

"Ah Honey, it's nothing serious, really." He smiled and sat down to his place. "What's that wonderful smell?"

After supper, Pete Pritchet picked up his pipe, filled it with tobacco and headed for the veranda, "You got a minute, Hank?" he asked.

Hank got to his feet and followed. On the veranda, the two men talked in such low tones that Grace could hardly make out what was being said from the dining room, where she and Hank's wife were clearing the table. She could catch a word or two every now and then, but nothing that made any sense.

"Hank, I'm telling you, these three Watson riders dead to rights. I rode up on them, changing brands and before I knew it, they had guns on me. They held me until their boss, ole John, himself, came along and they told him I was changing them brands. Before I knew what kind of a pot I was in, they had me under a tree with a rope around my neck. I just knew I was a goner, and then this stranger rode up and faced the four of them down, without blinking an eye. Well, when they backed down, I got out of there as fast as I could, soon's I got that damn rope off my neck. It was the damndest thing you ever saw."

"Do you have any idea who he might be?" asked Hank.

"Not the slightest," said Pete. "But he's the kind of fellow you would want on your side in a fight. I'm telling you Hank. You should have seen their faces. Watson looked like he had just soiled himself and might have for all I know, I didn't stick around long enough to smell the air to fine out."

The two men sat for a while, a little curl of smoke trailing off into nothing above Pete's pipe. Somewhere in the distance, the yelping of a bunch of coyotes broke through the stillness of the night as Pete pondered how he was going to handle the trouble that seemed to be coming, no matter what.

He was sitting there in thought when Grace strolled out onto the veranda, a lace scarf over her head. The wind caught the corners of the scarf and whipped them back and forth in front of her face. Pete thought how much she looked like her mother. He found himself thinking how her mother would have been so proud of her had she lived.

"You look lovely tonight, Grace," he said.

"Daddy, what were you so upset about when you came home?"

He repeated the story as he had told it to Hank.

"Oh, Daddy, you could have been killed," she said. "Do you not know who the stranger might have been?"

"No," said Pete. "I only noticed one thing about him, out of the ordinary. He had a silver steer head on the band of his hat."

"Why, that's the same thing I noticed about the stranger I met on the train from St. Louis to Dallas, said Grace. "I wonder if he is one in the same."

Pete drew slowly on his pipe. Then taking it from his mouth, he said, "Well, whoever he is, I am surely glad he came along when he did. Now Grace, tell me all about your trip."

****

The next morning broke bright and clear. The wind was blowing ever so slightly with a chill on its crest. Everyone was up and at their normal routine when Grace awoke and got dressed. Martha Childress, Hank's wife greeted Grace when she walked into the dining room.

"Have you seen my father?" asked Grace.

"He's with the men down at the catching pen, branding the new calves," said Martha. "Can I fix you some breakfast?"

"No, thanks, I'm going for a ride. Perhaps I can work up an appetite while I'm gone," said Grace, slipping on her hat and pushing the bola up under her chin. She put on her gloves, picked up her riding crop and headed for the stables. She much preferred wearing spurs to fooling with a riding crop but her father said it was not lady-like for a woman to wear spurs so she used the crop to please him.

****

Cladderbuck slept late and was two hours into the sun before he slipped on his boots. He had decided to relax for a day; after all, there was no rush. For that matter, getting away from the rush was what his trip west was all about. He saw nothing wrong with a little relaxation every now and then. Besides, he had a good book with him and enough time, it seemed to him, to read a few pages. Time would come, sooner than he knew, that there would be very little time to read, or anything else for that matter.

Cladderbuck sat in his camp and watched the smoke from his fire curl up and swirl against the cliff side. He thought how beautiful the different colors were as they blended to form the patterns in the rock face. He had forgotten just how beautiful the things of nature were and they seemed amplified in the American west. He couldn't help but wonder at the browns and tans and the multitude of shades in and around both colors.

There was wildlife everywhere, and nowhere, Cladderbuck spent the day relaxing against the beauty of the land, wondering why he had ever left the west in the first place. Along about mid afternoon, the wind began to stir and move the tumbleweed and mesquite. It was a cool wind and from the clean fresh smell of it, Cladderbuck knew that it was blowing in off a thunder storm. Before then, he had not noticed the dark clouds hanging over the foothills across the small valley between him and the mountains. They were not really mountains, but the locals called them that. A bolt of lightning reached its blue hot fingers across the sky and the low, dull rumbles of thunder rolling across the valley. He was glad that he had the large flat rock overhang that covered his camp site.

Tomorrow, he would go into Santa Rosa but take his time in doing so. Once more, the woman on the train crossed his mind. He wondered where she was and what she might be doing. On the opposite side of the coin, he thought of the loner he had seen on the train also. The one, other than himself, that lived by his wits. The one that looked hungry and mean.

The wind was much stronger and a few drops of rain spattered on the flat rocks nearby. Cladderbuck thought of how glad he was that he had decided to stick it out in his present campsite. He had some jerky to chew and a pot of coffee sitting in the edge of the fire.

There was still enough light to read by and Cladderbuck took advantage of it. As the afternoon light faded with the approach of the thunder storm clouds, he put his book away, leaned back against the rocks and watched the rain.

Soon it was dark and the rain trailed off and then finally quit. The clouds broke up and vanished into a clear, night sky and the bright stars twinkled at him until he fell asleep.

****

Grace lay awake, it seemed, half the night, thinking about the tall stranger she had met on the train. He seemed to be on her mind a lot and for no apparent reason. Finally, she too, drifted off to sleep.

****

Cladderbuck's eyes eased open about the time that the sun topped the crest of the mesa and flooded the wall of many colors that made up the background of his camp-site. It was a cool, crisp morning and the rays of the sun felt good as he stirred, slipped on his boots and then raked a stick across the ashes of the fire that was still smoldering. A few small twigs brought it back to flame. He made coffee and sat watching the colors of the cliff side change hues as the sun climbed into the morning sky.

He finished his coffee and doused the fire with what was left in the pot, and steam spewed into the air. He kicked sand onto the coals to finish off any chance that the fire might later revive and spread. He didn't want to be responsible for a prairie fire. He had seen them before and what they did to the countryside and wild life was no pretty sight. He stuck a wad of jerky in his cheek and started to saddle his horse. Once saddled, he wasted no time. He put his gear on board, mounted the saddle and rode off toward the southwest of camp.

****

The land office records in Fort Worth had shown no record of anyone ever filing a claim on the land in the valley where she and her father lived, when Grace checked but the man in the Fort Worth office indicated that there might be a record of filing in the larger office in St. Louis.

"Finding out that information would take a little bit more time," the land office clerk said. "You check back with me in, say, two or three weeks."

That was what had prompted her trip on to St. Louis. Without any further information forthcoming there, she had returned home.

Although he had not said anything, Grace could tell that her dad was disappointed at the news. He wanted to know for sure that the land in the valley was his. Grace had taken filing forms with her to Ft. Worth and on to St. Louis, but the clerk in St. Louis had refused to honor them until he could make a complete search of the records and that would take time, time he didn't have so her request would have to be put in line with the hundreds of other requests. She would be notified as soon as possible. With all this information up front, Pete Pritchet intended to go on with the running of his ranch, but he would be a little hesitant in making permanent improvements to the place.

CHAPTER 19

Cladderbuck had been in and out of town for four days since the boys arrived with the herd from Texas and he felt it was time to move the herd into his valley. He was sitting in a straight legged chair, leaning against the wall of the saloon when he heard the rumble of wagon wheels come around the livery at the end of the street. He peered from under the brim of his Stetson to see a buckboard coming down the dusty thoroughfare. The hooves of the horses that pulled the buckboard were pounding out puffs of dust as they pranced past. The driver was obviously a cowhand and there was a woman seated beside him. As they went passed, he realized, all of a sudden, that the woman was GP, the one he had met on the train during his trip from St. Louis. 'Of all people,' he thought. He almost fell out of this chair and had to catch himself to keep from hitting the porch floor.

She was helped down from the buckboard by the driver after stopping in front of the mercantile. She had noticed Cladderbuck sitting by the saloon as they passed but had not recognized him, but did notice that, whoever it was, his chair seemed to be a little unstable.. She turned to enter the mercantile and with a graceful sweep of her skirt, she entered. Pepper could contain himself no longer. He just had to find out who she was. What did the GP stand for? The memory of his encounter on the train had haunted him long enough. He made up his mind. Rising from his, unstable, chair, he strolled down the street to the mercantile, fighting a strong urge to hurry. Upon entering, he saw her standing by the counter, talking to the owner. This was his chance. Surely the owner would introduce him to her. He walked right up to them.

Turning, the owner smiled at Pepper and said, "Well, good morning, Mister Cladderbuck. I'd like for you to meet Miss Grace Pritchet. Miss Pritchet, Pepper Cladderbuck."

"How do you do, Miss Pritchet?"

"We've already met, Mister Satterfield. Mr. Cladderbuck was on the train that I returned on from St. Louis."

"Well, almost met," said Pepper. "We spoke but I never did find out what your name was. All I knew was that your initials were GP."

"How did you know that?" she asked.

"I saw them on your luggage when you got on in St. Louis."

"Oh," she said.

"What are you doing in this neck of the woods Miss Pritchet?"

"My driver is taking me to, or was taking me to Amarillo for a visit and we got off on the wrong road, if you can believe that, and wound up here. I was just asking Mister Satterfield which way it is to Amarillo from here," she said.

He had thought often of this woman and had even imagined what it would be like to settle down with a woman who was oriented to the west. She was a fine looker and Pepper felt a little intimidated by her for he had never really thought that much of himself, at least as a good catch for a woman.

Once she had gone, Satterfield turned to Cladderbuck. "I have all the supplies you ordered ready whenever you want them."

"Thanks. I'm sure there will be a couple more days before we leave for the ranch."

"You know you're going to run into a lot of trouble if that land turns out to be what ole Pete Pritchet is claiming is his.

"Yeah, I figured as much," said Pepper.

"Well, I didn't mention it with Grace here. I figured it was your place."

It was at that moment that Pepper Cladderbuck realized that Grace was the woman he would marry. This was the woman who would bare his children who would share his hopes, his dreams, his very soul. This was she.

****

The weeks passed quickly, during which time, the problem of moving his cattle to the valley where Grace and her father lived, was resolved. The oranges, reds and yellows of fall, with the leaves turning loose and falling to form a beautiful blanket of color, covered the countryside. They swirled through the cool autumn air, blown to and fro by the winds that were beginning to sweep in from the north. This was nature's introduction of winter on the land. Soon there would be snow in the mountains and occasionally in the valleys. He felt as if they had put plenty of hay aside for that eventuality but he knew he could never be sure.

Winter was about half gone when Cladderbuck took a turn in town. He had not wanted to go because he felt that if he ran into Grace, he would not know how to handle the situation. The cold winds that seemed to be always on the plains were whipping the corners of his coat collar as well as the mane of his black, snapping him in the face. The horse had the long shaggy hair of a winter coat and really didn't look like the same animal. He rode into town. The hooves of his horse making a crunching sound as his weight plus that of the man sent them through the frozen ground. It was so cold that what little moisture, there was in the ground, spewed forth to form little castle like crystals of ice standing one to two inches high. The sun reflected from them like a thousand sparkling diamonds that had been strewn across the earth. In a way, Pepper thought of the beauty of it as something he had admired all his life. As a child, he had walked through the same kind of ice formations and had listened to the crunching sound. He thought, "What things we remember."

His black was blowing steam like puffs from his nostrils that looked like smoke, into the air that surrounded them. He reined up in front of the Pork Chop. He hoped he was not too late for breakfast, being late in the morning. Surely Rachael would have some bacon, eggs and biscuits to go along with a few cups of strong, black coffee. He tied his horse to the hitch rail and stepped upon the boardwalk. He had already taken in the other side of the street as he rode in. Now he observed the side of the street on which he stood. He looked both ways. True, that most men never look up too high, but he cast his vision along the rooftops. From force of habit, he satisfied himself that all was normal. He turned and went into the café.

Much to his surprise, Grace was there, waiting tables. She lowered her eyebrows when she saw him and he took note of the fact. He went to a table in the corner where he could see the door as well as most of the street through a window.

"What would you like," she asked, with a chill to the tone of her voice.

"I'll have half a dozen eggs, some bacon and some biscuits. I'd like some gravy too, if you have some."

"We do," she said as she poured a cup of coffee and put it in front of him. She then placed the pot on the table and returned to the kitchen. He had trouble keeping his eyes off her as she walked away. She had a way of walking that stirred the inner man.

Before too long, she returned with his food and placed it before him. As she turned to leave, he caught her arm. She held very still for a long moment, then turned her head and looked into his eyes. The spark of anger was still there in her eyes, but she read something in his eyes that she had never noticed before. For an instant, the anger in her seemed to dampen.

"I would like to talk to your father," he said. "Would you tell him I want to see him?"

"I'll tell him," she said as she slowly pulled her arm free. "He might not want to see you, though." She hesitated for a moment longer. "I'll tell him," she repeated as she turned to go.

Later, when he had finished his breakfast and two more cups of coffee, Pepper stepped onto the boardwalk. He was wondering how long she would keep the burr under her saddle. The sky was a beautiful light blue and the sun felt good on his face. The rays of the sun only served to accentuate the steam issuing from his horses' nostrils as well as his own. He swung his arms around his body a couple of times in habit against the cold and rubbed his hands together, then blew into them and stuck them into the big pockets of his sheepskin coat. With his collar pulled up around his ears, he headed for the office of Carl Palmer, the owner of the local newspaper. He wanted to find out what had been going on since he'd been snowed in.

CHAPTER 20

The sun was climbing higher in the sky when Pepper entered the office of Carl Palmer. Carl was up to his elbows in paper, ink and type. He looked up at Cladderbuck with a friendly face and said, "I saw you going into the café. Did you enjoy your breakfast?"

"Sure did. Ma Pratt knows how to put on a feed."

"I couldn't help noticing how cool Grace was the last time I mentioned your name," said Carl. "She blames you for them losing the valley."

"I've been giving that a lot of thought and I can see her point of view," Pepper said as he sat sidesaddle on the railing that separated the lobby from the work area. I think things can be worked out if Pete will just give me a few minutes of his time."

"Pete Pritchet is a stubborn man, and proud, but I think he'll listen to what you have to say."

"I hope so," said Pepper. "What's been going on since I was in town last?"

"Well, Watson has been systematically buying up the small ranches around. He took up where that fellow Metcalf left off. A funny thing though, he makes his offers right after the ranch has been attacked and burned by a band of renegades. Some folks think that the renegades work for Watson."

"What do you think?" asked Pepper.

"I can't say but it seems really strange. By the way, you wanted to talk to Pete Pritchet. He was in here to see if he had any answer to his ad on the cattle and said he was going to be busy this week inventorying his lumber supply. Most of it is stored down by the river, at the saw mill. That may be where you can find him."

Pete Pritchet was at the saw mill tallying his lumber. Even though the cold of winter was heavy on the land, he was sweating from his work. He squinted against the sun and tried to make out who rode toward him. He was still squinting when Cladderbuck stepped out of the saddle and ground hitched his black.

"Howdy, Pete," said Cladderbuck.

"Howdy," was the response.

"Have you found a buyer for those cattle of yours?"

"No. Not yet. I've advertised all over, but no takers."

"That's what I heard, and you have a buyer," said Pepper.

"What are you talking about?" Nobody has made me an offer to buy my cattle. When they do, I'll get them off your place as soon as I can."

"I am," said Cladderbuck.

"You?" Pete asked.

"Yes. Me, under one condition," said Pepper.

"What condition?" asked Pritchet, wiping his face again?

"Under the condition that enough of your men come along and run the ranch."

Pete stood there for a long time in thought. He wiped his face a third time and picked up his canteen and took a swallow of water.

"You're a cattle man already. How come you're willing to mix my breed of cattle in the same valley with your cows?" I thought all you cattle men hated mixed cattle breeds. Lots say mixed cattle can't live on the same range and produce the best beef."

"It may shock and surprise a lot of folks, but I think they can," said

Pepper. "And I'm willing to give it a try, if you'll agree to my condition, and I'm sure JB will go along with it."

"What's the catch?"

"The catch is, your men will take orders from me, forth and found, like everyone else. I'm also adding five thousand dollars for the work you had already done to the place and you and Grace are welcome to live in the cabin we built on Sundance Creek, for as long as you want."

Pepper waited for Pete to make up his mind. It didn't take him too long.

"I'll take it," said Pritchet. "I sure hope you know what you're doing."

Pepper gathered his horses' reins and stepped into the leather. He wheeled his horse around and held for a moment.

Pete Pritchet stood with a look of shock on his face as Cladderbuck rode away. The shock slowly turned to a big wide grin. "Now, there goes a man to ride the river with," he said to himself. His heart was about to burst from his chest, he was so happy.

Grace was still not quite sure why Cladderbuck had done what he had done, but like her father, she didn't intend to look a gift horse in the mouth. This meant she no longer had to work at the café. She and Pete would be able to keep most of their furniture and personal possessions. Things were looking up for them and she looked at Pepper Cladderbuck in an all-together different light, as did Pete.

As time passed, there was plenty of hay stacked for the winter and the work of moving the stock to new grazes continued on through the cold months. Christmas came and went and the icy fingers of the north wind gripped the valley as well as the surrounding desert. Men gathered behind frosted windows around potbelly heaters and told tall tales of their life on the plains, deserts and in the mountains of the Rocky range and young boys listened with ears afire for the adventure of growing up.

Ice crystals spewed from the ground, and crunched under Cladderbuck's big black. He was seeing a lot of cows with fresh milk and no calves to suck. He stopped atop a knoll and leaned his coat collar into the wind while he lit a small thin cigar. Someone was making off with some of their unbranded stock.

****

"There's one thing for sure," said Laredo. "We keep taking them calves and sooner or later, they're gonna come after us."

"Let'em come," snorted Ron Kincade. "They bleed like anybody else."

"Maybe so, but you'd better have a couple of men backing you up if you tangle with that outfit. How many have we already grabbed?"

"I ain't counted'em, but looks to be about a hundred and thirty, give or take a few. It's a good thing we have fresh cows to put'em on. I sure would hate to try to bottle feed'em all."

"If the boss finds out, we've been using his fresh cows to feed our mavericks, we're gonna be in a lot of hot water," said Kincade.

"You let me worry about that," said Laredo

The two pokes continued their conversation as they entered the saloon but softened their voices inside so as not to be overheard. They were joined by a third owlhoot by the name of Joe Smart.

True, John Watson was ruthless when it came to taking and keeping range land for his cattle, but he, like most western men drew the line when it came to rustling other men's cows, branded or not.

During all the time Pepper had been in his valley, he had never covered all the ground on both sides. There were a lot of miles of ground to cover and to his knowledge, at least four waterways.

Stopping in a bubbling stream to let his black drink, Pepper sat his saddle in thought. He flipped his cigar butt into the water and pulled reins. Putting his knees tighter against the blacks' sides, he leaned forward as his horse went up the bank to level ground. He had seen no tracks that he could recognize and no definite trail to follow. He wheeled his horse around toward Amarillo. If he rode without stopping, he could make it to town by sundown.

He rode into town at a slow walk, the head of his horse bobbing to the beat of his hooves in the heavy dust of the street. Puffs of dust shot into the air from under each hoof fall. It was early spring but the air was heavy, and warm enough that the coat of his horse was even darker with sweat around the edges of his bridle and saddle blanket. He went straight to the livery. In the hallway, he unsaddled the black and gave him a rubdown with a burlap feed bag that was hanging over the stall door. He led the horse into the stall, turned him and removed the bridle. After closing the door to the stall, he put two large scoops of grain in the trough and then climbed up to the hay loft and forked down hay into the manger. A large rat ran out from under the loose hay and sought a crack in the wall. Cladderbuck turned his head and looked a large black and white cat, lying on one of the barn's rafters. *'Some mouser you are, or are you saving him for a special occasion?'* he thought.

He was climbing down when the hostler came through the barn door with a coal oil lantern in his hand, the orange glow of the light cast long dark shadows of the man's legs that scissored across the stall walls.

"See you've already put him up," said the Hostler. "Since I weren't here to rub him down and unsaddle him for you, I'll only charge you fifty cents for the first night but that'll be a dollar a night for any longer you stay and if you chose to do your own rubbing, well, that's up to you. It won't make any difference in the cost, it'll still be a dollar a day."

"I don't know how long I'll be staying, this trip, so I'll settle up with you when I leave, okay?"

"That's fine with me," said the hostler.

Pepper stowed his outfit in the tack room and headed for Ma Pratt's café. The sun was just down and the cliff side was shocked with a burning glow of golden light. The shadows of the buildings, falling upon each other, lent an eerie effect on the little town of Amarillo. Pepper walked past a couple of false fronted buildings before reaching the café. He stood on the boardwalk in front for a moment and thought of what this country, this town, this frontier would be like in ten years, twenty years. It was hard for him to imagine beyond what progress had been made just in his lifetime. Some day, he thought, this place will be peaceful and quiet. There will be schools, churches, and playgrounds for children, theaters and libraries. He reflected for just a moment longer then turned to enter the café.

Lucky for him, he moved when he did, for as he moved, the thud of a slug tore the door facing to his left and splinters flew in his face and side of his head. Then the roar of a rifle hit his ears. He spun to his right, dropped to one knee and without thought, had palmed his .44 and threw two rounds at the alley across the street where he had seen the suggestion of a whiff of gun smoke evidently from the rifle of the would-be bushwhacker. He heard a yelp, more from surprise than from hurt. He charged across the street to the building beside the alley and pressed against the wall. Inching to the corner of the building, he slowly looked around the edge into the alley. There was nobody in sight. He eased into the alley and pressed against the wall, made his way to the rear of the building only to hear the retreat of hooves as the would-be bushwhacker made good his escape.

On his way back to the street, he caught the reflection of something shiny in the dust by the corner of the boardwalk where it attached to the building. Bending down, he noticed it was the rowel of a spur. One of the large California type, used by the hands on some of the big Mexican grant rancheros of the Los Angeles area. He studied it for a moment and sticking it in his shirt pocket; he headed for the door of the café. Two or three had gathered on the boardwalk in front of the café to see what all the fuss was. Among them was Carl Palmer.

"What happened?" Carl asked

"Someone tried to bushwhack me from the alley," Pepper said as he stopped for a moment to check the door facing. The slug had gone through the facing and had lodged in the end of an adjoining log. He took his knife and dug it out. He looked at it and tossed it into the air and caught it. He then stuffed it in his pocket with the rowel. He and Carl went into the café and found a table in a corner so he could see the door and the street, through a window.

"Someone would like to see me out of the way," said Cladderbuck, "but who? Why?"

"Sure looks that way," said Carl.

"I can't figure it," said Pepper. "Who would stand to benefit from my death?"

"I have no idea," said Carl. "Maybe it's somebody who has a grudge against you."

"That's always possible; Carl, but I hardly know anybody hereabout."

"Could be one of Watson's men," said Carl. "Word's out that you're the one Watson had in mind when he sent for Laredo."

"If you're right, I've got news for him. But I don't think Laredo's a back shooter. Oh, he'd kill a man at the drop of a hat; even if he had to drop it himself, but I think he'd do it face up. No....if it was one of Watson's men, it was someone other than Laredo."

"What are you going to do about it?"

"Well, first thing is to have me a great big steak, a bunch of potatoes and enough strong black coffee to wash it all down with and then I'm going over to the hotel and get me a good night's sleep. That trail will be there in the morning and I think I'll go see where it leads."

****

Sunup painted the town in golden light, brushed the front wall of Ma's café, peeked in through the window and found Pepper sitting inside at his favorite table. Ma Pratt had just put a plate of bacon, eggs, biscuits and grits in front of him with a side bowl of gravy. He had already done away with half a pot of scalding coffee.

"Carl was in a while ago, Pepper. He said you were going after that would-be bushwhacker this morning."

"I guess so," said Pepper, "if I can find his tracks."

"You be careful, do you hear," she said. "Good friends are hard to come by and I sure don't want to lose one."

Pepper just smiled and nodded.

"By the way, you've never met my husband, have you?"

"No, Ma, I haven't. What does he do with his time, anyhow?"

"He works for the telegraph company. Out on the line most of the time," she said. "I'd sure like for you to meet him one of these days when he's in town."

"I'd like that," said Pepper. "In the meantime, tell him for me that I think he's a lucky man, having you for a wife."

"Ah, go on now," she said and chuckled with t bit of embarrassment and pride, all mixed together.

Cladderbuck finished his breakfast and went to the livery. His black nickered in recognition as he walked down the breeze-way of the barn. He stuck his soft nose against the brim of Pepper's Stetson as Cladderbuck approached to bridle him.

"Hey, Ole Son, are you ready to cover some ground with me this morning?"

The black twisted his ears as though he knew exactly what Pepper had said. Cladderbuck tossed the blanket on and then the saddle. He pulled the cinch tight and tied it off. Putting the stirrup down, he stepped into the leather and wheeled toward the door. The hostler came in about that time.

"Caught me again," he said. "I was out in the coral, feeding my mules. I got a pair of the prettiest reds you ever laid eyes on."

"Mules are good animals," said Pepper. "I'll be back later today so just keep a tab on what I owe you."

"Sure thing," the hostler said.

Cladderbuck rode around back of the barber shop where his ambusher had evidently ground hitched his horse. He got down and checked the tracks closely. He put the image of the shoes in his memory. A western man with trail savvy could read a trail like most people, who could read, would read a book. He would be able to recognize those tracks no matter where he saw them. He climbed back into the saddle and started off at a canter. The bushwhacker was in a hurry to get gone and the trail was as plain as day. He had made no effort to cover his tracks.

A few miles out and the trail became somewhat harder to see. Evidently, the bushwhacker had started to try and cover his trail and Pepper had to slow his progress a mite. Pepper had been taught by the best, his childhood friend, Screaming Eagle. It was said of Screaming

Eagle that he could track a snake across solid rock after the rock had been covered with snow all winter long.

Before long, Pepper realized he was tracking to the north of the range of mountains that bordered their valley. He continued through some of the roughest country he had ever seen. He had to pick his way around and through openings, over and under boulders, down falls, and patches of prickly pear. The scrub trees and bushes were very hard to penetrate, but the trail of the horse he followed was unmistakable. Whoever that was, knew where he was going and Cladderbuck was going there also.

Two and a half hours after he entered the rough country, Pepper pulled rein. He smelled wood smoke. There was just a faint wisp on the air but wood smoke non-the-less. He dismounted and continued on foot, leading his black. It was early spring, but the day was warm. The sun between the boulders and scattered cacti reflected off the countryside as if from a giant brass mirror. Pepper went on. And then, he saw it, a crude dugout in the side of a hill, almost like the entrance of a mine. There was a crude rail fence that formed a coral. There were three horses in the coral and no sign of anybody. Smoke rose from a chimney made of mud and sticks, sticking out through the top of the dugout in the back, where the structure seemed to join the hillside behind it..

Cladderbuck thought for a minute. Should he challenge the dugout or just wait for someone to come out? He decided to do neither. He worked his way around to the back of the dugout where the chimney stood. Access to the top of the chimney was easy from the slope behind and he looked for something to cover the chimney top and block the smoke. Not finding anything, he took off his shirt and wadded it in the top of the chimney.

Before long he heard some shouted curses and coughing, and the door flew open. Two men rushed out, coughing and fanning smoke with their hats. Both were dressed like cowhands but both had tied-down colts. One man had a Winchester in his left hand.

"You Gents got a problem?" asked Pepper in a matter of fact tone.

The two froze where they were, their backs to the dugout. They both spun at the same time, reaching for iron. Their guns were cocked, half rose to see nobody there.

"Up here boys," said Pepper, "drop'em."

The two slowly released their grips on their guns and let them tilt and fall to the ground. A third man, in his long johns, Pepper could not see, had come out of the dugout and was flat against the front wall beside the door. He could see Pepper's shadow on the packed earth in front of the door. He figured, whoever was up on top was standing almost directly above him. He had his .44 out and pointed up.

Cladderbuck almost heard the click of the hammer being cocked too late. When the slug tore through the shake roof, it would have hit him between the eyes if he hadn't moved just in time. Instead, it went through the skin on the right side of his forehead, slid along the skull and, like a mole, burrowed under the skin above his right ear and left a neat hole behind his ear and spun off into nothingness with a high pitched whine. That too is where Cladderbuck was headed, into black nothingness. He fell back onto the roof and the weight caused the roof to give. He went crashing through onto the dirt floor of the dugout. All he could think of was the sparkling lights that hung in a sea of darkness. He thought of the stars and wondered where the North Star was, then nothing.

CHAPTER 21

JB woke up well before first light. It was almost as if he had a rooster crowing in his head. He got out of bed and went to the pitcher and bowl on a small table by the window. He poured cold water into the bowl and splashed his face and eyes to finish the waking process. He got dressed, gathered his possessions and went to the lobby. The night clerk was sound asleep with his feet propped on a shelf under the desk. JB put his boot against the clerk's leg and gave it a shove, startling the man.

"Has my partner checked out?"

"Yes sir," said the clerk.

"I would like to have my saddlebags from the safe," said JB.

The clerk got to his feet and, taking the room key, looked at the number and went to the back office. He soon returned with the saddlebags and handed them to JB.

JB paid the final bill for the room, checked the contents of his saddlebags and satisfied, left the hotel. He walked to the livery, where he saddled his horse. The hostler was already up and going about his morning chores. JB paid for his horse's overnight stay, took the reins and led him out through the runway and onto the street. He mounted and rode to the front of Ma Pratt's café. There he dismounted, looped the reins around the hitch rail and went inside. He was a little earlier than he had planned. He walked to the corner table and sat down. In no time, Ma Pratt was by his side with a cup and a pot of hot coffee. He looked up at her and smiled. Then he spoke.

"Good morning Ma. Joe Collins will be here soon. You might bring another cup for him. I just know he'll want coffee."

"Sure thing, I'll be back in a minute," she said, setting the coffee pot down on the table. She turned and headed for the kitchen just as Joe Collins came in the front door.

Joe walked back, pulled out a chair and sat down. He reached over, took the coffee pot in hand as soon as Ma Pratt returned with his cup and poured it full of the black breakfast brew. He took a sip and let out a sigh almost as if he was totally satisfied.

"I've got everything ready," he said. "As soon as we get through eating, we can head out south and try to pick up Pott's trail. It ought to be light enough by then." Ma returned to the table and spoke.

"What'll you boys have?" She was looking at JB.

"I'd like a thin sliced steak, about half an inch thick and four eggs," he said. "Cook the steak well done and the eggs over medium with some fried potatoes on the side and plenty of hot biscuits with a smathering of butter and some wild honey."

"Okay," she said. Then looking at Joe, she said, "What about you, Joe?"

"I'll have the same thing JB is having except, soft scramble the eggs."

JB took the coffee pot and a split second later, turned it loose, "Ouch, that's hot," he said. Ma handed him a pot holder she had and he used it to lift the pot and refill his cup as Ma headed for the kitchen.

"Thanks Ma," he called, "you saved my bacon." She just chuckled to herself as she went through the kitchen door. By the time they finished that cup of coffee, Ma returned with JB's platter and a fresh pot of coffee which she exchanged for the half empty one on the table. She returned to the kitchen and brought Joe's platter. The two of them settled down to getting on the outside of breakfast. They talked while they ate, discussing their plans for the day.

With breakfast done, JB said, "I got it." He paid for the food leaving an eagle on the table and they got up and left the café. Ma was just coming out of the kitchen as they passed, headed for the door. JB turned to her and said, "That was a mighty fine breakfast, Ma." She just smiled and nodded. "You boys hurry back, now," she said.

It was cold outside and each man had a heavy sheepskin coat that came down half way to their knees. Taking the reins to their horses with gloved hands, they mounted. Joe had the rope to their pack horse tied to his saddle horn. Their horses' breaths puffed out like steam from an over worked train engine. They reined their mounts south and left in a slow trot. Each man had two sacks of grain, the tops tied together with a length of rawhide and balanced, thrown across the back of their saddle, behind the cantle. Each had enough to give his horse a double handful each day for three weeks. There were enough supplies on the pack horse to do the men for the same length of time.

There was which was usual for that time of year on the plains, a strong wind blowing which made it feel way yonder colder than it really was. Each man had a scarf tied over their head, down over their ears and around their necks. Their hats were atop the scarf and held in place by rawhide thongs. They rode with their faces almost concealed by the large sheepskin coat collars.

Outside of town, after leaving the street where the ground was chewed up with tracks, JB started casting in a semi-circle to one side and Joe to the other. Soon both determined that Potts' tracks were following the trail straight south. Once they decided which tracks belonged to Pott's horse, each committed the shape of them to memory. Each man was a tracker with many years of experience. Joe had more than JB but JB could hold his own when it came to following sign. They flanked the set of tracks and proceeded to follow.

"This guy hasn't made any effort at all to cover his trail," said JB.

"I'd say he probably don't know how," replied Joe.

They came to a point where the trail entered a stream some ten feet across. It wasn't deep and had a bottom of solid rock. It was immediately apparent that Potts had not emerged on the far bank. JB and Joe dismounted on the far bank and while their horses drank their fill, the two men moved around, swinging their arms in an effort to generate more body heat. JB cupped his hands and blew his warm breath into them.

"I guess I spoke too soon," said Joe. "It looks now like he's gone either up or down the stream in an effort to cover his trail."

"Yah, it does," said JB. "You go up stream and I'll go down, when either of us finds his tracks, fire a shot."

They mounted their horses and split, one going one way and the other going the other. They rode at a walk and kept close watch on the banks of the stream as they went. Although the bottom of the stream was rock, the banks were not. There would be a very noticeable disturbance of the bank where a horse passed. Thirty minutes went by with no sign of Potts leaving the stream. Then Joe noticed a spot where the bank had been torn up by the hooves of a horse. He followed them a short distance to be sure then recognizing the prints of Potts' horse; he pulled his .44 and fired a shot into the air.

Hearing the shot, JB wheeled his horse, left the stream on the south side, figuring Potts would have left the stream on that side to continue his route. He put his heels into the side of the Appaloosa and headed up stream at a fast gallop. He had gone about six or seven miles before he spotted Joe on the opposite bank. He crossed over and checked his horse next to Joe's.

"He came out here," said Joe. "It looks like he's headed around town. I think their hold up is another direction from town. He came south to throw any pursuit off."

"Let's ride," said JB.

The two of them put their horses in a mile eating trot that the big horses could hold all day if need be.

Both men had brush chaps to protect their legs from the many thorns and stickers they would encounter when riding through open country on the staked plains. Their trail was taking them north northwest of Amarillo and before too long, the buildings of the town could no longer be seen. Although there was no particular reason for doing so, JB and Joe both kept checking their back trail, mainly from force of habit. They had come across the remains of Potts' camp site. He had just let the fire die of its own accord and had not even put sand on it, much less water. They didn't even bother to dismount but instead, headed on out on the trail. By noon, they were some fifteen miles from Amarillo and the trail still headed northwest.

The lay of the land was such that a person could be just over the horizon and never be seen by pursuers. There were a lot of arroyos and washes in which a man and horse could travel and never be seen. There wasn't that much rain in that part or the country but when it did rain, usually it came down so hard that it formed gully washes that sometimes rearranged the Texas landscape to the tune of thousands of tons of earth being moved from one place to another. It was in just such a wash that JB and Joe spent the night. They had followed Potts' trail until it became too dark to see and had stopped to spend the night in the wash so they could build a fire and not be seen by their quarry.

With a small dry wood fire, they were able to fry some bacon to have with hardtack they had brought. It went mighty good with a tin of hot black coffee.

"I wonder how much farther we'll have to go to catch up with Potts and maybe Bert Rawlings. Assuming of coarse Rawlings is with him," said Collins.

"If there's two of them, it just has to be Rawlings."

"Well, probably so," said Joe.

The wind whipped across the plains and off in the distance, a coyote yelped over some scent or dead meal he had found and from another direction, the answer to his yelp came. JB thought he caught the soft flutter of the wings of a night owl close by. The fire flickered, casting shadows on the faces of the two men. They each sat with their blankets wrapped around them, facing the fire, sipping black coffee. Neither man stared directly into the flames for they knew from long experience that doing so would render them almost blind for a second or two after looking away. They each finished the coffee and rolled in their blankets, fully dressed except their boots. They both even kept their sheepskin coats on. During the night, JB roused a couple of times and fed the fire. He was sure Joe had done the same at different times.

When one of the horses nickered, JB eased his .44 from its holster that was lying beside his head and cracked his eyes open in a fine slit. He saw nothing. Looking across the fire into the face of Collins, he realized Joe was awake also. The two of them laid still and listened. Five minutes went by and there was no sound except the usual predawn sounds made by the living creatures of the plains. When the horses made no more commotion, the two men sat up and realized it was lightly snowing.

"That snow could have been what the horse was nickering about," said Joe.

"Yah, it could have been," replied JB.

The two of them rousted out and stirred about, getting wood for the fire. They built it up and soon had coffee boiling. JB got the horses ready while Joe sliced some bacon into a frying pan. They ate, cleaned the pan with sand and emptied the leftover coffee, what little there was, and the grounds onto the fire and then kicked sand on it to assure that it was out. They both knew what wild fire could do and though there wasn't much chance of one with light snow on the ground, they made sure, mainly, from force of habit. Joe tied the frying pan and coffee pot to the pack saddle and then he tied his bed roll with rawhide thongs to the back of his saddle. They both mounted and within an hour after first light, they rode out, picking up Potts' trail.

They followed the trail through the day and on into the twilight. When the sun was just sliding down the other side of the snowy horizon, they spotted the roof of the cabin over a rise in the land beyond the banks of an arroyo. Stars were blinking on by the time they circled and eased up to within range of the cabin from a downwind direction. There was no sign of life of man or horse. There was a small curl of smoke coming from the chimney. The cabin was situated against a bank of shell and was so close to the bank, JB figured there was no window on the back side. It had only one window, located on one of the sides and a door that swung from leather hinges. The window had no glass but was covered with what looked like heavy burlap or canvas.

"What do you think?" asked Collins.

"Except for the smoke, it looks deserted but you can never tell. Let's not take any unnecessary chances. You ease around the side of the house where there is no window and I'll pick my way up to the other side."

The two of them did so and when JB was against the wall next to the window, he eased his .44 over the edge and used the barrel to lift the cover. There was still enough light from the fire and the late after sunset reflection to show that there was nobody inside.

He stepped around the corner of the cabin and called to Collins. They met at the door.

"It looks like we've drawn a blank. There's nobody home," said JB. The chill wind moaned through nearby trees, complaining that the trees were standing in its way.

They went into the cabin. There was still a strong smell of bacon and whiskey inside. There was a set of bunks against one wall, a rough made table and two chairs. There were a couple of shelves on the wall, one opposite the window and the other on the back wall, next to the fireplace. There were food stuffs on the shelves and the cooking utensils were still in place.

"It looks like they are planning on coming back," said Joe.

"Yah, it looks that way," confirmed JB. "What would you suggest we do?"

"I say give it at least a couple of days. Maybe we can surprise them when they get back."

"That's what we'll do," said JB. "That arroyo we just crossed, let's see if we can find a place in it where we can see the cabin but one where we can hide a small fire. If we stay here in the cabin and try to keep the fire going to keep warm or cook, they will see the smoke and know someone has been feeding their fire."

"Good thinking," said Joe. "Let's get the cayuses and ease up that arroyo."

Leaving the cabin just as they had found it, the two men took their horses and went up the arroyo some three hundred yards before they came to a crook and an overhang that would hide their fire from view. They gathered as much dry wood as they could before dark and after unsaddling and picketing their horses, they built a small fire with the dry tinder because dry wood makes very little smoke. They built it under the overhang, under mesquite bushes that hung over the edge so any smoke that might be generated by their fire would be dissipated by the bushes, even though there were few leaves left on them. They decided not to cook for the odors might forewarn those they wished to surprise, so they ate jerky and hardtack and washed it down with water from their canteens. The night settled in and they soon rolled in their blankets to get some well deserved sleep. If the owlhoots returned during the night, they would keep until morning. JB checked the load in his .44 and laid it next to his head, just in case. The song of a whippoorwill sang them to sleep.

Morning came with frost lying like a blanket of sprinkled silver dust over the prairie plants. The fire JB and Joe had been warmed by, the night before, was a cold flattened out patch of ash. Joe stirred from his blankets first and was just beginning a new fire when JB rose up on one elbow.

"Well," said Joe. "I thought you were going to sleep all day."

"It couldn't be too late in the day, the sun's not more than a half hour high," said JB, in defense of his late sleeping. He had generated enough body heat to fill the area between his blankets and he hated to vacate his them.

Joe chuckled at his effort. Although there was a chance that the smell of coffee might give them away, he decided to make coffee. He put water into the pot and took out the beans. He put them in a soft leather pouch with a draw string, pulled the string tight and laying the pouch on a flat rock, he used the flat side of his hunting knife blade to crush the beans. Then he poured the crushed beans into the coffee pot, closed the lid and set the pot in the edge of the fire.

JB was pouring a small amount of water into his hand from his canteen. He splashed the water into his face and rubbed his wet fingers through his hair. He then put on his Stetson and went to move the picket stakes so the horses would have access to more grass. By the time he had done that, Joe had coffee ready. They ate jerky and hardtack with their hot coffee.

"I figured since we were on the downwind side of the cabin, the smell of coffee would not give us away," said Joe.

"I think you're right," said JB. "This jerky don't stay with you like freshly fried bacon. I just wish we had some biscuits instead of having to eat hardtack. Of course, hardtack is a whole lot better than nothing."

The men spent the day lying on the rim of the arroyo, in the shade of a mesquite bush, watching for the return of the two occupants of the cabin. That day rolled into night and another day and another night and still no return of the two they were after. The fire in the cabin had long since gone out

****

In the meantime, Rawlings and Potts, having run out of money, went looking for an easy target for a hold-up. They had ridden their horses to the Twin Buttes relay station, and waited for the stage to come in for a change of team. They waited until the horses were changed and then pulled their guns, robbing the passengers, relay employees and took the strongbox from the stage. They then made all the passengers and employees of the station board the stage and hightail it out of there. They mounted their own horses and headed for Amarillo, planning to buy fresh supplies and mounts and leave the country. They had gotten sick of being cooped up in the cabin and had no intention of going back to it.

****

After three nights and two days, JB and Joe decided to give up on Potts and his partner to return. On the morning of the third day, they packed up and got ready to leave. The past two days were sunny and the snow had melted off enough for them to find the trail of Potts and Rawlings' horses. Fortunately, snow don't wash away tracks when it melts. It just gradually seeps into the ground through and around the tracks, if anything, it makes them more defined. Casting around, they located the tracks and determined that they were headed for the Twin Buttes relay station. They followed.

"I wonder why they didn't come back," said Joe, "and why the relay station?"

"I have no idea," said JB. "It could be that they went to catch the stage when it came through. Maybe they figured the stage would be a slick way to leave the country."

"Could be," said Joe. "Your guess is as good as mine."   T h e y kicked their horses into a trot and rode off toward Twin Buttes. Their pack horse trailed along behind on a lead rope.

It was a beautiful day at the J-C Connected ranch. The outfit got busy whipping the ranch back into shape. Their first order of business was to get as much hay put away before the next snows came and that's just what they did. They then went about mending fences, corals and ranch buildings.

Clancy was glad to get back in his own kitchen and he showed his appreciation by feeding the outfit royally. He didn't want to spoil them completely so he only made his famous bear sign ever so often. Life was good on the ranch but the whole outfit worried about JB. They had heard nothing since he had sent them on to the ranch weeks before.

****

Hope Collins was in her shop, not only concerned with the running of her business but concerned for the two men she had locked in her heart. The two men she loved, her father and JB Johnson. She was preoccupied on the day that Jack Potts and Berton Rawlings came in. Before she could react or even know they were in the shop, Potts had subdued her helper while Rawlings wrestled Hope into the back room. He and Potts had her and the helper in the back room with the front door of the shop locked and the closed sign hanging on it. She started to scream and found Rawlings' hand over her mouth. He held his gun on the two women while Potts tied their hands behind them with pieces of cloth he had picked up from the counter. Rawlings removed his hand from her mouth and she only had time for a half scream before he had covered it with a gag. They lay helpless on a pile of cloth bolts and starred at the two with a mixture of fear and anger sparking their eyes.

"Well, my little hand iron swinging bitch," said Rawlings. "I owe you. That little bit of temper you showed in hitting me with that hand iron caused me a lot of grief." He grinned with a sinister smirk on his face and flashed a tobacco stained set of half rotten teeth.

"Rawlings, what are you going to do?" asked Potts.

"Jack, go keep watch for me and then I'll do the same for you."

Potts was grinning through his own greenish yellow teeth. He had a half inch growth of whiskers on his dirty face and tobacco stained his whiskers on both sides of his mouth. He pulled his hat tight on his head and turned to the curtain that separated the front of the shop from the back room. He stood there while Rawlings had his way with Hope, glancing over his shoulder and grinning at the prospects of his turn. Before long, Rawlings came to the curtain tightening his belt, grinning.

"Okay, Potts, it's your turn."

When Potts was finished with Hope, Rawlings came over and lifted her head up by lifting on the front of her dress. She had a stream of wet tears trickling down her cheeks. Bert drew back and said, "This is for the lick I took from you with that hand iron. He doubled his fist and hit her hard on the jaw causing her head to jerk hard to the side. They left her tied up and left the shop through the back door. They had gotten their supplies and fresh horses earlier and had them, along with a pack horse, tied behind the shop. They mounted and rode out of town.

CHAPTER 22

"What was that noise?" Pepper thought to himself. He wished someone would light a lamp or strike a match of something. He was in the dark and his head was aching worse than any hangover he had ever had. '*There...there it was again,*' he thought. '*Water dripping. Wonder what it could be?*'

He was laying on the ground, wondering how he got there. The darkness was so total. Maybe he had his eyes closed. He tried to open them but they would not respond. "That dripping, it couldn't be rain. I'm on the ground and I don't feel wet," he thought. "Oh, my aching head. I must have fallen. No...I was on the roof and....and I....I.... Now I remember. I was on the roof and one of those owlhoots shot me. Shot me? I've been shot, but where, my head. Yes, that's it. I've been shot in the head."

He tried again to open his eyes and gained a small slit only to see more darkness. It was night time. He could make out the sound of more water, more than a drip. Yes...it was raining and he was wet. Funny he hadn't realized it before. He raised his hand to his head and felt the stiff, matted hair, stiff from dried blood. He flinched as he touched the side of his head. Pulling himself to a sitting position, he fished an oil skin pouch from his watch pocket and shook out a match. When lighted he looked around. He realized he was in the dugout that he had been on top of. He pulled himself from under the hole in the roof to get out of the rain. He found a lamp but before he could light it, the match burned too close to his fingers and he lost the light as he jerked his hand and dropped the match.

He struck another and lit the lamp. As the light from the lamp searched the corners of the dugout to root out the darkness, he noted the four bunks, the table and chairs, only two of them and both in a bad state of repair. The fireplace was a crude one made of rocks, mud and sticks.

He was cold and wet. His head hurt and he was weak from loss of blood. Just how much loss, he did not know. He eased to his feet on shaky legs and made his way to the outside. With much effort, he climbed to the roof and retrieved his shirt from the chimney top. It was soaking wet. He went back into the dugout and found some dry kindling and wood next to the fire place. He put a small fire together and warmed himself. Placing the shirt over the back of one of the chairs, he set it close to the fire to dry.

He found an old crock that had been used to cook beans. He washed it in the rain. He thought about his horse. The big black would not have let a stranger approach him and maybe he was still close. He whistled. He waited quietly for a moment, and then whistled again. The black came out of the darkness. He was really not all that wet. He must have found some kind of shelter. Cladderbuck's rifle, canteen and saddle bags were still there, and the horse seemed glad to see and smell his master. He shied a little at the smell of blood but Cladderbuck was able to calm him with just the sound of his voice.

He caught rain water in the pot and placed it on the fire to heat. He needed to clean his wound and try to determine just what damage was done. From his saddle bags, he took some jerked beef and chewed on a piece while he bathed his head. He didn't rub the dried blood too hard for fear of restarting the bleeding. He found some coffee that had been left behind by the men who had occupied the dugout and after washing the crock well; he put on some water to boil and added the coffee.

After the coffee had boiled a while, he set it off the fire to cool a little and finding no cup or anything to use for one, he tilted the crock and drank the hot, black coffee from it. He felt much better with some jerky and hot coffee in his stomach. He searched the floor and found his .44 where it had landed when he fell through the roof. His Stetson was there also.

When his shirt was dry, he slipped it on and began to feel much better. Then he thought of his sheepskin coat he had taken off to remove his shirt. He had left it on a bush beside the chimney. It was still there but wet. A couple of hours over the drying chair and it was dry enough to put on. He had no idea, when he eased into his coat, how long he had been out from the gunshot. Was it yesterday or three or four days? He just didn't know, but no matter. However long it was, it was. He'd find out later. With no stars to see, he had no way to tell what time of night it was, so he decided to try and sleep. He was very tired and his head ached, not as much but ached none-the-less. He slept the rest of the night and well into the morning hours.

The rain had stopped and the sky was clearing. From the position of the shadows, he judged it to be around eleven in the morning. His first venture away from the dugout revealed a spring on the south side, about thirty yards away. It bubbled out of the side of the hill and formed a pool which overflowed into an arroyo before disappearing into the ground there. He filled the crock and his canteen. Then he returned to the dugout. The wind was very cool. His fire had long since gone out so he built another and heated the water in the crock and bathed his head wound. There was not as much soreness and his headache had reduced to a dull feeling. He had no sign of fever and he considered himself fortunate that he seemed not to have any infection. He washed out the crock and made more coffee. Then he slept.

He awoke the next morning about the time the sun came up and decided he wanted something other than jerky to eat, and since his strength was returning. He made the decision to track out of there. He had unsaddled his horse to roll and graze. He knew the big black and was sure that he wouldn't stray too far afield. He whistled for him and the black came right then. After saddling the horse, he stepped into the leather. With a flick of his tail, the black horse took to the trail that led out of the rough country where the dugout was located and headed for Amarillo. Cladderbuck now had two scores to settle, the stealing of his stock and the attempt on his life. He rode with extreme caution even though he was pretty sure the owlhoots that had shot him and left him for dead were clear out of the area. He hoped they had quit the country for as much as he wanted justice, he still didn't like the idea of killing, and would do so only of he had no other choice.

He was following the same trail taken by the three hard-cases without realizing it for a long time. The separation of the tracks is what sparked him to notice the trail. One of the three had left the trail and gone toward the Watson spread. The other two continued on toward Amarillo.

Pepper decided to return to the ranch. He could track down the owlhoots that tried to kill him later. He was interested at the moment in finding who was stealing their stock and more important, how. He was still weak and felt dragged out from the loss of blood and he figured a couple of good meals and a good night's sleep would greatly improve his state of health.

He arrived in time for supper and Curly had steak, potatoes, corn bread and sawmill gravy and after telling his story of the attempted ambush and the shooting at the dugout, Curly and the rest of the outfit was red hot to go after the owlhoots that had tried to kill their boss, for they were all men who rode for the brand. Pepper calmed them down and then explained that he wanted to find out how someone was getting away with their stock.

"I want everyone in the saddle come daylight," he said. "Bill, I want you, John, Shotgun, Noble and Jim to ride the west side of the valley. The rest of you will go with me and cover the east side. We'll be looking for tracks in number, going out of the valley and we might find it. If you spot any sign of stock leaving the valley and going toward the mountains on either side of the valley, let everyone know. Three shots ought to do it."

Come first light, everyone was at the breakfast table waiting for Cladderbuck. He soon appeared and pulling up a chair, he sat straddled it and went over his plan once more. He had his breakfast of eggs, bacon and biscuits. After eating, they all mounted, split up and rode out, leaving Curly and Shirley to clean up after them.

"I'd give anything if I wasn't all stove up and could ride with the rest of them," said Curly. "I miss being in the thick of everything."

"Ah, ," Shirley teased. "Do you mean to tell me you'd rather be riding with a bunch of hard-tails than to be here with me?"

Curly flushed from his collar up and Shirley laughed out loud. It was contagious for Curly laughed also. They turned to the work at hand.

The weather was beautiful and the countryside was something for the eyes to behold. The valley held most all the beauties of the natural southwest when there is water in plentiful supply. The grass of the valley was belly-high to the horses. There were a number of waterways that converged finally into the course that formed the deep canyon at the north end of the valley. Along those waterways, grew all sorts of trees, grass and brush. Hugh sycamores lined the banks of the streams and watercress grew in beds where the streams curved one way or the other. The water was teaming with fish and at night you could hear the sounds of a million frogs all up and down the banks. The sun was beginning to warm the earth and there was some dust, kicked up by the horses, floating on the soft breeze that tickled the leaves of the sycamores and hummed lowly through the needles of the Lodge Pole pines. Most of the growth along the base of the mountain was pine although from time to time they would see an oak or chestnut. There were not an awful lot of cacti in the valley but some could be found among the rocks at the foot of the mountains.

Rod Taylor was the first to spot the tracks. He was walking his horse around a large boulder when he came upon what looked like a deer or goat trail but a closer look revealed the tracks of young calves and horses. He gave out a yell and pulling his .44. He fired three shots into the air.

When everybody had converged on the spot, Cladderbuck

dismounted and walked the trail for about twenty or thirty yards, while some of the others dismounted.

"This is it," Pepper said. "Mount up. Let's see where these tracks take us."

They rode in a single file for a ways and the trail had two or three switchback turns. Then it went straight toward a cliff side, as if it went right through the solid rock. From their frontal view, the rocks seemed to be just a solid wall, but when they got to within a few yards and looking down at the trail on the ground, they could see where the rock face came out and over lapped the other face which was three and a half to four feet behind the front rock face. There was a crack almost four feet wide that went parallel with the rock face and wove its' way back into the cliff. There was just enough room for a horse to go through and sometimes the stirrups rubbed against the rock sides. It had a sand bottom that was pretty well chewed up and the only light came from straight up. The walls on either side were forty to fifty feet high with a path of blue sky above.

When they emerged from the crack, they were in the bottom end of a draw. They followed the draw up and over the crest. From the point they entered the crack to the crest of the draw, Pepper estimated to be about two and a half miles. On the other side of the crest lay a slope of talus that went down some two hundred feet and then scattered cedar and pinion sparsely covered the slope to the bottom. At the bottom they found a dugout and corral. It was the same dugout the three owlhoots had been using. Pepper knew then that whoever tried to kill him were stealing his stock and probably wanted him out of the way to keep from getting caught.

He led out and the outfit rode as one toward Amarillo. They picked up the trail of the hard-cases that had gone before and followed it to the point where the three had separated. One going toward the Watson spread and the other two went on toward Amarillo. Stopping for a moment, they all waited for Cladderbuck's direction. He studied the tracks for a moment, and then spoke.

"We're going after those owlhoots and we're going to put a stop to the ambushing and rustling. They've been making off with our unbranded calves. Now it's time to settle up. Shotgun, you take Jim, Jay and Jack with you and track down those two that went on to town. Bill, John and Noble, you three head on back to the ranch. I don't like leaving Curly and Shirley there by themselves, not with killers on the loose."

****

At that moment, Ron Kincade and Joe Smart were having a drink in the saloon in Amarillo and were about to sit in on a poker game. Laredo had gone back to the Watson ranch and was taking a nap in the bunk house. He awoke and swinging his legs off the bunk, he sat there for a minute, combing his mussed up hair with his fingers. He was thinking of how close they had come to getting caught. He thought about that uppity Grace Pritchet, how she thought she was so much better than him. He made up his mind. He was going to clean out old man Watson. At least all the cash the old man kept at the ranch. He would get the money, go after Miss uppity and leave everything else to the fools who he felt deserved what they got.

Laredo had no doubt in his mind that he was just about the fastest and deadliest man with a gun in the territory. He felt that nobody would try to stop him.

****

Cladderbuck arrived at the Watson ranch and found John Watson coming out of the corral. Watson closed the corral gate and walked out to meet him.

"Watson, I know we've had our differences but at least one of your men and maybe more have been taking my unbranded calves and leaving their mamas bawling out on the range."

"How do you know my boys are involved?" Watson whipped with a smirk.

"We trailed three of them from their hideout," said Cladderbuck. "One of them branched off and came here. Two others went on into

Amarillo. We tracked them out of my valley and I sent some of my boys on to Amarillo to round them up. I came here for the other one."

"I try to be a fair man these days," said Watson. "I've got too much at stake to get involved in rustling and I sure don't condone any of my hands being involved in such activities."

"The one I trailed here rides a horse with large feet and throws his left front foot out. It looks as if a notch in his left front shoe might be causing him to do that."

"There're only two of my riders that have been gone lately. They both rode out day before yesterday and one of them came in yesterday, packed his outfit, drew his time and left. He didn't say where he was going or where the other one might be."

"Who was that?" Cladderbuck asked.

"Laredo," said Watson. "He ain't been with me all that long. He's a dangerous man with a gun or his fists. The other one is Ron Kincade. I had trouble with Ron. He would draw his pay, light a shuck for town and stay two or three days and come back broke. He's a pretty good hand otherwise....as long as he's broke. He and Laredo usually stuck pretty close together. I about half way thought they were up to no good in some way."

"Mind if I take a look at the horses in your corral?" asked Pepper.

"No, I don't mind, go ahead."

After checking the left front feet of the horses in the corral, Pepper climbed back out.

"Well, none of those have a chipped shoe. What kind or horses were Laredo and Kincade riding?"

"They both own their own mounts. Kincade rides a strawberry roan and Laredo has a big gray, kind of a funny looking dapple gray. You can't miss him if you see him, stands out like a scarecrow in a corn field."

"One other thing, Watson, you may not approve but I bought those cattle from Pritchet and I'm going to run them on the same graze as our cows. I aim to find out for sure, on my own, what is and what is not open range and I intend to use any free range that is available. If that's going to be a problem for you, let's hear it now."

"There's no problem with me," said Watson, "as long as nobody starts branding my stock including calves of my branded cows."

"Then, you and I should have no problems, between us."

After Cladderbuck left, John Watson went into the house and when he walked into the living room, he discovered his strong box out, on top of the desk, empty. *'That damn Laredo,'* he thought, *'if I get that thief in my sights, I'll take pleasure in putting a bullet in his thieving hide.'*

When Pepper returned to his ranch house, the boys that had followed the two riders to town were still not back. He unsaddled his big black and rubbed him down with a piece of burlap. He put a couple of scoops of grain in the feed box and climbed up to the hay loft, disturbing a nest of rats and forked down some hay into the manger. He went on to the house where he found Curly and Shirley in the middle of making a wash tub of bear-sign.

"Hot coffee's on boss," said Curly. "Dig in on them bear-sign. They're still warm and they'll go awful good with a cup of hot coffee."

Cladderbuck reached and got a tin and Shirley poured him some coffee. He put his big hand into the tub and came out with four of five of the big bear-sign and sat down at the end of the big table where the outfit took their grub and had his doughnuts and coffee.

"Curly, I don't know for sure but I think your bear-sign are just a little bit lighter than Rachael's. But, don't you go and tell her that I said that. If I want her to know, I'll tell her." Pepper chuckled with a mouth full of bear-sign and coffee.

He was just about through with his second cup of coffee when they all heard the fast beat of hooves come into the ranch yard. Pepper looked out the window and saw Pete Pritchet hanging onto the neck of his horse, without a saddle. The horse came to a stop and Pete slowly slid off to one side. He hit the ground as Pepper bounded from the back door and headed for the man. The horse shied as Pepper ran up to it and Pete lay there with blood all over his head and clothing. He was out cold. Pepper and Curly picked him up and headed for the house. Shirley went ahead and held the door open. They laid him on the bed after Shirley yanked the covers down. She then went to the kitchen for hot water. When she returned, Pepper and Curly had his shirt off.

"It looks like he's only hurt on the side of his head," said Curly. "He must have fallen or someone hit him awfully hard."

They cleaned all the blood away and poured whiskey into the gash alongside of his head. He groaned at the burning even though he was out.

About an hour later Pete came to. He blinked his eyes and looked around as much as he could without moving his head. When he did move his head, he winced and groaned at the pain there. Shirley was there and was alerted by Pete's groan.

"It's about time," she said. "Pepper!" she called out.

Cladderbuck came into the room as Pete forced himself to a sitting position.

"Hey, Ole Son, take it easy. You've got a nasty arroyo across the side of your head. What happened?" Pepper asked.

"It was that Laredo, Pepper. He came by the line cabin and was sitting there just as pretty as you please, and then all of a sudden he started talking about leaving the country and then up and grabbed Grace by the arm and said she was going with him. I jumped at him and he pulled iron and whacked me across the head. I went out like a light and when I came to, he was gone along with most of our grub supply and Grace." Pete sat there a moment in silence and said with a quiver in his voice, "Pepper...he's got Grace!"

CHAPTER 23

Two days later, finding nothing out at the deserted relay station, JB and Joe Collins rode into Amarillo late in the afternoon. The sun was just down and the horizon was all aglow with the beauty of a western sunset. Closer, the landscape took on a purple tone that seemed fuzzy with haze. There were a few lighted windows in town and the livery had a lamp, lit, hanging beside the door. The hostler was the first to meet and tell JB and Joe of the attack on Hope Collins two days before. The two men were incredulous at the news.

"Where is she?" Joe spit the words through gritted teeth. A rage of fury churned in his guts. He looked at the hostler with wide burning eyes.

"She's at the boarding house," said the hostler. "Martha Williams has been staying with her these past two days."

Joe and JB went directly to the boarding house. It was almost dark by then and the flickering of the flame from the lamp was playing frightening shadows across the face of Hope Collins as she turned to face her father and JB. She ran to Joe and fell into his arms sobbing. He tried to console her, the best that he could but she had to cry it through. She did and finally her sobs turned to slight whimpering like a whimpering puppy that had been whipped.

"Honey, you get some sleep now and I'll be here when you awaken," said Joe.

"Alright father," she said. Nodding to JB, she left the sitting room and retired to her sleeping quarters with Mrs. Williams by her side. She barely realized that JB was standing in the room at the time. When Mrs. Williams returned to the sitting room after putting Hope to bed, she spoke.

"I think she will be able to sleep now. She hasn't slept more than five minutes at a time since it happened."

"Just exactly what did happen?" asked Collins.

Mrs. Williams relayed the entire story to Joe and JB as she had been able to get it from Hope. By the time she had finished telling it, the thought of what had happened was almost more than Joe Collins could stand. He leaned with one hand on the mantel above the fireplace and stared into the fire, gripping the mantel so hard that his fingernails actually dug into the wood. He was still standing there when Martha Williams and JB said their goodnights and left. JB went to the hotel and secured a room for the night. He took his key, ascended the stairs, unlocked his door and entered. He dropped his saddlebags and Winchester to the floor next to the bed and sat to remove his boots. He laid back on the bed, clothes and all and went to sleep. The news about Hope was disturbing to him but he was so worn out that even that couldn't keep him from sleep.

The first glimmer of daylight found JB standing by the window looking at the early morning mist that had settled just above the ground. There was a heavy frost on the landscape and the sight of the cold winter morning made him shiver a little. He went to the bowl on the small table against the wall, took the pitcher of water, poured a small quantity into the bowl, dipped his hands in and splashed his face. He ran his wet fingers through his hair and combed them backwards to lay his hair down before putting on his Stetson. He buckled on his gun belt, picked up his Winchester and saddlebags and left the room.

"What time does Ma Pratt open for breakfast?" he asked the
"She's been open for an hour already," the clerk said. He lifted the news
paper, he had been reading before lowering it to answer the question,
and returned to his reading.

JB walked out into the cold morning air. He stopped at the edge
of the boardwalk and squinted at the eastern sky. The wind, common
to the area had not picked up as it normally did each morning but it
would as the sun spread its rays across the plains. He heard a rooster
crow somewhere off down the street and as he stepped off the boardwalk
to cross over to the café, he saw the old blue tick hound that claimed
squatters rights to the streets of Amarillo. He stepped up onto the porch
of the café and opening the door, stepped in.

The café was warm and although there was a hat rack beside the
door, JB had just as soon keep his Stetson on his head. He walked to
the corner table and sat down. He could smell the rich aroma of fresh
brewed coffee and smoked ham frying. Ma Pratt approached him and
spoke.

"Good morning, cowboy, what'll it be?"

"Good morning, Ma. How about a steak with some eggs over
medium? Bring me some of those wonderful biscuits you bake and
some butter and molasses. Since you have that coffee pot in your hand,
I'd appreciate it if you'd pour me a cup of what's in it."

Ma laughed as she leaned over and poured a cup full of the hot
coffee. She sat the pot down on the table and returned to the kitchen to
see about JB's breakfast. Before too long, JB had finished about half of
his first cup when Joe Collins came in. Spying JB at the corner table, Joe
went straight back and pulling out a chair and sat down.

"Morning JB," he said, picking up the coffee pot and pouring himself
a cup full of the black brew.

"Morning, Joe. How's Hope this morning?"

"She's better, I think. She slept through the night and is still asleep.
I left Martha Williams with her."

JB sat quietly for a moment. He picked up his cup and took a sip and
putting the cup down easy on the table, he looked up at Joe and said, as
a matter of fact, "When are you leaving?"

"I'm leaving just as soon as I can get the pack horse loaded and my horse saddled. They have a two day head start on us and we can't waste any time, assuming, correctly, that JB was going with him."

JB sipped his coffee and looked up as Ma Pratt came from the kitchen with two plates of food. She spoke.

"I went ahead and brought you some breakfast, Joe. I figured you'd need it before you hit the trail."

"That's thoughtful of you Ma but how did you know for sure that I was going anywhere?"

"You can't do anything else, seein as what has happened," Ma said as she set the plates in front of the two men. "Everyone in town knows what has happened and we all know what you have to do."

"You're right, Ma," said Joe. "JB and I are leaving within the hour. Do you think Seth is open for business this early? We need some supplies before we can leave."

"Nah, he won't be open for two more hours yet, but he sleeps in the back of the store and I don't think he'll mind too much if you wake him now," Ma said over her shoulder as she headed for the kitchen.

They finished their breakfast and JB dropped an eagle on the table. JB picked up his saddlebags and Winchester and they left the café. They both walked to the livery to get their horses and the pack horse. The ground was frozen with ice crystals spewed up above the dirt and made a crunching sound as their boots pressed down on it. The old blue tick hound came to the corner of one of the buildings and peered around it to see who was walking through his town. Another dog barked off a few buildings away as the two men entered the runway of the livery. The lamp beside the door was still burning. JB pecked on the door of the tack room where the hostler's sleeping quarters were and in a moment, the man came out through the door pulling his second suspender over his shoulder. He rubbed the stubble on his chin and yawned through a toothless mouth.

"You Gents are up and out mighty early," he said through a second yawn.

"We wanted to get an early start," said Joe.

"You need any help with them hosses?" asked the hostler.

"No, I just wanted to settle up with you for the night," said JB. "How much do I owe you?" He started to reach for a coin when he stopped and as though in thought, looked at Joe and said, "What you say we get two extra mounts to rest them off times. We could make a lot better time if we don't have to stop longer than it takes to switch saddles."

"That's good thinking, JB." Turning to the hostler, Joe said, "We're gonna need a pack horse and do you have a couple of good mounts we can rent or buy?"

"Yah, I got a bunch of good mounts but I reckon I've got two of the best around for you Gents. I'll get them."

JB and Joe both led their horses into the runway and proceeded to saddle them. By the time they had their horses ready to go, the hostler returned with two of the finest horses Joe and JB had seen in a long time. He had them haltered and led them with a rope tied to each halter. The sun was just peeking over the horizon casting a sliver of silver light all across the edge of the world that brushed against the dark shadows on the faces of two determined men preparing to ride out on a vengeance trail.

"Let's go by and load up on supplies," said Joe.

They rode their horses, leading the pack horse and the two extra mounts to the front of the mercantile store. JB dismounted first and went to the door and taking the butt of his .44, he knocked hard on the door facing. Even though the sun was rising above the horizon, the shadows cast across the front of the store caused it to still be dark enough inside for Seth Williams to light a lamp before coming to the door and peeking out. He opened the door when he saw who it was. Swinging it open he spoke.

"I was expecting you Gents this morning. Come on in."

"We need supplies to last us a couple of weeks," said Joe. "First off, we'll be needing a thousand rounds of .44/.40 shells, a side of bacon cut in two pieces, twenty pounds of hardtack, ten pounds of coffee beans, twenty pounds of jerky and a small bag of sugar. Sack us up a hundred pounds of grain for the horses and split it into two bags. That way we can tie them together and sling them over the back of one of the horses."

"Will that be all?" asked Seth.

"No," said JB. "We'll need some tobacco and a box of Lucifers.

When all the supplies were placed on the horses and the two men ready to ride, JB turned to Joe and said, "It's a good day for skunk hunting. Let's go looking."

"You Gents might check out back of Miss Hope's shop," said Seth. "Hope's helper said that the front door was locked from the inside so their attackers must have gone out the back door."

At the shop, the two of them left their horses out front and walked through the shop to the rear. They didn't want their own mounts to mess up any sign that might be there. Before stepping out the rear door, they surveyed the back yard from the door stoop. Sure enough there were two sets of boot prints leading from the step to where their horses had been tied. Good sign in that the horse prints, even after a couple of days, were clear and crisp. JB and Joe, both, committed the prints to memory. They would be easily recognized by the two later on. Leading their mounts, they followed the trail to the edge of town on the south side. The owlhoots were headed south toward El Paso.

After five hours in the saddle, JB and Collins took a nooning in the shade of a small stand of Pinion trees. They changed their saddles to the spare horses while stopped. Each man poured an amount of water in their hats for the horses. They would have to find water before dark. They both knew that water could be found in many unlikely places. The blades of the prickly pear cactus held water that could be squeezed out once the spines were removed. The fruit, called tuna, of the prickly pear was good to eat. They were tasty and high in water content with sugar. They knew a man could stay alive by eating fifteen or twenty of those tuna a day.

A favorite place to find water by the Indians was to uproot a Yucca plant. When the plant was pulled from the sandy soil, it left a hole that water would seep into and could be used to drink and fill canteens.

"So far, the tracks haven't varied a bit. They are still headed toward El Paso," said JB. "With any luck, we'll catch up to them there."

"If they decide to go down into Mexico, our trail may be a long one," said Joe.

"Whatever or however long it takes, I'm going to find those two bastards and either I'm going to kill them or they are going to kill me," said JB with a gnawing anger deep down in his gut.

"You couldn't have said it better," said Joe. "I feel exactly the same way."

They rode side by side throughout the rest of the day. Late in the afternoon, they began to look for a place to make camp. Along about dusk, they came on some large boulders that were left over from years of wear on an up thrust of rock. There was a space in between three good sized ones with mesquite growing all around but the center looked like an ole buffalo wallow. They unsaddled their horses and gave them a rubdown with a handful of bunch grass and let them roll before putting them on picket for the night. There was no water there and they were thankful they had brought extra canteens of the life giving fluid.

JB took a canteen and with his hat, went around watering the horses. He then gathered a pile of prickly pear, knocked the spines off them and before long had squeezed a full canteen of water out of the cacti. In the meantime, Joe had gathered some dry mesquite branches and had made a fire. He had coffee on before long and was slicing bacon into the frying pan when JB finished his water retrieval. JB took a pan and shelled some mesquite beans into it, added a little of the cactus water and placed the pan on the edge of the fire. Later, the two men had themselves a fine supper of bacon, beans, hardtack and coffee.

After supper they took the pans, plates and forks and rubbed them with sand and then splashed them with a little water. They poured themselves another cup of the hot black coffee and settled back to have a smoke, Joe with a pipe and JB with a cigarette. They rested by the fire in silence, each with his own thoughts. JB lay on his side, his saddle under his left arm and his left hand on the saddle horn, holding his coffee in his right hand. His hat was lying to one side. He had taken off his boots but left his socks on as well as his clothes. He spread a blanket over his legs and was as warm as could be with the fire built up to a good size but not big enough to attract unwanted attention. He looked at Joe and spoke.

"Joe, for what it's worth, I don't think Hope is going to have too much trouble from now on. When this mess is over and if I come out of it on top, I'm going to ask Hope to marry me and take up ranch life instead of city living. What do you think?"

Joe stared into the night for a long moment. He ran his fingers back through his gray hair, sighed and turned and looked JB in the eye.

"JB, I'm not that much older than you amigo but I'd be proud to call you son anytime."

With that, he cracked a short grin in one corner of his mouth and even though it was short, it was warm. He stretched out and pulled his blanket up over his shoulder and drifted off to sleep. JB lay awake for quite some time, lying on his back looking at the untold number of twinkling stars in the black night sky. Finally, he drifted off to sleep, too.

The frost settled lightly on the countryside and JB awoke to the smell of coffee. He had a shiver run all over him for he had kicked his blanket off during the night. His back was to the fire and he rolled over to look into the smiling eyes of Joe Collins with a cup of scalding coffee outstretched to him. He took it and sipping it, winced at the hot.

"How long have you been up?" he asked.

"Oh, I crawled out about a half an hour or so ago. I'll have some bacon ready in a few minutes if you want to relieve yourself and wash up to eat."

JB walked off into the bush and soon returned, buttoning his Levies. He washed up and by then the food was ready and the two men sat down by the fire and ate. They broke camp and saddled their horses after loading the supplies on the pack horse and slinging the grain sacks over the back of one of the extra mounts. Climbing into leather, they rode off toward El Paso, the sun shining on their left cheeks. The trail they followed had picked up the stagecoach route that was well established as a two rutted road with knee high grass growing in the center. There had been no stage along the trail since Potts and Rawlings had gone that way so the tracks were as clear as a bell.

"You know that we're going to lose these tracks as soon as we hit El Paso," said Collins.

"Yah, I know," said JB. "We're just going to have to look till we either find our men, or ask around until we find out where they are or where they've gone. One way or the other, they're going to pay the price," he spoke with dogged determination.

Four days later, Joe Collins and JB Johnson rode into El Paso. They stopped at the livery, unsaddled their mounts and gave them a good rubdown with a piece of burlap sack. They had the hostler put them into stalls and give them a double ration of grain each. Then they took the supplies off the packsaddle and unsaddled the pack horse. He too was rubbed down, stalled and given a double ration of grain, along with the two extra horses. Leaving their trappings in the tack room, JB and Joe took their saddlebags and Winchesters and headed for the hotel a couple blocks from the livery. It was just before noon and the streets were lively with horses, wagons and people. They walked up the boardwalk at a slow pace, stepping aside for locals coming and going and took in the town as they walked along. They came to an intersection where a side street left the main street and when crossing, they had to jump upon the opposite boardwalk to keep from being run over by a couple of horses as men rode them at a full gallop around the corner from the side street to the main street.

"Folks don't have too much respect for others around here, huh," said JB.

"You find that just about everywhere you go these days," said Joe. "Not like it used to be. I believe it's this younger generation. They haven't been taught any better."

They reached the hotel, went in and approached the desk. The clerk was a short chubby man with a clean shaven face and a pair of spectacles sitting down on the tip of his nose. He had short chubby fingers and he used them to hand the pen to JB for him and Joe to sign the register. Looking at the register, he spoke.

"You Gents from Amarillo, I see."

"Yes," said Joe. He had a look on his face that said "don't ask any more personal questions."

"How long will you Gents be staying with us?" the clerk asked.

"Don't know," said JB. We'll just have to wait and see. We'll need two rooms."

"Yes sir. That'll be rooms three and four, top of the stairs, to the right. Both rooms overlook the street," said the clerk as he handed the keys to the two men.

"I'd like to have a hot bath," said Joe. "Do you have a tub here in the hotel?"

"We sure do. It's in the room at the end of the hall, past your rooms. I'll have the water brought up from the kitchen."

"What about you mister...uh." The clerk stuttered as he looked at the register to see what JB's last name was. "uh...Johnson?"

"I don't think so, not right now. How about getting some hot water later, say six o'clock," said JB.

"Sure thing mister Johnson. I'll have hot water brought up at six."

After getting his bath, Joe went to his room, cleaned his weapons and then took a nap. JB was already asleep in his own room. Later in the afternoon, Joe got up, put on his gun belt, checked the load of his .44 and went out to check out the town. JB got up around four thirty and went about taking his Winchester and .44 pistol apart and cleaning them both. He eased down the hall about six and found the tub full of hot water. He stripped off and crawled in. After bathing, he put on a clean shirt, he took from his saddlebag. He finished dressing after he returned to his room. Buckling on his gun belt, he went to Joe's door and knocked. Joe was back from his walk around town and answered the door.

"What say we get a bite to eat and circulate around town and ask a few questions," asked JB.

"Sure thing just let me get my hat."

CHAPTER 24

Snow was already blanketing some of the high up mountains although it was still pretty fall weather in parts of the valleys. Before heading out, Pepper packed his saddle bags with plenty of hardtack and jerky. He was worried for Grace but knew it would do her no good if he went into the mountains unprepared. He rolled his bed roll along with his sheepskin coat and an extra blanket. He took his coffee pot, tin cup and a cloth bag of coffee. He loaded all of this on his big black, gathered the reins and stepped into the leather.

"Try not to worry, Pete," he said, knowing they were useless words. "I won't come back without her."

He rode out at a trot to conserve the energy of his horse and headed for the Sundance creek line cabin. He rode through meadows of tall lush grass that would be turning brown before too long. His cattle were grazing everywhere. They were getting fat on the lush valley grass. He rode down into a stream of cold clear water. Cottonwoods lined the banks and he saw a fish jump as his black stepped into the water. He sat there a while to let his horse rest. Then they went up the opposite bank and out into the open. Just a few more miles and he would be at Sundance Creek. He would not be able to reach the line cabin before dark.

As the sun dropped behind the mountain range to the west of Sparkling Water Valley, long, gray to black, shadows were cast out across the valley floor. The effect was a sight to see with a background of uneven ridges of black against a pale blue sky with golden streaks shooting up from behind the darkness. By the time Pepper reached the line cabin, it was too dark to find any kind of trail so he set about putting a fire together. He would spend the night in the cabin and start at first light to locate the trail Laredo and Grace would have left. He was glad that there had been no rain and glad that it didn't look like any for the next few days, at least.

He added fuel to the fire and sliced rashers of bacon, he had found in the back room, into a frying pan. There were potatoes there also. So he sliced a couple of them into the bacon grease and fried them until they were a crisp, golden brown. By the time he had the potatoes done, his coffee had boiled long enough to be ready and he moved the pot off the fire to let the grounds settle. He ate the bacon and potatoes and washed it all down with half a pot of scalding black coffee.

Then looking around, he came across some hardtack. He finished the coffee as the night time hours passed. It was way past midnight when he stood on the front porch, leaning against a post and finished the last cup. He wasn't a bit sleepy but he realized that he needed to get some rest before daylight. He stretched out on one of the bunks and wondered if it was Grace's. He thought about Grace and what Laredo might do to her. Finally he fell asleep with only a couple of hours left till dawn.

He awoke as if a trigger had been set to pull him from sound sleep to wide awake at an unconscious preset time. Looking out the cabin door, he could see just a faint glint of light in the eastern sky. He went to the bench just outside the door where a bucket of water sat next to a large tin pan. The pan, he thought, was the kind used to pan for gold, serving a different purpose. He splashed cold water into his face and rubbed the sleepy out of his eyes. Pouring the water out in the yard, he went back inside and checked the fire. There were still a few faint glowing coals under the ashes and adding some splinters of kindling soon brought them back to flame. He added more fuel and soon had a nice fire to knock the morning chill off. He fixed a breakfast of bacon and potatoes while his coffee was brewing. After finishing his meal and drinking almost a whole pot of hot black coffee, he put together what grub he thought would come in handy and loaded it in two cloth bags he found in the back room. He divided it so that the weight was equal between the two.

Looking out the door again, he determined that it would be light enough to find the trail soon so he went out and saddled his horse. While he was saddling the black, he wondered to himself why he had assumed Laredo would have gone to the mountains. Maybe it was what he would have done himself, under the same circumstances. He had learned a long time back that if you want to know what someone else will or will not do, you must first place yourself in their shoes, and this, he could do very well.

Finished with the saddling, he tied his outfit behind the saddle and swung the sacks of grub over with one hanging on each side. Stepping into the leather, he began to cast around for the trail. There was just enough light to see by when he found it. Sure enough, they had headed toward the mountains to the east. He put the black into a mile eating trot that the big horse could hold all day if he had to. Laredo was in such a hurry, he hadn't even bothered trying to cover his trail. Cladderbuck was sure that once he had time to think, Laredo would take the time to do so but for now Pepper could follow at the pace he had set.

"We're going to catch them, horse," he said aloud.

Cladderbuck left the flat land of the valley and started to wind his way through the boulders and scrub growth that was the fringe of the meadow. Beyond that fringe he entered the Lodge Pole pine forest that layered the sides of the foothills. The trees were virgin and grew so thick that he had to weave back and forth so that he almost lost his direction. Onward and upward the black climbed.

Reaching the top side of the forest growth Cladderbuck emerged into more boulders of varied sizes. All of a sudden, the trail disappeared.

Pepper dismounted and started casting around for some sign. It took a while but he found it, a scrape on the side of a rock that had been moved from its bed. He mounted and went on. Finding more tell-tell signs, Cladderbuck was able to trail them to where they had spent the night. Not much sign of a camp, but enough to know that they had spent the night there. By then, it was getting hard to find sign because it was getting too dark. Cladderbuck decided to camp for the night.

He set about getting ready for sleep. He was so tired, he felt as if it had been months since he had slept. Never-the-less, he would be looking for some sign of light from their new camp. He was thinking that Laredo would not risk a fire but he just might. There was no sign of a fire in the altitude beyond him and he finally went to sleep.

Laredo was standing in the mouth of the canyon where he and Grace had stopped to spend the night. She was back in a dimly lit corner crying. He had his way with her during the night and she felt dirty. Laredo was looking through the snow-covered terrain for any sign of pursuit. He figured someone would be coming after them sooner or later and he had made up his mind that he was leaving the woman behind for she was slowing him down and, after all, he had gotten what he wanted already. He didn't want to leave a live witness but he couldn't risk a shot. He thought he had killed her old man with the blow to his head. He knew the sound of a shot would carry for miles in that country. He would have to use his knife come first light and then be gone.

"You'll not get away with this," said Grace. "Pepper Cladderbuck will be on you like a duck on a wounded June bug."

"He don't have the sand to come up my back trail," Laredo snarled. "If he does, I'll leave his stinkin carcass here on this mountain to feed the critters."

"Just you wait and see," Grace said with confidence.

Laredo turned with a back hand thrust at the face of Grace and knocked her back flat on her back.

"You little spoiled bitch....You keep your mouth shut."

Grace lay back without further word to prevent more physical abuse as Laredo packed his bed roll and the supplies that he would take with him. He loaded the supplies on the horse Grace had been riding. She looked on, wondering what he had in mind. He had brought the supplies tied behind his saddle to this point. When he had finished readying the horses with blankets and saddles he turned to Grace.

"I'm leaving you here," he said, as he stepped close to her.

"What am I supposed to eat to stay alive?" she asked.

He had taken out his knife and held it half hidden behind his leg. He turned with a thrust that sent the knife into her mid-section. She had gotten to her feet and now she stood there with wide eyes, looking at Laredo with disbelief that he would have done this to her.

"Who said you were going to stay alive?" he grinned through tobacco stained teeth. He shoved her backwards, off the knife blade. He wiped his knife and placed it back into its sheaf. He left her laying there, mounted his horse and rode out into the snow. He had always wanted to see southern Arizona Territory so once clear of the foothills down the western slope; he would point his horse southwest.

It was cold and the air was crisp with the smell of new snow. Pepper Cladderbuck was up and saddled by first light and taking his horses' reins in hand, headed up the draw on the bank of a small brook that babbles over the rocky bottom of its bed. The snow had quit falling and the sun was peeking through to reflect in millions of snow flakes and looked much like diamonds that had been strewn across the land. His big black was putting his feet down easy for he couldn't see what lay beneath the layer of new snow. The trail was not that hard to determine because the wild life of the area had been using it and the limbs of small growth along the sides of the trail were worn back.

By mid morning, Pepper came upon the trail of Laredo. Noting that one horse seemed to be carrying light, he decided to backtrack and see why. He had a feeling that something was bad wrong. He tried to suppress the feeling but his mind would not let him. He went down the bank of the stream, through the water and there found the ascending trail that Laredo had just come down that morning. He headed up the bank, leaning forward on his horses' neck for the trail was very steep.

All of a sudden, the trail leveled off and went around the side of the mountain. Before too long, he came on the entrance of the canyon. He dismounted and slowly approached the mouth. Easing into the darkness of the canyon from the snow covered outside, he could hardly make out the features of the opening. It took him a minute or so to recognize anything. Presently, though, he noticed Grace leaning over, holding her hand tight over her mid section. She moaned and he rushed to her side. He could see the bruises on her face from the reflected light off the snow outside the canyon. He could also see the red, blood soaked, front of her shirt.

"What happened?" he asked.

"Laredo...he....he raped me during the night and then after beating me off and on, he stabbed me and left me here to die. I'm so ashamed. I'm so cold."

"Hold still now and let me have a look at that wound," said Pepper. "You have nothing to be ashamed of, Sweetheart."

He leaned over her and eased her shirt out of her jeans. She had a bad stab wound in the left of middle of her upper stomach area.

"You've lost a lot of blood, but it looks like the bleeding has stopped. Pepper brushed the ashes from a few orange glowing coals in the fire and adding some dry grass and twigs, was soon able to rekindle it. He added fuel from what was there in the canyon but realized that he would need to gather more before too long. He took his coffee pot and filled it with snow, then placed it next to the fire to melt and heat.

"You're going to have to come out of that shirt," he said. "I'm going to have to clean that wound and get it bandaged against possible infection. It's lucky I brought a bottle of whiskey with me."

He went to his saddle bags and recovered the bottle. When the water was hot, he took a portion of her shirt that was not soiled, and bathed her wound with the hot water and then with the whiskey. It had started to bleed slightly and he made a bandage out of an extra shirt he had in his pack and soaked it with whiskey, then bound it tight to her, covering the wound and tied it in place with the arms of her shirt.

"You may have a fever before morning and if you do, I'll need to get some of this whiskey down you. Fever may even hit you before nightfall."

Grace was very weak and showed signs of sleepiness so Pepper placed her between the fire and the back wall of the canyon so the heat would reflect off the wall to warm her on both sides. He then left the canyon to look for more fuel. He would have to keep the fire going at all times and it would take a lot of fuel.

The day wore on slowly and by nightfall, Grace was out of her head with fever. It had come on her sooner than he thought it would. He raised her head and forced her to drink from the whiskey bottle. He got a goodly amount down her and he laid her back down and let her go back to sleep. He built the fire up a little and stretched out with his head close to Grace's so he would be able to hear the slightest sound she might make. He was pretty sure that he had snaked up enough wood to last the night.

He lay there and watched the shadows flicker on the walls of the canyon as the flames licked into the air in their consumption of the wood he repeatedly added. He thought back to the train ride when he first saw Grace. How he, at the time, wondered who she was and noting how beautiful she was. He thought of Ma Pratt and her bear-sign and how good a fine meal of steak and potatoes would taste and finally he eased off into a light, restless sleep. Sleep so light that he could still hear the crackle of the fire in his subconscious mind. In the middle of the night, Grace stirred and moaned to awaken him and upon checking, he found she still had fever. He lifted her for another round of whiskey. She gagged at it but he was able to get what he thought was a sufficient amount down her. Then she slept.

First light paled the sky to the east and the sounds of the wildlife of the area could be heard as they went about their normal routine. Pepper awoke to a fire that was on its way out. He quickly added twigs and dry grass and blowing on the coals, soon had the flames eating the wood he piled on as though hunger was something that more than people and animals felt. He soon had coffee made and was slicing rashers of bacon into a pan when Grace raised her head and spoke to him. Her voice was even paler than her skin.

"Pepper," she said. "How did you get here? How long have I been out?"

"I rode in yesterday. You were in bad shape. How do you feel?"

"I feel awful," she said. "My head feels as big as a barn. What did you give me?"

"I gave you just a sip or two of good raw whiskey. You'll have a headache for a while, not being used to the stuff."

"Right now," she said, "what I need more than anything is a drink of water. My throat is so dry I can hardly swallow and it hurts to talk."

Pepper gave her his canteen he had filled with snow the night before and the water was still cold. She drank slowly but long.

"That bacon smells good," she said.

"It'll be ready in a minute. Meanwhile, have a cup of this coffee."

He poured a tin full and handed it to her. Cupping her hands around it for the warmth, she sipped it slowly while Pepper held her part of the way upright. After having the coffee and eating some of the bacon, she laid her head on the blanket and went off to sleep again.

The second day, Pepper worked on a barrier to cover the mouth of the canyon to help keep the cold air out and the warm air in. After weaving young saplings to form a framework, he laced boughs of cedar in the framework which formed an almost perfect barrier to the cold. With a good supply of fuel, he and Grace kept very warm in their little hide-a-way. Within five days, Grace's stab wound was showing signs of healing and her bruises were beginning to disappear. She was cool toward Pepper as though she was ashamed and seemed to find it hard to face him.

"What's bothering you, Grace?" Pepper asked. "You seem to be a million miles away."

"Nothing," she said in almost a half sob and half whisper.

He took her by the shoulders and felt her body tremble. She was shaking like an Aspin leaf in an early winter whirlwind.

"Yes, there is," he said. "Now what is it?"

"I am just so scared," she said.

"Scared of what?" He asked.

"Of what you must think of me," she sobbed. "I'm used goods. I've lost all I ever had to offer a man."

"Hush now," he said. "You're still the same woman; I think now, that I fell in love with a long time ago on a train out of St. Louis."

"How could you?" she asked. "After what Laredo has done to me."

"Grace, I don't care anything about that. I realize, now, that I love you and I want you to share my life, raise my children and grow old with me."

"Oh, if only I could believe that," she said

"If you believe anything, believe that," he said.

She looked up into his eyes and large tear drops overflowed her warm eyes, sparkled with the flickering light of the fire, and then ran down her cheeks. She was at that moment, the loveliest woman that he had ever seen, and he took her in his arms, held her close and kissed her softly but long.

Finally, after the ninth day since Pepper had found her, Grace seemed sure she was up to riding back to the Sundance Creek line cabin. Pepper put their things together, divided equally between the black and the pack horse. He put Grace's saddle on the pack horse and saddled the black. As the sun was peeking over the crest of the mountains, they headed for the Sundance.

They camped that night in a canyon off the rim-rock and were glad to be down out of the snow and cold wind. There in the canyon, the wind was blocked from camp and they sat long next to the camp fire and talked over a pot of hot, rich coffee. Grace went to sleep with her head on Pepper's shoulder. He sat there with his thoughts. Far off a coyote called to another and received an answer. A stick fell in the fire sending sparks swirling in the night air. All seemed at peace. Pepper ran his hand over Grace's hair and he leaned over and kissed her lightly on the forehead. He closed his eyes and drifted off to sleep.

It was close to supper time when they rode into view of Sundance Creek, and half an hour later, they were greeted by Pete Pritchet with tears in his eyes. He hadn't shaved since Grace had been taken and he had a ragged look about him but the glow of happiness showed through it all. He wasn't a crying man, normally, but seeing his daughter safe got the best of him. The look of thanks he passed to Cladderbuck said more than words ever could.

Pepper was up at first light the next morning and headed for the ranch house. Upon his arrival at the ranch, he was greeted by howls and whoops as the outfit gathered around to hear what had gone on. Pepper told his story as if he had reached the end of a bad trail but inside, he knew there was one loose end yet to be tied up and he could not rest until that had been done.

Winter was coming on again and there was still work to be done before first snow flew. There was hay to be gathered, stacked and stored. Yet there was only one thing that dominated Cladderbuck's mind. He had made up his mind to go after Laredo. The trail would be gone by then and Pepper knew it. He would have to start at the separation of the trail he had seen just before he found the canyon where Grace lay. He would head in that general direction and hope for a break, a word here or an action there. Someone had to have seen Laredo pass their way; someone.

Once decided, he wasted no time. He picked out a good mountain horse for a pack and loaded supplies on its back. The black would serve him well in the chase, he had no doubt. Early the next morning he gathered the outfit together with instructions on buttoning up for the winter. They were to finish the hay and drive the cattle to winter pasture at the proper time. Afterwards, he stepped into the leather and started his vengeance trail. He would not return until Laredo was made to pay for his violation of Grace.

CHAPTER 25

JB and Joe Collins walked down the boardwalk, their spurs jingling, to the café recommended by the desk clerk at the hotel. The town was alive with all kinds of people. There were prospectors, teamsters, cowboys, gamblers, gunfighters, drunks, whores, Indians and local town folks, all coming or going places, and a shit pot full of Mexicans. The street was somewhat loaded with traffic but most of the movement was on foot. Being winter the days were short and it was coming on close to dark by six thirty or so. After covering a couple of blocks of false fronted stores and shops of all kinds, including three saloons, they came to the café.

They went inside and looked around for a table that would put their backs to a wall. Both men had learned a long time before that it paid to play it safe. They pulled out chairs and sat down. Before too long a man came to their table and spoke.

"What'll you Gents have?"

"What do you have on the menu?" asked Joe.

"Don't have a menu," said the man. "We got steak, potatoes, snap beans the wife canned this summer past and biscuits. For desert, we got blackberry cobbler. If you don't like steak, we can substitute roast beef or chicken. We don usually sell a lot of chicken."

"I'll have the steak and the works plus the cobbler and coffee," said JB.

"I'll have the same," echoed Collins.

The waiter went to the kitchen and in a minute or so the man returned with a pot of scalding coffee with two cups. He placed the cups in front of each man and poured them full of the hot black brew.

"Do you Gents want any cream for your coffee?"

"No," they said as one. Then JB said, "This sugar here on the table is enough to doctor this mud." He chuckled for he knew as well as did the others that he referred to the coffee as mud only because he liked it strong. The waiter smiled and left the table to wait on others.

"When we get through with chow, we can mosey on down the street to the end and work our way back toward the hotel, checking out each saloon," said Joe.

They would check in the saloons for the saloons were noted for being an information spot and if you wanted to find out what was going on around town or even the county territory for that matter, you most likely would hear it in a saloon.

After they had finished their last cup of coffee and had a smoke, they paid their bill and left the café. They turned on down the street and after passing two more intersections of side streets, they came to the saloon that was the farther most in that direction, 'The Last Chance'. They went in through the batwing doors. The inside of the saloon was lighted by coal oil lamps and it was so dim, it was hard to make out many faces except those seated around tables where there was a lamp on the table. There were a couple of tables where poker was being played and a string of men standing along the bar that ran from just inside the front door to the back wall, on the north side. There was only enough room at each end for the bartender to pass through. There were two bartenders, one seemed to be taking care of the people at the bar and the other seeing to the Gents seated at tables. They both had long sleeve shirts with garters holding the sleeves pulled up and dirty white aprons tied around their waists.

JB and Joe eased over to the bar and picked out a spot that would accommodate the two of them. Neither man was in a mood for drink but to make it look as though they were there for that purpose, they both ordered a mug of beer which they intended to nurse until they could get the answers to a few questions before checking out the next place. The best way to get questions answered is not to ask the question in the first place. Joe and JB were well aware of this fact and their method was to slant the conversation in the direction they wanted it to take it. They were doing just that when the name Rawlings popped up. They had been talking to the bartender in the third saloon they visited and one of the men standing at the bar was telling the man next to him about running into an old acquaintance named Rawlings. He was shocked to see him since he had heard that Rawlings had been shot in a gunfight in Dallas just a couple of months before.

"Rawlings? Did you say Rawlings?" asked JB.

"Yah, Rawlings, Bert Rawlings," said the man. "Why? Do you know the Gent?"

"Seems I heard of him somewhere," said JB. "Did you have a chance to talk to him?"

"Yah," said the man. "Me and ole Bert used to play poker together a lot back a couple of years ago, down in San Antonio. I tell you, he was about the slickest card handler I ever ran across."

"Is he still in town?" asked JB.

"Don't think so," said the man. "He said something about stocking up on supplies and heading down toward San Antonio. That was day fore yesterday. I spect he's well on his way by now."

"Let me buy you a drink stranger," JB said in a friendly tone.

"Why sure," said the man. "Always glad to drink with a gent like yourself."

JB bought him a drink and after he and Joe finished their beers, they said their goodbyes and left the saloon. They went to the hotel and sacked out for the night. First thing in the morning, they planned to have breakfast and get on the trail as soon as possible. The next morning, just a little before daylight, they left the hotel together and went to the café where they had eaten the night before. They had eggs and steak with fried potatoes, biscuits and gravy. After eating all that and finishing off a whole pot of coffee between them, they left the café and went to the livery for their horses. After saddling their horses, they loaded what was left of their supplies on the pack horse. They took the lead ropes of the extra mounts and pack horse and led them, along with the horses they were going to ride, up the street to the Mercantile. The owner was out sweeping off the boardwalk in front of the store.

"We'll need a few supplies," said JB.

"Sure thing," said the store owner. "Be right with you."

After replenishing what supplies they had used up from Amarillo to El Paso, they loaded them on the horses and climbed into leather and rode out of town toward San Antonio. Not far out of town, they spotted the tracks of Rawlings' and Potts' horses. They were on the right trail.

"One good thing, Amigo," said Collins. "They didn't turn south into Mexico."

"Yah, we can be thankful for that much, anyhow," said JB.

"I know the sheriff in San Antonio," said Joe. "He's a good man. He's fair and I think it would be a good idea to fill him in on what we're up to if we find those two there."

"I think you have a point there," said JB.

They rode on. For the sake of having plenty of water, they decided to forsake the trail and swing down close to the Rio Grande river and follow it most of the way. Then cut up to San Antonio and go in from the south. On the second day out of El Paso, JB picked up followers on their back trail.

"Joe, did you notice that we have company?" JB asked from the corner of his mouth rather than turn his head. "We need to maneuver them into a position where we can get the drop on them before they know what hit them."

"How many do you make it?" asked Joe.

"I'd say at least seven. Not many more than that."

"Let's cut down to the river," said Joe. "Then swing into the water and the first bunch of river bank growth we come to, that's big enough, work our way up into the bush and wait. We should be able to catch them by surprise."

"Sounds good," said JB.

They rode to the water's edge and urged their horses into the river. Riding downstream, they covered about a quarter of a mile before they came to what they were looking for. Swinging their horses up into the bush, they encountered a sand bar high enough to hide the horses from view from the river. They dismounted and ground hitched the horses, tied the lead ropes of the extra mounts and the pack horse to the saddle horns of their horses and eased up to the top edge of the sand bar. Looking over the top, they were no more than twenty feet from the water's edge. They laid their Winchesters down across the top of the bar and waited. There was an area of open space just south of the river bank growth that would afford them clear shots at their followers.

Before too long, the men that were following them came down the river, their horses' knee deep in water. They splashed past the growth on the edge of the water and were soon exposed through the clearing.

"Just rein up and sit still. Put your hands where I can see them," said JB.

The men were taken aback at being caught with their guard down. They were not used to having the drop gotten on them. They reined their mounts down and stood still. Nobody made a move as Joe eased down to the water's edge and motioned the men ashore with the business end of his Winchester. Coming ashore, the men kept to the tight group Joe had indicated.

"Why have you pulled down on us stranger?" asked one who apparently was the leader of the group.

"Don't make me laugh," said JB. "You Gents have been trailing us for over an hour. Why?"

"We ain't trailin you. We just happen to be going in the same direction"

"Joe, take all of their guns and check their saddle bags. I don't mind them following us as long as I know they can't shoot us in the back."

Joe started making the rounds, picking up their weapons.

"You're not going to leave us out here with no way to defend ourselves, are you?"

"You'll make out okay," said JB. "I'm sure you Gents have been in worse situations before. Probably won't be the last time either."

"You Gents keep your distance from now on or we'll shoot you on sight if you get close enough. You're just lucky we don't turn your horses loose."

There was true, deep anger in the eyes of each man in the group but the leader was the one with the light of killing in his stare. He spoke.

"You and I will meet again, Amigo. I will kill you for this."

"That's funny," said JB. "That's something I have never seen."

"What?" asked Joe?

"I've never seen a dead man kill someone," said JB, with a promise in both his eyes and the tone of his voice.

The leader of the owlhoots felt a cold chill run up the center of his back all the way up to the top of his neck. He nevertheless resolved in his mind that he would one day kill this cowboy. He reined his horse around as did the rest of the men in his group and headed back up river. JB and Joe watched them out of sight, tossed their guns in the river and then mounted their horses, took up the lead ropes to the extra mounts and pack horse and headed on down river.

"I have a feeling we haven't seen the last of the leader of that bunch," said Joe.

"I think you're right," answered JB. "I think it'd be a good idea to stand watch from here on in. We can take turns. At least until we get to San Antonio."

They made camp by the river that night and laid a couple of false bed rolls and went back into the bush to sleep. They were getting farther south each day and the nights were not near as cold as they had been, making it bearable to sleep back from the fire with only a blanket. Two days later, without any more trouble, the two of them rode into San Antonio in a pouring rain. They had slipped on their slickers and water was coming off the brims of their hats in a sheet which made it hard for them to see.

Their horses' hooves splashed in the puddles in the street. The street was mostly mud where before the rain there was only dust. They found the livery and rode their horses into the runway through the open door. Darkness had just set in and the only lights in the livery were a couple of oil lanterns hanging on planks nailed to the uprights and hanging out into the runway. The smell of fresh horse manure and hay intermingled was a welcome odor after being on the trail so long. They dismounted and unsaddled their mounts. Then they stripped the pack horse and leaving the animals standing in the runway, took all their gear to what appeared to be the tack room. Storing their things there they returned to the task of rubbing their horses down with pieces of burlap they found in the tack room.

The hostler came in about the time they were through with the rubdown.

"Howdy Gents," said the hostler. "Thet'll be fifty cents a night for each horse and thet includes grain and hay. It normally includes a rubdown but I see you've already done thet."

"That's okay old timer," said Joe. "We kind of like to rub our own horses, but you can put them in a stall and feed them. It won't hurt my feelings a'tall."

"Where is the best place to get some grub here?" asked JB. "We're both starved for some good ole home cooking."

"Well, the best place for price is the saloon just up the street, but the best place for taste is Mildred's Café. It's up two blocks, just past the Alamo. Turn left and it's two doors down thet side street."

"Thanks," said JB.

"Think nothing of it," said the hostler. "The only reason the food is cheaper at the saloon is they expect you to buy a drink and Rollo King, thet'd be the owner, makes his money on the rotgut whiskey he sells. He makes the stuff out back in a shed. Some say he chases all the rats he can find into the mash and throws in a dozen plugs of chawin' tobaccy in each batch for flavor." He chuckled. "Don't get me wrong, I drink the stuff cause it beats most of the swill you can buy in this town."

JB and Joe picked up their saddle bags and Winchesters and left the livery. They walked along the boardwalk, their spurs jingling, checking out the store fronts as they went up the street. Before going to the café for grub, they stopped at what passed for a hotel and got a room for the night. They went to their room and washed up in the large bowl on a table against the wall. They left their gear stacked in a corner of the room, locked the door and went out of the hotel.

"Let's go eat and then stop in for a drink afterward at the saloon where Rollo sells his rotgut," said Joe. "I'd be willing to bet you a dollar to a hole in a donut that he's got some good Kentucky or Tennessee whiskey hid away."

"No bet," said JB.

Before long they rounded the corner at the Alamo and espied the café right off. It had the picture of the head of a cow painted on the window in front and as soon as they had turned the corner, they could smell the food cooking. They entered and found a table against the back wall, close to the kitchen.

"If their food taste as good as it smells, we're in for a treat," said JB.

"I know what you mean," Joe responded, his mouth beginning to water.

The waiter approached their table. He had a white apron tied around his middle. His sleeves were pulled half way up his arms and held in that position by two lacy garters, probably trophies from past adventures.

"Howdy, Gents," he said with a big broad smile that showed two gold teeth in front. His smile appeared between a set of pork chop shaped sideburns. He had a walrus mustache and a twinkle in his dark green eyes. He spoke with an Irish brogue that had a layer of the blarney spread all over it.

"What do you have to offer?" asked Joe.

"Well, let me see now. We have steaks and pork chops, fried potatoes, beans and some of the best sourdough biscuits you ever let melt between your teeth. We serve the steaks covered with onions sautéed in wine, if you like."

"I'll have the steak with everything you named," said JB.

"Me too," echoed Collins. "Bring us a pot of scalding black coffee and two cups." He looked at JB with a questioning look on his face. "That okay with you JB?"

"Sure is," said JB, "the sooner the better on that coffee."

"I have some good Irish whiskey if you'd care for a tad in your coffee," said the waiter. "I call it 'coffee royal'."

"Yah, that'd be good," said Joe.

The waiter left the table and soon was back with the coffee and a small glass filled with the whiskey. He put the coffee pot down with the glass and went for cups. When he returned, he said with a note of pride on his lips, "Me woman has made a large fresh apple pie and she's itching to try it out on someone. So, save room for a slice."

"Sounds good to me," said JB.

The two men sat and enjoyed the meal, topping it off with the apple pie, then coffee and each had a smoke. They left the café with a complete feeling of satisfaction, the kind of feeling that makes a man want to lean back and go to sleep. That feeling was magnified by the sound of the rain on the porch roof. They stood on the boardwalk, under the sheltering roof and watched the rain for a long moment.

"Well Joe, lets ease over to the saloon and see what's going on around town."

They both pulled the collars of their coats up around their necks and stepped off the boardwalk into the muddy street. The rain was coming down hard but there was very little wind so their hat brims were enough to keep the rain out of their eyes. They entered the saloon taking off their hats. Shaking them to remove most of the water, they turned and hung them on a hat rack along the wall just to the right of the door to let them dry a bit while they were in the saloon. They slowly turned, surveying the large room. There were a few men at the bar with a couple of dance hall girls. The bartender looked up with a side glance and looked back to pouring a drink for one of the men at the bar.

They noticed the piano player in the back corner, the men and women at the bar and the few that were seated at the tables. Some were playing cards and some were just talking and drinking. A couple of them were eating. One of the men, a young gun slick got up from the table he had been seated at and strolled over to the end of the bar. He had a questioning look in his eye. He looked Joe over real good. Then he ordered a drink. When he had received his whiskey, he took a small sip and set the glass down so hard it splashed some of the brew out on the bar. Everything got quiet. Everyone was looking at the slick.

"Ain't you that fast gun Ranger from Austin," he said with a smirk on his face broken by a tight grin. He had a hog leg buckled around his hips and tied down.

"I don't know about that part about being a fast gun but I was a ranger out of Austin," Joe spoke softly. He knew what was coming. Here was another young man with an attitude. He fancied himself fast on the draw and was just itching to prove it at the expense of someone else. He'd seen them all over the west. Most of them wound up in boot hill before they were twenty five years old. He turned and spoke directly to the young man.

"Listen son, you don't want to do this," he said.

"I ain't your son and I say all you rangers are a bunch of yellow bellies!"

"Think what you want," said Joe.

"I think your old man was away from home when you was thunk up," said the slick.

Joe turned his left side to the man and in doing so must have caused the slick to think that he was pulling iron and the man's hand flashed to his gun butt. Joe caught the movement in the corner of his eye and turned, drew and fired with blinding speed. The gun slick had no more than cleared leather when Joe's .44 slug caught him in the teeth. It blew teeth, brains and hair out the back of his head, spraying them all over the wall behind him. The exiting matter actually caused the man to be impacted forward and he fell like a board, face first, to the sawdust covered floor. There was a pool of dark red spreading around his head. Joe picked up his drink and knocked it back.

"They're all alike," said Joe. "They draw and shoot a bunch of bottles and cans sitting on a fence and they think that's all there is to being a gunfighter, sad, very sad."

"The only thing that saved me from being like that was some hard, straight talking from you," said JB. "Remember?"

"Yah, I remember," said Joe. "But you listened. Most of them don't."

The Sheriff came through the batwings and took a quick look around.

He walked over to the bar and spoke to the bartender. He hadn't noticed Joe that closely until the bartender indicated him with a nod.

"Why, Joe Collins," the sheriff exclaimed. "What happened here?"

Joe had been listening to the bartender explain what had gone on to the sheriff and agreed that it was true, he shrugged his shoulders and spoke.

"It's pretty much the way the man said Tom." .

The Sheriff turned to a couple of locals and said, "You boys take that man over to the Doc's office. If Doc's asleep already, wake him up."

"A doctor won't do him any good," said JB.

"We;;, Doc is also our undertaker,

Then turning to Joe, he said, "What in the world are you doing down here in San Antonio, Joe. I thought you had retired and was living up in the Pan Handle."

"You've got that right," said Joe. "Me and my friend are down here on a hunting trip." Turning to JB, he said, "JB, I want you to meet Tom Winters. Tom, this here is JB Johnson. He has a spread up in the Pan Handle. He's going to be raising a cross between Missouri Shorthorns, White Faces and Texas Longhorns."

The Sheriff stuck out his hand and JB took it in a friendly, firm shake.

"I'm glad to know you, Mr. Johnson.

"Just call me JB," JB said.

"You say you're down here on a hunting trip, Joe?" the Sheriff asked.

"Yah, but the varmints we're after are the kind that claims ownership to other folk's cattle. They killed some good men in the process of taking those cattle. To top it off, they raped and beat my daughter."

"I can't abide trash like that," said the Sheriff. "What can I do to help?"

"Just be there when things break loose if we find the bastards here in San Antonio," said Joe.

"If you spot the ones you're after, let me know where and when you intend to confront them with it and I'll be standing on the side," said the Sheriff. "Hell, I'll even shoot them for you, if you like."

"We'll let you know," said Joe. "What about that gun slick."

"Don't worry about that. We all know what happened and you are in the clear as far as I am concerned."

Questioning of the bartender revealed that he indeed knew Rawlings.

"Yah," said the barkeep. "Rawlings used to hang out at the Vista de la Sierra saloon. He played poker there and was sweet on one of the girls that work there. That is if you're talking about Bert Rawlings."

"That's the man," said JB. "Just where is this Vista de la Sierra saloon?"

"I'll take you there," the Sheriff said. "Is Rawlings the varmint you're after?"

"Yah," said Joe. "Him and a sidekick named Potts."

"I know them both," said the Sheriff. "The world would be better off without them."

"Come on, Sheriff, let's go find those skunks."

The three of them left through the batwings and Joe and JB fell in behind Sheriff Winters. They headed for the Vista de la Sierra. Their spurs were jingling as they walked down the boardwalk. It was dark in town and the windows of the homes and some businesses were lit with orange light from the kerosene lamps. A dog barked off a ways and the wind was blowing a little stronger, whipping the rain in their faces and snatching the sound of the dog from their ears, making it sound like an echo.

The railroad had come to San Antonio and it had split the town into two distinct sections. The section on the south side of the tracks was where the riffraff hung out and where most of the crime in San Antonio was perpetrated. The Sheriff knew it well. He spent most of his official hours on the south side. They crossed the wooden planked ramp over the tracks and soon were in front of the saloon.

JB took out his .44, opened the loading gate and spun the cylinder, stopped it on the empty chamber and pushed a round into the vacant spot. He checked the action, let the hammer down easy and returned it to his holster. Joe did the same.

"It's been a long time since I've seen Rawlings," said JB. "We may have to depend on you, Sheriff to point him and Potts out if they're in there."

"No problem," the Sheriff said. They all three entered the saloon through the front door and all stepped aside from the door to survey the crowd. The Sheriff, checking the back table, recognized Rawlings and Potts seated at the table, playing cards with three other Gents. Before he could call them to the attention of JB and Joe, Rawlings recognized JB. He using the smoke filled room as cover, sliding his chair back, twisted through the support posts to the back door and was out of it and gone. Potts was busy talking to a dance hall girl and didn't see Rawlings' move to the back door. He turned around and saw that Rawlings was gone, and rested his stair on the Sheriff as he approached with two strangers. He knew, from the expressions on their faces that something was wrong. He felt a surge of bile in his throat. He knew that one of the men had to be JB Johnson. Shoving his chair back, he tipped the table over between him and the three oncoming men, grabbing for his gun in an awkward stumble backward into the wall. His pistol came clear of leather and a sudden smile of triumph sprouted from his face. He just knew he had them beat and he was going to kill them all before they could get their weapons into play.

He felt a thud in the stomach and thought that someone had thrown a shot glass at him. He was furious as he lifted his pistol to finish the job but something was wrong. Something was very wrong. His pistol was too heavy. He couldn't lift it. He thought that he was going to have to buy a lighter weapon. He looked down at the blood on his belt buckle. *'Damned fool, throwing that shot glass at me. It must have broken and the glass has cut me.'* He thought. His eyes glazed over and his pistol swung down, spinning on his finger and dropped to the floor. He sank to his knees and stayed there for a moment and then fell forward, face down on the floor. His body still, his soul in Hell, his muscles relaxed and his bowels and bladder empted into his jeans..

"Rawlings went out the back door," said the Sheriff. About that time they heard the sound of horses' hooves. JB and Joe, both, headed for the front door, hurried down the street to the livery for their horses. They got to the doors of the livery and JB caught Joe by the sleeve. Joe turned and looked at JB

"It's no use," JB said. "We can't see a thing in this darkness. I know the rain will more than likely wash away his tracks but we can't help that. We'll have to wait until morning." They were on their way back to the hotel when it stopped raining. Joe looked up into the dark sky and all of a sudden saw a star. He spoke.

"It looks like we're in luck, JB. If the rain is through, we'll be able to find that outlaw's tracks without any trouble. Let's get some sleep. As soon as it's light enough, we can be on him like fir on a wooly worm." They left the Sheriff and headed for the hotel.

CHAPTER 26

A fter only thirty minutes on the trail, Pepper could no longer see the buildings of the ranch headquarters. The floor of the valley had the effect of looking flat with the grass belly deep to a horse, but there were arroyos and swells that hid the outlying countryside. Then too, there were groves of trees that went from a few trees to acres of them and all Pepper could see on his back trail was a panorama of beauty. Only the thoughts of his mission kept him from enjoying the scene that spread all around him. He was instinctively checking his back trail for any sign of pursuit, a lifelong habit. There was none.

He made camp the first night in a small stand of poplar trees on the bank of a stream that eventually emptied into the Sundance. He would get to the Sundance by midmorning the next day and the line cabin where Grace was recuperating by early afternoon. He made camp next to a deadfall that broke the wind which blew out of the northwest. There was a chill on the air and Cladderbuck felt the introduction of winter in the valley. Although there was snow in the high up country, there had been none on the floor of the valley but he not only felt the coming of a white blanket, he seemed to be able to smell it. He only hoped he would be able to cross the mountain pass before it got too deep. He recalled that there were a couple of feet already in the pass when he had found Grace. He would be able to stop and see how she was doing but he could not linger. The pass would be snowed in just days away if not already. He sat by his fire and warmed himself. He drank his coffee and had a smoke. There were a few stars out but a dark bank of clouds hid most of them in the direction of the mountains.

He thought of the first time he had spoken to Grace, that night on the train from St. Louis, when he offered her coffee from the pot on the potbelly heater. It seemed like only yesterday but he realized, with thought, that it was a long time back. He was thinking on that as sleep overtook him and his thoughts transformed into dreams.

When he rode into the packed dirt yard of the cabin, Grace was sitting on the porch, enjoying the afternoon sun. She had a blanket pulled up to her waist and draped down over her legs to block the chill air. She smiled as Pepper dismounted and walked to the step.

"How do you feel?" he asked.

"I feel okay," she said, "although I'm still a little weak in the knees. Sit down, Pepper. It's so good to see you. It warms me that you are here."

"I can't stay too long," he said. "I've got some riding to do."

"Oh, Pepper...you don't have to do it," she said, knowing that he was going after Laredo. Knowing also that what she said was like water off a duck's back.

"Yes I do," he said, "if I want to be able to live with myself."

They sat for a while and talked. The subject of Laredo never came up again. He only stayed an hour and then he was on his way. He left the valley through a stand of Lodge Pole pines and took the trail up the side of the mountain. The wind pushed its way through the needles of the pines with a chilling song of winter. He pulled the collar of his buffalo coat high around his neck and ears. There, too, the wind sang its song. The trail on which he ascended the mountain was one that dated back years. It was probably formed by wild game or Indians. There was no way to know for sure how many years before. At some places, the ledge was only a few feet wide and at others, as wide as five or six feet. His horse was mountain bred and seemed to have little trouble keeping his footing.

As nighttime closed in, Cladderbuck was looking for a place to camp. He was about to give up on finding a suitable place when he saw a small tendril of smoke rise from the side of a cliff. Could there be a camp there? Sure, it had to be. He proceeded with caution to within forty or fifty yards of the cliff. He could see the smoke very well from there but hadn't seen any sign of human existence. A few more yards, he thought, would put him close enough to see.

Something warned him that he was at a moment of turning. He did, just in time to catch the Indian as he came off a boulder in a spread eagle leap that covered Pepper and they both went sprawling down a slope of talus. Rolling to the bottom of the slide, he scrambled to gain his feet only to be looking into the muzzle of a .44. As the dust cleared from his vision, Pepper was looking into the eyes of Tawkawa. Upon recognition, Tawkawa flashed a wide brace of white teeth that shined through the dark skin of his face in a wide grin.

"You almost loose hair, Pepper Cladderbuck."

"Tawkawa! What...how...." Cladderbuck was at a loss for words. Then he took Tawkawa's extended hand. "Where in the world did you come from," he asked.

"Tawkawa on his way to find you," said the Indian. "The enemies that sought to kill Tawkawa are dead, all dead. I come to help my friend build his ranch."

"I have started to build," said Cladderbuck. "But now I must find a man, one who must pay for his crimes. A man called Laredo."

"Come to my fire," said Tawkawa. "Tell me of this man, Laredo. I have coffee and rabbit to share with you."

After eating the rabbit, Pepper and Tawkawa sat by the fire, drinking their coffee and talking. The night was half gone when they finally rolled into their blankets and slept.

Cladderbuck awoke two or three times during the night and put more fuel on the fire. He was sure that Tawkawa had done the same. Finally, when the first speck of light peeked over the eastern horizon, they were both awake and moving about as one to secure from camp and be on their way. Pepper had not meant for Tawkawa to join him in his search for justice, but there he was. He could not hurt his friend's feelings by telling him that he was not wanted. So he decided to let it stand as it was, and play the hand as it was dealt. They headed for the pass.

"I just came through that pass two days ago," said Tawkawa. "It will still be passable for maybe two of three more days. You have seen the clouds in the Northwestern sky?"

"Yes," said Pepper. "We'll make the pass by noon, tomorrow. We should be there ahead of the storm."

They moved to single file for the trail was narrow at that point and they stayed in single file for the rest of the day. That night, they camped in the canyon where Pepper had found Grace after Laredo's departure. While there in the canyon, Pepper related the whole story to Tawkawa. Telling the story only caused the anger he had, to burn anew and increase. He must ride this trail to its finish. When he found Laredo, he knew one or both of them would die. It was good to know he had Tawkawa to watch his back.

Half a mile short of the pass, on the second day, the snow started to flake in the faces of both men and horses, and by the time they reached the crest of the pass and started down on the other side, the snow was falling so hard it was difficult for one rider to see the other.

"We need to find shelter and quick," said Cladderbuck.

"I know of a place I saw a few days ago, when I was on my way to the pass," said Tawkawa. "Follow me." He then lead the way to a canyon that took them off the main trail but once in the canyon, the snow and wind was blocked by the rim rock above. Instead of blowing in a straight line, the snow was swirling with the wind bouncing off the walls of the canyon.

They found an overhang with the remains of previous camp fires. There was even some dry wood piled in the back of the area with which they soon had a fire started. Pepper scooped enough snow to melt for coffee and he soon had the chill of the snow filled air equalized and the two old friends broiled bacon, broke out some hardtack and had their meal.

Pepper offered Tawkawa a cigar. They sat in quiet fellowship enjoying their smoke and a final cup of coffee before turning in for the night. Off in the distance, they heard the howl of a wolf and from the opposite direction, came an answer. Pepper got up and brought the horses in closer and tied them between themselves and the back wall of the overhang. If they kept the fire going, there was a good chance that the wolves would not bother them. Finally, as the night drew on, the two men rolled into their blankets and slept, lightly.

Later in the night, Tawkawa opened his eyes to see the fire was just about out. The slight flicker of light from it showed him that the horses were standing stiffly with their ears pricked. They stared into the darkness with eyes rolled so that the whites shown. Looking in the same direction, Tawkawa could see the red eyes of at least three wolves reflecting the faint light from the failing fire.

He took his Winchester and nudged Pepper, who quickly grasped the situation. They both had their Winchesters and the eyes of the wolves made perfect targets. They fired as one and two of the fanged beasts dropped to the snow. The third lingered for a couple of seconds and realized, too late, that he had made a mistake and hung around too long. Tawkawa's second shot caught him as he turned to run and he tumbled in the direction he had started. They both had jacked shells into the chambers of their Winchesters but as they waited in snow-covered silence, there were no more sign of wolves that night. Soon they were able to recapture sleep and slept with rifle in hand.

The fire had all but gone out when the two began to stir as first light crept through the brush. Cladderbuck was just fanning the coals of the fire to ignite the small pieces of tender he had gathered from the ground in the back of the overhang when Tawkawa lifted himself to one elbow and squinted through the haze of early morning. He looked at the bodies of the wolves in the snow, reddened by their life's blood. He shook his head and turned to Cladderbuck and spoke.

"It's a shame such beautiful animals have to die but in the everyday life of survival, it's the one who does the killing who survives."

"Yes," said Pepper. "The difference is you feel pity for the wolf. The wolf never feels anything about his victim. All he's concerned with is eating."

"Yes, I know," said Tawkawa. "It is still a pity, though."

After a breakfast of bacon and hardtack, Pepper and Tawkawa saddled their mounts, loaded their supplies on the pack horse and headed on down the trail. The snow had let up quite a bit and it seemed a good idea to get down the mountain as soon as possible, while the getting was good.

They left the high country and moved out onto the desert that was central Arizona. They traveled from can till can't with a couple of hours of siesta in the shade of a mesquite bush from about one o'clock to three, to avoid the hottest part of the day in the sun.

Eleven days later they rode into Laredo, Texas. Laredo was normally a good sized dusty western town but when they rode in, it was during a thunder storm and the dust of the streets had become a muddy quagmire. The town boasted two hotels, one a two-story rough board sided structure and the other a long one story building that was built like a bunkhouse. There were at least twenty saloons, some with brothels upstairs but mostly they consisted of drinking and gambling only. The one and only bank stood on the corner with the entrance facing the center of the intersection. There was a jail, a freight office in conjunction with the railroad station which included a telegraph office.

Coming to the livery, they rode their mounts into the breeze way of the large barn. There was a coal-oil lantern hanging on the wall just inside the large double doors that cast long shadows against the stalls that lined both sides of the breeze way.

The hostler came from the darkness in the back of the barn as they dismounted.

"Howdy Gents," he said. "The rate is a dollar a day, which includes grain. I'll store your saddles and gear in the tack room, yonder" He indicated a door to one side made of wide rough boards with one-inch wide cracks between them. "How long you Gents figger on stayin?" he asked.

"Day or two," said Cladderbuck. "Don't really know, yet, depends."

The old man knew better than press. It was none of his business and many men took offense at being questioned about their personal affairs.

Cladderbuck and Tawkawa slipped their bed rolls and saddlebags off their horses, and then they took their Winchesters and headed through the rain and mud to the hotel that was closest to the livery, the shotgun building that could have passed for a bunkhouse.

The clerk looked up when the door flew open and the howl of the storm rushed in on a sheet of blowing rain. The entrance of Cladderbuck and Tawkawa was punctuated by a flash of lightning and as the clerk looked at them, a loud explosion of thunder that rattled the glass of the hotel windows rolled and bounced between the walls of the town's buildings. Then the rumble rolled out of town toward the open plains sounding like the ball of a six-pins game being played on an upstairs carpeted wooden floor.

Cladderbuck removed his Stetson and slung the rain from it, laying a path of wet across the floor. He walked over to the desk and laid his Winchester on its top. He turned the register book to fill in his name.

"We'll need just one room, Tawkawa here sleeps on the floor anyway," said Cladderbuck.

"Do you know how long you'll need the room?" asked the clerk.

"No, not exactly," said Pepper. "We'll be wanting a bath. Do you have a tub?"

"Yes, we do. It's in the room at the back end of the hall. I'll have it filled with hot water right away."

The clerk handed him the key to his room and turned to go and find his man to fill the tub. Cladderbuck picked up his Winchester and was followed by Tawkawa down the hall to their room. He had looked at the room keys hanging on the peg board behind the desk and noted that they were all alike. One key fits all, he thought as he inserted his key in the door and opened it. They would need some alarm system because the walls of the building insulated them from the natural sounds of the open so every sound in the room would be alien to their normal pattern. A drinking glass balanced on the door knob would do just fine. They stowed their saddle bags and Winchesters in one corner of the room and after Tawkawa splashed a little water on his face, they picked up their hats, left and locked the door to their room and went to the front desk.

The clerk verified that their bath water was ready and Pepper was not at all surprised that Tawkawa had decided to skip the tub bath.

"You take bath," Tawkawa said. "I go and sit on porch and watch the rain."

"Okay," said Pepper, picking up the towel, the clerk had laid across the desk.

"That'll be two bits extra for the bath," said the clerk, almost as an afterthought that he seemed hesitant to voice.

Cladderbuck reached in his shirt pocket, brought out a two-bit piece and tossed it across the desk to the clerk. He flung the towel over his shoulder and went down the hall.

Tawkawa eased out the front door onto the covered porch in front and sat down in one of the straight back chairs and leaned back against the wall. He pulled his Stetson down over his eyes so that just thin slits could be seen between his cheek bones and the hat's brim. The rain came down slowly now that the wind had died down and the soft sound of the rain on the roof of the porch blended with the sounds of the night.

A cricket chirruped from somewhere under the porch. A dog barked a couple of times and then went silent. Tawkawa settled back to wait for Cladderbuck to finish with his bath. They had not had their evening meal and had planned to go to the café on the opposite side of the muddy street after the bath. Awhile later Cladderbuck pushed the door open and stepped out onto the porch. Tawkawa still had his slicker and after Pepper put his on, they waded into the mud of the street and crossed to the café.

The frequency of lightning flashes had decreased and what few were left seemed to all be cloud to cloud and each flash stretched flickering shadows throughout the town. They entered the café and found that most of the supper customers had been there and gone. They found a clean table in a back corner with a full view of the front door.

"What'll you Gents have?"

Looking up, they were confronted by a large, dark-haired woman with a checked apron on and a pot of hot coffee in her hand. She assumed

278

rightly that they both wanted coffee as she put two cups on the table and filled them.

"Is it possible that you have a tad of Irish whiskey to flavor this coffee?" Pepper asked. "You know, a little something to warm the chill of the rain."

"I sure do," she said. "I'll be right back."

In less time than a rooster can crow, she was back with a dust covered bottle and poured a snifter in each cup.

"What do you have cooked that's good?" asked Pepper.

"Well, you can have steak and potatoes, or you can have potatoes and steak," she said with a friendly chuckle. "Everything that comes out of my kitchen is good."

"I think I'll have the steak and potatoes," Pepper said with a broad grin on his face. "Bring my friend the potatoes and steak," he grinned. Tawkawa just nodded agreement, and the woman headed for the kitchen, giggling to herself.

After supper, they returned to their room and after Pepper placed a drinking glass on the door knob, they stretched out and went to sleep. Pepper took the bed and Tawkawa placed his bed roll on the floor. The dawn broke with a bright array of sunshine soon after first light. The rain clouds had completely disappeared, leaving the countryside damp from the rain of the previous day and the street was still a quagmire. There were a few people on horseback moving in the main street with two wagons parked along the side, one in front of the mercantile. There were a few horses standing three legged at the hitch rails.

After a late breakfast of steak and eggs, the two of them went to the Red Dog saloon. It was early for the regular drinkers and the only two in the place was the bartender and a man, evidently a drunk, swamping the floor.

"It seems like we have the same mess on the floor every morning," the barkeep said as Cladderbuck stepped up to the bar. Tawkawa lingered by the front door and watched the street.

"What can I do for you?" the bartender asked.

"We're looking for a man you might know," said Pepper. "I know it may sound funny, being here in Laredo but he goes by the name of Laredo."

"Not funny at all," said the barkeep. "We have three men in town from time to time who go by that name."

"Could you put me on to them?"

"Sure, one of them works for the Double K and the other two have a place of their own, one up Capland Canyon and the other on the flats down by the river.

"How long have they been in the area?"

"The two that have their own places, both came into the area over ten years ago. The one out at the Double K blew in here just a week or two ago looking for work. I recommended the Double K and I understand he rode out there and went to work the same day. He's a big fellow wearing a cross rig with two Navy Colts, butts forward. He struck me as being a dangerous man."

"If he's who I think he is, he is dangerous," said Cladderbuck. "How often does he get into town?"

"Well, let's see." The barkeep rubbed the stubble on his jaw. "The last he was here was last weeks, said he got an advance on his first month's pay." The barkeep leaned one elbow on the bar and wiped a shot glass with a towel usually found over his shoulder. He squinted up one eye and looked through the slits and drawled, "What you want him for? Has he done something he ought not to?"

"Let's just say I owe him and he's not going to be happy until I pay up," said Cladderbuck, "how about a couple of beers?"

The bartender drug two mugs out from under the counter, where Pepper had figured him to have a shotgun, probably sawed off. He filled the mugs and slid them down the top of the bar, leaving a small streak of foam trailing each.

"Which direction is the Double K from town?"

"West," the bartender said, "due west of town."

Pepper and Tawkawa finished their beer and went out through the batwing doors. The sun was almost directly over head and Cladderbuck pulled back a chair and sat, leaning against the wall. Tawkawa sat on the porch and leaned against a post, facing more or less to the east, watching the end of the street and checking the tree-line of a grove of pinion that grew blocking a creek bed which ran past that end of town. At the same time, Pepper was checking the west end of the street. There was no sign of riders so Pepper suggested that they find some grub. The café was close by so they got to their feet and walked across to it. The mud in the street was beginning to dry and stiffen a little, causing the walking to be a little uneven.

"You know," Pepper said as they sat down at a table in the back with full view of the door, "It might be a good idea to let the local law know what's going on. I think I'll look the Sheriff or town Marshal up after we eat."

Tawkawa nodded as the big woman walked up to the table.

"What'll you Gents have?" she asked.

"Do we have a choice this time?" asked Pepper.

"Sure do," she said with a grin on her face. "Jake, that's my cook. He trailed in here a couple of summers ago with a herd of longhorns. He was cooking for the crew and I offered him a deal he couldn't refuse. He came to cook for me. Best bargain I ever made. Wound up marrin the old coot and now he does all the cooking around here; keeps my feet warm when old man winter comes calling."

Pepper nodded that he understood but said, "What's the choice?"

"Oh! Well, Jake has put together a big pot of trail stew with plenty of gravy. I serve it with sourdough biscuits."

"That sounds good to me. What about you Tawkawa?"

"Trail stew would be good for a change," he answered.

Pepper turned back to the woman. "We'll both have the stew with plenty of them sopping biscuits and a pot of hot coffee."

Three days passed and still no sign of Laredo. Pepper casually mentioned that fact to O'Hara, the bartender. Cladderbuck had found out that he was the owner of the saloon.

"This is payday out at the Double K. He should be here tonight or tomorrow night for sure," said O'Hara. He busied himself with wiping the tables, expecting the crew of the Double K to come in for their usual monthly drinking and gambling. The first couple of days after payday, they could be seen in and out of town as their work permitted. Then the visits tapered off as their money ran short, then you only saw them one or two times till the next payday.

Pepper went to the hotel and laid down a while then he and Tawkawa went to the café for an early supper. There was some of the stew left over but Cladderbuck wanted a steak with potatoes and biscuits. Tawkawa had the stew again.

"Like being back on the trail with this kind of food," Tawkawa said.

They finished and walked out into the street just in time to get in the path of the Double K riders, pushing their mounts to get to the saloon. The two of them had to step back against the hitch rail to keep from being run down. A streak of hot resentment flushed through Cladderbuck's mind but he held and let it pass. After talking to the Sheriff, they went to the saloon. When they were in the saloon and leaning at the end of the bar over a couple of beers, O'Hara just casually asked the Double K riders at the bar, where ole Laredo was.

"He's in love," whispered one of the riders.

"Yah, he's took a fancy to the boss's daughter and he stayed back at the ranch to do a little courtin before coming in for a drink."

"One'll get you ten he's unfaithful to her soon as he gets here and sees another woman," said one of the other cowboys.

"You're on," said another. "I've been lookin at the boss's gal myself and I wouldn't mind giving her a poke. It might be good enough to keep a man's mind off other women, at least for a while."

Cladderbuck had heard all he needed to hear. He touched Tawkawa on the arm and they finished their beers and eased out past the line of men at the bar and out the batwing doors.

"I'll wait for him across the street. You stay here and don't let any of his friends interfere."

Tawkawa nodded and sank back against the wall next to the batwings.

The sun was just beginning to fade behind the ridge when Laredo walked his horse into the west end of town and slowly came up the street toward the saloon. As he left the saddle and had both feet on the half-dried mud, standing there with his reins in his hand, Cladderbuck called to him.

"Laredo!"

Laredo turned and stared into the dim light of the late afternoon to see who had called him. He stepped away from his horse and dropped the reins. He moved a couple of steps to the side and then realized who had called his name. Sweat popped out on his forehead and started to trickle down his face. Cladderbuck had moved to the street and stepped closer to the man he aimed to kill.

"I had little doubt it was you who took her and when I found her alive, she confirmed it." Cladderbuck said with a dry, level tone. "Now it's time to pay the piper."

Without another word, Laredo dropped his hand to the butt of his gun. He lifted it clear of leather and felt it buck in his hand. Twice it bucked and then he felt the impact of a chunk of hot lead pushing his belt buckle back into his guts. Then a second slug caught the tag of his tobacco sack string just below the top of his left shirt pocket. His pump stopped and he still had enough oxygen in his brain to whisper to himself '*Oh shit!*' He knew no more.

****

The wind blew the curtains of the window across the small table that sat against the wall. There was sunlight filtering through them and the smell of fresh baked bread floated on the air. Cladderbuck opened his eyes and looked at the curtains for a minute. He then realized he was somewhere familiar, but where?

"Well, it's about time." He heard a soft voice say, and turning his head he saw Grace standing at the foot of the bed he was in.

"What happened?" he asked.

"Well, for one thing, you were hit by a bullet and you've been unconscious for the past two and a half weeks. It was touch and go for a while but your fever broke last night and I felt you were going to make it."

"What about Laredo," he asked?

"He's dead," said Grace. "It's finished. Tawkawa brought you home in a wagon two days after we moved our furniture in. I was glad that we had a decent bed for you when he got here."

"Come over here," said Pepper. Grace moved to the side of the bed. He took her hand in his and looked into her eyes. "We have a lot to do," he said. "We've just started to build a ranch here."

She looked deep into his eyes and whispered, "There's plenty of time."

CHAPTER 27

The next morning, a little while before first light, JB and Joe were in the café having breakfast which consisted of steak, eggs, fried potatoes and scalding coffee. To top off such a breakfast, they were served biscuits, butter and wild honey. They ate in silence and when through, got up, left the café and headed for the livery. They had brought their gear with them and after saddling their horses, they led them along with the two extra mounts and the pack horse out into the street.

The supplies they had were not too far gone that they needed more at the moment so they stepped into leather and rode to the back of the saloon where Rawlings had been and started casting around for tracks. Before long, they had the track and the rain hadn't done much damage at all. It was the same tracks they had followed out of El Paso.

They had only followed for an hour or so when they came on the sign where Rawlings had made camp. JB dismounted and looked the campsite over.

"He made his camp here okay, but he ain't got an awful lot to eat. He left in too big a hurry and he didn't have too much stashed on his horse. It looks like he just saddled up and rode with maybe a handful of jerky and a canteen of water."

"He won't get far on that," said Joe. "It looks like he's headed for Brownsville. He can be there by noon tomorrow so he won't get too hungry."

JB stepped back into the leather and wheeled his Appaloosa to the south trail left by Rawlings, Joe beside him. They put their mounts in a mile eating trot that the horses could hold for an entire day without getting all that tired. They intended to trade off to the extra mounts as they had done since they started on this trail. They had enjoyed being on fresh horses all the way. They stayed in the saddle until the western sky became aflame with the refracted rays of the sun as it slid behind the horizon.

By the time they had gathered wood for a campfire, the landscape to the west had taken on a purple hue that was a wonder to behold. They unsaddled their mounts and allowed them to roll before giving them a rubdown with a handful of bunch grass. Joe took the horses to an area, well covered with bunch grass and put them all on picket. When he returned, JB was well on his way to having coffee and bacon ready. They sat when grub was ready and ate their fill of bacon and hardtack soaked in the bacon drippings. After supper, the two relaxed by the campfire with a tin of scalding black coffee and a good smoke.

They had gotten so far south that they didn't need their coats or their blankets to be comfortable. The next day saw them well on their way to Brownsville and by early evening, they arrived. A night of velvet soft black had settled in like a blanket over the town of Brownsville. The skies were clear and an uncountable number of stars were shining brightly though. The night air was humid and sultry. They rode up to the front of a saloon and dismounted. There were a number of figures that could be seen sitting and leaning in front on the boardwalk under the roof covering. The dim orange light of coal oil lamps filtered through the door and two front windows. Upon entry, the two had a hard time seeing in the dimly lit room with all the tobacco smoke that hung in the air.

They eased up to the bar which was a couple of wide planks lying across three wooden cracker barrels. The floor was covered with wood shavings, probably from a saw mill in the area. They each ordered a beer and when served, sipped them as they let their eyes move around the room. There was no sign of Rawlings so they finished their beers and left.

"You know, Amigo, if our man is sitting in one of these joints, he is probably going to see us before we can see him, us walking in with the light dim and the place filled with smoke," said Joe. "Maybe it would be better if we hold back from going in and observe for a minute or two through a window or door. What do you think?"

"I'll go you one better," said JB. "You ease around and find any back way in and once you're inside, show yourself and I will come in the front."

"I'll buy that, JB. "I'm just glad I thought of it." He chuckled at the expression on JB's face.

When they had gone through that routine at two more saloons, Rawlings was nowhere to be found. They had just about decided their efforts were a waste of time and energy when JB spotted Rawlings crossing from a café to the saloon across the street. He watched as Rawlings went in the saloon.

"What did you see?" asked Joe.

"Rawlings," said JB. "He just went into the Texan Saloon. It's been a while since I've seen him but there's no mistake, it was him."

"Well, let's go get the bastard," said Collins.

They decided to use the same routine as before, with Joe going around back to block any escape by Rawlings in that direction. JB waited until he saw Joe ease in the back door and stand beside it before he went in. When he walked through the door, he spied Rawlings right off. He had made his way to a table against a side wall where there were four other men at poker. He asked if he could sit in and with approval nods, took a chair.

JB walked to the bar and placed himself in a position so his right hand was clear for fast action. He stood there for a long moment, thinking about what he must do. He removed the thong of rawhide from the hammer of his .44 and walked to the center of the floor. Rawlings still had not seen him.

"Bert Rawlings," he called.

Rawlings turned in his seat and slowly rose to his feet. He knew he, himself, was fast with a gun and it had come down to who was faster, him or Johnson. When he was fully erect, he kicked the chair from him. With a smirk of a smile on one corner of his mouth, he spoke.

"Well, what can I do for you Mr. Johnson?" There was a mocking tone to his voice.

"I've come to settle a debt with you for killing five of my men and for your violation of a good woman in Amarillo."

The room became so quiet you could have heard a bug burp. All eyes were moving from one to the other of the two men facing each other. Sweat beads popped out on the forehead of both. Finally Rawlings shrugged his shoulders as if giving up the fight when his hand swept for the butt of his gun. He was fast. Like lightening he had his weapon clear of the holster and coming up to face a .44 that was more like greased lightning. JB's first bullet tagged Rawlings just above the belt buckle and his physical reaction was just enough to pull his shot off and his slug hit JB in the upper left shoulder.

JB's second shot punched a hole in the center of Rawlings' breastbone exploding bone fragments all through his lungs and upper body, ventilating his heart. The chunk of hot lead continued on, taking out Rawlings' spine as it zinged into the wall behind. Rawlings was dead when he hit the floor. JB stood there for a second to make sure, Rawlings was through. He replaced his empties, holstered his gun and held his shoulder. Joe rushed over and helped JB to a chair. He looked up at the barkeep and asked him to send for a doctor. By the time the doctor arrived on the scene, JB had passed out from both shock and loss of blood.

"See what you can do for him, Doc," said Joe.

After an examination of the wound, the doctor spoke.

"Looks clean," said the doctor. "I don't believe any bones got broken but I need to get that bullet out." He turned to one of the locals and said, "Help this man carry him over to my office."

Joe and the other man took JB's arms and legs and carried him to the doctor's office which was the front room of the doctor's home. The doctor led the way and opened the door for them.

"Put him on that table in the middle of the floor," the doctor said.

He worked on JB for about half hour or so and finally turned to Joe and said, "He'll be alright. He just needs a few days rest. Give me a hand. I want to move him to a bed before he comes to. I used a little chloroform on him and he'll be out for a little while."

"How long before he'll be able to ride?" asked Joe.

"Oh, in about a week," the doctor said. "It all depends on how quick a healer he is."

Four days later and JB was chewing on the bit to get on the trail so on the fifth day, they rode out. A week and a half later, they rode into Amarillo. It was the middle of the afternoon, on Monday. Joe and JB found Hope in her shop and their reception was more than JB had hoped for.

JB returned to the ranch a hero. His outfit was jubilant at the sight of him riding up the road toward the ranch house. He was weak for a while but eventually he regained his strength and was able to act as best man at the wedding of Pepper and Grace. As time went by he was able to take on more and more duties as a rancher. His cross breeding program went on as the years went by and after five years of natural gain, he bought out Pepper Cladderbuck's half and had one of the most successful and one of the largest ranches in the Texas Pan Handle. Pepper and Grace turned Sparkling Water valley over to Pete who started raising sheep. The two of them then moved to Dallas to live.

Amarillo grew and became a thriving community. JB kept his promise to Joe that he was going to come calling on Miss Hope and eventually she became Mrs. JB Johnson. He moved her to the ranch where she blended right in. Buck Parker and Jocke Atchley never got married. They spent the rest of their days working the ranch. Vicious Dog took an Indian maiden and settled down to married life in a cabin there in the valley. He continued to work and scout for JB on his cattle drives. Joe Collins died five years after JB and Hope were married but he had the pleasure of holding two of his grandchildren who would eventually inherit the J-C Connected Cattle Company. JB kept the C in J-C Connected in memory of his ex-partner and friend.

Look for more Books
By
James Richard Langston

'Byrider' [Western]

'Lobo Loma' [Western]

'One Bullet More' [Western]

'Trail to Vallecitos' [Western]

'One Under The Bridge' [Poems]

'Two Under The Bridge' [Poems]